D0102285

884

A SPOONFUL OF SUGAR

Liz Fraser has three young children, a degree in Psychology and Neuroscience from Cambridge University and is the best-selling author of *The Yummy Mummy's Survival Guide* and *The Yummy Mummy's Family Handbook*. She has worked in television for ten years both in production and presenting for the BBC and Channel 4 among others, and is now a regular guest on BBC Breakfast, GMTV and many other television and radio programmes as a family and parenting expert. She lives in Cambridge with her husband of twelve years and her very funny and never, *ever* boring children!

Visit www.liz-fraser.com to read exclusive extracts from her books, her blog and much more.

The Yummy Mummy's Survival Guide
The Yummy Mummy's Family Handbook
(also known as *The Yummy Mummy's Ultimate Family Survival Guide*)

A Spoonful of Sugar

Old-fashioned wisdom for
modern-day mothers

LIZ FRASER

HarperCollins*Publishers*

1

A catalogue record for this book
is available from the British Library

ISBN: 978 0 00 728477 1

Printed and bound in Great Britain by
Clays Ltd, St Ives plc

Mixed Sources
Product group from well-managed
forests and other controlled sources
www.fsc.org Cert no. SW-COC-1806
©1996 Forest Stewardship Council

FSC is a non-profit international organisation established
to promote the responsible management of the world's forests.
Products carrying the FSC label are independently certified
to assure consumers that they come from forests that are managed
to meet the social, economic and ecological needs
of present and future generations.

Find out more about HarperCollins and the environment at
www.harpercollins.co.uk/green

For Granny, with love.

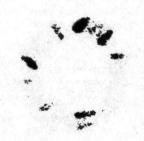

CONTENTS

Liz Fraser, aged three

Author's Note

This book won't make you or your children perfect. It won't solve all the problems of parenting; it won't stop kids writing 'Suzy has big nokkers' on bus stops or flicking snot into the freezer compartments in Tesco's. It won't answer all of your parenting prayers or make your husband's tongue more agile. Sorry, but it really won't.

What it *will* do is offer a whole host of practical, simple, common-sense solutions to many of the dilemmas faced by all those of us who, despite trying really jolly hard indeed to raise decent citizens of this world, feel we might just be making a dog's dinner out of it.

Those of us who feel hemmed in by public opinion, government legislation, rules and regulations, by the pace and stress of modern life, technology and consumerism. Those who have had enough of the Negotiation Generation, of the early sexualisation of our daughters, the cotton-wool parenting of our sons, the loss of respect and manners, of not feeling that we *can* parent our own kids: who feel something precious has been lost and who are equally worried and saddened by what is happening to the people we love the most. In short, those of us who want our children to be allowed to be *children* again.

What I hope is that this book can make the experience of childhood better for thousands of children growing up in this country today, while making the job of parenting them a good deal easier and more enjoyable for you.

Sometimes you need to look back in order to go forward. Talking to my grandmother – and thereby to a whole generation of parents gone by – has been the most eye-opening and helpful experience I've ever had where child-rearing is concerned. I just hope we can pass some of our combined experience and knowledge on to you, too.

Take your pick and see what works for you. Children are only young once and they are our future – so listen to those who have done it before, and then give it your best shot!

Liz and her Granny, 2008

Introduction

One late-August day, I receive a phone call from my Granny: she has recently had an operation to improve the feeble circulation in her leg and foot, and, although she is trying to sound upbeat about it, she is clearly very under the weather, in pain and unusually weak. I decide immediately that a spirit-lifting visit is required, so a week later I, my husband and our three children all pile into the car for a 480-mile drive to the highest inhabited village in the remote Scottish highlands, which Granny calls Home and I call Far Too Bloody Far Away.

As we squash our bottoms into cellulite pancakes all the way up the M6 and beyond, I am more anxious than ever to get there and with every passing motorway service station I have a growing regretful, guilty, wretched feeling that I should have spent more time visiting her in the past. Like most pissed twenty-somethings and self-obsessed thirty-somethings I have been too selfish to make time to visit her; to connect with someone who, suddenly in light of her illness, seems such a vital connection to my children: through her, through my dad and then through me.

As the car hugs the last few miles of mountainous road, my daughter vomits into a carrier bag for the third time and Granny's village twinkles into view at the end of the final valley, I sense that this visit is going to make quite some impact on my life.

I just don't know yet that it's going to fundamentally change how I raise my children, and how I feel as a parent.

Meet Granny ... and what you're in for

Before we meet her, I feel I should give you a brief description of my granny, so you know whose child-raising tips you're getting along with my own.

Born on the 8th November, 1923, in chilly Aberdeen, Granny was the second daughter and youngest child of a lawyer and a teacher. Not a bad start, then. (Apart from the 'chilly Aberdeen' bit, obviously. Brrrrr.) The story goes that her parents were engaged for twelve years before finally being in a position to tie the knot.

By the time Granny came along, her dad was fifty and her mother forty-six, ages which would raise an eyebrow or two even today. Nevertheless, two healthy baby daughters came along who are now the proud holders of the title, Oldest Members of the Family. (And also Most Likely to Buy Junk from Catalogues, but we don't mention that often.)

Granny met my grandfather when she was about nine years old, on one of her family's annual holidays to a village in North East Scotland called Tarland. After a mere fourteen years of hide and seek in the bushes, giggling on the tennis court, secret liaisons, separation during the war and making sure they were very, *very* sure, they finally married in 1945. Blimey, he must have been a catch! And he was.

My granddad was an impressive man: intelligent, sporty and as handsome as any Hollywood star of the day – though, to be brutally honest, a star who'd been eating rather a lot of pies in his latter years – and when I knew him he smelled sweetly of pipe tobacco, had white hair and bushy eyebrows, a huge model train set in the attic and a musty study crammed with artefacts from ancient lands and strange objects from his science labs. He ate lots of cheese and biscuits by the fire in the evenings, and had more stories of faraway places and eccentric characters to tell than anyone I've ever met. He also carried a mystical air of unpredictability that meant you never quite knew how far any childish silliness would be tolerated before he'd make it very clear that he wanted you out of his hair. *Now*, Lassie! In short, he was in every way the perfect grandfather in my eyes, and I still miss him and wish I had spent more time talking with him.

He died four years ago of a heart attack, just after walking the dogs across the moor. All that cheese and biscuits didn't help, they reckoned.

I digress . . . Granny studied languages at Aberdeen University but spent the last years of the war code-breaking at Bletchley Park, a time she never talks about except to comment grimly on the lack of mountains and fresh air and the intolerable excess of English people. (I did once try to point out that Bletchley is actually *in* England, hence the English people, but that went down like a lead balloon.) When she finally escaped back to Scotland she completed her teacher training and then taught for two years, before having her first child – my dad – and settling down into a life of motherhood from then on.

I'm not sure if this true, but certainly it seemed to me that for at least the first twenty years of my life Granny thought I was a silly, giggly, empty-headed, directionless ninny. Certainly my love of daydreaming and making up dance routines when there was a table to be laid didn't help matters, but I think the clincher was when I started watching *Neighbours* in my teens. That, dear reader, in my granny's eyes, won me the Idiot of the Year title hands down.

As a consequence of this grandmotherly disapproval, at least as I saw it, we spoke very little; I didn't really know her, and what I witnessed of her quick tongue and lightning-fast reactions made

Liz, aged five, her brother Andrew and Granny, 1979

me a little nervous around her. But about ten years ago everything changed: in a move that shocked even the most radical, optimistic thinkers in my family, I met a fine young chap, got married, had a baby, and all but gave up work to stay at home and be a Mummy. Ka-pow. The New Liz was born.

Suddenly, Granny and I found common ground: motherhood. Our shared experience of having kids young, working hard to keep the family together, our children happy and healthy and our outside interests going without going bananas during the process created a bond between us that had been woefully absent previously. We started talking on the phone about schools, violin lessons, what my kids were up to and any worries I had about them. The children sent her little pictures. She sent them back letters in old-fashioned handwriting that they couldn't read.

What I gradually realised was so special about this growing mother-daughter-like relationship was, crucially, that she was *not* my mother. Mothers can say more to their daughters in one look than the entire script-writing team of *Desperate Housewives* can in a series. Oh, you feed your baby like *that*, do you? Oh, she still sleeps in *your* bed, does she? Grrrr. My mum is actually brilliant at letting me raise my kids my way but still, as we all know, the subject of child-rearing can be prickly indeed, even in the kindest, most caring hands where mothers and their daughters are concerned. But a grandmother stands apart from this, and can dole out advice, criticism and support free from any compli-cating undertones. She's your gran – just listen to the lady, and be glad she's still here sucking pear drops!

And so there grew, over a number of years, a camaraderie between Granny and me that I never imagined I'd feel, and we have become firm friends.

She's still a tough cookie with a fierce brain though, and it's a brave person who contradicts her, or says anything stupid in her presence. Allegedly . . . This lady suffers fools about as gladly as I suffer my own stress-related dandruff, and I've learned a thing or two about being idiotic in front of her. Thing one: don't. Thing two: see thing one.

I realised, as our friendship grew stronger, that I was in the very lucky position of being able to ask my grandmother all the questions about her life, and about how she raised her children, that many mums of my generation either feel they can't ask, or don't have the opportunity to ask because their grandparents have passed away.

This wonderful old lady, this suddenly ailing powerhouse, this mine of information who had successfully raised four strong, independent people, could be the key to answering the question asked by thousands of stressed, confused, desperate parents every day: **how has it gone so wrong for our children and what can we do to put it right?**

If you need evidence that something *has* gone wrong – and you'd really have had to try hard not to have heard any of this before – then consider the following:

* In 2007, a Unicef report on the wellbeing of children and young adults put the UK bottom of the league of twenty-one economically advanced countries.

* The same report found that children growing up here suffer greater deprivation, worse relationships with their parents and are exposed to more risks from alcohol, drugs and unsafe sex than those in any other wealthy country in the world.

* Only forty per cent of the UK's eleven, thirteen and fifteen year olds find their peers 'kind and helpful', which is the worst score of all the developed countries.

* More than thirty per cent of fifteen to nineteen year olds are not in education or training and are not looking beyond low-skilled work.

* According to the children's charity NCH in 2007, one in ten young people suffers from significant mental health problems, and the prevalence of emotional problems and conduct disorders has doubled since the 1990s.

* According to a Children's Society survey in 2008, a quarter of children say they often feel depressed, and seventy per cent of fourteen to seventeen year olds say they feel under pressure to look good and are on a diet some or all of the time.

British children . . . are more tested, more punished, more imprisoned, more unhappy and more generally disliked, distrusted, feared and demonised than they are pretty much anywhere else in the developed world.

Deborah Orr, writing in The *Independent*, June 2008

Yikes! The grim, bleak picture painted above is one that many of us already suspected was there, and fret about daily. It starkly illustrates that our twenty-first-century children are losing out on one of the most important phases of their lives; a time that sets them up for life; a time that is irreplaceable and invaluable. In short, children are missing out on a proper *childhood*.

Now then, before we get too depressed, it's important in any discussion about childhood in times past to be very careful not to mythologise it – to see it through the rose-tinted glow of Time; to imagine it was perfect and lovely and happy and jolly for all children. It wasn't. Times really were tough for many kids, even fifty years ago. There was *real* hardship. We may remember our own childhoods as a time of sweet innocence, uninterrupted hours of playing with hand-made toys, cooking with mother, climbing trees and watching *Fingermouse*, but it wasn't all wonderful! Things our kids take for granted like hot water on demand, central heating making every room in the house toasty and cupboards full of fresh food whenever they're hungry were not the norm for many of us growing up.

But children were at least given the chance to be *children* and to enjoy this childhood beyond their fourth birthday – and that's what's missing now. Getting that experience back for our kids is the crux of what we're going to be seeking to do in this book.

Asking where it has all gone wrong is all very well, but what we really need to ask is, how can we put things right? How do you ensure children have a happy childhood these days? *Why* has it become so difficult and so complicated? And is there anything simpler from previous generations that we could try to implement in ours?

In a bid to answer these and many other pressing questions of the day I decided to ask Granny, while I still could. I talked to her at length about all of this over a period of a year, while her toe-related illness went through it ups and downs, and it's *these* conversations that are recounted in this book. I wasn't sure what I would get: maybe a few snippets of useful information here and there, a funny story or two about tin baths or halfpenny sweets, or a memory dug up from the depths.

What I actually got outstripped all expectations – Granny's stories and details taught me so much about the *essential* elements of child-rearing that all of us could put into practice today, and in doing so, remove much of the stress, worry and hair-tearing that seems increasingly to accompany modern parenting. Of course the world is very different now and I've allowed for twenty-four-hour TV, internet chat rooms and fast-food chains in my own tips and advice. But I'm now completely convinced that there is much about raising kids and about family life in general we can and *should* learn, simply by talking to the oldest generation alive today. They generally offer biscuits and limitless tea while they're at it, so it's not such a bad deal really.

I hope some of it proves useful and effective to you and makes your experience of raising your own troublesome brood a good deal simpler and more enjoyable than it was proving before. Who knows – we might even manage to raise a generation of kids who can spell 'No ASBO for me today, thanks' properly.

I also hope it makes you think about where *you* come from, how you, and your parents before you, were raised and how you might try to use some of their wisdom and experience in your own children's upbringing. It's best to discard the 'kids up chimneys, regular beatings with sticks and general misery' and try to stick to the good, sensible bits instead.

But they're your kids. You decide.

Liz and her Granny in Scotland, November 2008.

Chapter One

CHILDHOOD

The very basics

The first day of our holiday! And what a day – the sun has made the unprecedented move of coming out for a whole hour (no, really) and my children have missed it all by their own unprecedented move of sleeping until nine o'clock. Typical. I blame the mountain air.

When I finally turf them out of bed with the cunning promise of hot chocolate – if and only if they manage to get dressed in something moderately presentable without being asked more than six times – it is well and truly time for a morning coffee. And so it is that we make our first trip down the road to Granny's house.

We have a somewhat perfect set-up here: we're staying in my parents' house, and my parents are not. Result. To cap it all, Granny only lives three doors down the road so we can see her as often as we like – without having to stay in her house. The reason this is such a good thing will become very apparent later. You've been warned.

By the time we get there, our children have already said their brief hellos and are tearing down to the bottom of the garden. I am *so* happy to see Granny, and to be back in the place where I spent most of my childhood holidays: falling out of trees, getting lost, terrorising the cats and getting into trouble. A lot. For her part, Granny's broad smile and sparkly eyes show she is over the moon to see us too (can't think why – we are nothing but noise and mayhem) but she looks frail, unsteady on her legs, and generally as though life has just dealt her a nasty few months.

'Well you look *great*,' I say, giving her a big hug. 'I thought you were ill? Are you malingering, or is there really something wrong with you?'

She laughs, and prods her foot with the garden fork she's holding. *Why* she has been gardening in her condition I can't say, but that's just the way she is. You can't argue.

'Oh well, it's just my silly toe. Means I can't walk, but you know, I'm fine apart from that. So who's for coffee?'

Ten minutes later my husband has been discharged, caffeinated beverage in hand, to play with the little people, leaving me alone to have a good natter with Granny. Shrieks of laughter and excitement fly up from the garden every so often – and the kids seem to be having fun too.

Having fun: now there's a thing. Surrounded by all of our incessant – and often quite unnecessary – rushing, working, worrying, buying, cleaning and general obsessive *busyness*, it seems to me that our children are left with remarkably little time for what being a child is surely all about: having FUN. Having the freedom to muck about, dig in the earth, find little bugs, stick them down their sister's neck, and not worry about anything; being able to just BE.

Granny notices this too.

'Just *look* at that lot – happy as ducks in water down there, adventuring. It's beautiful. You don't see so many kids these days just playing freely like children should, without an adult or a piece of silly legislation to spoil it all for them.'

There's a pause, while I think of a neat way of asking the question that pretty much sums up the core of this entire book. Drum roll . . . Deep breath . . .

Splish! A suicidal greenfly lands in my coffee.

Fishing the squirming insect out with my little finger, I try again.

The big rush

'Granny?'

'Yes?'

'You know there's a lot of concern these days about what's happening to our children's health and happiness, and that many kids aren't having what we consider to be a proper childhood any more.'

'Oh yes?'

'Well,' I pop my drowning friend on the corner of an old copy of *National Geographic* so he can take some time to reconsider all his life choices. 'What do you think childhood is actually *for*?'

There is a long pause, as she searches for a tactful way to answer this that won't make me feel as stupid as a remarkably stupid person sitting a remarkably difficult nuclear physics exam.

'Well,' she offers at last, giving her coffee a little stir. 'Firstly, I think childhood is for having TIME. Time to think, time to learn, to process, to experiment, to grow into yourself. There seems to be so little time available to kids these days for any of that. It's all rush, rush, rush.'

'Yes, but that's just how it is in modern times, Granny, isn't it? So much can happen at once, with email and mobile phones and BlackBerrys – that's a kind of phone by the way, not a fruit – that we never get a chance to just *stop*.'

'Exactly, and there's your problem. Adults can rush about if they like, but rushing children means they lose that important freedom to play properly. You have your whole adult life for such responsibilities and constraints – they're not for children. How can they learn through play, using their imagination, if they are stopped every twenty minutes to rush on to the next task?'

OK, here I am guilty as charged, and, dare I say it, you quite possibly are too. My kids are constantly being told to 'Stop doing that now, it's time for . . .' and if that sentence doesn't end in 'school' then it's ballet or dinner, or homework, or bed. Or *something*! We all know kids who are marched from pillar to post, in a supposed bid to give them the 'best' childhood, whatever that means.

Granny isn't done yet.

'And it's not just the pace of their lives that takes their childhood away. It's also what they're exposed to and how they are treated. Childhood is a heavenly time and you should try to make it last as long as you possibly can for them – so why dress your three year old up like a pop star or coach your little ones for university or stage school? There are plenty of years ahead for that, and the early years of childhood are not the time. You don't need to cram it all in before they're ten!'

4

The curse of worrying

She stands up gingerly and hobbles to fetch a box half full of what looks like they might once have been ginger biscuits. When offered, I take one, nervously. I'm reasonably sure you can't die from eating a ten-year-old ginger biscuit, so let's keep an old lady happy.

'When I was young,' she continues, sitting down again and taking a suspiciously chewy bite of something that should be rather crunchy, 'we didn't *worry*. We really didn't. **We had very few *things*, but what we did have was the freedom to live happily and to grow – without worry. Kids seem to have so much to worry about now – but *why*? Why put that on them?'**

It's true indeed that there is far more for children to fret about than even when I was growing up ages and ages ago . . . in the 1980s. My children worry about everything: from getting their five portions of fruit a day to what they wear, whether they'll pass their ballet exams; whether they have even a tenth of the myriad technological gadgets on offer in Tesco's; what's on YouTube; if they have seen all the latest films; whether the world is about to burn itself into a crisp; why they haven't received any emails for a month; if they are the only kids in the class to go to bed at eight o'clock, and a million other things.

Much of this has not come from me (especially the five portions thing, which the school curriculum seems to obsess about and it drives me crazy) but from school and their friends. So what can we parents do to alleviate some of this concern?

Over to Granny: 'Well, you don't have to heap so much responsibility onto their shoulders, do you?'

'Responsibility? Like what?'

'Like all of your own worries. If you are worried about how much exercise they take, then just fit some more into their daily life, without making a big deal about it. Don't have a long talk with them about how bad it is not to exercise enough. They don't need to know that until they are well into their teens, and if you've got them into a healthy routine they'll do it as part of their normal life anyway. Stressing kids out about what they eat, and all the bad things that are happening in the world, and how much work you have to do, and deadlines and things going on in a marriage are not at all for children's ears.'

'So, basically you're saying we should chill out more and protect them from a lot of our worries?'

'Yes! It's about as simple and easy as that. It even extends to all the little responsibilities you give them, like what they wear, what they eat, what they watch. Children aren't designed to take so much responsibility on board – they sometimes need to be told: this is the way it is, so eat up, or put this on, and that's the way it is!'

Granny's Pearl of Wisdom

Worry is a terrible thing to load onto a child and causes all manner of problems. They should be free to learn without any responsibility and concerns that belong in the adult world. They don't need to be bombarded with information and offered hundreds of choices – tell them what they need to know, make sure they have what they need, and leave the rest to the grown ups.

The issue of work and marital issues is one many of us can identify with: I get really crotchety when either of these is causing me grief (usually it's both, but let's not dig too deep into this!) and I know my kids pick up on it very fast. The same was true when we moved house and started to have financial concerns recently. My usually delightful and sunny temperament (a mild note of sarcasm here . . .) was replaced by that of an irritable and decidedly un-jolly witch, and I know my kids were all affected by the general stress that floated on every dust particle in the entire house – and given the state of the building work, there were millions of those.

Of course, family stress is nothing terribly new – who doesn't remember overhearing a blazing row between parents and waiting upstairs with bated breath, convinced they were either about to kill each other with frying pans or file for divorce before bath time? But the difference is that any worries we may have had were lessened because we had more freedom *elsewhere*. Having talked to many adults about this, it's pretty clear to me that a significant majority of us had plenty of opportunity to get away from it all and be kids: to run about unsupervised and loosen our knots out properly, in the fresh air, and in relative freedom from the Adult World. These days it happens far less as children are contained, controlled and generally smothered and squashed from every direction.

Or, of course, they seek refuge in the wonderful, though equally worrying for reasons we'll come to later, two-dimensional world of the internet.

So am I right to want to get some of this sense of mental and emotional freedom back for my children? Certainly the way things are doesn't feel quite right to me – and I know it's not what

7

many other parents I chat with on a daily basis want for their kids either. Perhaps by putting some of what Granny suggests into practice we can make things better for our pressurised children, and so far Granny's thoughts have given me plenty of ideas of how to do this. Wonder what else she has up her sleeve . . .

When push comes to shove

A small child I think I recognise comes to the door pasted in a brown, slimy substance and looking very pleased with himself.

'Charlie!' I exclaim, dreadful thoughts of which drain/ditch/bog/dead animal this slime could possibly have come from flying through my head. 'What on earth have you been *doing*?'

Granny, meanwhile, is chuckling away happily.

'Oh, just look at you! I think someone's been having a *very* good time – haven't you, young man?'

Vigorous, proud nodding is then accompanied by, 'Mummy, Mummy, I've made a pond! Do you want to come and see?!'

Before I have a chance to reply, the bog baby disappears happily behind the huge spruce tree again. Granny, meanwhile, has another tip for me about childhood.

'I think something you young parents would do well to bear in mind is what you think you are trying to achieve.'

'What we're trying to *achieve*?' If you must know, what I'm mainly trying to achieve is not drowning in the whirlpool that is my daily life, and if I could stop these bloody crow's feet from spreading across my entire face that'd be a bonus as far as I'm concerned. I wisely choose to keep these musings to myself.

'It seems to me that a lot of parents today spend a huge amount of time ferrying their children from piano lesson to cricket club to I don't know what else, and they think they are doing their kids a favour.'

'Well, they sort of are, aren't they? Learning to play music, and dance and do sport is all part of their education, and it's fun.'

'Oh yes, some of it is fantastic. But it's the *scale* of the thing now. When your child is so tired she can't stay awake at the table for all the activities she has crammed into her day – and because her parents won't enforce a decent, early bedtime, but that's another matter – isn't it time to let a few things go? You have to think of the child and what she is actually getting out of it all.'

Granny's Pearl of Wisdom

If you fill every waking moment with clubs and lessons and activities, where is all the time for childhood – for free, creative, imaginative play?

It's a vital point, and I'm interested in *why* this intense activity-cramming is happening.

Why are all we meddling, fussing parents so frightened if our kids can't speak eight languages and compose symphonies by the time their milk teeth fall out? Who are we trying to impress? And who are we doing it all *for* – the kids themselves? I'm not so convinced.

I've known children in the Reception class at school who are only given toys if they learn their times tables. Aged four!! Of course it's a great idea to teach basic maths and literacy as part of their everyday lives, and we do it all the time – adding up the peas on the plate, learning how to write 'sausages' and so on, but why teach it in such a pressurised, results-driven way? It's rather unnecessary, I think. But there are many kids under this kind of low-level, constant pressure these days, as so many parents worry about giving their children 'the best chance'.

And there's the nub of the issue. What *is* the best chance? I put the inescapably meagre case for the defence to Granny.

'I think what's happened is that we've lost confidence in ourselves, and we've got confused about what the "best" is for our children,' I venture.

'Oh, then let me help you out. 'Best' doesn't mean sent to the most classes. "Best" doesn't mean getting the biggest prize. The best thing you can do for your child is *be there*. And that's where much of this pushing and shoving comes from.'

'What do you mean?'

'Well, so many parents aren't there, looking after their children as we used to be. So you feel guilty, understandably, and you try to make up for it by creating some "wonder child" who *has* everything – including extra French lessons and Tai Kwon Do. It's supposed to show what a good parent you are, I suppose, when really you just need to be at home more.'

Aha, a masterful play of the guilt card. And, though I feel it's unjustly aimed mainly at the womb-bearing half of the species, it's still a winning one.

'There seems to be a belief,' she continues, 'that if you put them into enough classes and courses and get them all the grades, achievements and skills, that will in some way make up for your absence and give them the ticket to a good life.'

Granny has raised an important point about guilt and making up for our absence, but I think she's missed an even greater one raised by two mothers below:

> ❝ I just can't believe how many extra activities some kids do – and yes, I do feel under pressure to not let mine fall behind. But at the same time, I want my kids to have more time at home to do what they want, and not have to do cello practice or Spanish verbs. They are at primary school, and it doesn't seem right to me to take so much of their play time away. ❞
>
> **Helen, mother of Suzanne and Tom**

> ❝ We were expected to be bored sometimes when I was a child. Now, we stimulate our kids all the time. I over-plan like mad!! Sometimes I can't arrange a play date for my daughter and her friends for months because they're all so busy. With all the alpha mummies or alpha daddies there comes a lot of 'Oh, is she in Japanese class yet?' We don't have to raise our kids this way: a six year old doesn't need a PA! ❞
>
> **Linda, mother of Jessica, six**

The pressure from other parents not to 'fall behind', and to 'keep up' is immense. A lot of our manic 'activity-doing' with our kids is *not* to alleviate guilt, but because many parents feel under unspoken pressure to keep up with everyone else. And I know from my own kids that much of it also comes from the children themselves: if their best mates are playing the piano, they want to play the piano too!

Between the three of them, my own children do four ballet classes a week, plus violin, cello, football, chess and choir. And they're all at primary school. So am *I* a pushy mum?

Well no, I don't think I am, because they *want* to do all of this. If any of them wanted to stop, they could at any time. They have asked to do all of these things, and they absolutely love them. In fact, they have asked to do a good deal more activities and classes that I've had to say no to, just to keep some time free for us all to be together. So maybe the well-intended push turns into unacceptable shove when the poor love wants to play the trombone about as much as he wants to eat his own poo. Each child to their own, but **beware the considerable pressure from other parents; you let your child do what is right for *them***, and sod the irritating show offs next door whose son plays cricket for the Junior England squad, while his sister's got a part in Steven Spielberg's next movie. Good luck to them, and good luck to yours, too.

So, how can we stop the pressure cooker from exploding?

∾ *GRANNY'S TIPS* ∾

Don't over-schedule your children. Let them have some free time that isn't planned or time-constrained.

Be brave and resist pressure from school and peers.

Allow your (young) child to have plenty of time at home. Their childhood will be over in a flash.

Playing by the rules

So far Granny has advised not rushing too much, not worrying too much, not studying too much, not pressurising too much… anything else?

Yes, one more thing. Didn't you just know it?

'But you know,' she says with her oft practised and amazingly effective 'listen to your grandmother now' stare, 'I'm not saying you should just give kids a free rein to mess about all the time!'

'Oh, right. I thought that didn't sound much like you.'

Granny has a sharp tongue and a firm hand and has been known to use both on children who step out of line. Not that I would know, obviously.

'At the same time as all this freedom you have remember the other thing childhood is for.'

What's that then – making tiny models of squirrels out of your own snot? Saying rude things at full volume about people ahead of you in the Post Office queue and then having them say how sweet you are, instead of clonking you on the head with a jiffy bag? Eating sweets until you throw up into your sibling's lap? Turns out Granny has something else in mind.

'It's the time when you learn the rules.'

'What, the Rules of Life?' (I think I may have been absent when some of these were spelled out . . . Sorry, Mum.)

'Yes, if you like. **There are a lot of rules that we all have to understand and abide by if we are to all live together peacefully. And childhood is when we learn the very basic ones, and learn where the boundaries are, from our parents.**'

And presumably, I say, when children overstep those boundaries, as they so often do, they need to know about it . . .

'Oh yes, of course they do. You have to teach that to a child, by disciplining them when they're naughty. It's not cruel, as some people say now. It's part of what parenting is about.'

13

Granny's Pearl of Wisdom

Rules give a child's world boundaries and allow them to feel safe. If you can't get the rules straight and clear in your child's mind and teach them that their actions have consequences when they are very young, you really set yourself up, and the people around you, for a tough time ahead.

Granny has a few last thoughts on the importance of childhood and I start taking notes, lest my befuddled, knackered parent's brain has trouble retaining all of this valuable stuff.

Letting kids be kids

Granny takes a good slug of coffee and settles back in her chair.

'You asked what has gone wrong with the way children are raised today – well, I think lots of you are doing a very good job, actually.'

Oh, well, thank you very much. Time for a communal pat on the back methinks . . . Oh, hang on – hold the patting, there's a 'but', . . .

'But one of the main things that's happened is that you have stopped treating children as they need to be treated.'

'What do you mean?'

'Well, as so many of you seem to have forgotten somewhere along the very busy line, childhood is the time *before* adulthood.

That may sound obvious, but it doesn't seem to be the case any more.'

It doesn't?

Granny's Pearl of Wisdom

Childhood is the time to be a child, to be treated as a child and not to be treated as equals with adults.

Ah yes. The old 'treating kids as equals' habit. This worrying trend is one I have noticed increasingly in the last decade, and it disturbs me. Kids often seem to be put on a level with their parents now: they're asked what Madam would like for dinner, what time Sir would like to go to bed, what her Ladyship would like to wear, what Mummy can do to make her offspring's lives absolutely perfect in every way, in fact.

Talking to some of my mum friends and just listening to conversations around me in the street I observe the same concerns, but it seems few people feel safe to say that they don't want to treat kids as equals. That they feel there should be a 'place' for children, and another for adults. Perhaps there's a fear that they'll be seen as unkind, or cruel or even – Heaven forbid! – Bad Parents.

But hang on, give the self-flagellation a break: is asking what your child wants for dinner really treating him like a mini adult, or are we just trying to give kids a voice, and to listen to their opinions? That's surely not a bad thing. I mean, they may poo their pants for several years and everything, and make your hair fall out, but they have feelings and we can listen to them!

Granny thinks it's more to do with role clarity.

'I think that in many ways the line between childhood and adulthood has become so blurred and this is causing a lot of problems, because you lose your authority.'

'Such as?'

'Well, where to start? The clothing that's made for little children that looks like it's fallen out of a seventeen-year-old pop star's dressing room, the fact that parents cannot discipline children for fear of being told off themselves, the number of tiny tots who are dragged out to cafés every weekend to have a cappuccino with their parents – that's no place for a small child! They want to play, and muck about, not sit in cafés while Mummy and Daddy read the newspaper.'

Now hold on – I happen to agree that there are far too many kids being hoiked off to Starbucks several times a week and are all but ignored while they're there or given gargantuan muffins and pastries to keep them quiet. It's very depressing actually. But we do it from time to time, and I consider it valuable – no, *essential* – grown-up time, and there is absolutely nothing wrong with having a nice sit down over a latte while my kids read a book, or draw a picture. Or, as we do most of the time, actually talk to one another without emptying the dishwasher, hanging out the laundry or picking up thousands of bits of Bionicles from the kitchen floor. Going to cafés means having unadulterated family time, and that's a good thing.

But Granny doesn't mean only this. She sees it as one example of the many ways children have crept into an adult world. Being given the same responsibilities and choices as we have.

Granny is surely not saying it's better to ignore children's feelings and opinions? Even she wouldn't go that far!

'No, but sometimes it's absolutely fine to tell a child that they just have to do as they are asked. They are children, and you are adults. Period. You don't have to treat children as though they are about to fall apart – or as though they are your best friend. Sometimes life is tough, and unfair, and understanding this is part of childhood too.'

Oh, how many of us have fallen foul of that wonderfully tempting business of treating our children as our best friends? They're cute; they like shopping; they don't bitch about you behind your back (much) and they love staying up late having a good chat. What's not best friendly about all *that*?

We are to touch on this sticky issue again in a few months but for now it's very handy that it crops up here. I'm not sure if it's a totally modern phenomenon – for all I know Roman mothers used to hang out in the Grandus Shoppingus Mallus with little Julius and Athena – but wanting to be 'bezzy mates' with our children, particularly mothers with their daughters, is something that seems to have taken over families of late and it's not an entirely good thing. Mothers out on shopping trips with their five year olds, having girly lunches with their ten year olds, getting their hair done together – even having *facials* together when their child could be off reading a good book or inventing something involving toilet rolls and Sellotape. (Interestingly, this is still what many little boys seem to like doing . . .) All this adult-like behaviour is . . . well, it's kind of weird, no?

Sometimes I desperately want to feel like a best friend to my children, but let's be perfectly honest here: the reason many of us do this is either because we didn't have the relationship with our own parents we would have liked and so we want to create this pally-ness with our kids, or because we're desperately trying to recreate a *good* relationship enjoyed with our parents. Both are dangerous games to play. In many ways I actually do feel like a best friend to my children because they will always come to me to talk about things that are troubling them, to tell me something funny or to cry. But I feel it's also essential to maintain some kind of authority, and for me to feel and behave as though I am their *mother*, their parent and therefore in some way responsible for them and in charge of them.

Does Granny think this is important in order to keep our kids under control?

'Well, partly. **But don't forget it's also because children need certain securities when they are growing up and one of them is knowing that they have parents who are there to act as guides, as role models and as protectors. Being best friends removes this safety net and that's very unsettling for a child.'**

This is a point I had never thought of. If you are over-friendly with your kids, far from making them feel happier and more secure, it can actually have the *opposite* effect because the role that they so need from you – that of the person in control, and where the buck stops – is missing in their lives. It establishes boundaries and draws out an invisible 'safe zone' within which they know what's what and know they'll be OK.

It takes a while to realise the importance of this, but it's worth taking that time and remembering it.

Granny's Pearl of Wisdom

Childhood only happens once, and it's terribly short as it is. Be their parent. Be in charge, and give them everything they need to be children. It's the foundation for everything that's to come.

So what do some other parents think childhood is for?

66 *Watching clouds.*99

Don, 58, father of two

66 *Childhood is for growing memories. It is for having as much fun as you can fit in. Childhood is a time for 'doing' without being judged; for laughing when you know why and when you don't; for learning to trust; to be free.*99

Rebecca, 40, full time mother of four

Childhood is for simply being a child; for growing up and learning about the world, and learning about survival as well as how to dream – even Einstein says, 'Imagination is more important than knowledge'; childhood is also a call on a parent to be properly human: to be less selfish and more humble in the face of new life; to be strong and yet feeling, protective and prepared to let go.

Jeremy, 40-something, father of two

I love thinking myself back to early childhood for the sheer feeling of acceptance with everything as it was – no intrusive expectations or judgments of character. My brother and I just played and played and played in our own world and it was wonderful!

Jane, 63, mother of four and grandmother of four

Now then, did you notice as you were reading the thoughts above that the word 'judge' cropped up in various guises? We'd be well advised to think about that more often in the way we raise our children. We are very quick to give judgement, to offer our opinion, say what we think, compliment and criticise, but actually sometimes it's best just to shut up, listen and not judge at all.

These thoughts, all of them beautiful, moving and true, along with Granny's own suggestions from another time, form the very backbone of what you read from here on. The idea is never to wish ourselves back to times gone by – that way madness lies (and bad haircuts).

What I will seek to do instead is to find ways of putting some of this carefree and happy and, if such a word can be used here, *successful* childhood back into today's world.

After this first chat I feel ready to start tackling some of the issues we raised in greater depth, and to really dig deep into the vast pool of knowledge Granny has from her child-rearing days, and that continues to this day, of course: fifty year olds still need their Mummy sometimes!

But not right now. A slimy pond awaits, and I'll be in the Naughty Mummy corner before you can say 'last one covered in mucks' a rotten egg!' if I don't go and check it out, as promised.

Chapter Two

HOME SWEET HOME

Family life starts in the home, so that's what I want to talk to Granny about next. I'm a great believer in the importance of home. Not a house, but a *home*. It doesn't matter what this home looks like – whether it has one or five bedrooms, a dedicated playroom or a corner in the kitchen for some toys, matching crockery or charity shop mugs – whether you spend most or only some of your time there, or even *who* lives there with you. What matters is that it *feels* like home, and by that I mean it feels safe, familiar, and full of love.

As times have changed, so the way we live in our homes has too. No longer do we eat in formal dining rooms: instead it's more common now to have an open-plan living area where we cook, eat and play in one big space. Children often have a bathroom that is separate to their parents' bathroom, and you're as likely to see an office in a corner of the lounge as a place to sit and read.

Given the frightening statistics we've already seen about children being apparently so unhappy and troubled, is there something we can learn from the past about how to run a happy family *home*?

Household chores

As I pass through Granny's creaky iron gate the next morning on my way to talk with her about the importance of Home Sweet Home, I have a nasty run-in with a wild and exceptionally vicious climbing rose. This unpleasant altercation results in part of my left ear looking like Mike Tyson didn't get enough breakfast, and, wiping the blood into an old scrap of Costa Coffee tissue I find squashed in my pocket, I decide that I will have to tidy the garden up a little for Granny before either she or I kill ourselves tripping over a flowerpot or getting lost forever in the bindweed.

To my great surprise, Granny accepts my offer of horticultural help (I have offered innumerable times to tidy her house up a little and have been met on each of these awkward occasions with bristling mutterings about it being fine, and what nonsense, and couldn't I just sit down and have a cup of tea) and puts me to task immediately with the somewhat vague instruction to 'clear up that messy patch of the left flowerbed and leave the buddleias some room to breathe'.

I can't tell if it's the excitement of being let loose in the garden, the pleasure of doing a job for someone else or the quiet revenge I seek on that blasted rose, but either way within half an hour I find myself standing next to a pile almost as tall as I am of what I assume to be bindweed, grinning broadly at my heroic efforts and sweating profusely despite the autumn chill. I am doubly pleased with my efforts, because this bindweed had been smothering to the point of suffocation a rather attractive bush with thick, dark green leaves, which my hard work has spectacularly exposed. Granny will be so pleased.

I am just on my way to the bonfire, my arms full of metre

upon metre of the nasty, smothering weed, when Granny hobbles gingerly out of the porch to take a look at my efforts.

There is an unexpected and rather unnerving silence, as she inspects first the sizeable hole I have just created in the flowerbed, and then what I am holding.

'Oh!' she says at long, long last, looking at the mass of greenery in my arms. 'I see you've taken out my favourite Clematis.'

This story is not so much to demonstrate how rubbish I am at gardening – though for anyone who invites me round for the weekend that's a warning worth knowing – as to bring us to the troublesome issue of chores.

I remember doing chores around the house when I was a child: setting and clearing the table a little, making my bed (badly) and tidying up my room occasionally – though mainly this involved shoving everything into my cupboard. My brother and I also did odd jobs for our grandparents when we were there – washing the car, fetching the groceries, getting the newspapers in the morning, that kind of thing.

We weren't saints and we did do some of this for money rather than out of the goodness of our own hearts, but we still had chores and we did them, and so did many adults of my age when they were kids.

After I've cleaned myself up a bit and feel I can face Granny again, we settle down for our daily chat, and I get straight to the subject of the day: household chores. I am fairly sure she would have been given her fair share as a child, and would have set her own wee ones to task as well. In what looks set to be the theme of the day, I am proved wrong yet again.

'Oh, I'm afraid I'm going to disappoint you, Elizabeth – because we had absolutely no chores at all! We got up as late as possible, we played a lot, and we had a lovely time. Chores were not a thing for us as children. We were just children!'

I am dumbfounded. I expected a list as long as my arm of jobs they were made to do; not quite shimmying up the chimney, but the more daily domestic chores like cooking, washing and so on. I imagined that's what childhood was like 'back then' when times were tough, kids were disciplined, no meant no and sweeties cracked your teeth before they had a chance to rot them.

'But, I thought you would be doing lots of things to help your mum around the house. Wasn't that what all the discipline, and the "do as you're told, work hard" ethic was all about?'

'No, not at all,' she corrects, opening the door a little to let Mica, her small ginger and white cat, out. 'Doing things to help others was just assumed. It was part of respecting others, and doing your bit. But they weren't *chores*, or jobs, and we weren't asked to do them. We loved our mother, and we had huge respect for her and our father, but we didn't need to do chores for them, to show this respect. We just behaved well, and were polite – and mainly tried to stay out of trouble!'

Granny's Pearl of Wisdom

The housework is not part of a child's life at all.
They should be free to play while they can.

25

All of this surprises me so much that even I am silenced for a few moments. It dawns on me that maybe I've been wrong all this time to try and get my kids to help with the washing up, to fold away their clothes and to scrub the kitchen floor till I can see my face in it. (OK, not that last one. Jeeez, you were calling the police weren't you?)

So maybe Granny is right, and that the concerns many of we parents have to try and instil a 'work ethic' in our children, to make sure they 'chip in', pull their weight, stop taking us for granted and jolly well pull their finger out on the home front is entirely counterproductive.

Maybe letting kids be kids, and simply raising them to do things for others because they instinctively understand and feel it's the *right* thing to do, rather than insisting they make their bed and put away their own clothes aged five, is a better way to go.

Granny and her sister were allowed to *play*. They were children, and they had freedom, and time and opportunities to play in a way kids today can only dream of.

While this does sound fantastically idyllic, and something we should all strive to provide for our kids today, I do have to disagree a little with Granny here. I think that, after the age of six or so kids *should* be asked to help out at home a little bit. Teaching kids to muck in and appreciate what we do for them by giving them some jobs to do themselves, not only makes them realise how much work there is to do around the house, and how much effort goes into looking after a family, but it also teaches them a lot of useful skills for later life. I wouldn't know how to change a bed in two minutes flat if I hadn't had to strip and make my own for years as a child! Nor would I be able to cook, or clean a bathroom properly, or iron a shirt well if I hadn't watched my mother do it a million times, and then had a go myself.

But I do like the idea that children helping out at home was just done if it was seen to be necessary, without them being chivvied along every twenty minutes with a 'do this', 'do that' attitude, and it's one I decided there and then to try and adopt a bit more for my own children. Helping out because you want to, because you respect the person you are helping, is a much better way to be going about it.

∞ *GRANNY'S TIPS* ∞

Childhood is a time for playing and learning through play, not doing household chores.

Children should respect their parents enough that they help out instinctively, not because they are told to.

—— LIZ'S TIPS ——

Some degree of helping out around the house is a good thing, as it teaches children to value what you do for them, and gives them the skills they'll need one day to look after themselves.

Don't start the 'chores' too young. A child of five doesn't need to set the table, but one of nine can easily put her own clothes away!

Routine, routine, routine

When I left home at the grand old age of seventeen I felt a colossal sense of loss. Really, it was like having a huge hole ripped out of my stomach, and I felt totally rootless for a while. Of course, I loved that I was finally going out into the great big world by myself – that was the most exhilarating feeling ever for an adventurous sort like me, and as soon as I could I packed a huge rucksack and set off around the world on my own for six months – but leaving the place I grew up in was a painful wrench and when my parents sold the place a decade or so ago I couldn't even go back to help them with the move. It had to stay in my mind just as it was: patterns in the cracked paint that had been there for years making shapes that became my companions, of strange faces, animals or faraway islands; marks on the walls where, in a moment of wilfulness, I'd scribbled the name of someone I fancied; the smell of the lounge carpet in the sunshine; the reflection of the bay window on the top of the piano – all of it had to remain just like that.

What made me so attached to my home was, oddly enough, not the people who were there (they are still around, even though they're in a new place now), but the incredibly strong sense of routine that was present: every day, from the age of six, I'd get up at the same time, catch the school bus at the same time, come home at the same time, have dinner, a bath, go to bed, read and sleep. Weekends were for music lessons and practice, walking the dog, homework, jobs around the house and family time. The same things, every week, for years and years. It was constancy, a familiar, known rhythm, which gave me a huge amount of comfort and security when times weren't quite so rosy. Even through the turbulent teenage years when I was, according to reliable sources, 'a bloody nightmare' to live with, my routine changed very little and my house – the building itself – was a passive, non-judgemental observer of all who lived in it, which made me like it all the more.

I wonder what Granny thinks about routine and the importance of setting out some patterns and rhythms in a house with children? Is it good for them, and should we be trying to stick to routines that work for us? Or do they need more flexibility and irregular patterns in their lives?

'Routine is vital for a child, oh yes,' she tells me emphatically. 'And the most important one is bedtime.'

'Why?'

'Well, just think about it: I hear of parents who just cannot get their kids to bed in the evening – but they're watching the television until two minutes before bed! How can they ever sleep then?!'

Granny's Pearl of Wisdom

You have to establish a very clear routine of calming children down in the hour before it's time to go to bed – the same every day. A child will learn that and then settle down very easily.

Mica, who has been out for all of about five minutes, now wants to come in. Maybe that's part of his routine, and Granny's is to open and shut the door.

'So what kind of a routine did your kids have before bed?'

'Well, the most important thing was to get some *peace* before bed time. It helps to settle them. So they'd all have a bath together – by the end of the day they were filthy! – and I'd give them all a good soaping. When your dad was born we had no electricity and he'd be bathed in a big zinc tub in front of the fire.'

I feel a brief moment of 'ohhh, poor little thing!' before remembering this is my dad we're talking about, and he was hardly a shrinking violet – the pictures I've seen of him as a baby suggest the zinc bath was likely to come off rather worse than he did. Bless his cotton socks (if they had any back then . . .).

'And did you have a rigid bedtime?'

'Oh yes. The children were all in bed by half past seven until they were at least ten or so. Then we started to let it get a little later – they had homework and music practice. But you have to have a routine in place; otherwise they'll stay up half the night and get exhausted.'

This point about exhaustion is one I discuss *ad* flipping *nauseam* with my eldest who seems to think that she is the 'only person in my whole claaaass!!' who goes to bed this side of midnight. (She is not. I've checked.) Sadly, what happens when she gets less than ten hours' sleep for two days running is that she gets shadows under her eyes that could well land me in jail for child neglect and cold sores on her mouth that are both unsightly and painful. The fact is that she needs sleep, and thus needs to go to bed early!

THE SCIENCE OF SLEEP

The amount we need to sleep changes a lot with age, and also with how much activity (mental and physical) we do. Each person is different, and the amount we need varies from day to day. Know your child, and what he can cope with, and adjust accordingly.

An average toddler needs about eleven hours' sleep per night, plus a nap in the day of an hour or so, while a child of ten doesn't have a nap in the day at all, but still needs about ten hours' sleep. By the time they hit adolescence children can get by with about eight and a half or nine hours' sleep per night, but many don't get half that amount because they're up late, watching telly or out with friends.

School-aged children need to get enough sleep so that they can concentrate on their work, learn and behave well at school. Establish a sensible bedtime which enables this amount of sleep, and stick to it as much as possible.

Sleep is a basic need of the human body and prolonged periods of not getting enough can result in serious difficulties concentrating, working and keeping well. Kids are growing and learning at a phenomenal rate and generally using up a lot of energy all the time – they need sleep to recuperate!

Getting enough sleep can become a real battleground as kids get older because they want to stay up later to feel 'grown up'. Sadly this does them no good if they are becoming sleep-deprived. Try to explain that sending them to bed is not a punishment – it's what they need to learn, grow and be healthy. Even if you can bring bedtime forward by fifteen minutes, that's a good step.

Now, all of this routine is something I believe in very strongly, but, to be quite honest, I think a completely rigid and unmove-able routine is not so very helpful. Children do need to learn that sometimes things change and we can't always do what we'd like, or what we usually do. It teaches them flexibility; the ability to cope when things change.

For me, there was probably a little bit too much routine, though I'd say at least half of this was self-imposed, and I did develop some rather obsessive-compulsive tendencies from quite a young age that I used as a safety net. So long as the alarm clock rang six times, I got out of bed with my right foot and the bath-room light went on before I stepped into the room, all was well. That kind of thing. It can be hard to adapt to 'unknowns' if you are brought up with immoveable routines, so I'd advocate having a clear system throughout the week, but letting this shift ever so slightly as new things present themselves.

We still stick to a 'no screen-time after dinner, bath, stories, lights out' routine every night and have done for over ten years so far – but if there's the odd one where we're travelling or we've got friends round then it all goes out of the window for a day. Life is too short to be totally anal about these things – one night a month isn't going to harm your kids!

So bedtime routine is important. What about other routines in the family home – is it helpful to have systems in place, patterns of activities and some kind of a rhythm in a home?

Granny thinks it is: 'Listen, you don't want to run a home like an army, with Mummy blowing her whistle when it's time for dinner, or time to do homework. But if you can have some kind of routine each day it just makes life so much easier!'

'For whom – the children or you?'

'Well, for both actually. If kids have homework every day, or even every week when they're little, have a "homework time". That could be Saturday afternoon, or each day at 4 p.m. Whatever fits your family. That way it won't get forgotten, and eventually it becomes a habit: Four o'clock is homework time. Then there's no pushing and forcing them to do something – they know that's what they do at that time. It's clearer for them, and much easier for you.'

Granny's Pearl of Wisdom

Routine is vital in a child's life. It needn't be unnecessarily strict, but a basic pattern of what happens when provides a very important and useful structure to their lives, and helps to get them mentally prepared for each part of the day, for example, playtime, homework, bed.

Talking about the importance of routine with Granny has come at a very useful time for our family: as the kids are starting to get more homework and also have music practice to do each week, taking Granny's advice and putting a certain time aside each day for these things has meant we actually get everything done, and aren't scrabbling around with homework diaries the morning it's due in! It even means weekends are more relaxed because I know we're on top of things. Such a simple tip and such good results! Wish I'd thought of it ages ago . . .

Illness

Something that happens in a family home with remarkable and frustrating frequency is that someone gets ill. If it's not a baby with diarrhoea it's a toddler with chicken pox or a teenager with flu. Or, worse still, Daddy with a cold. Lord save us all! Illnesses fly through families like WAGs through a department store, and just as one person is showing signs of recovery, the next is sniffling and coming down with it. What should take three days for one person turns into a month of hell for everyone, and then we all start again with the next lurgy.

But here's an interesting thing: once upon a time, people knew how to deal with common illnesses. If a child had a cold you'd feed her home-made chicken soup, give her a hot bath and put her to bed for a week. For stomach bugs you'd eat nothing at all or nibble on dry bread, keep the fluids going and wait till it worked its way out. For flu, my grandfather used to wrap us up in a freezing cold, wet sheet, causing our bodies to go into a kind of panic, sweat profusely, almost pass out and then sleep for twenty-four hours – before waking up with no symptoms whatsoever. Except possibly a desire to shout at him very, very loudly. (He was a medical man, incidentally, so it wasn't quite as bonkers as it may sound, though I would urge you NOT to try this at home!!)

Old wives' tales and 'secret remedies' passed down the generations, and, bar some nasty outbreaks of smallpox and the plague, many people did just fine with home remedies and bit of common sense.

Here's a favourite family story: when I was six years old my entire family spent Christmas with my aunt and uncle at their home near Edinburgh. Also present were their three children all under the age of five, my grandparents, two other sets of uncles and aunts and their various infant offspring, three beagles, two Labradors, four cats, two kittens and a budgerigar. And nine kilts. It was, as you can imagine, a jolly, noisy, colourful gathering, but no one could have predicted the fall-out that this event would produce.

I am certain that the warm glow of my aunt's pride could be felt as far away as the Outer Hebrides, as she served up the now infamous salmon mousse starter. It was pink; it was light; it was delicious.

It was also chock-full of salmonella.

Over the next twenty-four hours every member of the family spent time getting to know their toilet bowl better, and, as one of the youngest members of the Fraser Clan, I was the first to go. As luck would have it, this coincided with one of the very few occasions my parents were supposed to be going out for the evening, and something as inconvenient as a daughter at death's door wasn't going to stop them. Fair enough.

I was left alone in the house with my granny looking after me. And what fun it was! She tucked me up in bed with an entire year's collection of *Oor Wullie* and *The Broons*, brought me water every so often – and watched to make sure I drank it – and largely let me get on with trying not to be sick any more. I wasn't fussed over, she didn't call a doctor, I didn't require urgent medical attention. I got time and rest and peace. And I got better.

Health scares

These days a child with a severe stomach bug is more likely to be either packed off to school with a smile and an 'Oh, she's totally fine now – just a twenty-four-hour thing!' or be bundled off immediately to the doctor who would be expected, and most probably pressured, to say something conclusive at the end of his three-minute examination, prescribe some ointment/pills/tonic or treatment that was guaranteed to rid the patient of all her woes within six hours and do so without looking the slightest bit as though the adult bringing her in was totally barking and should take a chill pill herself.

The level of concern, worry and even occasional panic levelled at the health of our children seems to me to be deeply ironic, given that kids have a far higher chance of survival today than they have ever had. We are bombarded with news stories every week telling us of yet more 'killer bugs', poisonous food, deadly additives or hidden nasties just waiting to zap your kids into oblivion.

As well as actually getting ill less frequently than ever, we also have more understanding of the causes and cures of most of the common ailments that befall our little darlings than anyone could have dreamed of fifty years ago. We can do more than ever to avoid illness and treat it effectively if it does strike, and yet we worry like nervous fleas about our children conking out at the first sign of a sniffle or sneeze.

We are a nation of health obsessives who pop pills as though they're going out of fashion and live on a diet of hysterical, often misinformed or exaggerated health-scare news.

So what can Granny tell us about dealing with common illnesses in her day that might calm our nerves and save the NHS spending several billion pounds a year on unnecessary antibiotics?

'Well, we had all sorts of childhood diseases that, thanks to vaccinations, you lot don't come across so much any more.'

'Good point. And would you call a doctor about those straight away – they could be very serious.'

'Not always. You knew chicken pox when you saw it and there's not much you can do about it until it goes away. If anything you wanted the whole family to catch it and be done with it!'

Aha, the famous chicken-pox parties; very sensible idea I think. Nothing more annoying than spending one entire summer holiday seeing Child A through chicken pox only for Child B to get it in time for Christmas.

'You had to be careful of a child with mumps,' she recalls, with a somewhat sterner than usual expression, adding another line to her already time-worn but still beautiful face. 'You had to keep them in the dark, as the mumps really affected their eyesight, and they had to be warm. Mine all had mumps, but it didn't last long. You just expected it then.'

My mother-in-law has told me of the fearful time when my husband contracted mumps as a child. When he was four she could get the thumb and index finger of one of her hands to meet around his thigh bone. She still speaks of it as one of the worst episodes of her life, and it's a terror I can only hope I never come to experience – that of believing you might lose a child. And to think that I recently panicked because I'd run out of Calpol when one of my kids had a slight fever – what a nincompoop!

Granny goes on, rubbing her ankle in the hope of getting some blood into it. It looks totally lifeless, cold and white – much like the doctor who allegedly prescribed her a dose of aspirin and a hot water bottle would look now if I could get my hands on him.

'Now whooping cough was a nasty one. Such a noise they made! I put Ken and Alison in a room together, just whooping

37

and whooping away they were. Such a racket. And German measles – we used to have German measles parties as soon as one of the girls got it. We didn't have the vaccinations then. And we certainly didn't mollycoddle them.'

She looks straight at me now, not in an accusatory way, but I feel she's trying to drive a point home here about the level of fussing we modern mums do.

Granny's Pearl of Wisdom

If our children had a fever, we kept them warm and in bed for a few days. We didn't go to the doctor and demand pills. A child gets ill, so you nurse it better.

'It took time, but that doesn't matter. We had the time to keep them at home and nurse them back to health, and if things got really bad then of course we'd take them to see the doctors at the practice. But it started by keeping them at home and resting for the first week, and usually most things got better in that time anyway.'

Stop right there! Having a child at home for a *week*?! What, is this lady *nuts*? Does she have the kindest employer in the world who doesn't mind her taking five days off to mop her child's brow and thus miss out on two board meetings and a client deadline? Does she not have grocery shopping to do, or ludicrous amounts of dashing about between toddler groups and ballet classes and trips to the bank and visits to Zara just in case something exciting has just arrived on the shelves?

It's then that a penny about the size of a small island drops, taking with it half a ton of guilt to choke even the most adoring parent: **one of the main reasons we dash off to the doctor so often for a miracle cure for our offspring's ailments is that we don't have the time for them to be ill any more**.

That day when you bundled your daughter off to nursery even though she had a stinking cold and probably infected the entire class before biscuit and juice time. That day I sent mine to school with impetigo claiming it was a rash brought on by some new bath wash. That week the entire Year One class got nits when Johnny came in crawling with the little buggers, because his mum was at a conference in New York and his nanny promised to get the nit-comb out for him but didn't. All those times.

Let's be honest: how many working parents do you know who can take time off every time one of their children is ill? One? Two? Probably three at most, and they're probably the idiots like me who work from home as freelancers because they were too lazy to get a proper job. (Oh, I'm kidding, fellow free-lancers!) Many parents are forced to take unpaid leave to look after sick kids, and they worry about their chances of holding on to that job if they are doing this more than two or three times a year, which is almost guaranteed even if you have only one child.

And for those who have a nanny to hold the reins, what are parents supposed to do when *she* is ill? Can't she have a miracle cure as well so we can all get back to normal?

I put all of this, in a slightly gentler, explanatory way, to Granny. There is some more shaking of the head. She stops rubbing her leg and looks at me with a mixture of disbelief and deep sadness, making me half wish I'd kept such an admission to myself. Too late.

'If you can't look after your child when he's ill, what sort of a mother are you, Elizabeth?'

Granny's Pearl of Wisdom

Your primary role as a parent is as carer, whether your children are well and ill, absent or present. A child who is unwell needs their mother or father there to care for them – and no job should come in the way of that.

Clearly we can't just drop everything every time Jack or Josephine comes home from school with a chest cough. But it's a heartless parent indeed who honestly thinks it's OK to pump her child full of Paracetamol and pack him off to school when quite clearly he needs to be in bed, warm, comfortable, and with whoever it is who normally looks after him to make him feel better.

I would like to add one thing about illness and families: while I agree that we need to calm down a little and not panic at the first hint of a cough, it is of course vital that if you really think your child needs medical attention you seek it as soon as possible. Also, prevention is as important, if not more so, than cure, so banish soggy, bacteria-laden hankies and use tissues instead, don't cough all over each other, get a flu jab if someone in your family is particularly at risk and wash your hands regularly.

These simple things can stop infections spreading like wildfire through a household.

The jury is still out as to what caused my entire family to fall foul of the vomiting bug all those Christmases ago. But my money's still on the salmon mousse.

∽ *GRANNY'S TIPS* ∽

When your child is ill and needs looking after, one of his parents *must* be there to look after him. And let him be ill – don't expect him to get up and get dressed!

Many illnesses just get better within a week or so – don't rush to the doctor immediately, unless you are really concerned.

Know basic first aid and how to treat the most common ailments yourself.

And one secret remedy? For bad skin infections, a bread poultice works miracles. I used one on Ken to draw out the poisonous pus in a nasty shoulder infection, much to the astonishment of the local doctor when it worked like a dream within twenty-four hours. Boil some water and when it has cooled from boiling to hot, pour onto thick slices of white bread. Lay the bread on the infected area and wrap in a clean sheet and then some oil silk (OK, since you ask, it's silk treated with oil to make it water-tight, such as raincoats are made of. You learn something new every day . . .) to keep the moisture in. Leave overnight and in the morning, when you remove the bread, you'll find all the poison has been drawn out into the bread and sheet.

Make your work work for you: Many employers have a policy that states employees are allowed to take time away from work to care for dependants – make sure they stick to this and do NOT force you to take it as annual leave.

If your child is looked after by a nanny, make sure you have agreed how you'd like your children cared for when they're ill, which medicines they can take and so on. And if *you* can't take the day off to be with your child, that's fine, so long as they're happy to be looked after by the nanny. We don't need you wallowing in guilt!

Sending a child to school who is ill is not only cruel to that child, it is also irresponsible. Children seem incapable of keeping more than five millimetres apart from each other for the entire school day and of not coughing, sneezing and wiping their germs over everything that moves – and everything that doesn't too. I don't want your kid's bugs in my family, so keep them at home please!

'Feed a cold' is one of my mum's favourites. If your child has a cold, try to keep him warm and resting, offer plenty of fluid (water or juice with high vitamin C is best) and regular snacks. And yes, home-made chicken soup really is a good place to start!

For gastric problems, avoid offering fatty foods or anything spicy or 'complicated'. I used to get dry toast (no butter, as it's hard to digest), plain white rice or just dry biscuits until it passed. Extra fluid is vital to avoid dehydration.

Remember that a raised temperature is actually performing an important function: by raising its core temperature the body is trying to kill off some of the bugs. If you cool it down all the time, this can't work. If a child has a temperature it's a good idea to try and keep it down if it is prolonged, using something like Calpol or Nurofen for Kids. My granny tells me they used to use Baby Aspirin, which is considered unsafe now, so who knows what they'll find out about our current methods of body temperature and pain control in years to come. Use medication wisely, and only when necessary.

The great outdoors

From where I am sitting in Granny's porch I can see the top of a mountain called Morrone, with its five cairns like pimples on the horizon. I remember being marched up to the top so many times I know every stone and patch of heather like the moles on my hands. And that was only a short walk. There was nothing at all unusual about our packing the tents and walking for nine hours a day into the mountains, anywhere from Scotland to the Indian Himalaya. Complain though I did – all the way up! – I always came bounding down the mountain pink-cheeked, invigorated, covered in muck and scratched till my legs bled – but I was full of health and life. And I was rarely ill.

Children need fresh air. It clears the head, works out some of their troubles and keeps them fit, which is a very good start to being healthy. Those who think fresh air is what they get by watching nature programmes and keeping fit means using a Nintendo Wii are missing a very important trick. Not convinced? This should help:

* Time spent in green spaces is sometimes jokingly termed 'vitamin G time', and kids who get more of this have been found in some studies to have lower stress levels, more success in school, and fewer Attention Deficit Hyperactivity Disorder symptoms.

* Simply being in sunlight triggers the skin to make vitamin D, which could help to prevent cancer.

* Being in the fresh air can turn grumpy children into happy and energetic ones remarkably quickly, and it also helps them to sleep better at night.

> " As families are forced to tighten their spending, more people are looking to their local communities for outdoor activities and with a large variety of activities on, it's easier than ever for everyone to get outdoors and get active. Outdoor adventure and activities have numerous benefits – including helping to tackle obesity and providing opportunities for young people from all walks of life to enjoy new experiences. This can be as much as climbing a mountain in the Lake District, to experiencing their first time camping at a music festival to playing football with their friends in the local park. "
>
> **Peter Duncan, former *Blue Peter* presenter and Chief Scout**

Granny remembers spending the vast majority of her childhood in the fresh air, despite living in the often bitterly cold East of Scotland.

'We were outside all the time! There was little to do indoors – we had no telly or radio or even many toys – so we played outside: making dens, skipping, throwing a ball. Simple things like that. Our mother would have to call us in for our supper.'

'But it's hard to get kids out nowadays. There are so many temptations – the computer is always there, even if it's off; there's the telly and they have games and toys coming out of their ears. Going outside is "boring" so they often tell me.'

'Well, throw them out then!'

Granny's Pearl of Wisdom

Children need fresh air every day, and all you have to do is get them out. Once they're there they'll find something to do – to keep warm if nothing else! Just open that door, and send them out for an hour.

And there's more:

'If you can get your children to enjoy the feeling of being in the fresh air as kids, it'll stay with them forever and the benefits cannot be overstated. Just look at you now – it's hard to get you inside! You're always walking or cycling or running outside. And that's because you were raised to enjoy the Great Outdoors – camping, hill walking and just playing outside.'

She is so right. I like being outside so much I'd live out there if I could (so long as I had a comfy bed, a hot bath and a television, obviously. I'm not *mad*). And I can already see the same love of the outdoors starting to take hold in my kids. Yes, it's almost impossible to get them out there sometimes, but once they *do* finally leave the comfort of the sofa and get outside they're as happy as teenagers in a pub. (A pub garden, of course.)

What may have seemed like hard times, being forced up hill and down dale by 'unsympathetic' parents were actually far better times than many kids experience today, sitting for hours in front of their TVs and Gameboys, with their toys and videos and clothes and *stuff*.

∾ *GRANNY'S TIPS* ∾

Children need to go outside for a time every day, even if it's only for ten minutes.

If you can **give children a love of the Great Outdoors** it's something you can never take away from them, which will bring them a lot of good health and happiness in their lives.

If they don't want to go, just be tough and **send them out anyway**. Not for hours, but for some fresh air time. They'll find something to do.

—— LIZ'S TIPS ——

Make it a family affair. If your kids are really reluctant to do anything outside then get involved yourself. Go sailing; cycle together on a Sunday or go for a walk, which ends in a pub lunch. Anything to make it *fun*.

Even ten minutes is better than nothing. If the weather is awful then get the wellies on and go for a short walk – even around the block or to the shops. This can be enough to shake away the 'fug' of the day at school.

Set a challenge. 'This year we'll walk up small mountains', or 'let's try a one mile fun run all together'. Something small that you can work towards can really excite and motivate children.

Lead by example. I love being outside and my kids can see the positive effect it has on me. So they want to do the same.

Chapter Three

EAT YOUR GREENS

We really *are* what we eat

After a brisk morning walk up the nearest hill, which all but kills the lot of us, I leave my children playing 'attack the cute, fluffy rabbits with pieces of dry twig' in our garden while their dad tries to set up some kind of internet connection so we can check our email – sigh – and toddle off down the road again.

Squeezing through the gap in Granny's French doors and making my way past the piles of catalogues, binoculars, weed killer and cushions, which fill the sun porch, I finally enter the kitchen and am somewhat alarmed to find her cooking an enormous pot of Scotch broth. This, in itself, would not usually be any cause for concern: she is, after all, a Scot, and broth is the panacea of the pennywise unwell: cheap, warm and highly nutritious.

But when I tell you that she is doing this otherwise entirely sensible activity in a room containing approximately six hundred badly stacked and never quite properly washed pots and pans, at least twenty-five opened herbal tea packets, fifty cereal boxes – some pre-dating the Queen's coronation – the entire Lakeland catalogue of

47

'Handy Kitchen Gadgets' (none of which appear to be particularly handy as they are almost all still in their packaging and are merely cluttering the work surface, such as is visible), several kilos of bird food, yesterday's shopping – still in bags – two cat litter trays, a jungle of house plants, not all of which are still alive, a motley collection of sad-looking fruit and nowhere near enough space to swing either of the cats who are helping themselves to some chicken remains on the sideboard, then you will perhaps understand why my eyebrows come to rest at my hairline.

Experience tells me not to even think of asking if I can be of assistance. If there's one thing my grandmother isn't, it's helpless. This Scotch broth *will* be made, by her, in this environmental health catastrophe, and I *will* be having some.

She looks up as I enter, her eyes softening at the sight of uncomplicated, friendly company. But then, the frown.

'Oh – and where are your lovely children?'

That's me feeling special, then.

'Getting to know the local wildlife a bit better, Granny. Best left to it, I think.'

She gives the bubbling liquid a final, vigorous stir, just to make sure there's nothing either alive or with any nutritional value whatsoever left in there as seems to be the custom with ladies of a certain age, and picks up a ladle.

'Well that's a shame. Still, *you'll* be having a plate of soup, will you?'

It seems wholly appropriate, as we spoon the thick, surprisingly delicious liquid into our grateful mouths a few minutes later, that our conversation should turn to the nutrition of our children. It's a subject that spills into our newspapers almost daily, and, like the waistlines of our little darlings, shows no sign whatsoever of decreasing. It has come to obsess the nation, fill more column inches than Jordan's chest, and bring to their knees a good number of parents who are simply trying to feed their family, but haven't got a clue what's OK to eat and what's not any more.

Before we even start, some facts and, erm, figures.

FACT BOX

OBESITY AND FOOD-RELATED PROBLEMS

The number of children developing Type 2 diabetes – which normally affects overweight people in middle age – has risen tenfold in the past five years.

A Government-instigated survey recently showed that across England almost twenty-three per cent of children aged four to five were overweight or obese, rising to over thirty-one per cent of children aged ten to eleven.

A further 60,000 children are thought to be suffering weight-related metabolic syndrome – a combination of conditions including high blood pressure, raised cholesterol and increased fats in the blood.

Obesity in children causes problems with the joints and bones (such as slipped femoral epiphysis and bow legs), benign intracranial hypertension, hypoventilation, gall bladder disease, polycystic ovary syndrome, high blood pressure, high levels of blood fats and diabetes.

There are also marked psychological effects leading to low self-esteem and obesity is also one of the prime targets of bullying.

The problem is clearly huge. So huge, in fact, that the Government, terrified of the enormous bill the Health Service will face when all of these kids start getting very ill indeed – or possibly because they really do care about the kids in this country. Who knows – is starting to do its bit to help. A £372 million strategy to help everyone lead healthier lives was published in 2008 by Alan Johnson, Health Secretary, and Ed Balls (hee hee. Oh stop it), the Secretary of State for Children, Schools and Families. It pretty much sets out to try and 'create' a healthy society, from improving school food and food education, encouraging sport and physical activity and even covering planning and transport issues.

Providing healthy school food is obviously one crucial factor in improving what our kids eat, but for parents there is a much more direct way we can get a grip on our children's double chocolate muffin tops.

✳ A study published in December 2008 in the journal of Paediatrics found that one in four children aged four to five in England are overweight and most of their excess weight gain happens *before* school age – in other words, it starts *at home*.

This result starkly illustrates how vital it is that we start making things simple and healthy again on the home front.

It's time to make things simple again on the home front. So what, according to Granny, should our children be eating, what is good for them, what's bad and why oh *why* are so many of them so revoltingly, dangerously, unnecessarily rotund?

'Well,' she says, stirring her broth. 'People often seem to focus on how *much* food children consume, you know, but really, just as big a problem now is *what* they are eating.'

'I'm not sure you'd get many kids these days eating anything as good as this soup, that's for sure,' I remark, with a great dollop of tact, a peppering of sincerity and a dash of 'smart-arse'.

Her spoon comes abruptly to rest at the side of her bowl with a loud clank.

'*Soup?*' she echoes, with disbelief. 'Auch no. Not *soup*. Children eat nothing but *junk*, Elizabeth. I see them on the way to school eating crisps or chocolate bars. They haven't had any breakfast, and they'll be down at the chippie for lunch. Or their parents post burgers through the playground railings. It's no wonder they're all obese. They're not eating any proper food.'

'Now hang on, Granny, children are certainly not *all* obese, and there are plenty who don't eat junk food all day long, yet are still getting fat. And there must have been fat kids when you were little too, no?'

'Well, there were of course some children who were bigger than others, but just look at the old photos of kids back then – school photos and the like. Do you see so many children who are fat? No – we were all eating enough, and very healthy.'

She's right. In my own school photographs from the late 70s and early 80s, there in the rows of dodgy haircuts, mean outfits and shocking front teeth I can't see more than three out of a year of sixty who are what you'd even call fat, and none who were obese. But we did eat – I ate a LOT when I was little! – so how come we weren't fat?

'Its simple: if you eat real food made of natural ingredients – cooked at home – you won't get fat, even if you eat quite a lot of it. If children live on manufactured this and reconstituted that, they haven't a hope.'

Ah, the curse of processed foods. When did it all get so complicated?! Food was once just that: FOOD. Not pretend sugar, or hidden fat, or energy-boosting chemicals, or life-enhancing additives. It was just FOOD. Grown in a muddy field somewhere, or straight out of the back end of an animal, or dangling from the branches of a tree. The farmer gathered it, the shop sold it, we bought it, and we ate it. Simple.

These days finding anything natural or unadulterated means either turning your garden into a farmyard or having more money than you could shake an organic stick at. Either way you need an extraordinary amount of time to grow your own or to actually locate any natural products between the millions of jars of ready-made high-salt sauces, and packets of water-filled meats, and not all of us have that time. Fast food is . . . erm . . . faster, so that's what we turn to time and time again. Until the scales break and we move into velour tracksuits. Mmmmm.

> ❝ I contend that most of what we're consuming today is no longer, strictly speaking, food at all, and how we're consuming it – in the car, in front of the television, and, increasingly, alone – is not really eating, at least not in the sense that civilisation has long understood the term. There have been traditional diets based on just about any kind of whole food you can imagine. What this suggests is that the human animal is well adapted to a great many different diets. The western diet, however, is not one of them. ❞
>
> **Michael Pollan, author of _In Defense of Food_**

Let's be honest here: who of us can have failed to pick up on the fact that processed food, fast food and 'un-natural' food generally contains high levels of salt and that this can lead to high blood pressure – and that's a risk factor for heart disease? None of us, that's who. And yet we consume more food, with more salt and refined sugar already added, than ever before.

FOOD NASTIES TO LOOK OUT FOR

If you want to make sure your kids eat better quality and healthier food, you just need to know what to look out for when you're shopping. You don't have to go mad, checking every label – it'll soon become quite clear what's OK and what's not, and you'll change your buying habits accordingly.

Colourings are one of the top offenders. A study of 300 youngsters by the Government's Food Standards Agency (FSA) found they lacked concentration and became more impulsive after drinking a mixture of artificial additives. Used in a number of foods, including soft drinks, sweets, cakes and ice cream, these include:

Sunset yellow (E110) – Colouring found in squashes
Carmoisine (E122) – Red colouring in jellies
Tartrazine (E102) – New colouring in lollies, fizzy drinks, sweets and sauces
Ponceau 4R (E124)
Quinoline yellow (E104)
Allura red AC (E129)

Other things to avoid

Trans-fats. The artificial hardening of vegetable oils by hydrogenation can form some unhardened, so-called, trans-fats, which cannot be properly digested by the body. These have been linked to coronary heart disease, and the simplest advice, since labelling is often not very clear (products such as cakes

continued overleaf . . .

and biscuits that include hydrogenated fats in the ingredient lists do not often mention trans-fats) is to avoid all foods that list hydrogenated or partially hydrogenated fats or 'shortenings' on their labels.

Salt. Young children's kidneys can't cope with too much salt. Babies need less than 1g per day, and even eleven year olds should have no more than 6g. There is enough in the food they eat anyway so you should never add more, and always choose reduced salt options.

Added sugar. If it has added sugar, find an alternative. It's that simple. Fizzy drinks are full of added sugar, and even fruit juices aren't the best as they cause tooth decay. If kids are thirsty, get used to offering water or milk. Snacks can just be fruit or crackers. It doesn't have to be a biscuit or chocolate bar!

Sodium benzoate (E211). This is a preservative, commonly found in soft drinks. Some research has shown that benzoates could make the symptoms of asthma and eczema worse in children who already have these conditions.

Sulphur dioxide (E220). A preservative found in a wide range of foods, in particular soft drinks, sausages, burgers, and dried fruit and vegetables. It has been linked to asthma, but in very rare cases.

Preparation: products that have been deep fried are clearly less healthy than those that haven't, as they're coated in batter (chicken nuggets, anyone?) or covered in a sticky sauce, like BBQ chicken. If you can, choose foods that have been adulterated or processed the least.

So does Granny have any suggestions as to how I can start feeding my kids more wholesome ingredients again, without chatting up the Time Lord, who'll whiz me back to 1925, or moving to the South of France for daily trips to the oh-so-healthy Marché? Yes she does, and it all comes down to shopping. Wahey. We like shopping.

'The thing that has changed is the *way* you shop. We used to visit the local butcher, the local greengrocer and the local baker. Everything was made that day or came from nearby, and it hadn't been messed about with by anyone. Nowadays you all go to the big supermarkets and fill up on stuff to last the whole week, or even longer. And, how do you think it lasts so long before it goes off?'

Scientific wizardry? Better fridges? Botox?

'It's not real food any more!'

Granny's Pearl of Wisdom

If you buy local, and buy fresh, you'll cut out on most of the junk in your diet immediately and not have to worry about how much you eat – you'll be healthier and happier.

The good news

The very good news, for our children's dress size, the country's local businesses and the planet itself, is that the embarrassingly simple activity of buying local is finally becoming *à la mode* again. Farmers' markets are now hotter than St Tropez, darling, and where have you *been* if your marrows don't come with clods of local earth attached?

Buying local

* Local shops sell a wide range of great products at affordable prices and shopping there can save you money. Once you've added in travel, parking costs, fees to transport larger items home and your time, the overall cost can be higher in out-of-town supermarkets.

* Buying local means buying food at its prime. It hasn't sat around on shelves or on lorries for days losing nutrients and taste, so it's as good as you can get it.

* Food from local farms has usually undergone minimal processing, so it's healthier and looks, smells and tastes *real*.

* Shopping locally also retains our communities and distinctiveness, creating vibrant town centres where people can socialise as well as shop, and is vital for the local economy.

66 *Local food economies are of the utmost importance to the sustainability of rural communities. They bring great benefits to the countryside both in terms of safeguarding rural jobs, sustaining local retailers, providing outlets for local produce and conserving the British countryside. If we are to ensure the survival of our rural communities and regional food heritage, we must build positive relationships between our local food networks and the global food chain. This would be hugely beneficial for farming, for rural businesses, local jobs and for the conservation of the countryside as a whole.* 99

Jimmy Doherty, TV's *Jimmy's Farm*

The recent and welcome growing trend to try and purchase fresh produce locally is not just down to our desperate fat-busting requirements, but for three other main reasons:

Carbon footprint. The way we buy much of our food today (flying raspberries halfway across the world when we could just wait and have British raspberries in August when they're good and ready) is mind-blowingly stupid, selfish and environmentally damaging. I've done it and you probably have too, but it's now really time we stopped, or at least cut down drastically. The trend for all things Green means many of us are trying not to buy anything that has travelled more than a few miles, and this is nothing but a damned good move!

The best things come to those who wait. Many consumers have finally realised that what they thought they wanted (everything being available all the time) is actually very crap and unfulfilling for one simple reason: nothing has any sense of 'specialness' or excitement any more, and there is consequently now a yearning to get back to a time when you had to *wait* for something, and then enjoy it all the more. When winter meant apples and oranges, summer meant strawberries and asparagus, lamb came in the spring, berries in the autumn and all the seasons were *different* and special.

Fashion. Love it or hate it, what's fashionable does dictate how many of us live, and shopping locally is *the* thing to be doing these days, once again. This is one trend we should ALL be following if we are to start feeding our kids something real for a change.

Granny's Pearl of Wisdom

Growing some of your own fruit and vegetables
is an easy way to feed your family well. We all did it
out of necessity during the war, and you don't need
a huge garden. Just a few pots for tomatoes, or a small
bed for potatoes or runner beans. It's very cheap and
it also teaches kids where some of their food
comes from.

The bad news

The slightly less good news is that, while this local shopping and home growing is all very admirable, healthy and fun, we have to keep it real: shopping once a week in a big supermarket is just the easiest way for many people. End of story. When I stopped work to look after my kids at home I could shop locally every day and I even managed to tend the crappy vegetable patch we had – it was something for us to do for goodness' sake! But now that my kids are all at school and I'm at work almost full time, shopping isn't an option most days of the week. And for those who work more than me it's nigh on impossible at any time other than the weekend. Quite apart from anything else, the big shops are actu-ally *open* at a time people can get to them – local ones often shut at 5 p.m. or even earlier.

So what's to do?

Strike a balance

Shop in supermarkets when you have to, and certainly for the big basics like washing powder, tins and so on, and for the Mothers Emergency Kit of freezer favourites like fish fingers – honestly, who is really going to be bothered to *make* those every time? – but while you're there try as far as possible to choose healthier, more natural options with less processing. The occasional big supermarket shops aside, try to make as many trips to local shops in between, for fresh seasonal produce like vegetables, as you possibly can. Saturday mornings are a possibility for many, and Sunday markets are open on . . . um, well, on Sundays, so that's another day you can probably manage.

Until food manufacturers promise, promise, *promise* to stop filling our daily bread with sugar, saturated fats, and salt it's going be very tricky to reverse the obesity trend and get the nation's children back into their skinny jeans again. But Granny has another suggestion that we can all try out, and this time it means coming out of the shops, and back into the kitchen . . .

Cooking from scratch

Just as I am wondering whether anything is safe to eat any more I am shown a newspaper cutting Granny has put aside to illustrate her next point.

'Just look at this,' she exclaims, waving the paper dangerously near my almost empty bowl. 'Children at a school in Fife have been banned from bringing in home-made cakes to the School Fayre, in case of any allergic reactions. They're being told to bring shop-bought ones instead. But what's in those?'

I make a face that I fear sums up the words 'Ummm . . .' and 'I don't know' perfectly. Granny clearly has no difficulty reading the look in my eyes.

'Well, that's just it: they don't know either. They've no idea!'

Granny's Pearl of Wisdom

When you cook food at home, you know what's in it because you do it yourself. Flour, eggs, salt and sugar – and that's IT! No hidden extras. If you buy everything from the shops your children consume a terrific amount of unnecessary things that are bad for them, without realising it.

Granny has finished her lunch now, but not her attack on the way we eat these days.

'There's nothing home made any more, like soup, or bread or a roast dinner, and many people don't even know *how* to make them, and you know why?'

'Because we're all lazy and watch too much telly?' Mmmmm, telly . . .

'Well, there's a bit of that, certainly, but it's mainly because parents are both out at work all day, and haven't the time or energy to cook when they get home. So they open the freezer and heat up any old shop-bought junk they find in it. Tins, packets, jars – you name it. I was at home looking after the family, so I had plenty of time to cook a healthy meal. That's what the trouble is now. '

Aha – so *this* is how it feels to be one hundred per cent guilty of every charge thrown at you. Mummy works: guilty. Too tired to cook: guilty. Opens freezer and removes 'any old junk'? Guilty. Crikey, she's going to put me away for life.

As I struggle to reconcile the undeniable sensibleness of what Granny just said with the fact that it somewhat undoes most of what the Women's Liberation Movement achieved and that allows me to be sitting in front of her at this moment researching my latest book, rather than chained to the stove baking cookies for my adoring children, she tells me a story of an American schoolgirl who came to stay with them as some kind of exchange programme, back in the 1960s.

One afternoon Granny was in the kitchen, doing something exciting with the aforementioned flour, sugar, eggs and so on. The poor, unsuspecting visitor asked Granny what she was doing, and received the swift reply, in a voice I can only imagine was so far beyond terse it was teetering on the brink of bone-crushing, that she was 'making a cake!' According to Granny, her American guest's eyes nearly popped out of her head.

'"Oh", she said to me. "Do you mean you *make* them – *from scratch*? You don't buy a packet and just add water before cooking it?" She'd honestly never seen anyone bake before, Elizabeth. And she was fifteen if she was a day. I'm sure she thought we were either very hard up or just strange! It was so sad.'

Now then, nobody but the disgustingly virtuous, irritatingly time-rich or bored beyond words can be expected to bake every loaf of bread and cake they eat. Even Nigella must nip down the in-store bakery once in a while! And nobody, least of all me, is asking that all mothers stop working to stay at home and bake! But making a simple, healthy meal from scratch needn't take more than ten minutes, quick enough even for the busiest of us, and learning to cook is one of life's absolute essentials – one we must, *must* pass on to our kids. If we never show them how to cook, or where their food comes from, what chance do they have to spot what's healthy and what is a vacuum-packed heart attack in the making when they come to choose food for themselves?

FACT BOX

HOME COOKING VS READY MEALS AND FAST FOOD

* We spend around £2 billion a year on ready meals.

* In 2006 Britons spent more than £52 billion on food – with more than ninety per cent of that money going on processed food. Ugh.

* In 2007 we spent £39 billion on fast food in Europe's top ten outlets.

* Home cooking is cheaper, healthier (you control the amount of fat, salt etc) and you even get some exercise preparing the meal and cleaning up!

* Cooking can relieve stress and it's satisfying (assuming you don't burn it all like I often do).

66 *The evidence is now undeniable that poor nutrition is putting children's physical health at risk. Many children are now expected to die before their parents – as a direct result of their unhealthy diets and lifestyles. Many children's diets are high in sugar, refined starches and the wrong kinds of fats, as well as artificial additives. They are high in calories (energy), but lacking in essential nutrients. The risks to physical health of such a 'junk food' diet are now recognized, [and] the effects of food on behaviour are . . . very real.*99

Dr Alex Richardson author of
They Are What You Feed Them

Fewer and fewer of us spend time cooking in the kitchen with our children, which is sad enough from a bonding and life-skills point of view – children learn not only how to look after themselves, but also how to count, measure, weigh, and look suitably irritated when it all goes wrong – but what makes it even worse is that it's been shown that when kids help prepare a meal, they are much more likely to actually *eat* it. It's a complete no-brainer in other words!

And just look at what all of this ready-meal culture has done to our kids' education: In a study in 2007, eleven per cent of eight year olds didn't know that pork chops come from pigs, eighteen per cent had no idea where yoghurt comes from (it's from bats' teardrops, obviously . . .) and eight per cent of children growing up in cities didn't know that beef burgers come from cows. And when you realise that two per cent of children think that eggs come from cows, and that bacon is from cows or sheep, you really are left wondering: do they even know what food IS?!

The facts above are not so much surprising (and, let's admit it, more than a little funny) as brow-wrinklingly depressing. When more children think honey comes from Tesco's than know how to crack an egg, you know something's gone seriously wrong not only with their education, but with their home life. I'm not suggesting we should all keep our own bees and hens, of course, but when you cook with a child, even using shop-bought basics as most of us do, you can have those lovely little conversations where matters such as bee keeping, pollination, and Great, Great Aunt Muriel's perfect method of egg beating crop up, and where such knowledge is passed on to the next generation. And if time for cooking (or the lack of it) is a big issue for you then try this one for starters: go without the television and computer games for a week. Seriously, try it. If you don't find at least an extra hour in your week to cook together, I'll eat my hat (and it's a nice one).

Spilling the beans – was it *really* all home made back then?

Much as I am enjoying the discussion, I can't help noticing that in this picture of domestic bliss, something smells fishy. And it's not fish. Much as I am prepared to believe that Granny cooked almost every meal for her family from basic ingredients and slaved over the stove more than I ever will, surely even morally upstanding people Back Then used to skip the home baking and indulge in a little corner-shop Battenberg or Victoria sponge every so often? Surely they too occasionally cried 'Oh to hell with these bloody domestic chores' and gathered around the wireless instead? Granny thinks about this for a moment. I wait for a confession.

'Well,' she says at last, 'it was a little of both, I suppose, but only where you couldn't make things yourself. You'd never have *thought* of buying a cake, for instance, and I always made sure there were home-made sweet treats the kids could eat. But we'd buy butteries (the Scottish equivalent of croissant – in other words as much fat as science will allow you to squeeze into a pastry before it explodes – and possibly even a little bit more delicious) from the bakery, and bread was usually bought, but that was it.'

Granny's Pearl of Wisdom

You don't need to be a genius to cook for a family. People get so frightened about it, but anyone who can read a cookery book can produce something edible. You just have to have a go!

I am beginning to feel more than slightly inferior now. The last time I baked was only about a fortnight ago, but I'm fairly sure that was under duress because I had someone else's children round for tea so I was just showing off, and not because I particularly wanted to have a big family cookathon with my kids.

I *still* want to find some imperfection in this picture of family bliss. Something naughty. Something you and I do on a regular basis.

What about takeaways, I ask? And eating out? Could she put her hand on her heart and tell me that they never treated themselves to the 1950s equivalent of a cheeky Friday night curry, a Sunday pub lunch or a chip butty on the way home from school? Here, at last, I find a chink of reassuring sloppiness.

'Oh, no, we had our treats! We had a fish supper every Saturday.'
(A 'fish supper' is what those of us hailing from South of Quite
Far North would call fish 'n' chips, incidentally.) 'It was a weekly
treat, and there was certainly no worry about it being *bad* for us,
or making the kids fat or unhealthy. Everything else they had was
home made or natural, so having fish and chips once a week was
absolutely fine. They needed the extra fat to keep warm and
growing – it's cold up here you know, young lady!'

∞ *GRANNY'S COOKING MEMORIES* ∞

'I learned to cook at Brownie camp where we cooked over a
fire. We made liver and bacon, and little scones. In the 1920s
and 30s, we had little indulgences like Rice Crispies and
Cornflakes [my, my, they *have* been around a long time!] but
there was no "snack" foods or "junk" foods at all – eating
between meals just didn't happen. Crisps were virtually
unheard of, and chocolate bars were either too expensive or too
hard to come by when my children were growing up. There
were simple biscuits, and snacks by then were a buttery or an
apple. Everything else was made by hand, at home. From the
scones themselves to the jam that went on them, food was
simpler – we'd added salt ourselves, which is frowned upon
today, but it didn't matter because there was no salt hidden in
everything from bread to beans. And my children were happy,
healthy and enjoying life to the full.'

At this moment I suddenly realise that the house we're sitting
in is a good deal colder than it probably should be for an elderly
lady with no circulation in one leg to be sitting in. Having cleared
the soup bowls to the kitchen, I go to fetch some more logs from

the wood shed to stoke the lounge fire. When I return, Granny is sitting in her favourite chair, surrounded by a year's supply of newspaper supplements and with a large ginger cat on her lap.

(Don't) supersize them

As she strokes and he purrs, she tells me her last tip about feeding children well.

'There's one more thing that has made your children all fatter, you know, and that's how much you give them. Why must you all feed your children – and yourselves too – as though they aren't going to see food for the next month? They are *children* – they're small! So give them small portions for goodness' sake.'

Amen to that. Just as everything technological is getting smaller, so everything nutritional is getting bigger. Muffins are the size of basketballs, chip portions are like giant sacks of felled trees, and crisp packets are larger than bin liners. A 'standard' loaf of bread is now several slices bigger than it used to be, and 200g bars of chocolate have magically grown to 230g! Where will it ever stop?

The crazy thing is that, whatever food suppliers might be doing to portion sizes, on the home front we have complete control over this, because we can choose to give our children whatever portion size we feel is right for them. And yet we often don't seem to exercise this control one jot: I see kids sitting down to meals with more food on their plate than *I* could eat and then watch them listlessly munch their way through the whole lot, under the unwavering gaze of their parents – who then have the audacity to complain that their kids need more exercise because they're overweight . . .

Granny has her theory on this one:

'All of this overeating is only a result of having too much money, you know. When we had to count every penny, and when there were rations, we didn't waste it on huge portions that nobody could eat. We gave our children just as much as they needed – which wasn't a lot when they were young – and there was no wastage. Any left over we used the day after, and we never piled our children's plates up so high that they couldn't finish. You all waste so much now – it's horrifying.'

Do we ever?! Money, we have been raised to believe, can buy us whatever we want. And, we've been told, we're *worth* it. Well, the funny thing is that money has also trashed all the things we wanted, and, with tougher financial times a reality for many of us now, it's going to be up to us now to change our ways and use our money more wisely.

THROW-AWAY BRITAIN

* Every day, we Brits throw away 220,000 loaves of bread, 1.6 million bananas, 5,500 chickens, 5.1 million potatoes, 660,000 eggs, 1.2 million sausages, 1.3 million yoghurts and 4.4 million apples.

* Every year, we throw away over £10 billion of wasted food.

* Daily food waste costs an average home more than £420 a year and for a family with children (that's us then) this rises to £610. Madness! (stats from 2007)

But hold on a second: you don't want to waste food, of course, but neither do you want to *under*feed a child – they are growing and learning so fast, after all. We are bombarded with information about how important it is to make sure our kids get enough of this and enough of that in their diet lest they develop scurvy, diabetes, behavioural problems or a silly walk (OK, possibly not that one) and this has almost certainly led to us feeling the need to offer our kids gargantuan portions on their plates. Here: look at all these wonder-nutrients – eat, child, *EAT*!

Granny has little time for this, and argues her point in her usual clear, no-nonsense way:

'Oh you hear so much about nutrition this and healthy diet that. But children are very clever, and they will eat as much or as little as they need or want on that day. Some days they want more, and other days they want very little. It's the *balance* that's important. Instead of worrying about what a child eats during the course of a day, think about what a child eats over a week. It usually all balances out.'

Granny's Pearl of Wisdom

Just give them a little portion to start with – if they want more they'll come straight back and ask for it, mark my words!

This is so refreshingly simple that I feel calmed at once. Granny has raised four very healthy children this way, and that's the only evidence I need to know it works.

So where does all of this lead us? The three main points about feeding children healthily I've learned from Granny today are as follows:

* Children need to eat REAL food not processed foods full of hidden fats that make them fat.

* Food preparation should be done at home, with your children where possible, with time and love as important ingredients.

* Children need to eat child-sized portions, and will tell you if they need more.

No amount of muffins, biscuits or burgers we buy our children to alleviate our all consuming guilt for our frequent absences and hectic lifestyles, or because we simply can't be *bothered* to cook them anything better, will make them any happier. The soup I have just eaten was better than anything I could have bought from the best food shops in the country, partly because it was healthier as it was home made, but also because it was made for *me*, with love, by my granny.

Before she returns to the wonderful world of the National Geographic Channel, Granny gives me one last piece of old-fashioned advice.

Granny's Pearl of Wisdom

People think they can buy affection, buy happiness and buy love. But they can't. Cooking for your family is one of the best ways of making a loving home.

Or, as my mother would put it using a favourite Czech expression: 'Love goes through the stomach.' Provided the food doesn't get there via the takeaway counter or the deep freeze, I think she has a point . . .

∾ *GRANNY'S TIPS* ∾

Cook as much as you can at home. It needn't be anything fancy, as long as it's home cooked.

Teach your kids to cook. Even boiled eggs and toast is better than nothing, and watching you is almost as good as doing it themselves.

Shop locally and buy fresh, seasonal produce.

Don't eat snacks or junk food. What's wrong with an apple?

Keep the portion sizes to children's sizes, not elephants'!

—— LIZ'S TIPS ——

Cook in bulk. Set time aside at the weekend to make home-made meals and freeze them if you won't have time in the week. Take a meal out in the morning before you go to work, or the night before and put it in the fridge. All you need to do is heat it up in a pot and you've a home-made meal ready to go in minutes!

Think of your wallet. According to www.moneybasics.co.uk, a ready-made meal that costs £4 or more would cost no more than about £1.50 to make at home, and that's before you factor in the leftovers potential. Pre-packed sandwiches are priced at around £2.50, over four times the cost of making your own and just by making a packed lunch, cooking supper at home and avoiding coffee bars all week it could save you around £200 per month.

Think of your health. Ready meals contain more saturated fat, salt and sugar than food you make at home. You could be eating twice the number of calories you need just by not bothering to make your own food!

Keep it simple: learn to make soup. Soups are ridiculously easy for you and for your kids to make, and are so healthy it hurts! Once you've cracked the basics, you'll wonder why you never did it before.

Basic meals need only have three ingredients. If you have rice, pasta or potatoes, some kind of vegetable and something for gravy or sauce like tomatoes you're away. Add some meat or fish and it's a feast!

Chapter Four

PLEASE MAY I GET DOWN?

Animals feed, humans dine. Which are you?

A few days of warm, sunny autumn weather pass quickly by. Granny looks pretty well, all things considered, but she still insists on driving the 200 metres from her house to the coffee shop to share some carrot cake with us and takes naps in the middle of the day, which I've never noticed her doing before. Honestly, anyone would think she was old or something. Slacker.

Before I know it it's Thursday already, and I've barely managed more than a few chats with her. Time to put that right, and quickly.

Another of the joys of staying so close to Granny is that we can invite her over for dinner. This is not only because her house resembles a museum exhibit entitled: Every Object I've Ever Owned, Have Mostly Not Used Since The Last Millennium But Cannot Throw Away, and as a result we can barely all fit around a table – even if we could find one – but because it's such a pleasure to be able to cook for *her* once in a while, after she has spent so many years cooking for us all. She is also terrific company, and after a wee dram can usually be persuaded to recount funny stories from her past until she drops. Also, the thought of Granny eating her tiny meal all alone every day always makes me feel a little sad, living as I do in a family where dinner times are a tranquil and civilised mix of *Pop Idol* meets *House of Tiny Tearaways* meets *The F Word*.

So I pop down the road on Thursday morning to issue the formal invitation: dinner, tonight, six sharp. I find Granny in the kitchen, trying to stuff small white bags into a freezer that already contains enough food to keep her going through several long periods of severe rationing, and am reminded by their contents, as the smell that greeted me at the back gate already should have, that Thursday is Fish Man Day.

On Fish Man Day, half of the village waits in eager anticipation for the 'beep, beep' of a horn, as a small, white van splutters over the last hill and swings gratefully into the car park, laden with fresh North Sea marine life, at precisely 11a.m. The other half of the village, I assume, doesn't give a damn about fresh fish and is having a fag out the back of the local bar. More fool them. Like many old people whose metabolism has slowed to the pace of a snail carrying a grand piano on its back, Granny eats so little it's a miracle she doesn't disappear altogether, and most of *that* passed its sell-by date before the Berlin Wall came down. But if she can consume fresh fish several days a week, I think she'll be healthy for a long time to come.

'Got your fish then, Granny?' I enquire, subtly removing half a brown banana from the sideboard and slipping it into the compost bin.

'Oh, Elizabeth! Good morning. Yes, yes, got my fish. Oh, he

had some *beauties* in there today – did you not get any for your-self? And those poor wee children of yours?'

My 'poor wee children' love fish, but as we are heading down South in a few days and still have more food in our fridge than the British Olympic team could trough in a week, I didn't think it was wise to buy anything that needs eating within twenty-four hours. Ten-hour car journeys are bad enough as it is with three kids decapitating each other on the back seat, without half-rotten herrings joining the fun.

'Nope, no fish for us this week, Granny. But we do have some chicken curry that desperately needs eating – fancy joining us for dinner tonight?'

'Oh – a meal with the family? Sounds *lovely*. You're not to go to any trouble though. Just something simple and some good *company*. That's what mealtimes are all about.'

It is *indeed* what mealtimes are all about. *How* we eat, as opposed to *what* we eat, has become the subject of much dis-cussion and debate (though sadly not around the dinner table, of course – this being the root of the problem) as eating on the hoof, munching on the bus, scoffing in the bath and chomping in front of the telly have become the normal way to get grub into our wobbly bellies these days. It's a far cry from the big family gatherings of old, and, truth be told, it is also just a hazard of modern-day life for many of us: we'd quite like to have an evening meal *en famille*, but the members of that *famille* are all miles apart, stuck in traffic or off to football practice.

The main question of course is: does any of this *really* matter? Is eating together really such an important thing? Food is just food after all, no matter *how* you get the stuff down your throat. No?

I pass Granny another couple of bags of haddock and sole and ask for her opinion.

'Oh yes, eating together does matter, and you know why?' She looks up, leaning on the freezer door for support. 'Eating together cements a family bond. There's so much panic about *what* people eat, which is of course very important, but eating *together* really matters too.'

Slamming the door shut with some considerable force for a lady of her stature, she stands up slowly, before continuing.

'It's when you're sitting around a table together that you learn so much about each other. Children talk about their friends, what they get up to at school, especially when they're talking amongst themselves. If you sit and listen you'll learn a lot about what's happening in their lives.'

Has the family meal-time really declined so much in recent years? Here are some thoughts you may recognise, and some facts in the box opposite:

66 *We have started trying to eat together most evenings in the week but I've given up actually trying to eat at the same time, as the spillages, demands for drinks, more/less of this, trips to the loo and people going AWOL make it impossible. But in theory we do, and the children seem to enjoy it and behave better.* 99

Camilla, mother of three

66 *One person is usually missing from breakfast and the children will often eat earlier if friends are around. We always try and have lunches together at the weekends, in the garden when possible but the timing of popular TV programmes causes a lot of friction.* 99

Nikki, mother of three aged between five and twelve

FACT BOX

FAMILY EATING HABITS

According to the 2004 National Family Mealtime Survey, twenty per cent of those asked sat down to eat together just once a week or less. The poll, by parenting organisation Raisingkids, found children often had meals alone in their bedrooms while watching TV or playing computer games. Of those who did eat *together*, TV was the preferred dinner guest, with seventy-five per cent eating while watching it.

Child psychologist and parenting expert Dr Pat Spungin, founder of Raisingkids, says the benefits of family meals are far-reaching, and should not be underestimated. The organisation is running a Back to the Table campaign to get families eating together again.

* Some estimates put the percentage of children who now eat in front of the TV in this country at fifty per cent!

* Kids who eat in front of the TV don't pay attention to what they are eating or exactly how much, and are thus less likely to respond to their own bodies' signal for hunger, and overeat.

* According to www.talkingretail.com on average, Britons cook from scratch three times a week, which is a slight rise on four years ago, BUT the number of us who use ready meals *every week* has doubled to fifty per cent in the last five years.

66 *Both of us working means we have to make appointments to eat with each other, let alone the kids. And teenagers only let you know they are around for dinner by turning up and complaining there isn't enough for them. But you have to find a way to make it happen – the kids would happily accept a pizza pushed under their bedroom door otherwise – and it's the best way to find out more about each other's lives, without the embarrassment of having to text them to find out!* 99

Lisa, mother of two teenage boys

OK, so while many people are making an effort to eat together – a very good sign! – family mealtimes are still either a battle-ground or an impossibility for many. And when so many of us use the kitchen table as an office, general dumping ground for junk and art table, how can we be expected to sit down and eat a meal at it – even when the TV is finally switched off?

Even without knowing the stats, anyone worth their Jamie Oliver cookbooks must have noticed that families don't eat a home-cooked meal together half as much as they used to. It's all microwave this, ready meals that and TV dinners the other. There are even children now who don't know how to use a knife and fork because they've never eaten anything from a plate. Ye gods!

It's not that mealtimes have totally *vanished*, of course: *most* people manage to sit down once in a while and eat together. But the days of the whole family enjoying three hearty, home-cooked meals round the dinner table every day are just O-V-E-R for most of us, however hard we beat ourselves into a scramble about it. So what *were* real family mealtimes like fifty years ago, and is there anything we can do to put a little lovin' back into the way we eat?

Once upon a breakfast time

Granny has now picked her seat of choice for the morning – with the best view of some gorgeous tits (oh, stop it) pecking away at a seed block hanging from the bird house. We begin our discussion with breakfasts: the most chaotic and troublesome meal of the day, surely?

'Well now, we always, *always* had breakfast together,' she recalls, smiling. 'It wasn't the quietest affair, much to your grandfather's annoyance, as we were also hurrying to get ready for school, and someone – usually your father, of course – would always knock something over or need to get up and fetch something from the wee hatch to the kitchen. That drove Gordon [my granddad] mad. He was not the best morning person, you know – didn't like noise or fuss.'

This image of kids getting up: spilling stuff, being noisy and generally causing more chaos than a group of runaway baboons at the zoo, sounds comfortingly familiar to me, and may chime with you too. Maybe we're not doing such a bad job of it after all . . .

'And was it important to you to have breakfast together, even if it was a bit hectic?'

'Oh yes. Essential.'

> *Granny's Pearl of Wisdom*
>
> Start the day off all together, because whatever chaos comes later in the day, at least you've all said good morning and have been together as a family before the rush of the day begins.

And don't we all know about the rush of the day! Most of our days are more hectic than sports day in a bee colony on unlimited double espressos, and starting them at 300 miles an hour without so much as a 'morning' to the people you share a home with isn't the most family-oriented way to begin.

Starting the day with your children, talking through what they need to take to school, what they dreamed about, how they are feeling this morning, how many scabs they picked off in the bath last night and so on is essential family time. Quite apart from the bonding aspect of this, it can really focus their minds on what they've got coming up that day and it's often the time we realise we haven't done the homework due in today – again. Quick – grab a pencil . . .! Breakfast is an especially important time for parents who work and may not be able to get home in time to share the evening meal with their kids.

Now, I can hear what you're thinking already: what if there really *isn't* time? Is it OK to skip breakfast and make up for it later? Absolutely not, says Granny:

'A child has to have breakfast. I hear all this nonsense about children going to school with nothing inside them – it's ridiculous. They can't learn, they can't behave – and they can't grow!'

This point, as those of us who've been living on Jupiter for the last half a century might have failed to notice, is the 'breakfast is the most important meal of the day' one. Seems our forebears knew about it long before Top Scientists told us so. It's not just that the first meal of the day kick-starts the metabolism and gets some goodness into our bodies; it's also because when we adults are in a rush in the morning and have to get by on some fruit and a cuppa until the Hungry Bug really kicks in at around ten or so that's fine. We can get something to eat then. But kids don't have that luxury, and if they don't eat some decent food before they leave for school they'll get nothing for hours – and that can lead to some serious learning and growing issues . . . If you're hungry you can't concentrate, learn, behave properly or grow, and kids need to be able to do all of those at the same time. Poor them!

Now then, I fully acknowledge that everyone's lives are just the *weenciest* bit busier than they were when aprons were the fashion of the day for fine young gals. My own home life is positively tornado-like at times, as we all zip about at breakneck speed. But, hand on heart, how many of us can honestly say that eating breakfast *at a table*, *with* our children, *sitting down*, is completely impossible, on any day of the week? Really? *Impossible?*

Of course, there is the commute for many, or the morning jog (obviously not for all of us, that one, but I hear there are remarkable people who manage to drag themselves out of bed and actually *run* before they've had a coffee. Respect), or just trying to get book bags, packed lunches, violins, swimming bags, coats, brains etc etc ready before the school run. But *every* day?

Even the busiest of us can manage a breakfast *en famille* occasionally without causing a national disaster. It just takes some effort, some planning and some major re-jigging. But it's worth it because a good, family-oriented morning sets the tone for the whole day.

∞ *GRANNY'S BREAKFAST TIPS* ∞

A child has to have breakfast. Try to have breakfast all together and start the day as a family.

If you let children make their own breakfast, insist they sit at the table and eat together, rather than eat it as they stand around.

Don't worry about *what* they have too much: something is always better than nothing.

Get up ten minutes earlier if you have to!

Find that time. If getting home in time for the evening meal is a problem (many people have the nasty habit of getting stuck in the office till late while trains have the nasty habit of being delayed . . .) try going to work later on some days and coming home later, leaving breakfast time available.

Sit down and eat with them. It's no good just putting food on the table for them to eat and then walking off to have a shower. How do you know they're eating any of it, and what message does it send to your kids? Sitting *with* them means you can check that something healthy and sustaining passes their lips before they kiss you goodbye, and your kids will see you as more than a slave who doles out food! And *eating* with them is even better.

A healthy start . . . Granny's point that something is better than nothing is a really good one to remember if you're freaking out, but breakfast is also a great opportunity to get something *healthy* into them, especially if you worry that your kids aren't getting such a good meal at lunchtime because they're too busy chatting or school dinners are still planned around the deep fat fryer. We always offer fresh fruit with breakfast: they're so hungry in the mornings they'll eat anything they can lay their hands on, and this way you know you've done your bit to stave off scurvy. If they don't want it every day, don't worry!

Offer a choice. Breakfast is the one meal of the day where I think you can, and should, offer a choice. We've had such trouble with one of our kids who just hates cereal, toast and almost anything else I can offer her, and went for years hating breakfast. It was a real battleground every morning, but now we've discovered she likes pitta bread with ham and melted cheese, and she gets through three of these in one sitting, making it herself and loving it! Everyone likes something different for breakfast, and it's hardly any effort to offer a choice of cereals, toast toppings, eggs etc. What's important is that they eat – and enjoy it.

Organise to save time. If your kids have a packed lunch, make it the night before so you just have to grab the boxes and go. Lay the breakfast table; get the school bags, shoes and even their clothes all laid out (unless, like mine, your kids like to choose what they wear every morning. Bring on the school uniforms!). Basically anything you can do the night before that gives you more time free in the morning for breakfast time is worth doing.

We had got quite lax about our table habits before I spoke to Granny, but since then I've made far more of an effort to sit with my kids while they eat, rather than making their sandwiches for the next day or doing the washing up quickly, and we've had better mealtimes together. It's not perfect, but it's better than it was. Just doing a simple thing like this, and also remembering to let them cook with me more often, has made family mealtimes and the way we all eat considerably better than it was. Hopefully you can have some similarly positive results . . .

Lunchtime, what **time?**

For children, lunch on a week day means one of three things: pre-schoolers generally have lunch at home (or at nursery), while those at school have the choice of a packed lunch or a school dinner. (Why not a school *lunch*? Answers on a postcard . . .)

Granny's experience of school lunches is a world away from what kids know now:

'Oh, when I was a girl we always came home for lunch. We had from 12.50 until 2.15 I think, for lunchtimes, and as we all lived so close to the school we all went home for lunch with our parents: we'd have mince, potatoes and peas, or some stovies. We had carrots and cabbage for vegetables too.'

Phew! This sounds to me like a proper meal, not some thrown-together snack in the middle of the day like we so often have.

'Oh yes – this was often the main meal of the day,' she agrees, picking up her binoculars for a better view of a chaffinch who's just landed on the bird table. 'And Dad always left the office and came home to join us. It was quite normal – people didn't work eighteen hours a day non-stop you know. They could take time out of the day to *eat*!'

Hold that thought . . ., hold it a little longer . . . annnnnnd let it go. Welcome back to the twenty-first century. The idea of having lunch together as a family is so outdated that it's not really worth worrying about at all. If my husband said to his boss: 'Right, I'm off home for two hours now to have lunch with Liz and the little people. Again,' he'd be out of a job before he could say 'Mine's a burger and chips please.' And the same is true for just about everyone else I know who works. Not to mention the small matter of the commute just to get home . . .

We can't change our work/life set-up completely and just have to accept that kids will have lunch at school these days – and just hope they eat it! What we *can* do, is to try and make the *weekend* lunches special. This doesn't mean a huge roast, or lots of effort: just something simple like bread, cheese and salad is fine so long as you are ALL there together. Even if you can only do one of the weekend lunches because of ballet classes, or football practice or whatever, one day is better than none – so make a meal of it!

The evening meal – nervous breakdown anyone?

f *The more we can get together around the table and share each other's company, the closer and more strongly knit we can become – even on the days when nobody can agree on anything!* ™

Tana Ramsay

Getting bums on seats

The typical family evening meal is a time of more stress, noise, worry and argument than just about any other time of the day. See if you recognise anything in the following scene:

Mum is cooking while simultaneously emptying the lunch boxes, writing two cheques for school and answering the phone. The kids meanwhile are shouting at a hundred decibels about who sits where and how much they hate what Mum is cooking – especially the broccoli; Mum gets cross because nobody likes what she's made (even though they loved it last week, which is why she bothered to make it again), worries about her kids developing iron-deficiency diseases and hangs up on the British Gas man who's just phoned for the third time that week, calling him an arsehole under her breath as she does so; the kids refuse to lay the table, switch the computer off or wash their hands; Mum gets crosser and burns the sausages; child A says child B hit him; child B says child A is a 'stinky fucky arsehole pig'; Mum tells her off, explaining that four year olds shouldn't say nasty words like that, even if they're justified and even if they did overhear Mummy being naughty and saying the very same word thirty seconds ago; everything descends into a scene of carnage; Mum opens another bottle of wine . . .

What's sad is that this is barely an exaggeration of what occurs in thousands of perfectly normal homes every day when dinner is being made. What's even sadder is that eating together *at all* is now so rare.

But hang on – we can't be the first generation of parents to have rowdy mealtimes! Surely *some* of this sounds familiar to Granny? Or were family meals fifty years ago in her household truly more refined, less argumentative and more . . . well, more 'perfect'?

'Oh we had plenty of commotion at supper time – there were four children, don't forget!'

'But was there shouting, and moaning, and kids getting down every three minutes? In our house, every time I turn my back another child has vanished to pick something up off the floor or is pulling faces at a sibling. And I know from talking to so many other mothers that they have the same problem – and it drives them nuts too.'

She pauses for a moment, careful not to answer without remembering what scenes on the home front were *really* like.

'Well no, there certainly wasn't shouting, but there *were* arguments and there was plenty of chatter and noise – just as there should be at a family meal. But there was no getting down from the table during the meal.'

What none *at all*? This seems incredible to me: I do try and enforce the 'two bum cheeks on the chair at all times' rule, but it all seems to descend into madness very quickly. So how did Granny get her kids to sit down so well, and can it work for us?

Granny's Pearl of Wisdom

You have to sit with them, even if you're not eating with them. This way you lead by example and they copy you, sitting down and eating properly.

The importance of leading by example where eating is concerned really cannot be overstated. From what you eat, to how, your attitude towards food and your table manners – it's all 'watch and learn' where kids are concerned. And there's another bonus, according to Granny:

'Sitting with them means you are right there to say "no" as soon as they start to misbehave.'

'And then . . .?'

'Well, if they are being rude at the table they can just sit there waiting for the rest of you to finish. Sending a child to his room is what he wants if he's misbehaving at the table – then he can play! Sitting still is a far worse punishment. And he'll probably wish he could be eating with the rest of you after a few minutes anyway, so he'll not do it again.'

Even though this technique almost certainly ruins the meal for everyone else – having a moody, wilful child at the table never helps the digestion I find – it's certainly a good deterrent and if you try it a few times it'll probably stamp out the worst tableside offences.

But making kids sit at the table for the duration of every single meal can be very counterproductive, and far from improving the atmosphere it can ruin it completely. We've found that mealtimes are much more pleasant if the little ones can get down and play when they've had enough to eat, but only if they've asked to get down, while the rest of us finish up. Then they can come back to the table for pudding. So long as it's controlled in some way and people aren't getting down whenever they like, it's fine.

The most important point is that you are sitting down and being a part of the occasion somehow.

Who's at the table?

In the picture Granny has described to me I've caught a glimmer of something many of us recognise today: Granny was eating with her children early in the evening because her husband was not home from work yet. This is the case for many mothers and stay-at-home dads I know, and it's how we eat at home quite often too.

66 My husband works in London and is never home before eight, so I feed the children earlier. I always try to sit with them, but it's hard not to pick at their food, and often I have little appetite left for my own evening meal – or I end up eating both and put on weight! Sometimes I just swap and eat my tea with them, and just sit with my husband when he gets back and has his. Each day as it comes . . . !99

Becky, mother of Cameron, Lewis, Findlay and Dylan

Was this a similar story for Granny, and how did she make this work for her family?

'Oh yes, during the week Gordon was rarely home for dinner – often not even until the kids were in their bath, or being tucked into bed. But we just got on and had dinner together and he'd come home when he could. This was where having a main meal in the evening started, you know? Once eating together at lunch stopped being a possibility we just changed our routine: the kids had a packed lunch at school and I gave them their main meal in the evening, with me. That way I knew what they were eating.'

While this sounds eminently sensible and practical – and it is! – there are two facts that Granny seems to have overlooked here, which I think are important to consider. Firstly, young children tend to eat early because they go to bed early, and there are few adults who like to have their evening meal at 5.30. (I'm one of them, incidentally, but perhaps I'm weird.) Secondly, the effect on a marriage of having kids is not always entirely positive and if one parent only eats with their kids, and never with their partner then the flames of romance are certainly not going to be kept very hot. The ritual of sharing a meal with the person you love – yes, you love your kids too, but not in *that* way – is an important one.

The answer is simply to mix and match, and, as ever, try to keep everyone happy. Sometimes you eat with the kids; sometimes you merely keep them company and enjoy some grown-up table-time later on. Oysters optional.

But Granny's central, simple point holds true: that the evening meal is very important for children and they should eat it with an adult sitting down with them at the table.

Granny's Pearl of Wisdom

If kids supposedly have a main meal at lunchtime in the school canteen and nothing proper at home, you've no idea what kind of a diet they're getting, have you? Then the evening meal becomes most important.

66 *Eating between meals should be kept to a minimum: just one snack at elevenses, and beware of bad family eating habits. Fat children tend to be members of fat families, because the whole lot of them eat rubbish – it's not a genetic thing! And be disciplined about what your kids can and can't eat: too many parents just give in because it's too much like hard work to have a fight over the biscuit tin.* 99

Dr Rosemary Leonard, GP, TV doctor and author of
The Seven Ages of Woman **(Bantam Press)**

I guess I already knew that mealtimes were important, and I've always tried to get all of us around a table every dinner time at least. But just hearing it from Granny was enough to really remind me of that importance, and to spur me on to try harder to find ways to make it work for us and to feed my kids as healthily as I can. She could, I can, and you can too!

Eliminating fussy eaters

Fussy eaters are now as common as nits. Where no more than a couple of generations ago they were a rarity – almost an anomaly, thanks to the joys of financial hardship, tough-as-nails parenting and rationing – now they inhabit every home in the land. Won't eat peas, don't like carrots (unless they're raw), can't have 'bits' in yoghurts, don't like mushrooms (unless they're cooked), hate fish, love fish *fingers* . . . the list goes on and on and it's enough to drive any parent round the bend! So is there any hope? How did people manage in the Old Days before fussy eaters took over our kitchens?

'Children have always been fussy about what they eat – it's nothing new,' Granny tells me as she rubs some warmth into her bad leg with a marked old hand. 'But they always ate *something* and I tried to give them what I knew they liked.'

'Does that mean you asked what they wanted for tea, or offered a choice?'

I'm thinking of the times I've heard of people serving up two or even three meals in one sitting, to cater for each child's individual tastes – not something I've ever done, I have to say. My kids get what they're given, and that's that! Given her reaction, I immediately surmise that Granny will agree.

'Offer a *choice*?! Oh no – they were out on the road playing and had no say in what I made – and they didn't care! Why on earth cook more than one meal, Elizabeth? To hang with that! It's a *family* meal – they can share it with the rest of the family, like it or lump it.

Granny's Pearl of Wisdom

Cooking individual meals for fussy children just makes it worse – and they'll never grow up and learn to be grateful for what they're given.

While this is a very good plan in theory, I have found more success with making one meal, but ensuring there is something in it that *everyone* likes. This could be the rice (some have it with sauce, others have it plain) or the meat (you don't have to eat it, but at least you like the potatoes it's with) and so on. Forcing kids to chomp through a meal they hate every part of, just because it's 'all you're getting' is deeply unhelpful and can cause bad relationships with food. And with the chef!

I did an interesting experiment a few years ago, with some startling results. We spent some time with friends whose children all wear the Fussy Eater badge: one won't eat cheese, the other no tomatoes, the next no vegetables and so on. None have allergies, you understand – just dislikes. They never eat with their parents, their dinner is cooked separately and the youngest will literally stand over the pots as dinner is being served, picking out every item she doesn't like.

Well, not when I'm cooking! My experiment was as follows: what would happen if these four fussy children spent a few days with us, all being served the same food as everyone else and eating together with the adults?

On day one the suspicious looks of the children were outdone only by the nervous glances of their parents: they would *never* eat that! Was I mad?

But guess what? They did eat it. Each supposedly 'fussy' child bravely tried a new food – every day – and managed to eat some of it. By the end of the stay they were tucking into their food, no longer scared of what nasties it might contain. The parents were shocked, and told me they had never seen their kids eat so well.

My conclusion: if you all eat together, and all have one meal, kids will just eat what they are given – and leave a few bits they don't like, but don't we all? It's as simple as that.

❝ We're talking about a contemporary style of parenting, particularly in the middle class, that is overindulgent of children. It treats them as customers who need to be pleased. A meal is about sharing. (When) parents are preparing different meals for each kid ... it takes away from that. The sharing is the compromise. Not everyone gets their ideal menu every night. ❞

William Doherty, professor of family social science at the University of Minnesota at Minneapolis and author of *The Intentional Family: Simple Rituals to Strengthen Family Ties*

And you're not getting down till you're finished

Many adults remember being pressured to finish everything on their plate as a child. Playing 'pea hockey' from one side of the plate to the other for what feels like an eternity; hiding the fish under the potato skin (my technique); sneaking bits of potatoes to the dog . . . lucky mutt.

So what does Granny think about making children eat up their meal? My assumption was that she'd approve wholeheartedly. 'Waste not, want not', and all that. I am stunned to discover that my assumption is completely wrong.

'Making children eat up everything on their plate is totally counterproductive in my opinion. You can try to encourage children to eat up to a point, but there's no good in forcing a child to eat. It just causes problems where there needn't be any.'

On cue, she offers me some cake, which I politely decline. Biscuits, I like. Cake I generally don't – especially if it has been at the back of a cupboard for five years . . . I'm also frowning too much to enjoy cake, because I'm confused:

How is this 'don't have to finish what's on your plate' thing going to work? If I were to let my kids eat what they wanted and leave the rest, one would eat no vegetables, the other no potatoes and all of them would eat only pasta and cheese given half a chance! How can we make sure our kids get the nutrition they need and don't just live on the bits they like?

Granny has a very simple answer to this:

'I always found that by the end of the week their diet had balanced out with enough meat here, potatoes and vegetables there and fruit in between. Your Uncle Ken was the worst: he'd eat no meat for days and then no potatoes . . . but it all panned out and he was perfectly healthy. The most important thing is to offer them good food – not processed *rubbish* – and NOT TO WORRY! Ignore as much as you can of their little fusses and refusals and you'll see: they'll be fine.'

Granny's Pearl of Wisdom

Making children eat up everything on their plate is not helpful at all. Give them less, avoid snacks and they'll eat what they need.

HONESTY BOX

I was guilty of repeating this 'finish it all up' behaviour with my kids, before I talked to Granny about it. I just felt that if I'd made it, they should finish it up, and I also felt this was one way I could make sure they were eating enough. You know the score: 'Just three more mouthfuls…' and the poor kid is sitting there about to throw up – and still getting told off for it! I often wondered if it was the right thing to do. Now I realise it wasn't.

And for dessert: a serving of realism

We are nearing the end of our chat for the day, and I feel I have really picked up some simple, workable tips for making family mealtimes more frequent, more successful and less like a competitive slanging match. But I want to know how Granny thinks we can do this in *our* world. Does she know how much harder it is to eat together every day, and can she suggest anything to make it easier?

'The thing is, Granny, people just can't live like you used to any more: eating every breakfast and every evening meal together. People don't work down the road – they commute, often for hours at a time, and because we're all so busy during the day, especially those of us where both parents work, many of us have to use our time *after* work or on the way home to get some exercise or do more work at home, or just do the shopping to ensure there's anything to eat at all! So this ideal of all eating together just isn't workable for loads of families any more.'

Granny leaves her leg alone for a minute and shakes her head sadly, as if I've just summed up all the evils of the modern world in one sentence.

'I know. I know, it's a terrible shame and it's just the crazy world you live in. I don't envy you, I really don't.' Then the fire lights up in her eyes again. 'But with a little common sense and some effort, you can make it a lot better.

Granny's Pearl of Wisdom

If you teach your children to eat well at home they can take this with them into the world and behave properly at other people's houses, in restaurants, on holidays and so on. It's a vital social skill!

And one final thought to take home with me to my unruly brood, before attempting to put all of this into practice tonight:

'Eating together binds a family, and that's what's missing now – there's very little that *binds* people. No sense of love and time shared, all together. *That's* what you can get from eating together.'

As I feel the guilt of a thousand parents pile onto my shoulders like ten tons of uneaten chicken nuggets, she adds a sprinkle of honesty that lifts the weight considerably.

'But you mustn't think that we were perfect – we weren't! We didn't always manage to eat together – and it only gets harder as the children get older: they have after-school clubs like football, swimming, orchestras and so on, so they often can't be sitting down at a table every evening. That's why you just have to try and do it as often as you practically can, and make the most of the early years when their lives aren't so chock-a-block. And if you spend this time with them when they are young, they'll come back all the more as they get older – mine are still coming home for a meal with me now!'

Hurray! We are *not* useless failures who have no idea how to make a decent family meal: these issues have been there for years, and it's just a part of family life to try and juggle things and work out a way to spend time eating together, as the world changes and our lives with it. The point is to *make that happen*, make it enjoyable and not just flake out in front of the telly every night with a takeaway. Every *other* night will do . . .

If we can't manage to eat together we have to change the way we live and make that time for the sake of our children and our family life. It's as simple as that.

I put away my notepad and get up to leave.

'Right – I must get back to my lovely little hooligans now. We'll be seeing you at about six then?'

'Aye – six o'clock. Just remember now: I want to be back home by eight. There's a *super* programme about tigers in Siberia and I don't want to miss it.'

Perfect. We can eat together and then watch telly – a fine combination of the times we've all lived in. Three generations, two cooks and one chicken curry – should be a lot of fun.

∾ *GRANNY'S TIPS FOR MEAL TIMES* ∾

Only offer one choice of meal. If they don't like it, they'll be hungry and eat more at the next meal.

Sit down and eat with your children where possible. They learn to eat by watching the way you do it, so show them how!

Don't worry if they don't finish everything on their plate. Making an issue of it or forcing kids to eat causes problems later on.

Give small portions. Why give a child an adult's portion?

Let the conversation flow! Table talk is where you find out a lot about your family.

—— LIZ'S TIPS FOR MEALTIMES ——

Don't feel you have to eat together at *every* meal: just once a day, or even once every other day is better than nothing. But once a week is leaning heavily towards 'not often enough at all' . . .

Make it part of the day's schedule: if mealtime isn't treated as importantly as work meetings, then it won't be thought of as important. It is, so get it in the diary and schedule other things around it – not the other way around.

Prepare as much as you can at the weekend or in an evening and freeze it. We can't all cook a fresh meal every day, so this way you can just take portions out of the fridge or freezer the day you need it.

Have a proper table to eat around, ideally in the kitchen so that you aren't relegated to a room by yourself to cook and it makes it much easier to serve the food and then fetch seconds, cloths, more water and so on, which you're bound to be doing.

Find the meal that works for your family: it could be breakfast or dinner: not everyone can be there at both, but *one* of them shouldn't be beyond the bounds of most families out there. If it isn't, make some changes to your routine to make sure it can be.

If all else fails, block out the weekend meals. Sunday lunch is the only time that works for many, so make sure you stick to it and eat together. Take your time, enjoy the event, and talk to each other!

Don't make them clear just their own plate. This teaches them to only look after themselves – much better is to get them to all clear *something*, no matter whose it is, until there's nothing left on the table. That way they are helping as part of the *family.*

Chapter Five

BECAUSE I SAY SO

The importance of discipline: at home

The evening went well. So well, in fact, that we ended up making a xylophone of sorts out of our variously empty wine glasses, drinking or replenishing as required to make the exact notes, and Granny played an impressive version of Happy Birthday on it, without the B flat. She was laughing, and chatting and a picture of good health – until it came to walking home and she realised she couldn't do so without leaning on my husband all the way home. It's the first time that's ever happened, and it comes as a sad surprise.

Much of the conversation over dinner was about discipline – hmmm, I can't imagine why – and it is this *core*, divisive, controversial subject that I decide to tackle further with Granny the next day. As we are reminded every time a person over the age of sixty opens their mouth, children used to have a lot more discipline back in times of yore, so my task for the day is to ask Granny how things were back in her day and see if there isn't something from those times I can learn and put into practice in today's world, ruled as it has become by the so-called and much-maligned Negotiation Generation for whom the word 'no' seems to mean 'perhaps you'd like to tell me how you feel about this'.

I find Granny listening to a Bach cello sonata on the radio at full volume and leafing through a mail order catalogue from the RSPB. There is something about old age which makes people become more concerned with small animals and plants than with their own wellbeing – or perhaps she's just suffering from a geriatric hangover after last night . . .

The item of interest in the catalogue today is a bird feeder which allows the user to reach the nuts only after performing some kind of *Krypton Factor* challenge with levers, buttons and a small mirror – presumably so it can see just how irritated it looks. I try to look very impressed with this contraption as she writes a shaky number 2 in a small box beside the photograph, and I know that next time I come to visit there will be two of these techno-feeders in the garden, to complement the other twelve. Unearthing the amplifier from behind several piles of *Reader's Digest* catalogues, a pair of binoculars and five packets of lemon drops, I turn the volume down several notches, leaving Bach to get on with it while we do the same.

Granny looks very tired and is clearly having trouble walking even a few paces without wincing, but she's still able to smile and laugh with me just as ever and I wonder if I will possibly manage to stay so strong-spirited and positive when I am all but falling apart at the seams myself. The smallest hint of a headache and I cave. Old Age sure does come with some major downsides, and those of us who moan when they run out of our shoe size in the Office sale had better get ready to toughen up.

'So, young lady,' she says, swapping catalogue and pen for what looks like lukewarm herbal tea. 'You want to pick my old brain for information again. Fire away – what's the subject? I'm all ears.'

Her directness is unnerving even for someone who feels so comfortable around her, and I can feel her beady, sharp eyes demanding an answer out of me quick-smart. No time for dawdling. This lady is ready for business!

'Right then. Well, last night we were talking about discipline, and I'd like to follow that up, really. About discipline at home and at school, which most people agree has all but disappeared, and how you managed to instil some in your kids.'

Drawing the line

'Discipline? Oh, aye. I can tell you lots about that. We had plenty of it, and it never did us any harm. In fact it almost certainly did us all a lot of good.'

As she nods her head up and down a little, thinking perhaps about all the times she was called upon to break a ruler over my dad's bottom, I tell her that I want to understand why so many children don't give a damn about what they're told any more. It's not just the ones running about local shopping centres (dressed, *bien sur*, in the very fabric of all perceived modern malaise: the dreaded hoodies) who don't seem to have the slightest notion of discipline, collect ASBOs like I collected stamps and are more than likely to tell their teachers off than the other way around. No, even perfectly sweet kids who behave reasonably well and look like butter wouldn't melt in their pretty little mouths have developed immunity to all forms of discipline and can be pretty much uncontrollable at times.

'Well, you know,' she says wistfully, putting down her cup, 'it just makes me sad. These kids have no sense of discipline at all because they've never been told "No" and they've never been taught that there's a line you just don't cross.'

She hits the palm of one hand with the side of her other, marking out an imaginary line across the deep, story-telling wrinkles. 'So now they're just wild, and there's not much anyone can do about it – it's too late.'

She continues, after another sip. 'It's quite normal and healthy for a child to want to overstep the line. But if there's no line beyond which lies trouble, there's no opportunity for the child to learn where to stop. They have to learn when to stop – how else can they ever learn to say 'no' to *themselves*?'

She's absolutely right, of course; setting the boundaries is exactly what children need in order to a) break through them and b) learn that they can't go around doing what the hell they like all the time. Saying no to a child isn't being unkind; in fact, *not* saying no is, because you're not teaching them anything about how the real world out there works. And then one day, when the nice man at Tesco's says 'No, you can't actually pay for those in Monopoly money' your poor teenager will be stumped that he can't do as he pleases.

If you don't show that you are a parent who's in charge, they almost feel short-changed and probably wonder why you're so crap at it, not why you're so wonderfully lenient. So be in charge, have some rules and enforce them – it's part of what you're there for!

Granny's Pearl of Wisdom

Kids need a line to be drawn – it makes everything clearer for them: they know where they are and they can then try to see how far they can take things – try to push the boundaries.

A child doesn't hate a parent who sets reasonable rules and sticks to them. They know that's just one of the roles of parents: to be in charge. There's nothing wrong with saying 'do as you're told' sometimes.

Discipline: where are we now?

If we're going to talk about discipline, it'll be rather useful if we're all agreed on what the word actually *means*, and what exactly the point of disciplining anyone is. So let's see . . . According to the Oxford English Dictionary, 'discipline' has a number of meanings.

As a noun it is, among other things:
'maintaining of order among those in one's charge'
(that'll be those pesky kids then)

and as a verb it means:
'train to obedience and order; punish'

Taken to its extreme I think we can safely say that the latter is *not* the purpose of what we're trying to achieve. Nobody wants a child to feel they are being trained to be obedient. They're not dogs! For children, discipline is *not* about squashing all of their own ideas, desires and wishes so that they obey your every command like a robot, nor about punishing them until they give up all hope of having a better life – without you – but about teaching them that we all live together in a society where we have to comply with certain rules, otherwise everything would go a bit loopy, and *that* means that sometimes NO means NO: they will just have to do as Mummy and Daddy say, and that's the end of it. *How* we go about this we shall soon discover . . .

The accusation that 'Kids these days have absolutely no sense of discipline at all, and cannot be controlled' is made with depressing frequency by the media, on the tube and in the smelly prescriptions queue at Boots. Indeed, if you listen to the loudest part of common public opinion children are nothing but out of control, spoiled, hoody-wearing little hooligans, the lot of them. They don't hold doors open, or say please and thank you, or listen to their teachers or do anything to help others, or apologise when they fart the theme tune to *The Simpsons* in the library. If they ever go there any more, that is. *And* they're smelly, messy, rude, lazy and, in case you missed it, fat to boot.

You know the kind of thing.

This is, of course, not the case for many millions of kids – and probably yours – who are reasonably kind, thoughtful and polite. It's just that, for fairly obvious reasons, we don't hear much about them; we hear about the loud, rude, ill-disciplined ones. But even the milder cases, are growing in number. And it's not simply a case of class, social background, geography, or wealth. It's a general growing trend across the board. So we're *all* involved.

But here's the weird thing: despite the way we discipline (or don't) our children being one of the hottest topics on the parenting grapevine these days, I hear very little about it being discussed by parents in the school playground. This seems to suggest that either we are all burying our heads so deep in the sandpit that we have convinced ourselves it's not happening – or at least not to *our* little darlings – or that we are all far too embarrassed to speak out and say something about it.

Assuming the latter, allow me to say a lot about it and get this festering sore out in the open so it can mend . . .

There are three main types of parents where it comes to discipline:

TYPE 1: THE ANTI-DISCIPLINARIANS

These parents believe their kids have a right to do whatever they like, and don't discipline them – ever. Mummy and Daddy's little cherubs control *them*, not the other way round, and by the time he is two years old there is just nothing his parents can do to stop Tommy darling dropping his new MP3 player out of the second-floor window or de-tailing the neighbour's cat. The only course of action is to ignore the whole affair, continue trying to convince themselves that they are doing their kids good by allowing such freedom of expression with the kitchen scissors, and drown their growing despair in cheap wine. Hic.

TYPE 2: THE OVER-DISCIPLINARIANS (AKA BULLIES)

To counteract those kids who ignore Mum and Dad completely, and are never, ever disciplined lest their blessed human rights be infringed, is another sad bunch who are continuously abused by vile parents who either treat their kids like little soldiers in their own private army *à la* Captain von Trapp, or who see smacking, hitting, slapping and much worse as the only way to communicate with their unwanted offspring. We've all seen such parents in supermarket car parks and, quite frankly, they make my skin crawl; I'd like to do a lot worse to them if I could.

TYPE 3: THE CONFUSED

I, like many conscientious, concerned parents fall into this latter category. These parents were raised to understand right from wrong by parents who disciplined them sensibly. They believe strongly that they in turn should discipline their kids if they misbehave. Unfortunately they're not sure what's socially acceptable any more and so try desperately not to discipline their kids in public for fear of being frowned at/outcast/ arrested. Some are also unsure how many of their own adult hang-ups stem from their upbringing and want to try to do things differently – negotiating and compromising at times, and disciplining at others. Despite their efforts they still seem to have ended up with kids who are sometimes not very well behaved, want to negotiate rather than apologise and seem at times wilful, rude and out of control. These parents occasionally feel lost and could do with some self-confidence and guidance, for fear of slipping into either of the types above.

Clearly neither of the first two ways of tackling children's bad behaviour is going to yield anything other than a walking, shouting, swearing, pregnant disaster, and even the last one sounds like it could do with some help. What's needed – and what I'm going to offer in this chapter – is more sensible, practical and socially acceptable solutions to putting back some discipline, based on old-fashioned principles and without getting a call from the Social Services.

So whatever type you are: read, think, and apply as required.

Crime and punishment. *What to do when they cross the line*

All this talk about 'drawing a line' leads, inevitably, to the question of what lies *beyond* this 'line that must not be crossed but that is quite often crossed anyway'. We live, thankfully, in a gentler society than half a century ago, and we've learned the hard way that punishing kids harshly, offering empty threats that are not followed through or disciplining kids too much is not very helpful and can leave lasting emotional and behavioural scars. But surely this doesn't mean we *can't* tell kids off any more.

What does Granny think we should do when an unruly child takes a flying leap across the dreaded line?

'Well, you have to tell them off of course! That's what you're there for, you know, not just to kiss them and tell them you love them twenty-four hours a day.'

'Even if you do love them . . .'

'Oh, aye – *especially* if you do.'

Granny's Pearl of Wisdom

A parent who truly loves a child is going to discipline them and tell them off when they're naughty with a sharp, clear word because they know that this is helping the child, not hurting it.

'It's hard to remember that, though,' I point out, thinking of all the angst felt by so many parents, who want desperately to tell their child off but somehow feel they can't in case it's damaging

108

them somehow. 'Nobody likes to scold, so we reason, plead and lecture instead, and the result is that "you'll be told off" simply has no power any more.'

'But it's what a child *expects* from someone in authority. If you let them get away with murder the whole time they are let down badly because you aren't doing what parents are supposed to do! If there are no lines to be crossed, and there's no way of getting into trouble, or being naughty, then a child is missing something. Silly as it may sound, getting into trouble is a very important part of growing up.'

> ❝ I respect my parents when they do say no, and I know they mean it. If they threaten a punishment, I know it will materialise. Without this balance, young people will just walk over the freedom given to them – much like we walk over society knowing it can't punish us. Kids used to be disciplined at home and at school. Nowadays parents aren't allowed to smack and at school kids know teachers haven't got a leg to stand on or they'll be sued if they discipline a child severely. A child is more likely to get a 'please darling, don't do it again' from many parents when a good telling off is due. Don't kids need a line to be drawn that they know they shouldn't cross or they'll be in trouble?? ❞
>
> **Jellyellie, 18-year-old entrepreneur and author of**
> *How Teenagers Think* **(White Ladder Press, 2007)**

'And if a raised voice or sharp word have no effect and your child carries on ripping the wallpaper – what then?' I ask Granny, knowing the answer already.

The last of the tea meets its end more abruptly than it may otherwise have, following this question.

'Well,' she scoffs, swallowing hard, 'you can tell them off, and threaten this and that, but if they're really misbehaving and they know it, a quick smack on the bottom, so long as it's at the time you catch them, is the best way. They learn very quickly, and won't do it again.'

Ah, thought we'd get here eventually. Smacking.

Smacking. Oh here we go

The debate about smacking rears its ugly head every few years, and generates enough debate to fill a year's worth of *Question Time* programmes. It's a thorny, emotional and heated issue with people arguing strongly on both sides: either for their right as a parent to decide how to raise their children or for the right of the child to be protected against any physical punishment. Which order you put these points in rather decides whether you agree with smacking or not.

> *I have smacked only to stop a child doing something dangerous, or as a last resort when dealing with bad behaviour, and I haven't found it particularly effective, probably because the child has sensed that it's a last resort. I try never to threaten to smack as it makes me uncomfortable because it doesn't seem an enlightened or intelligent way to guide children towards desirable behaviour, but also possibly because the orthodoxy now is that it is always wrong to smack. I'm not convinced smacking deserves all the bad press it gets, but the problem is, where does it belong in one's armoury of parenting techniques? Not as a first response, I wouldn't think, nor as a last one for the reasons above.*

Louise, mother of three

HOT TOPIC

SMACKING

—∿∿∿—

The situation in the UK now is this: parents in England and Wales who smack children so hard it leaves a mark face up to five years in jail.

In 2007, Government Ministers rejected calls for a complete ban on smacking in the UK. This was met by opposition from children's charities.

Those for a ban say: Children's Commissioner for England, Sir Al Aynsley-Green, said in an article for *The Guardian* in October 2007, 'There is no good reason why children are the only people in the UK who can still be lawfully hit. They are protected from assault in most other settings. By not changing the legislation, we continue to send out confusing messages to parents about the acceptable use of violence across society.'

Several European countries have outlawed smacking, including Sweden, Austria, Denmark, Finland, Germany, Norway and Iceland. Nordic societies commonly agree that children are better educated with words than with violence.

Those against a smacking ban say: Good parents may be criminalised; the rights of parents to discipline their children would be eroded by state control; physical discipline is considered an effective tool for teaching children a lesson.

continued overleaf . . .

The problem with smacking

Quite apart from the obvious issue many people would raise – that it's just wrong full stop – the other problem with saying 'smacking is sometimes OK' is that, for every parent who smacks their child once in a lifetime there's another who's not quite so well restrained. In other words, some indescribably vile people smack their kids as a matter of course – or for their own entertainment. I witnessed a young mother outside my window only yesterday shouting at her (crying) little boy 'If I hear one more noise I'll smack ya!', only for him to receive a nasty, clearly painful smack across his bare legs moments later – even though he hadn't made any sound at all. It was heart-wrenching and I really wanted to run down to the street and tell her what a stupid child-abusing bitch she was, only I didn't really want her to see where I live and come back with the club-wielding big boys. I felt like such a coward.

Legislation about smacking runs into difficulty, firstly because many people believe it is the right of the parent to decide how to raise their own child, and secondly, even if you did manage to come up with some kind of Smacking Law, how could you *possibly* regulate what goes on behind closed doors?

The jury for now is still very much out in this country as to whether smacking children has any place in our society or if it should be outlawed. No doubt the debate will run and run. What's important is that *you* think about it and decide what you feel is right for your child.

> 66 *I can't remember smacking either of my daughters but I may have done, and I don't disapprove of it in principle. I was smacked for pretty awful behaviour. I don't think it should be illegal per se, but there could be clear legal guidance about what is considered too much.* 99

John, father of two

In a disturbing and confusing way, Granny's advice about smacking sounds very sensible: if a child misbehaves, a quick smack should quickly teach them it's wrong, and they'll not do it again – right? Erm, no, not entirely. Inconvenient though it may be for tyrants and control freaks, we *are* living in the twenty-first century, and that's where the old 'smack a child if she misbehaves' theory runs into difficulties: kids are no longer shoved up chimneys or made to eat gruel, and it's now also acknowledged they have things called feelings and human rights. Crazy, I know! Next you'll be telling me they like computers and chocolate . . .

All joking aside, I put this little hiccup in the plan to Granny. Can she not see that this kind of child-rearing has had its day and that smacking should now only be used as an absolute last, last resort, if indeed ever?

'Smacking is seriously frowned upon by many now, Granny. You can't just smack your child in Sainsbury's or someone will arrest you by the frozen peas, even if he *has* just scratched six cars with his coat zip then nearly run under a bus. And anyway, it's a good thing that we can't smack kids any more – it's not exactly very *nice* is it?'

'Well that's just *nonsense*. Utter nonsense, Elizabeth. Whoever came up with the idea of disciplining your own child being a problem?'

I get the full 'look into my eyes and listen carefully to what I'm saying' treatment now, as she prepares to give me the punch line – so to speak.

'The only thing a quick, sharp smack hurts is a child's *dignity*. Not its bottom; its dignity. If it's done quickly and at the time they're being naughty, there's no harm in it at all. Really. They only care that they've been embarrassed, not about the smack itself.

She raises her eyebrows, and continues.

'*You've* had a smack or two in your time I dare say, and look at you – you're not "damaged" or "troubled" by it, are you?'

I was indeed in trouble much of the time as a child, despite every effort to the contrary. Honest . . . There was the somewhat kak-handed episode resulting in a wrecked record stylus (OK, *three* wrecked styluses) . . . and the time I set fire to the living room because I was trying to rub the colour off the end of the match while watching *John Craven's Newsround* before attempting to put out the considerable flames with my woollen slipper . . . and the day I walked fresh mud over Mum's newly varnished kitchen floor . . . OK, I was in trouble quite a lot, and I got the occasional tap on the backside, though it was *very* rare and, by anyone's standard, less than I deserved.

But as for 'damaged' or 'troubled' by any smacking that came my bottom's way – well, I really can't say that I am. Any 'difficult' periods as a teenager were quite normal I'd say, and I'm doing OK just now, thanks for asking. Similarly, if you talk to people who received the occasional smack as a child, very few will say they think it affected their lives dreadfully, or that they considered it child *abuse* in some way. Most say it did them no harm, they knew they were being naughty, and they still love their parents very much.

> 66 In Italy if a child misbehaves – my God he knows about it! They get properly told off, and yes, they get smacked, but we don't make a big deal of it. The funny thing is, they love their family so much more than I see children love their family here. If you smack them they don't hate you, so long as you are consistent and you show love the rest of the time. They understand and it's part of a childhood – kids are naughty! 99

Antonella, mother of Gabriella and Tomaso

But just watching a child being smacked and screaming is enough to convince many that this practice is just not acceptable in any situation, and certainly some people are adversely affected by being smacked as a child.

> 66 I was smacked as a child and I certainly remember the times it happened and feeling terrified, shocked and frightened that it would happen again – sometimes I might have deserved it but I'm not sure it was always justified. 99

Helen, 45, mother of four

HONESTY BOX

—~~~—

I have, at various moments of overwhelming 'being pushed to the limit by a wilful, naughty, cheeky, rude child' maternal eruption, smacked all three of my kids – probably once or twice each, in total. When my eldest daughter tried to stick a metal fork into a socket; when my son ran full tilt up to the edge of a busy road, after I told him three times not to, and he came within three inches of the underside of the Number 1 bus; when my youngest daughter thought it was a good idea to make a mask for her baby brother out of a Sainsbury's carrier bag. That kind of thing. I fully acknowledge that all of these smacks were probably my reaction to the shock and fear of what *almost* happened, but I don't regret them, as none of the children ever did anything like it again so I've probably saved their lives!

And yes, I have also said to each of my children at some point 'If you do that one more time I'm going to smack your bottom!!' And in some cases I did carry this out, if only because I said I would and didn't want to look like an idiot and lose all credibility. Did I feel good for saying or doing this? No, I felt horrible. But we all do it sometimes because we are driven to complete insanity and rage by our kids and by life in general sometimes, and I really don't think we need to feel too dreadful about it. It's life. It's not the worst crime against humanity, so deal with it and be lovely to them the rest of the time. Please.

> f I have smacked my kids though not recently and yes, on those occasions I have felt absolutely like the worst, cruellest, nastiest, meanest mum in the world and hated myself for losing it. Typically they've been at times when one of the children was pushing me to the absolute limit and behaving particularly badly. I definitely see it as a failing in my own character more than theirs. ™

Sara, mother of four aged between five and eighteen

It stands to reason . . . or does it?

So there you are. I've smacked my kids. No enormous harm done, I don't think, except to my conscience.

But disciplining a child, however you decide to do it, is only worthwhile if they *learn* from it. Otherwise you have a sore throat, they have a sore bottom, and you're back at square one within ten minutes. And this is where reasoning with children, explaining *why* they are in trouble and trying to understand why they did what they did, comes in.

Oh come off it, you say. How can a child of three reason with an adult about bad behaviour? They can't reason at that age!

Well, I think they can, and that preventing a child from having any chance to defend herself can be deeply upsetting and damaging, a point that I put to Granny:

'Being smacked or really told off doesn't hurt much – not physically anyway. But what I remember hurt the most were my *feelings*, when I felt it wasn't my fault, and that nobody was listening, you know? When it wasn't fair, or justified and I felt I had no power to defend myself. And that kind of frustration and anger is as bad as physically hurting someone I'd say.'

117

Granny finds a piece of greenish blue ginger cake on the rug and tosses it out of the window at the small gathering of birds on the lawn.

'But Elizabeth, you were just being a *child*, and sometimes children get into trouble unfairly – it's part of life, and it continues right into adulthood so it's best to get used to it early: Life isn't always fair! People say they should "reason" with these tiny tots – well, what a waste of breath!'

Really? Let's ask a child psychologist.

&6&6 *Smacking a child is never the answer, if you have smacked your child remember how you felt afterwards and think about the look on your child's face. A child is left thinking 'how confusing, someone who loves and cares for me can also hurt me.' A parent's job is to teach their child right from wrong. We all need reasons for why something must not be done. As an adult you wouldn't stand for it if your work colleagues told you off for no reason! It may take a bit longer but if you explain to a child why they should not do something they can begin to learn to self-regulate: next time they're in a similar situation they can think before acting, especially if they know that there will be a consequence for their unacceptable behaviour. If a child is never given a reason they may feel unduly punished and confused about what the rules and boundaries are in the home. Setting limits and sticking to them is one of the most helpful things that you can do.*99

Laverne Antrobus, child psychologist

So reasoning is very important after all. But, like skinning cats and losing tummy fat, there are many ways to reach your goal. (In the case of tummy fat, by the way, the only way to reach your goal is to lower your target and accept that it'll ALWAYS wobble after you've given birth. And who cares?! There's always George Clooney to cheer us up.)

Just so we get things right in the reasoning department, here's how NOT to do it:

* 'Honey, if you don't take that bag off your sister's head very soon Mummy is going to be upset, OK?'

* 'No, I *know* you don't want to go to bed, but it's after midnight now and Mummy is starting to look just a little bit scary around the eyes. Shall we say Night Night, Sleep Tight, to Mr Nintendo?'

* 'So, you're telling me that it hurt your feelings when Daddy told you off for making a Dalek out of the new leather sofa, are you? OK, let's talk about that for a while ...'

* 'Now then, darling, can you please tell Mummy *why* you flushed her gold watch down the toilet just now?'

I honestly once heard a lady ask her three-year-old son this last ludicrous question on a train. It was everything I could to stop myself from turning around and saying: why do you *think*, you moronic woman? He was being a three year old! He was experimenting. He thought it would be fun. He thought it would be naughty. And it was all of those things and now it deserves a jolly good telling off – followed by a call to your insurance company – *not* a deep philosophical discussion with someone who thinks Spiderman could easily get it back for you. And why did you give him your gold watch to play with while you went for a wee anyway?? Are you *mad*?!

The above are all good examples of exactly the sort of thing that makes many people, such as my grandmother, roll their eyes at the very idea of reasoning with young children, and this is a terrible shame because you *can* reason with them. They're not stupid. They do understand – they just don't understand in the same way as we do, nor should they.

If a child can come away from a post-catastrophically bad incident with a box of matches thinking '*That was shit. I won't be doing that again in a hurry*', then you've had a successful chat. Expecting them to come away thinking, '*Hmmm, well my actions did indeed cause much distress and pain to my dear, long-suffering mother, whose breasts I made so droopy that Daddy doesn't like them any more, even though he says he does. I really think I ought to make more of an effort to make her happy and fulfilled and stop burning the house down,*' is farcical.

It's pathetically easy to shout at or hit a child in a moment of frustration or irritability. Any mean fool can do it. What's more difficult is to employ more intelligent, thoughtful and communicative ways of teaching a child a lesson, which is one reason why we have to try harder to: difficult things are almost always the most rewarding.

I think it's vital to explain to my children why they are being told off and to ask for their side of the story. This does *not* mean I let them off or retract what I've just said or done. Sometimes – indeed often – I apologise for my rants, but I still hold firm and make sure they understand why it happened, and that it was in some complicated, adult-ish way justified. If children feel we can all open up to each other this way, they will feel happier and more secure as they hit teenage-hood and the troubled waters of the school disco, clothes that aren't cool, hair that won't do the right thing and bastards who take your virginity and then laugh about it over chips at lunchtime. (You know who you are.)

Silencing children makes them angry and frustrated – emotions that aren't helpful to anyone, let alone young children. To negate their side of the story completely is to render them utterly powerless and this is very unhelpful. Just think how you last felt when someone – a boss, a husband, a parent – refused to listen to how you felt about something that had annoyed or upset you, and just totally ignored you. Not good, huh? So don't do it to them.

Out of sight, out of order

Granny reaches for her blanket and throws it over her legs as she continues her explanation, aware that I am looking deeply unconvinced by her 'smacking is the best way' theory.

'I can see you don't agree with me, Elizabeth, but I'll tell you what the problem is now: people are *scared* to discipline their kids because they're so often away from them. If both parents are out at work all day, every day, then not only are they not around to establish and maintain basic codes of behaviour and rules during the day, but when they come home they don't want to spend what little time they have together arguing. So they let the kids get away with murder.'

Now here we *can* agree. I doubt there's a single working parent in the land who can't identify in some way with this. So many of us work, work, *work* all week, and weekends are a whirlwind of catching up on the housework, the garden, the laundry and the shopping –- that when the time comes for us to actually spend any 'quality time' with our kids (and yes, I think it's a term that

121

does have a place in today's world, like it or not) arguing over whether they've made their bed, said thank you for their tea or put their filthy shoes on the sofa *again* just doesn't seem worth it. So we ignore it, tell them we love them anyway, and they never learn any better.

Another challenge for parents

* According to research this year, forty-six per cent of UK parents admit to spending less than an hour and a half a day with their children, blaming the pressures of modern living.

* According to a survey in 2005, Britons put in £36 million hours of free overtime each year with one in three refusing to take all their holidays fearing a backlog of work when they return.

* Britons work the longest hours in the European Union.

* The number of dual-income families is at an all-time high: in over two-thirds of couples, both parents work.

* In nearly nine out of ten working families where both parents work, at least one parent works unsocial hours. This is, crucially, often in the time when they would be with their kids – at weekends or evenings.

The lack of parental control is a real vicious circle too: the less time we spend with our children the less we feel inclined to discipline them or teach them any decent manners, so the less well behaved they are. And the less well behaved they are the more we have to tell them off, which we don't want to do because we see them so little. We have so little experience of correcting them, we just ignore the behaviour again and hope it'll all just go away with time.

Which, of course, it doesn't. It just gets worse until we find we are living with a bunch of rude little shits who wouldn't take 'no' for an answer even if they knew the *meaning* of the word. And then, in a classic case of modern-day buck passing we blame anything and anyone we can think of for our own shortcomings on the parenting front: teachers, the Government, *High School Musical*, the media, fashion, pop music, the pace of modern life, the London transport system, the British Olympic bid, Disney merchandise, coffee bars, the internet, credit cards and the continuing demise of family values. (This last one being mainly our doing too, but never mind . . .)

For those who do stick to their principles and apply some rules in the roost, it's not so easy either:

> 66 *My wife and I both work and don't spend as much time with the kids each evening as we'd like. I really regret that the little time we do have is wasted having to discipline them sometimes, but if you do one job right, it has to be making sure they do the right thing – letting them off creates little monsters who run riot. It's not how I would prefer to spend my limited time with them though!* 99

Dave, father of Daisy, eight and Louis, ten

I feel we've hit a rather important nail on the head (if that hasn't been outlawed as well) with this point about parental absence and consequential guilt. Sadly, unless we all decide to give up working there is little we can do about it: it's modern life, and short of turning back the clock to a time when women weren't allowed to exchange their aprons for school books, mortgages didn't require two salaries and commuting didn't exist, we are stuck with having less time at home with our kids than we used to.

What we *can* do, however, is try to use what 'quality time' we can find as productively as possible, to actually be *together*: before school at breakfast time, after school at dinner, doing homework *with* our kids, or making something, or playing football in the garden for ten minutes – that's all it can take sometimes: just ten minutes to say 'Stop! I'm not going to put the laundry away or reply to these emails. I'm going to sit down with my child *right now* and play pirates, because she's been waiting all afternoon to do this with me, and this is more important.'

Yes, it sounds like something straight out of *Oprah*. And yes, like many irritatingly simple and 'worthy' suggestions, *it really works*. Because this way, when you *do* discipline your child:

* You don't have to use such unnecessary force as smacking them – just a sharp, well-chosen word or two will do, as it makes a big impact from the quiet, calm you playing with them.

* You can be more consistent with your disciplining because you're with them more often.

* You don't wallow in guilt for a month or feel annoyed that the only time you have with your kids is taken up by telling them off for putting BluTack in the washing machine.

* They have seen enough of the 'nice' you to forgive the 'ranting, spitting witch' impression you give when they nick your mobile to call an Australian game show.

The *principle* of what my grandmother is saying holds good: children need discipline, and need to learn, at home, in context and in a way that they can clearly understand, what goes and what doesn't and that there will be consequences if they overstep the mark. What's new is that the *way* we discipline has changed somewhat. Some of this change is unquestionably a good thing – it's now generally acknowledged by even moderately humane adults that children have feelings and emotional needs as well as bottoms which need smacking. Where once children were seen but not heard, and then given a wallop or two for good measure, now we understand that giving them a voice and a place **in** our lives, not on the sidelines, is vital to their emotional wellbeing, and that disciplining involves much more than just physical punishment.

What we modern-day parents are left wondering about discipline is just **how much is too much, and how little is too little**? Of course each child is very different from the one picking his nose at the next table in class, but still – what is the 'right' amount of discipline? Well, the answer is that there **isn't** one, of course, but I think there is one crucial factor in teaching our children how to behave that we all need to focus much on more: TIME. Our time.

If we're to avoid having hoards of either over-disciplined kids or anarchic little monsters running about the place, we need to give them some of our time and attention – not the kind we so often give our kids, through half an eye while ringing the plumber and emptying the dishwasher. Proper 'I am now yours' kind of attention, because **children often misbehave simply because they are neglected and are seeking that attention**.

THE TEN-MINUTE RULE

This is a great way to ensure you give your kids some undivided attention for a specific amount of time, and I know some working parents who find it especially successful when they've got in from work and have very limited time with their children. Let your child choose whatever she would like to do for ten minutes and (within reason!) you do what she wants you to. This way she gets some fantastic 'you time', but you don't have to give every second of your available time over to her. That's called being ruled by your kids and it takes you on a fast track to the Dark Side.

So try it: really get into the activity you're being asked to do, and see if it makes your relationship better and your ability to discipline where necessary easier.

So, lovely play time aside, when the little darlings *do* break the DVD player, call the postman a penis brain or wee in the neighbour's drive, how *can* we discipline them in this complicated, litigious, politically correct world, and what are the most effective methods to teach kids that they can't do whatever they like? Somewhere between caning them and letting them get away with murder must lie a middle ground that works, which isn't considered cruel or old-fashioned in the extreme, and that those of us with insanely busy lives and a guilt complex bigger than Greater London can actually implement in public without being castigated by Society At Large, whoever that is.

Well, here are some suggestions to get you started:

Top Ten Tips for disciplining children today

1 **Tone of voice.** This does not mean raising the volume! In fact, often if you lower your voice considerably and use a more stern tone instead, it can have a very dramatic effect.

2 **1, 2, 3 rule.** I don't use this method much because I feel a bit like an idiot counting down while my child looks at me with a cheeky little smile, but I know many people for whose kids it really does work. 'If you don't stop that by the time I count to three . . .' etc, usually followed by 'you'll get no pocket money/won't go to Tom's house/can't watch *Dr Who*.' *Most important thing*: follow through with your threats or you lose the battle in ONE attempt.

3 **Explain yourself.** I'm equally staggered and depressed by the number of parents who tell their kids to stop doing something or order them to 'come here now!' without even explaining *why*. If you can start with 'We have to leave the house in five minutes to catch the bus . . .' or 'that Ming vase is made of china . . .' then any order after that is in some kind of context and is so much clearer and more effective. *Most important thing*: ask if they've understood what you've just said.

4 **Pick 'punishments' that work for each child.** It can be earlier bedtime, no pocket money, cancelling a play date, taking something back to the shop . . . whatever that partic-ular child will feel miffed about.

5 **No naughty step!** I am a passionate disbeliever in the long-term effectiveness of the naughty step. I know many people

continued overleaf . . .

who swear by it, but I still cannot help looking into the eyes of kids who are there, putting myself in that position and thinking how very, very cruel it is. If you can't explain to your child why he is being naughty and why you are angry at the time he's doing it, then something's not working. Humiliating and ignoring him is a harsh, cold and damaging alternative, and I'd go so far as to suggest that even a quick, sharp smack would be preferable. At least it's over quickly. That's my view – take it or leave it.

6 **Pick your battles.** If it's not worth getting angry about, leave it. It makes the times when you really *are* angry, about a thousand times more effective. Ditto nagging at husbands by the way, but that's for another book!

7 **Keep calm.** Remember: you are the adult, so act like one.

8 **Reward the good.** This is as important as telling off the bad. I so seldom hear parents saying 'well done!' after their child has behaved well, and can't count the number of times I've heard them being shouted at for behaving badly. It can leave them feeling totally unappreciated and understandably quite angry.

9 **Keep eye contact.** Very, very important. You can far more easily control and calm a child if you are looking right at them, especially close up.

10 **Get down to their level.** This only applies if your kids are smaller than you, obviously! Little children respond very well to your words if you crouch down until your eyes are on a level with theirs.

The way we parents discipline our kids has certainly changed a lot in recent times. In fact it's been changing for hundreds of years, and as each generation makes a pig's ear of it, the next tries to come up with more successful methods.

What *hasn't* changed is the role of discipline: to teach children that they don't function in isolation but that they are part of a society and they need to behave in a certain way and abide by certain clear rules, in order for that society to function properly.

Since talking with Granny I have really tried to remember what she told me about children simply being told that 'no means no' sometimes, and how I can make things easier for myself, and for my kids, by sticking to simple house rules and not allowing myself to be talked, or negotiated, out of what I know to be the right thing to do. The results have been fantastic – there's less arguing, less badgering and pleading, and far less of me tearing my hair out because nobody does what they are told. My kids seem to understand perfectly that certain rules are there, like it or not, and I'm being fair in sticking to them. I'm not being mean – I'm just telling it like it is!

Whether at home or in public, we have to teach them these rules, and make it clear to them that stepping over the line is not OK. If we don't, we have a disaster on our hands.

∞ *GRANNY'S TIPS* ∞

The role of a parent is to be in charge – so *be* in charge!

Children respect authority – they don't hate rules or the parent who sets them.

Children need a clear line to be drawn so they know there are limits.

Be fair and consistent.

Kids need to know when no means no, but if you find it hard to stick to a hard and fast rule *every* time, don't fret. So long as you have house rules and can stick to them as much as your patience, willpower and exhausted mind can manage, it's a very good start. We all lapse sometimes, so try as hard as you can, but accept defeat occasionally. You're only human, and so are they.

Give them time. We need to give our children some proper, undivided attention and time at home every day. Not *all* the time, but some of it.

Share the load. Unless *both* parents get a chance to spend good quality time with their kids and *both* do some of the disciplining, one is inevitably the disciplinarian while the other is always the kind, 'nicer' one – this is a recipe for marital catastrophe!

Smacking is never the best way to discipline a child. If you ever do (for example when they run out into the road) don't worry too much, but keep a close check on it and try to resist if possible. Speak to someone if you are concerned that you are not managing to discipline in any other way. You are certainly not alone.

Be consistent. Inconsistency leads to insecurity, and we don't want that, please. Rules is Rules, baby, so they'd better learn to stick to 'em!

Don't be afraid to discipline your child in public. If your child knows you won't tell her off in town she'll play up and you'll have no chance of controlling her. And if she thinks you're embarrassed, she'll try as hard as she can to achieve this – it's all part of testing the boundaries. Be firm, be calm, be fair, and do what needs to be done to send the lesson home.

Keep a check on your own behaviour. Sometimes you can find you've started shouting at your kids or even smacking them more than you realised, especially when there are other major stresses in your life such as marriage problems, work stresses or financial crises to push you to the limit. Having a really strong reaction to a child's naughtiness two or three times a year or so is pretty understandable given what most kids can do to a normally calm human being in a seventeen-hour day. Once a week and you are in dangerous territory. Once a day, and both you and your child need urgent help.

Discipline is useful not only for your own home life, and to ensure that you don't end up killing each other/divorced/grey/bald before your child's fifth birthday, but also because it lays the foundations for what happens *outside* the home. The idea is that if you've done your job properly or even *semi*-properly, you should be able to take Thing One and Thing Two down to the local playgroup quite happily and not have them winding up in custody after a shoot-out in the sticky pictures area.

The first place any 'outside the home' disciplining is likely to happen is at a toddler group or the playground, where being able to control your child enough to stop him using a toy car to crack open his playmate's skull is rather useful. The second place a little discipline comes in handy is at nursery, and then, finally, at school.

It is here that we encounter a kind of symbiotic relationship between school and home: without discipline at home the teachers have no hope at all in the classroom, and without any disciplining going on at school the less chance you have of keeping order at home. The problem comes when one of these two breaks down. And our problem is that they both have.

Chapter Six

RESPECTFULLY YOURS

All of this discussion about discipline may have still left you to asking the following: 'Why do we have to discipline our kids anyway? They are *children*, they should enjoy childhood and be left alone to play and discover and just muck about while they can. Life is tough enough as they get older without us shoving rules and punishments at them so young. Leave them alone!'

Well, I suppose it would be lovely if children could grow up without ever being told off. If they could be free and happy and left to develop their cute habit of destroying phone boxes and calling Daddy a dumb-arsed jerk, and we could save ourselves a lot of energy telling them not to all the time.

But there are two problems with removing discipline: the first, as we've already learned, is that children like and *need* a line to be drawn so that they can have clear boundaries marking the framework in which they grow up, and the second Granny is to tell me shortly.

This being Saturday, Granny is treating us all to a trip to the local coffee shop. Forget everything you might imagine about coffee shops in remote Highland villages: here all traces of tartan, cream buns and cheap coffee have been replaced by the funky local owners of Taste, as it's appropriately called, with bang up to date décor, a mouth-watering menu and huge glass windows to admire the awesome views. They even do such shockingly modern things as cappuccinos, salad and good wine. (Though not all together.)

Within five minutes my kids have made more mess than I feel able to excuse, but it's a jolly gathering and Granny loves these times with her great grandchildren. She watches them with a smile as they chat with her, spill their drinks, share their cake and fold their napkins into little fans. But when there is no more cake to drop and restlessness sets in, they head home with their dad, leaving Granny and me to stay behind to clear up the debris and have a chat.

I ask her what she thinks the problem with removing discipline is, and I get the word I've been looking for. A word that is mentioned time and time again in reference to the Yoof of Today. The fourth 'R', as I like to call it.

'The main problem with removing all discipline,' she says, mopping up some milk from the table with an unfolded napkin, 'is that you lose all sense of respect. If you let children get away with murder, you stop treating them as human beings who have to abide by certain rules and laws, and they consequently respect nothing.'

Granny's Pearl of Wisdom

Without respect it's almost impossible to have any discipline, because nobody cares that they're being told off. Nobody feels bad about behaving badly and upsetting others, so they just carry on regardless.

Ah, there it is: RESPECT. The cornerstone of civilised society. The missing link. The magic ingredient. It's all about respect, innit.

Entirely sensible though this sounds, I feel we have entered a worryingly circular argument here, and put this to Granny.

'Hang on – if you don't discipline kids and keep them on the straight and narrow they have no sense of respect, but once they've lost all respect for others you can't discipline them? That sounds a bit hopeless to me.'

'No, it's not hopeless, but once you've let things slip as far as they have it is a challenge. Here's how you can tell that respect has gone missing: because despite having more rules, laws, advice, guidance, handbooks and regulations than we *ever* did, children are far less well behaved than they used to be. How can that work? If you respect others you don't *need* to be told what to do – you do it because you just know it's the *right* thing to do.'

'And you'd say it all starts in the home, with discipline?'

'Well of course. Parents have a huge responsibility to make sure their children don't run riot, and teach them that they are not in control – *you* are. For now! That's partly what makes them children, and not adults. Once a child has lost all sense of respect towards others you've really lost the battle, but you have to try and get some discipline and authority back into their lives.'

Oh hell – but I don't *want* to lose the battle! I want to try and win it – for our children's sake as much as our own – by solving the problem and finding ways to put some respect back.

Time to go back to basics and look at just what kind of a situation we're dealing with here, before we tackle the solutions.

First though, a word from jellyellie, our voice of the MSN generation:

> **"** *My friends and I often feel that respect has disappeared among young people today. Even we can see the decline in respect between us and kids just a few years younger than us. When adults talk about young people having no respect, it's always seen as a dig against the young people and their parents. In reality, the young people are victims of today's society.* **"**

Where are we now?

RESPECT:
n. deferential esteem felt or shown towards person
v. treat with consideration; refrain from offending

In other words, respect is a sort of courteous regard for others, which you *feel*, as well as show, and means you don't go around being rude or offensive towards them. Sounds sensible enough to me, bitch-face. (Sorry, couldn't resist.)

Respect is not a given; we don't have the *right* to be respected; nor do children innately know how to respect others unless they spend time learning about other people, by interacting with them and being told 'no' if their behaviour isn't cool any more. Respect has to be both earned *and* learned, through our experiences of others and our place in relation to them.

In other words, not everyone earns or deserves respect: a shite parent who neglects a child or beats him every day doesn't deserve any respect at all; neither does the weird old man at the end of the road who throws little stones at children as they walk by so they turn around and see he's got his sad little willy out. He's a wanker, literally, so why should I respect him – just because he's older than me? I think not.

> ❝ *I suppose it's part of the breakdown in society, the fact that we stopped having respect for figures in authority partly because those in authority didn't command it.* ❞
>
> **Diana Mather, etiquette coach**

The trouble starts when such disrespect is felt – for reasons we'll get to later – by thousands of children towards their parents, and then towards authority in general. Because when it's reached this stage all hell breaks loose – in fact, it pretty much already has. What has started to take over every park bench, school playground and shopping centre is a new *breed* of disrespect.

A loud, in-your-face, visible and tangible disrespect, not just for those who are pretty annoying or abusive, but for *all* people and *all* things, especially those in authority. It's a deep, rock-hard disrespect that crosses age, sex, class and postcode and it's what makes Outraged from Tunbridge Wells shake her bonnet on an increasingly frequent basis before calling *The Daily Rant* to complain about all those 'Young People' hanging around her cul-de-sac.

Annoyingly, she has a point. Ironically, she is missing the main one.

These ever-present, loud, unstoppable young creatures are so far beyond having any respect for anything that it's very hard to see any chance of taming them. You *cannot* discipline someone like this because they just don't care. You can't punish them or reason with them because they are, quite literally, unreasonable.

And it is thanks to the thousands like them that Catherine Tate's best-known and initially dislikeable character Lauren (or, to use her proper name, Dame Lauren Alesha Masheka Tanesha Felicia Jane Cooper) became, curiously, so loved by millions when she blurted that soul-withering phrase: AM I BOVVERED?

Lauren's impenetrable attitude of utter disrespect and hopelessness sums up the mentality and sad situation of a whole generation. We've met Laurens in the park, at the cinema, on holiday, at the cash point, by the bus stop and in the swimming pool – and no, they literally aren't bovvered about a single damned thing.

They don't care what they look like, how they behave, how they speak, what their effect on others is, whether they are despised, or liked or vilified. They just *are*. So fuck off everyone else.

And now we need to ask, HOW has this happened, and what can we do to help them out of it?

How has it got this way?

Jeepers, this is enough to make anyone want to jump off the nearest high building. Enough! Instead of being disgusted by disrespectful children, laughing at them, punishing them or ignoring them altogether, perhaps we should try to find out how this has happened, and what we can do to ensure it doesn't get any worse. And, for the self-interested (and that's all parents to a large degree, let's be honest) ensure that it doesn't happen to OUR children.

So, with this mission in mind, my questions for Granny are simply these: *how*, from her position of grand old age and experience, does she think we have reached the point where so many young people – people who should be looking forward to going somewhere with their lives, and achieving something and bettering themselves – feel they have nothing else to say than 'I don't care'? And what can we do to put some BOVVER back into our children?

Granny has several suggestions, starting with the obvious:

'Well, I think a lot of the blame lies with television and film, I really do.'

'Not all TV, I hope. I know there's a lot of mindless dross around – in fact, about 100 channels of mindless dross – but many films and documentaries *reflect* society, rather than shaping it, and there's still plenty of excellent programme-making for a young audience.'

'Well, yes, that's maybe true, but I'm talking specifically about television dramas and soaps. What I've noticed with time is that in these the youngsters started to always know best, or show no respect for their elders. The older characters are shown as victims, as *frightened* of the younger ones. And this filters into real life, and we hear it in the news all the time that kids are terrorising older people and being rude to their parents and their teachers.'

This suggestion, that television, film and the music industry may have changed our children's behaviour for the worse, certainly isn't new, but it's something that has been debated a fair amount in recent times and may well have some mileage.

A LITTLE RESPECT ON THE BOX

———⊶∞⊷———

Violence on the up: a study in the US in 2007 found that an average American youth witnesses more than 1,000 murders, rapes, and assaults per year on television. Nice.

The type of violence on TV has changed: when Popeye beat up Bluto we cheered, but much of it is now much darker and more realistic than when Jerry set fire to Tom's tail and finished the job with an anvil (or whatever it was). The violence is now more realistic and frightening.

Behavioural effects: children who watch large amounts of TV and play video games frequently and for long periods are more likely to act more aggressively with peers.

A survey in 2005 by Ofcom found that soap operas and reality shows were responsible for a sharp increase in swearing on television before the 9 p.m. watershed, a time when many children are watching.

Many 'real life' dramas for kids today, such as *Tracey Beaker*, *Horrid Henry* (sorry, him again!) and Channel 4's *Hollyoaks* show children being rude to others as though it's totally normal and acceptable. Compare this with *Press Gang*, *Rentaghost*, *Why Don't You*, *Degrassi Junior High*, *The Littlest Hobo* – oh, I'm going all weepy now – and so on from our day, which generally showed bad behaviour as being 'wrong' rather than glorified.

continued overleaf . . .

Mum, you're fired!

There is a charming programme on television that you may have missed if you inhabit a cave in Outer Mongolia or the quieter lanes in Ambridge. This gem, this shining example of all things sensitive, enlightening and cockle-warming, is called *The Apprentice*.

The Apprentice is the perfect example of just what we parents are up against when it comes to teaching our kids about respecting others. Its basic theme seems to be (at full volume, please) 'I am the most incredibly talented and deserving human being in the entire universe! I *deserve* to rule the world, and will stop at *nothing* to make as much money as humanly possible. Move over, assholes! Nya ha ha ha ha!'

In their quest for the top spot, contestants employ such commendable tactics as back-stabbing, lying (as Sir Alan himself said: 'business is all about bullshitting.' Great) and scheming; good manners evaporate; and humility . . . well, it doesn't even feature. The contestants are, without any exception that I've spotted, egomaniacs on a truly staggering, eye-watering scale, and what's all the more horrible is that they are lavishly praised – even hero worshipped by some – for the 'success' their self-centredness brings. What they seek is fame and fortune at any cost, irrespective of dignity or consideration for others.

In fairness, (and that's partly what respect is all about) *The Apprentice* is only one of a host of leisure-time pursuits dedicated to the good of ME: reality TV, *Big Brother*, *Pop Idol*, Karaoke, even our internet friend Facebook and much more besides are all based on the premise of showing other people how great and interesting we are, making us little more than walking, talking CVs.

Now, I'm all for a bit of self-confidence, for believing in yourself, and having the confidence and determination to fight on and succeed. How else would we ladies ever have got the vote, or managed to wax our underarms? (That's a joke, OK!)

But we are raising our kids in a culture where ambition and drive have given way to arrogance and ruthlessness on a global scale, which is all very well if you want to be in the top five per cent of the most dislikeable people on earth but really rather horrifying when you're seven years old and learning how to get on with other people.

By growing up in this culture of 'All for me and me for all' our children are learning that boastfulness, 'bigging yourself up', shouting the loudest and abusing other people is the best way forward. Add to this the inescapable 'celebrity' aspect of our culture, which dictates that a person's success is measured purely in terms of column inches and bank notes, not talent and what they *do* with it, and it's no wonder so many kids say 'I don't need to work because when I grow up I'm going to be rich and famous.'

Why are we surprised they have no respect for anyone if they are exposed to this kind of thing? So heed this warning and be careful what you let your children watch and try to stem the 'Because I'm worth it, asshole' tide.

Granny's Pearl of Wisdom

Children learn so much of their behaviour from the television, in music videos and what they listen to on the radio that unless we can change what they see and hear on there or cut down how much they watch, we have real trouble on our hands.

It is, of course, not only what children *see* that can influence their behaviour: they are also affected by what they read and listen to as well. Just take this classic example that I can identify with one hundred per cent:

66 *We had to ban Horrid Henry books completely. Toby turned from a good-natured little boy into a complete pig within hours – spitting, poking fun at people, being deliberately naughty and nasty and provoking us at every turn. He saw Henry's behaviour as acceptable, and the fact that we read him the books and gave him the CDs to listen to (they came with a Sunday newspaper) we were endorsing this. A day after we took the books and CDs away, we had our Toby back again. We're sticking to* Swallows and Amazons *from now on!* 99

Sarah, mother of Toby, six

Almost every parent I've spoken to has had an experience of this nature, be it as a result of a TV programme, a film, a book or some music. And yes, quite a few of us would, in our more nostalgic moments, just *love* our kids to go back to reading The Famous Five and watching *Take Hart*. The problem is they can't – at least, not entirely. Times have changed, new media are out there and we have to strike some balance between keeping a close eye on what our children are exposed to, and letting them be a part of the new things on offer.

It just doesn't have to be programmes like *My Mum is a Slag*, games called *How Shit is your Dad*? or music from Death House. There's compromise and there's caving in. Make sure you do the former.

So **solution number one** is to curb the amount of exposure to unhelpful influences kids get from popular culture, where behaving with no respect whatsoever is portrayed as acceptable, or cool.

And *how*? Well, by taking a little more control over what you expose your kids to, and knowing what they're watching, listening and reading. For example, don't let your kids watch telly or use the computer in their bedrooms: how can you have any idea what they're exposed to in there? Have a *family* TV and computer and know what they are doing on it all the time. If you think what they're exposed to is inappropriate you have every right, and a duty, to say so and suggest an alternative. Same goes for music – if you think your four year old shouldn't be listening to Eminem or Lily Allen, don't let him. If your eight-year-old daughter is choosing books from the library you consider more suitable for teenagers – an issue we've had in our house recently – suggest she waits a year or so and take her to the book shop or library to choose some alternatives. Just because a child *can* read

143

something, it doesn't mean they should. Take control, be sensible, and make sure your kids are exposed to information that is suitable for their age.

So far so fairly predictable: It has always been thus, and we are simply the next in a line of parents who think new technologies will corrupt our children's minds – even the good old wireless was seen as potentially harmful by many when it first came out! But Granny has another theory about the disappearance of respect, which I *hadn't* expected.

Generation ME

'And then,' she continues, wrapping the end of her cake up in some tissue to take home with her for later, 'there was the end of the war, and I think this could have contributed too.'

'How do you mean?'

'Well that was the very beginning of it as I recall: parents started to say to their kids then, 'Look at the mess your parents' generation made of it. You can do better. You go and do better and make a better world.' Maybe that's where this notion that elders don't know better started from, and it just went from there. The Baby Boomers – your dad's generation – became the very first ME generation, and they just did what they liked. They felt they *deserved* better. And just look where it got you all.'

Just look indeed. The Baby Boomers were not only the first ME generation, but they also came along at a time of unprecedented economic improvement. For the first time, many ordinary people really had the chance of *making* it. Of earning money, of living a life they had only ever dreamed of, and of spending their hard-earned pennies on *things*. Consumerism hit the big time and the manufacturing of totally unnecessary but rather gorgeous products went bananas, as did advertising. A whole new obsession with SELF was born against a rather cushy background of little pleasantries such as a job for life, owning a house, guilt-free travel, worry-free sex, worry-free drugs, unadulterated food and proper seasons. You know – all that stuff we don't have any more (I'll take my embittered hat off now).

Another change that occurred around this time was that divorce rates went up: legal reforms in the 1960s and the introduction of the 'no fault' divorce in the 1970s, made divorce 'easier', and the number of divorces in Europe tripled from 1970 to the early 2000s, with Britain leading the field by the staggering amount of *double* the number of divorces per thousand families compared with our European counterparts. I would suggest that this increase is probably also related to the fact that increasing numbers of women had jobs and were therefore financially independent, and *could* walk out on men they no longer wanted to live with – something that had rarely happened previously. Although divorce rates are now falling (though, interestingly, not in the Baby Boomer category, where they are still splitting up from each other in ever higher numbers) this sad trend left a sudden glut of children growing up in single-parent families.

Granny remembers this trend well.

'Oh, I think divorce has so much to answer for. All those children growing up with no stability at home, and suffering so much. People used to see things through, even in tough times. For better, for worse, you know? And economics and society played a big part too: a woman would never have walked out in my day – she couldn't afford to for a start, and she'd be looked down upon. But suddenly along came a whole generation who wanted to have it all; they could, and they did, and they messed a lot of things up for their children.'

Ouch, Granny! Though there is undoubtedly some truth in this, it's also a fairly harsh judgement on what is a very sad and unwanted outcome for many. I know a number of people who are divorced, with children, and I can't think of a single one who wanted it to happen to them. It is certainly not a case of 'I'm a selfish pig so I'm going to shag the nanny and leave my wife' in the majority of cases. And in almost every break-up there is at least one party who is dreadfully hurt, didn't bring the break-up upon themselves and tries hard to make things work. To damn an entire generation as selfish for having more divorces than those before is just a tad extreme for me.

I would also argue that it is perhaps better for kids to be brought up by two single parents than in a household where mum and dad clearly hate each other and row every five minutes. Yes, our predecessors stayed impressively glued together through tough times like limpets to a rock, but there were probably thousands of them who endured miserable marriages simply because they had no alternative. I'm not so sure that's better than getting divorced and making a new, happier start for everyone. Apparently I'm not alone: in a recent poll for the *Sunday Telegraph*'s Stella magazine, sixty-six per cent of women asked said they thought it was better to get divorced than stay together for the sake of the children.

But, whatever the reasons for the increase in split-ups in the last thirty years, what does Granny think the *effect* of divorce is on children and how does this link to the loss of respect?

'Well, as soon as you have a split family you have children who don't know where they belong – with Mummy, or with Daddy.'

'Oh, I don't know. The children I know whose parents are divorced understand very well that they are still loved by both, and belong with both.'

'But there is such upheaval. And worse still is that often you see parents trying to make up for the damage they've caused by spoiling them, and by not disciplining the kids as much as they should. They start to *befriend* their kids, and let go of the important parent-child relationship, with its discipline, and that's where parenting really changed, and where respect got lost.'

'What, because kids no longer respected their parents?'

'Partly, yes. With the lack of discipline came the lack of respect. But even where respect remains, as I'm sure it does for many, there is no constant, solid framework any more. Everything becomes uprooted and unstable, and the clear guide-lines and constancy that kids need so much vanish.'

OK, so that was the Baby Boomers. But what about *us*? Are we – the products of this Baby Boomer generation and the parents of today's children – instilling any sense of respect in our kids?

GENERATION US

Well, the evidence doesn't look too good unfortunately:

* We work longer hours than ever, often packing in sixty-hour weeks (and even more for some, not including the long commutes so many are forced to make) with weekends playing catch-up with tax returns or expenses claims, instead of hide and seek with our kids.

* Despite the credit crunch we are seemingly addicted to consumerism, buying and discarding more than ever, leading to mounting guilt and debt as well as mounting piles of landfill.

* According to the Office for National Statistics in 2007, children in the UK are three times more likely to live in one-parent households than they were in 1972.

* A leading provider of child care staff, Tinies, reported in 2008 a sixty per cent increase in the number of families wanting after-school care for their children, believing this to be because parents, particularly mothers, are returning to jobs and working longer hours as the cost of living rises.

* Children in the UK are less happy and more stressed than ever according to recent surveys by Ofsted and The Children's Charity.

What this shows is a situation where parents are increasingly absent in their children's lives. If we're not working, we're spending and kids are increasingly being raised by an ever-changing mixture of after-school clubs and an assortment of adults who are not their natural parents. Many of us are not choosing to work this hard: in the same Stella poll mentioned earlier, eighty-two per cent of women said balancing work and home life was their biggest challenge, compared with only twenty-four per cent who thought having a fulfilling career was.

But whether we're choosing it or not, the upshot is that there is woefully little time set aside for '*family* time', and if we're not ignoring our kids because we're busy, we're spoiling them rotten to make up for it. And then there are all the times when we feel we're stretched to the limit making ends meet and simply want to do something enjoyable for *ourselves*! I've done it; you've probably done it. Some of it we can't help: bills have to be paid. But some of it we can: we don't *have* to raid Primark on a Saturday or book in for a facial, when the alternative is playing footie in the park with our kids once a week. Remember the definition of Respect above: 'treat with consideration'. That's what we need to do to our kids, so that they can learn to do it for others.

Financial times are tough for many of us now, but if we let slip time spent as a family, discipline and love then loss of respect will soon follow, leaving us not with a third ME generation, but an emotionally abandoned, spoiled, confused and increasingly angry 'And what about *me*??!' generation, who has, understandably, little respect for anything.

Granny's Pearl of Wisdom

If you think about yourself too much, you're going to forget your children. They are the ones who suffer through selfish times, and they don't feel respect for people who largely ignore them or spoil them rotten. Why should they?

Solution number two, then, is to try not to let our busy lives take over time spent *with* our kids. If you do find yourself raising a child alone, or with a new partner, don't pile on the guilt: just try extra hard to make sure you keep the basic rules and levels of discipline and respect where they need to be.

By replacing the guilt-gifts culture we all succumb to sometimes with one where we give our children our TIME, we can teach them about thinking of others. Read to them, play with them, bake a cake with them, pay attention to *their* needs sometimes, rather than obsessing over your own worries and desires. Most of these things are free and don't require much effort at all but the result – happy little people covered in chocolate, for example – is invaluable. It's a bit of 'what goes around comes around' really, and it works.

Manners

> 66 *To succeed in the world it is not enough to be stupid, you must also be well-mannered.* 99

Voltaire

A discussion about respect is really missing a trick if it fails to mention some fucking manners. You know: basic courtesies like saying please and thank you, not telling the check-out lady she's a fat slag, not nicking the last Ferrero Rocher off the Ambassador's plate. That kind of thing.

* In a recent survey for ITV1's *Tonight* programme more than half of Britons said they believed bad manners is the biggest problem in the country today with sixty-seven per cent saying that it is the root cause of anti-social behaviour plaguing society.

* Over eighty-six per cent of the respondents said Britons are ruder now than ten years ago and eighty-five and a half per cent said they would prefer to receive a 'please or thank-you' than £1,000,000 from a stranger. (Honestly, I'd take the million quid – wouldn't you?!)

* More than ninety per cent said they think many parents are failing to pass on basic manners to their children.

Before we start flagellating ourselves too hard, let's just take a tiny step back, and reassure ourselves that all of this is not new. Kids have been moaned at for their bad, sloppy, rude behaviour from the second generation. The following quotation is very well known, but it's still a shock every time to read it and think that it was written some 2,300-odd years ago:

> *The children now love luxury; they have bad manners, contempt for authority; they show disrespect for elders and love chatter in place of exercise. Children are now tyrants, not the servants of their households. They no longer rise when elders enter the room. They contradict their parents, chatter before company, gobble up dainties at the table, cross their legs, and tyrannize their teachers.*

Plato (attributed to Socrates)

It's pretty amazing, isn't it? And quite uplifting too – if things have ever been thus, then all is not, after all, down the shitter.

My personal theory is that some manners, such as holding doors open for people, offering a seat on a bus and so on, which did go on eighty or so years ago, rather took a knock when women turned around to men and said 'Listen, you arseholes, stop bloody patronising us. We'll open our own bloody doors thanks very much. Now piss off and leave us to our hairy legs.'

This is a shame. I like it when someone holds a door open for me, and don't take it as a slight on my capabilities as a human being. I take it as a welcome sign of humanity. Ditto if someone offers me a seat on an overcrowded train when I'm seven months pregnant and look like I might be about to explode. (Mind you, I also rather like it when builders whistle at me as I walk past, so maybe I'm just a desperate housewife!)

This kind of gentlemanly, courteous behaviour is not lost – in fact, I sense it is having something of a mini revival; or maybe that's just genteel Cambridge – and I think it is absolutely vital in a civilised society that we demonstrate such behaviour to our kids, and point out times when people behave rudely. How else are they going to learn?

But the other kind of bad manners, the effing and blinding variety, shows no sign of lessening whatsoever. Granny tells me that when she was a child, 'damn' was the worst word she ever heard anyone say, and that was only in times of extreme exasperation. Crikey – emotional times then.

These days, we 'fuck, shit, bugger, Christ, Jesus, dammit, bollocks and bloody hell' our way through tea time or the school run without a second thought. I've done it a fair few times when I forgot who was present, and I dare say your mouth could do with a good clean-out once in a while too.

> ❝ *I believe that my generation has a lot to answer for. The youth culture in the 60s and early 70s threw out every rule in the book, including conventions about acceptable language. I was working as a researcher on the programme in which Kenneth Tynan delivered the f-word for the first time on television in a discussion about censorship, and though that seemed very daring at the time, in the forty-odd years since, the floodgates have been swamped. Personally I don't think comedy or documentaries have been improved as a result. What we have gained in freedom we have lost in respect. I would not like to bring back draconian censorship, nor the quaint old deference, but certainly it would improve our quality of life to bring respect back, and I believe that would make everyone's life more pleasant.* ❞
>
> **Esther Rantzen, patron of Campaign for Courtesy**

Esther is of course right: swearing on television doesn't add much to the content or tone of a programme, and a little more respect would make everyone's lives better. The recent Ross and Brand kerfuffle over lewd remarks made on a Radio 2 show brought the whole subject of what is and what isn't acceptable to broadcast these days sharply into focus once more, with the wobbly line between oversensitive censorship and total lack of control being argued over for weeks.

Blatant offensiveness is of course to be avoided. But swear words are part of our language – an important, colourful part, I would argue, and one we should celebrate and enjoy with fervour, where appropriate. There's nothing like a good 'fuck' to really hit the spot sometimes, so to speak, and you can't even compare the satisfaction of a full-blooded 'bollocks' with a soulless 'Oh deary me'.

However, like plunging necklines or tequila slammers, there is a time and a place for swearing. Knowing when *not* to swear is as important as knowing how to swear, and there's the trouble where kids are concerned: they have no idea what the words mean, or when not to use them. All children go through a perfectly normal phase of loving swear words. They have no idea what they mean, though they are aware that they're a little bit naughty, which is why they have a go. The best way to deal with it is to IGNORE the word completely. Making a big fuss simply results in delight, and much repetition. If it persists you might like to move on to stage two where you tell them very firmly not to say that *ever* again. Laughing and saying 'Oooh, isn't he cute,' is a recipe for disaster.

66 *Children have never been very good at listening to their elders, but they have never failed to imitate them.* 99

James Baldwin, American writer and civil rights activist

This point is a very important one, and actually applies to everything we do in front of our children. They're like mirrors and they reflect everything we do.

But, let's be honest, some 'children swearing' stories are far too funny to get all po-faced about. Our friends' seven-year-old son recently commented on the silly nicknames he overheard me calling my daughter. Don't your parents call you anything funny sometimes, I asked?

'Oh yes,' he replied casually. 'They call me poppet, and bean. And fucker.'

His parents – who do not, *ever* call him fucker, incidentally – nearly died of embarrassment.

Similarly, when my five year old was given two matching cuddly bears recently, he instantly named then Nutty and Penis. Having regained my composure I pointed out that penis really wasn't a nice name for a bear. Charlie looked pensive for a while, relishing the moment, and announced proudly: 'OK. I'll call them Nutty and Cock.'

And when I left my kids to play in the bath with their sticky sponge letters yesterday, I came back to find they had written 'willy, turd, bum, fart, cock, nipples and penos' on the tiles. I was very cross about bad spelling, obviously.

All true stories, and all, I think, very funny. *But,* it's only funny if such language is not encouraged. We occasionally swear in front of our kids, but have the clear and oft-repeated rule that it's OK at home, and never ever OK outside the home. In general we ask them not to swear at all if possible, pointing out that life is unfair, so deal with it.

Liam Gallagher was photographed recently with his seven-year-old son, Gene, on his hip sticking two fingers up at photographers.

This was neither funny nor cute. It was the clearest indication, if any were needed, that children copy their parents.

Even the Government has tried to step in to improve the situation, with the announcement in 2007 by the Schools Minister of plans to make lessons in good manners compulsory at secondary school. This is a sweet gesture and everything, but isn't it just a tad too late at this stage? And wouldn't you just *love* to be the teacher who asks her class of thirty-five hormonal, arsey kids to repeat the proposed mantra: 'We are gentle, we are kind, we work hard, we look after property, we listen to people, we are honest, we do not hurt anybody.' It makes you cry just thinking about it.

Manners lessons may help a little, but setting the standard *at home* is the best way to tackle bad manners.

∞ *GRANNY'S TIPS* ∞

Manners maketh man, so teach your kids some decent manners from day one, and watch them grow into polite, kind human beings. It will make the world a far more pleasant, gentler place, and good manners will take them far.

Children who use naughty words at home to get a giggle are doing what normal children do. But watch your tongue and make it clear that swearing is not acceptable. It comes from you, so set the tone clearly.

A bell tinkles above the door as two more customers come into the café, looking (and smelling) as though they've just come back from a hard morning's walk in the mountains. As she struggles out of her jacket, one of them knocks over a pile of newspapers, which flops to the floor, scattering paper and adverts for Stannah stair lifts and breast surgery all over the floor. Granny is up like a jack-in-a-box, helping to pick it all up. She can hardly walk, and yet here she is, on her feet, helping someone else out.

It never ceases to amaze me how much people who need help themselves do for others. Granny was still delivering meals on wheels to 'the old folk' as she called them, well into her seventies!

Here, it turns out, is solution number three:

Thinking of others: spending time with the Real People

'I'll tell you another thing that breeds respect, Elizabeth,' she says, plonking herself back down on her chair. 'Doing good for others. Working together as a group and learning to work *together*.'

'What, like community work?'

'Yes, if you like. Or something as simple as joining the Brownies or the Cubs. These are organisations where *you* don't come first – where you have to learn to wait for others, and to be part of a team. Team exercises are vital for gaining a sense of respect, and I don't see so much community-based activity going on these days.'

On first thought, you may disagree with this: kids seem to take part in more activities than ever these days, and parents end up as little more than a taxi firm and a source of money! But if you think about it more, very few of these are truly based on working as a group. Most are based around each child's *individual* progress, be it in ballet, piano lesson, tap, judo or painting. Drama is the exception, where how you interact with others is key. So are there others? What about team sports?

'Oh yes, team sports are very good. Or joining an orchestra or choir. Anything where you have to be aware of others, and play *with* them. Not just doing things for yourself. **It's not healthy for children to believe they are the only thing that matters. And that's how they seem to think these days – that they are the best.**'

This self-centredness in our kids is mainly fuelled by their lack of contact with their fellow human beings but it is compounded by the amount of time they spend in their own head staring at a screen: from time-killing on the computer (yes, even the 'good' things they are doing on there, like school projects or just 'finding out about stuff') to watching telly, communicating with friends via websites or texts and generally inhabiting a two-dimensional, cold, emotionless world. They are a generation that understands and deals with *things*, not people. Almost all kids do from time to time, but some do for up to thirty hours a week. That's not living – that's semi-existing in a parallel universe. Scary.

* According to research conducted by the Institute for Public Policy Research in 2008, children in the UK are spending more than twenty hours per week surfing the internet.

* A separate study found that sixty-four per cent of all kids go online, *while* watching TV. The mind boggles. (Which is exactly the problem.)

* A report in 2008 from market research agency Childwise found that British children spend an average of five hours and twenty minutes in front of a screen *each day*, four out of five children have a TV set in their rooms (no, no no!!) and eighty-three per cent of kids turn the telly on the moment they get home. Can I cry now?

Granny has little experience of such a two-dimensional child-hood, of course, and only knows what she has seen on, er, the telly (oh the irony) and from what I've told her. But as I describe to her just what many children's lives are like after school and at the weekend, and how much time many spend hiding out in their rooms, sitting alone with their computer games, having more friendships in chat rooms than down their own street, she looks completely horrified. As well she might.

'But . . . but Elizabeth . . . that's *criminal*. *Why* are they in their rooms, talking to pretend people? Why are they locked up, not out there in the real world?'

'I guess because they can be – because their parents let them, and because their parents are busy working or shopping or just not wanting to bother to do anything else with their kids. It's awful, I know, but it's happening everywhere. Many children are now much happier and more confident in a digital world than a human world.'

Granny looks so flabbergasted that my concern shifts from her sore foot to her heart! Calm down, Granny . . .

'But how are they ever going to understand how people work? How people think and feel? You can't just grow up in two dimensions. You need to interact with *real* people. To help others, and be aware of others around you. Oh, it's just too sad!'

Yes, it is. But we can help.

SMALL STEPS – GREAT PROGRESS

—⁘—

Here's an example of how we can teach our kids to think of others just by the very smallest, simplest things we say and do on a daily basis. As a treat I let my kids have lunch from the self-service salad bar in Sainsbury's. Yeah all right, I know it's a rather sad treat and I'm very embarrassed! But it's the 'self-service, and very, very occasional' aspect that they like, so stop laughing at me – it *is* a treat! Anyway, there was only a small amount of Phoebe's favourite pasta salad left and she, naturally, wanted to take every last scrap for herself. I pointed out that perhaps she could take *some*, and leave the rest for someone else to have.

She looked rather crestfallen and cross (and I felt very sanctimonious and annoying) but I could see that she understood the point and knew it was the right thing to do. That tiny moment was enough to show her, and her siblings, to think of others. It's not exactly life-changing, but it's a small step to making them aware of respecting other people.

So, solution number three: get our children out of their dungeons and involved in activities – join a sports team or music group, do odd jobs for the neighbours or just play with the bored kid next door. It takes time and our effort, but it's worth it.

I mean, remember Bob-a-Job? Who does that now? Nobody, that's who, just in case they knock on the door of a weirdo, or get sued for breaking a plant pot, I guess. Well that's a bloody shame.

We'd do anything for a penny or two when I was a kid: washing people's cars (badly), cutting their grass (badly) and weeding the drive (badly). Sure we got some cash for it but it wasn't the earning or the helping that was really the *point* – which is lucky, as we weren't really helping or earning much at all! – it was the doing something for someone else, talking to them and knowing who they were that was the real lesson here.

Getting out there in the community and doing things with other people is one of the healthiest things we can encourage our children to do.

As a good friend of mine put it to me rather beautifully recently:

> ❝ *There is a sense of belonging that I think we have lost – a sense of connection to one another. Without it we live a life that is governed by the rule 'every man for himself' instead of the 'golden rule'. We don't have empathy for how others live because we don't even know our neighbours any more, and consequently we don't have respect for them or their point of view. By working side by side with other people from all walks of life, our kids will be humbled, feel connected to others and feel a sense of respect towards others in their community.* ❞

Amen to that.

Coming right back at you, Mum

The last thought on respect for this book comes, not from Granny, but from me, and it is this: if we want our kids to show some respect, we need to give them some first.

Listening to how many parents talk to their offspring in public, I think they show less respect than I would to an unusually lazy, stupid ant. They bark at them, snap at them, order them about, don't listen to them, never ask them what *they* want and generally treat them like more than usually smelly vermin. You can see the poor kids are there thinking: 'Hello? Can anyone see that I'm actually *here*? And have feelings? And thoughts, and desires? Anyone . . .?! No, sod it, I'll be an arsehole too, then.'

This is a slightly inelegant way of saying, again, that children replicate their parents' behaviour so we must lead by example. Interestingly, our friend Lauren's other well-known phrase is 'Are you disrespecting me?' The answer, I think, is yes. We *are* disrespecting her. Too many kids today have been let down by everyone: their parents, their teachers, all of us. If we want to break this cycle of disrespect and lack of discipline we have to go back to treating our offspring as *people*, not Inconveniences, Nuisances and Problems.

If we behave in a more supportive, positive and inclusive way *towards* our children, it will not only help to make them respect other people more, but to respect *themselves* more. This is absolutely essential if we are to break the tragic rise in the number of teenage pregnancies, childhood depression and, that ever-present problem on our streets: binge drinking.

The drinking culture, family and behaviour

If you've been out after 8 p.m. in any British city centre or have ever listened to the news in the last few years, you will know that we are living in a country with a horrifying drinking problem, which is having devastating effects on our health, our happiness and our society – and the same goes for our kids. If societies could become ill, then ours has chronic liver failure, high blood pressure, and severe depression. A trip to Casualty is well overdue I'd say.

I recently spoke with a friend of mine who lives in Germany but who grew up here and was back in the UK on business. He was almost speechless at the scenes of young girls falling out of the pubs and clubs in the wee hours, half dressed and shit-faced. Nothing like this went on twenty years ago when he lived here, or goes on where he lives now, and he was pretty appalled.

And before we start smugly tut-tutting at those enchanting young ladies who vomit in gutters and get so rat-arsed they can't find their way home – and so end up shagging someone they've only just met because he kindly offers them a bed for the night – it's not just the usual suspects; the people who *look* like they drink too much; the drunks; the people society gave up on.

Middle-class piss heads are just as bad, even if they are leaning on designer furniture and drinking very expensive poison, and it's as likely to be *your* teenage son or daughter in that gutter, simply because of the culture we live in. Remember Euan Blair?

If you regularly open a bottle of wine before your child's book bag, think little of drinking two glasses of the stuff a day or more, or think getting sloshed in front of your kids is OK, then you too have a problem that needs addressing.

* A Government-commissioned report in 2007 revealed that a quarter of adults living in some of the UK's wealthiest towns are drinking enough alcohol every week to damage their health.

* 'Hazardous' levels for women are between five and twelve large glasses of wine a week and for men between seven and seventeen glasses. How many do you put away?

✳ In the 2007 Unicef league table on child wellbeing, the UK comes bottom of the rankings by some considerable distance when it comes to young people's risk behaviours, including smoking, drinking, using cannabis, fighting and bullying, and sexual behaviour.

I realised a few years back that I almost never got through an evening without a tipple. Just a glass, mind you, but a drink nonetheless. Every day. Somehow, just thinking about that made me feel really pathetic – why did I have to drink *every evening*? Could I not enjoy myself without it?

I decided to go for two months without any alcohol at all, not because I thought I had a problem, but because if I *couldn't* then I would know that I had.

That was two years ago, and I have barely had more than a couple of glasses of wine a week since. I'm not trying to be po-faced or saintly about this: I do still find occasion to get inelegantly sloshed once in a while and I'm certainly not saying that giving up the booze is something one *should* do. But I am perfectly happy sans loopy juice, my skin looks younger, my brain is clearer, my waistline is smaller and my bank balance is healthier too – and I don't miss it at all. So maybe it's worth a try . . .

All of this talk about booze is related to respect, and to generally acceptable behaviour, because if our children see us getting pissed every Friday and Saturday (and Monday and Wednesday) and see that we take our first sip of the evening with a long *sighhh* – a clear indication that we're finally escaping the nightmarish day – then they can only repeat this behaviour, and we don't really have a leg to stand on (so to speak) when we criticise this. We drink; why can't they when they're teenagers?

164

Interestingly, in other European countries, especially the Southern ones, the problem isn't so great even though adults do drink freely in front of their kids. So what's the difference?

Well, while there have been quite a few theories about this, nobody seems to have come up with the definitive answer. We've tried extending pub opening hours longer to avoid the 11 o'clock carnage – but now people just carry on drinking all night long and end up in Casualty . . . and with no liver by the time they're twenty-five. We can't do anything about the lousy weather in the UK, so if that's a factor then we're doomed.

My own theory, for what it's worth, comes from having lived in a Mediterranean country for some of my childhood, and from visiting such countries many times during my adulthood: one clear difference between there and at home is that children are brought up in a culture that *values* them, that respects them and lets them be a part of society and a part of the family, not something to be put away and ignored. Adults who do drink (i.e. most of them) do so in a responsible way – they don't drink to get pissed, to remove themselves from their lives and their kids. They drink *with* their friends and families, with a meal, in a supportive, friendly environment. Drinking isn't bad – it's even said to be good for you in moderation. Good news at last! But when it's an activity in itself we're in trouble.

How to bring back a little respect

∞ *GRANNY'S TIPS* ∞

Beware the influence of popular culture. Don't expose your children to programmes, books, films or comics that teach that disrespecting others is acceptable or cool.

Working with others. Encourage your child to engage with other people who live near them, and to join team activities. Maybe there's a local park that needs tidying, or a neighbour who needs help with the shopping.

Lead by example. Say please and thank you to your kids, as you'd expect them to say this to you. Hold the door open for others; give up your seat for the elderly on the bus and so on. If they get used to all of this, they'll do the same one day.

Keep a strong sense of authority and hierarchy. If children feel they are on the same level as adults, calling them by their first names all the time, having as much power in the family as the adults do and having no sense that sometimes kids just have to put up and shut up because that's LIFE, it makes kids feel they can rule the roost. Well, they can't. **Respecting kids does not mean giving up all your authority.**

—— LIZ'S TIPS ——

Treat your kids as humans, not little robots who do what you tell them to. Give them a voice, and a chance to choose things for themselves, and listen to your kids. Sure, a lot of what they say would make Mr Nonsense look sensible. But an awful lot is beautiful, important and listening – PROPERLY – makes them feel valued, and respected.

Make your children feel valued and part of the family. They will pick up very quickly that you want them out of your hair if you are always desperate to pack them off to bed or say in front of them that you really need some time away from the kids. Make sure they feel that you love having them and let them join in with the grown ups sometimes, even if you'd actually rather they didn't.

Make things clear. Try to keep children within a family environment of stability and predictability – and this includes keeping the discipline up!

Watch what you drink, and how you drink it. If you drink every day, you need to ask yourself if you could do without it for a while and be happy.

I've tried to put some of Granny's tips into practice in the last few months and already I notice a small, positive difference in our house. By making a conscious effort to ensure ALL please and thank yous are said BY ME, not just by them, and also by asking them to help my mum out with something that was very important to her, despite this resulting in my daughter missing a birthday party she wanted to go to, I think the penny has dropped a little about thinking of others and respecting each other. It's a small step, but if it's as easy as that, then it's one I'm going to keep up. It just takes remembering and putting into practice as part of normal *everyday life.*

Chapter Seven

DRESSING UP

You're not going out dressed like *that*!

Once upon a simpler time, children dressed in children's clothes. I mean, they still do, obviously – they'd look pretty stupid wearing scuba diving gear to school. But my point is that many of the clothes children wear don't *look* like children's clothes any more: they look like small versions of adults' clothes. (Some even look like small versions of prostitutes' clothes, but we'll get onto that charming subject in a little while.) With fabulous trench coats here, clingy dresses there, wedges and lacy tights for girls, and polo shirts, waistcoats, jackets and army trousers for little boys, I'm left wondering what 'children's clothing' *is* any more. (The problem is far worse for little girls than for boys, so I will mainly be referring to girls' clothing in this chapter. Although many of us are frustrated by the unwavering dullness of little boys' clothes, and the fact that it's either skater-cool or Little Lord Fauntleroy from the age of about six, there still seems to be a healthy amount of long-sleeved tops, funky T-shirts and simple trousers in the boy department to keep them well-dressed for now.)

What's odd about this Mini Me trend is that it just seems to be growing ever stronger without so much as a 'Darling, do you *have* to wear that sequined crop-top to your violin exam?' Still less are we asking *ourselves*, 'Do I *really* want to buy that for my child??'

I also think it's worth asking the question: who is mimicking whom – are our children dressing more and more like us, or are we dressing more and more like five year olds, in our ballet pumps, smock tops, 'city shorts' and Converse – compare this with how many of our mothers dressed in the 50s and 60s, with ladylike dresses, heels and matching handbags and gloves – in a desperate bid to stop the clock and postpone that inevitable day when the lady gawping back at us in the mirror looks less like a sexy thirty-something and more like our mother. (Sexy sixty-something mothers aside, Mum.)

All will be revealed, so to speak, in due course.

With such questions in mind I follow my whistling brood down the road to Granny's house the following afternoon. They know we're only here for another day and want to make the most of her rope ladder, football collection, cake supply and company. Probably, if we're honest, in that order.

This being Sunday, Extreme Smartness has descended on the whole village: kilts of every colour are out in force, moustaches are waxed, hair is brushed and smart coats blow in the cheeky wind down the main street. Even the yappy Scotty dogs look more elegant as they poo on the kerb.

These days Granny's toe problems have forced her to give up wearing her Sunday best, as her leg would all but freeze off in a tartan skirt, and she now dresses very wisely every day in comfortable, brown cords, a pair of exceptionally warm Ugg boots ingeniously given to her by my very stylish (but now bootless) cousin Joanna in an attempt to keep that leg warm, and a simple, bright shirt or jumper. She is completely happy with this repetitive, unglamorous get-up, because one of the things Granny was not raised to believe in was fashion. For her, fashion comes to rest on life's long list of Important Things to Worry About somewhere between Evil Popular Music and brand new fitted kitchens. In other words, it barely registers at all. I know that she disapproves of dressing kids up in pretty clothes from many comments she has made about such fripperies in the past, and in general I tend to agree with her, though not entirely.

For herself, this is all very well. But I want to know what she thinks about the role of fashion where children are concerned: what *should* we be teaching them about the importance, or lack of it, of clothing, of fashion and of looking a certain way? What does the way we dress them tell children about themselves, about how others think of them; about who they are and about who, or what, we think they should be?

Is there, in short, a place for fashion in our children's lives at all?

Fashionista, baby

Granny has a new top on – a light, violet-coloured fleece, with a zip opening at the neck – and in this she could easily pass for a sprightly seventy. It is also my perfect cue to get straight in there and face the fashion jury.

Surely there was *some* interest in fashion in Granny's day? Some rebelling? Some custom-made hemlines and quick changes in the phone box on the way to school? And what does she think we can do to stop our kids – especially girls – wanting to dress up like a Grade A tart most of the time?

First up, what *does* she think about the whole notion of children wearing pretty, fashionable clothes? I might as well have asked what she thinks of ethnic cleansing . . .

'Well, isn't it just *horrible*?' Granny has the unique ability to say a word with such venom that you hardly dare breathe until she speaks again. In this instance, the word 'horrible' is uttered with a nose-wrinkling revulsion, the like of which I haven't heard since she last said 'ripped jeans' back in 1985. I'm thinking already that she doesn't like it much.

'In . . . erm . . . in what way?' I venture, trying to get a little more flesh on this half naked, though very confident opinion.

'In *every* way. Children don't need fashionable clothes. They need love. And education. Not fashion. What's a six-year-old girl doing thinking about clothing and how she looks? She should have more on her mind, she really should.'

Granny's Pearl of Wisdom

It's taking their childhood away to make them worry about fashion and what people think of them because of how they dress. These concerns creep in all in good time anyway, but being a child means being free to be happy without such silly worries.

I don't dare tell Granny that, sensible though this is, the children's fashion industry is now so huge you can't avoid it unless you opt to live in a yurt in Darkest Peru. If you live in a town or city there is

171

truly no escaping it: every billboard, double decker bus, shop window and advert has pictures of pretty kids in pretty clothes: the kids look happy, the parents look happy, the bloody dog looks chirpier than any retriever has a right to. And it's all – we're encouraged to believe – thanks to the clothes they're in. (Not the retriever. He's naked, but he's so happy because his well-dressed owners give him yummy biscuits that make his coat shine. See?) The fashion invasion has taken over for certain and we cannot pretend it hasn't.

FACT BOX

WHEN FASHION HIT THE SMALL TIME

Early children's clothing labels included such glamorous names as Mothercare, M&S, Clothkits and Ladybird. My, we *were* chic.

* Now our little darlings can swan about the playground in Junior Jigsaw; D&G Junior, Ralph Lauren, Baby Dior, Armani Junior, DKNY, Burberry . . . it goes on and on!

* High Street children's clothing lines have also increased massively in the last fifteen years, with Baby Gap, GapKids, H&M, Primark, Next, Monsoon and Zara tempting us with their beautiful kids' collections. This is almost certainly going to change now that the words Recession and Credit Crunch have hit the headlines, but don't expect to see hordes of kids in home-made pinnies for some time . . .

* A survey from financial services company, Mint, in 2006 found that the average spending on toddlers' outfits was £406 per year, with sixty-eight per cent of mothers spending more on their children's clothes than their own.

Money worries or no, kids' fashion is here to stay – and maybe that's not an entirely bad thing. Experimenting with different styles is one easy way for children to play with their identity, find their own unique style and just to dress up and have fun.

But really, who wants their child to stand in front of the mirror for an hour every morning trying to decide what to wear and then becoming miserable when they feel they don't look right in anything? Teenagers do that, but four and five year olds?

Luckily there are simple (and money-saving!) ways we can reduce the amount that fashion impacts on our children's lives listed at the end of this chapter . . .

Money, money, money

The true cost of having too much

It's fair to say that I was not the most fashionable girl on the block: I wore hand-me-down tracksuits from the Czech Republic (now über-cool retro 70s items; then hopelessly out of fashion . . . how unfair is that?!), smocking dresses painstakingly sewn by my mum from Liberty patterns she chose in the local sewing shop, anything my brother had grown out of and I could fit into, and so on. This woefully unfashionable state came about for two reasons: firstly, I was, just as Granny said, too busy being a child, getting my hands dirty in the local streams and bushes to care about *what* I wore until I was about thirteen; and secondly, money.

We had very little of the shiny stuff and so spending on little fripperies like clothing was never an option. It wasn't until I got a job at sixteen and had my own money that I could start to buy items of clothing I actually liked, though by then it was far too late of course and I had no fashion sense at all – ah well!

It turns out that Granny has something to say on the money subject as well, which could be helpful.

'In the old days we simply didn't have the money to spend on clothing, and it saved a lot of bother. If you have too much – and no sense to go with it – you can spend it on a whole lot of stuff you don't need, like fashionable children's clothing, instead of putting some away for a rainy day. And then where are you when you need some cash for a holiday, a school trip or a new pair of school shoes?'

'Stuck?'

'Yes! Totally stuck, but it's too late by then. The money's gone. We were forced to make do – and you lot could learn a lot from it. During the war, when I was older, my parents had coupons for children to get clothing. My tunic was so worn you could almost see through it at the bottom where I sat down, but we couldn't just get a new one.'

66 *We should concentrate more on adopting the 'elegance of enough' approach. Really stylish women don't have wardrobes overflowing with clothing they'll never wear: they have key pieces which last years and which suit the wearer. That is what kids need to learn as they grow up: that enough really is enough, and we don't need more and more and more and more, because you can never be truly happy that way.* 99

John Naish, the author of *Enough*

174

HONESTY BOX

―――∽∞∽―――

Come on now – hands up: how many of you are as guilty as I am of spending money on clothing your kids don't need? Thought so.

There is just no way on Earth that my children need all of the clothes in their wardrobes: dresses, blouses, T-shirts, long-sleeved tops, shorts, skirts, tights, socks, party frocks, weekend wear, tracksuits, jumpers, cartoon character tops – it really is enough to keep them going for several years, not just a season. I'm not the worst by any means, and I have seen some children's wardrobes that would rival anything Mariah Carey could offer. And that's just the shoes! But I do try, and I am always the mother you hear in Next saying 'No, we don't need that. Put it down and let's go.' (And my kids are the ones wishing they had a different Mummy . . .) But if nine times out of ten I only buy because they NEED something then I feel totally justified in going mad once or twice a year and buying them something they don't need at all but that is totally gorgeous. This way they are always so surprised and grateful and anyway, life is too short not to have some silly fun and the odd splurge can't hurt too much. It's keeping it to the 'odd' splurge, and not a weekly one, that's the important thing.

One argument that many of us make when we spend too much on 'stuff' is 'Yes, but it's my money and I can choose to do what I like with it. What difference does it make if I buy my daughter three Gap T-shirts and another pair of ballet pumps? She'll look so sweet in them, and anyway – who cares? They're cheap as chips so what's the problem?'

Well, quite apart from the whole FairTrade/Sweat Shop issue, which we *must* have cottoned on to by now ('Wow, this pair of jeans costs 1p. How *do* they do it, I wonder . . .?'), according to Granny, all of this spend, spend, spend also has a potentially harmful effect on our children because of the message it gives them:

Granny's Pearl of Wisdom

The only thing children learn from all of this is that material things matter, instead of education. It's indoctrination of materialism at the earliest age, and it will only result in disaster for the poor child concerned, who can never be happy thinking that way.

This is a really important point: there's no denying that if you raise a child to think that buying stuff makes them happy, they're in for a nasty shock one day when they find themselves sitting in a house full of 'stuff', still feeling miserable.

Let's turn back the clock and open Granny's old wardrobe . . .

GRANNY'S 1920S WARDROBE
(YOU COULDN'T MAKE IT UP!)

'Well now, we had one outfit for school, and another for the weekends. That was it. It was carefully looked after, and washed, and mended, and there was never any discussion about *what* to wear. You just wore what you had.'

'First of all we *always* had a vest. It wasn't the comfiest vest, but you made sure it was tucked right in, and that kept out the chill. *Then* we had a liberty bodice. It was a sort of corset, an all-in-one undergarment, made of itchy, scratchy material, with our black, woollen suspenders buttoned on to it at the bottom. It was the most uncomfortable thing you've ever worn, but we all had to wear it.'

'On top of this we had a tunic, and a blouse – square-necked for gym days and round-necked for other days – a school jersey and then a blazer, whatever the weather. And the boys had shorts, right up to the third year. We had three-quarter socks from Easter on, but I don't think we ever had ankle socks. And shoes were regulation, with lace-ups, or little ankle straps when we were older, and we had to change into school shoes when we arrived and put our outdoor shoes in a special box. We then had a trench coat for summer and a mac for the winter. And that was it – every day.'

'I had a kilt for weekends and maybe two dresses. On holiday I'd have a couple of shorts and shirts, and it was a similar story for my own children: we had very little spare cash for their clothing, so they had very few clothes and didn't care. It was very simple, and easy!'

I see, therefore I want

Listening to all this, I have a ridiculous image of the girls in my daughters' classes at school wearing some of this stuff – they wouldn't last to first break without going mad! Didn't Granny ask to wear anything . . . well, anything *else*? I was always wanting to have clothes I'd seen in magazines or in shop windows. Or things the other girls at school were wearing. I still do from time to time, if I'm quite honest.

'No! That's the whole problem – children seeing all this stuff when really they shouldn't at all. It just makes them want it all.'

Granny's Pearl of Wisdom

Clothing shops are no place for a young child. If they don't see it, they don't want it and that's that. Taking them shopping just makes them want more and more.

Now, please don't get your best La Perla knickers in the twist, ladies. I happen to think it's fine to take a child into a clothing shop – how else are they ever going to work out what they like and feel comfortable and individual in? And who wants to traipse all the way back again with something that doesn't fit when you could have tried it on your child while you were there?

But the point about seeing and wanting is so true; you know how it is – you go away on holiday somewhere remote with no shops and no television and you are happy as a bee on pollen. You forget all the material things you stress about and just get on with being YOU. Being HAPPY. And then you get back home and

WHAM! You see all this gorgeous 'must have' stuff in the shops, you see other people wearing all those lovely clothes and you suddenly feel inadequate and miserable, and a quick shopping fix is all that will cheer you up. (Temporarily.)

Kids are no different. If they aren't exposed to all this fashion, then they don't want it.

Shops have always been there, of course, and children have always gone 'Shopping With Mother' (remember that book? Lucky that hasn't dated at all . . .) but there's one thing that really *has* changed immeasurably, not just since Granny was a child – since *I* was a child. She is quick to put her finger on it:

'I almost never went near the shops when I was young – I would rather have been out playing than going shopping – how boring! But when I did go, at least there were none of those nasty magazines aimed at children. Not like the *Beano* and that sort, but *fashion* magazines.'

'Yes!' I exclaim, adding an 'Oh, don't get me started on those . . .' expression that's shared by a hundred parents I know who feel the same, while also catching sight of the poor cat making a bid for freedom from my daughter's rough but well-meant attention and peering disapprovingly at me from between the banisters in the hallway. 'The thing is, there are now magazines for kids of all ages with well-dressed, pretty or "cool" kids in them, and they're all at children's eye level and so cleverly targeted at them. It's almost unavoidable unless you read no newspapers and never take your children into town.'

An old hand slaps against a small, frail leg with enough force to produce an audible 'whack'. The cat scarpers.

'Well don't take them there then! And if you must, don't buy them those things!'

You are probably reading this and thinking, 'Yes, I agree, but *how*?' and it's a valid question. For many kids, peer pressure to 'fit in' starts at nursery, and those with older siblings tend to be, by default, far more advanced in such issues as fashion and general 'coolness' than those without. Short of keeping your child separate from every other child, is it possible not to let them feel under pressure to 'fit in'?

TIPS TO KEEP THE IMAGE CONCERN AT BAY

It is obviously not possible to shield your child from fashion and concerns about 'image' full stop but the point is to *minimise exposure* where possible and to teach children more positive ways of thinking. Children are taught by our society from a very young age that their looks matter. We're all guilty of saying to a three and four year old 'Oh, you're so pretty!' and giving her a big kiss. Reactions like this teach them that looking pretty can make people like them more.

Don't buy fashion magazines for kids, don't leave yours lying around when your kids are little and try not to speak of clothing and the way we look as something that marks us out as 'acceptable' or 'weird'.

Instead, praise good behaviour, or a kind thought or action; point out that the way somebody looks has no bearing on what kind of person they are; reinforce that just because someone has something it doesn't mean we all have to have it too.

Encourage individuality! Things as simple as this can have a huge impact.

Sexy baby. Ummm, isn't that exactly the problem . . .?

I feel we are seconds away from one of the big issues to do with children's clothing and fashion, and, sure enough, Granny gets there before I've had a chance to bring it up.

'And you know,' she scoffs, pointing an old, bent finger at nothing in particular, but successfully strengthening her point, 'I can't believe some of the things I've seen little girls wearing on the television, and now in the streets – tiny wee skirts, with barely enough fabric to cover their legs. And, what do you call them – *crop* tops?'

'Or boob tubes.'

'Well exactly. They're just bras for wee lassies, only they wear them on the outside. And they're all pink, and sparkly, with things written on them they can't even understand. Or they're skin tight. Oh, no, Elizabeth. It's just so sad.'

She is shaking her head now, looking sadly at a photograph on the mantelpiece of all four of her children taken in about 1950, at the seaside. There is a strong presence of vile woolly sweaters, long shorts and headscarves – but not a boob tube in sight or mind.

'And,' she resumes, still going with the finger-pointing, 'what are they teaching them, these parents who dress their children like that? What good is it doing them?'

Granny's Pearl of Wisdom

If you buy sexy clothes for your daughter you deserve what you get. There's no place for something like that in a child's life.

'Fashion magazines and sexy clothes just breed body image problems, and there's no doubt about it as far as I can see. We saw *none* of this fashion, no television adverts, no posters, and we had no "body image" at all – we never thought about it! – and no eating disorders caused by wanting to look skinny; no pressures to be thin and fit. If you're too skinny you can't fight off illnesses when they come. Body image is just another offshoot of all of this fashion business, and it's a terrible shame.'

66 *The merchandisers must aim their clothing at not very imaginative parents, and it is absurd how much Lolita-ish stuff there is for girls: TV advertising for this kind of thing aimed at children should probably be banned.*99

Nick, father of two girls aged thirteen and ten

66*Kids are definitely being sexualised younger now – less so with boys, but definitely girls. I work with kids' TV companies and they know exactly what they are doing with* High School Musical *et al, and it's not what I'd want for my daughters if I had any.*99

George, father of two boys aged eighteen and thirteen

66*I think there is a really pernicious trend towards sexualising young girls' clothes particularly. The thing that astonishes me is that people buy them! Children have always wanted to experiment/play at being older. I thought that's what dressing-up boxes were for *99

Lucy, mother of Hannah, seven and Finn, four

Whether Granny's accusation is justified or not, dressing ten year olds up in clothing more suited to girls of eighteen, or even adults, is indeed a very odd thing for a parent to want to do to his or her child. They are *children*! Why dress them up as sexually active older girls? They have neither the bodies for it, nor the mental age to understand the signals it gives off to people who do.

I remember a news story in 2008 when *Playboy* started to make stationery for little girls. It was pretty, it was pink, it had a cute little bunny on it, which just happened to be a globally recognised symbol of pornography! Now, clearly my daughters wouldn't know anything about the porn reference – to them it's just a cute notepad or folder – but merely the thought of such young girls carrying around the most famous brand associated with sex is abhorrent to me. If you let your kids have products like this, what can you expect (and how can they be expected to understand) when they get suggestive comments and looks from those older than them who *do* know its true meaning? Think before you buy.

f *It's not only girls who are affected by this early sexualisation: it affects boys too because it changes how they feel they should relate to girls. Simply, we've lost the balance that allows kids to stay young, and it really raises body issues for young kids. I didn't get interested in clothes till I was about thirteen. Now you see them being very self-aware, which comes from exposure to sexy, attractive clothes and at a very young age. It's all about glamour, growing up so young. And when I was a kid, TV presenters looked like mums – now they look like porn stars! They're there for the dads, I'm guessing. And TV shows are all about money and looking good now. There is so much emphasis on money, glamour and 'stuff'.*

'And have you seen those Bratz dolls??? It's all 'Oh your hair is so fluffy! Let's go shopping!' They're directed at nine year olds – it's so sad! Dora the Explorer did so well because little girls do have a craving for that kind of thing. She's not a skinny little doll who's into clothes and make-up – she's adventurous and cool. We need more Doras! ™

**Linda Papadopoulos, chartered psychologist
and broadcaster**

f *I am very conscious of trying not to buy my girls magazines aimed at their age group not least because they seem to be full of a lot of 'which boy do you fancy' kind of airhead nonsense. It's easier to buy good books and magazines for my nine-year-old son to read with proper adventure storylines, etc whereas so much of younger girls' literature is still about fairies and princesses and older girls' literature is getting into snogging and chick lit territory.* ™

**Fiona, mother of Chloe, seven, Alex, nine
and Evie, eleven**

THE SEXUALISATION OF LITTLE CHILDREN

In 2006 psychologist Dr Aric Sigman found that girls are reaching puberty eighteen months earlier than their mothers, and almost two years earlier than their grandmothers.

Research in 2008 by the New Girlguiding UK and Mental Health Foundation found that girls of all ages found the pressure to grow up before they felt ready was among the greatest influences on their mental wellbeing. Feeling compelled to wear clothes that make them look older, sexual advances from boys, and magazines and websites directly targeting young girls with messages they should lose weight, wear make-up and even consider plastic surgery, were identified as particularly damaging. Two-fifths admitted to feeling worse about themselves after looking at pictures of models, popstars or actresses.

Interestingly, although boys are also affected by influences that can make them 'grow up' younger, they are more likely to see this speeding up as a positive thing, because puberty for a boy means being stronger, bigger and more sexually developed. But they still need enough time to be children too!

We have to be careful here: there is a big difference between the way children *feel* about themselves as sexual beings thanks to outside influences, and any actual physical changes they may be experiencing. Just because a girl dresses up in sexy clothes doesn't mean she is going to hit puberty earlier. But there is some evidence, such as Dr Sigman's research mentioned above, to suggest that such a change is gradually happening, and, *if* it is, we need to look at how.

continued overleaf . . .

What factors *could* cause early sexual development?

Hormones. There is growing evidence that a broad list of insecticides, herbicides and fungicides, and industrial chemicals, such as dioxin, PCBs, mercury, lead, cadmium, alkyl phenols, phthalates and styrenes could be affecting sexual development, including falling sperm counts and early development in girls.

The media. The number of sexy images thrown at our children is simply eye watering. If it's not Britney oozing sex appeal while dressed as a schoolgirl it's some other child star seductively licking a lollipop or posing in racy underwear. It hasn't been proved that exposure to such things can make kids develop younger, but it's one theory that has been proposed.

Magazines, television, video games and music videos all have a detrimental effect on girls' mental and physical health, a task force from the American Psychological Association reported in 2007. According to the research there is ample evidence to conclude that early sexualisation has negative effects on cognitive functioning, physical and mental health, and healthy sexual development.

As parents, we can help by praising good *behaviour*, or a kind thought or action rather than what someone looks like. We also need to monitor not only what they watch on telly or on the computer but also the kind of reading books our children choose: Jacqueline Wilson, for example, is very popular among little girls, but some stories often tackle issues that are more suited to the minds of fifteen year olds, than nine year olds. Perhaps it's prudent to wait until they have the mature minds to handle the words their young eyes can see.

Clothing. If girls dress in sexually suggestive clothing they *move* and behave differently. They swagger, they stick out their chests (mainly to keep those inappropriate tops from falling off, if we're honest) and they have a look in their eye that is totally incongruous for a child who still likes Charlie and Lola. This is because they see older girls behaving sexily in this kind of clothing, so they copy it. Whether in the media or on the streets, young children see that sexy clothes mean grown-up, sexy behaviour and so when they wear the same stuff they just do what they think is expected. Except it's NOT!

Weight. It's not only what they are exposed to and how they dress and behave that could be making kids grow into adults before they can say 'puberty – no thanks' but also their diet. No, they're not guzzling the breast-enhancers, it's simply that as they are becoming more overweight, their bodies are laying down fat and developing sexually at a younger age. One theory is that puberty is triggered by the hormone leptin, which is produced by fat tissue, so the more fat you have, the more 'puberty hormone' you produce. It's no longer uncommon to see girls as young as eight or nine with sizeable breasts (although we have to be careful not to confuse what is simply increased amount of fat which *looks* like breasts, with what is actually the onset of puberty) or to hear of them starting their periods at that age. I was at *least* fourteen before I started developing at all, and this was by no means unusual my year. I may not have had the most staggering cleavage in my class (and still don't!) but at least it all started when I was ready – in so far as a young girl is *ever* ready to turn into a woman.

continued overleaf . . .

According to Sigman, early puberty is associated with many risks, for example vulnerability to depression, and behavioural problems such as taking up drinking, smoking or drugs. Young girls who suddenly start to mature sexually are also less able to control their impulses than those who hit puberty at a later stage. This might in part explain why rates of teenage pregnancy have risen in recent times. The **number of abortions** among girls under fourteen rose by twenty-one per cent from 2006 to 2007, according to Department of Health figures.

But WAIT! It is very easy to get swept up into a panic when we hear theories about what could cause so-called 'precocious puberty' and the early sexualisation of our children, but we shouldn't. Although there is evidence that children in the developed countries appear to be reaching puberty earlier – some girls at the age of seven – some medical and science professionals dispute the fact that this change is occurring at all.

Dr Rosemary Leonard again

66 *I did a lot of research on this for my book, and though the age of puberty (and for girls, first menstruation) did fall in the first half of the 20th century due to better health and nutrition, for the last 50 years or so it's remained pretty constant. There is a lot of anecdotal evidence that the current obsession with staying thin has meant that in some girls the age of puberty has actually risen. There increasingly seems to be polarization of young people's sizes into either too fat or too thin, with sadly a diminishing number who are a normal size for their age.* 99

Whether or not future research will show that our children really *are* developing sexually at an earlier age, what remains pretty certain for now – and most of us as parents have noticed this already, whether in our own kids or in other people's – is that the way they *think* of themselves and feel they should look and behave has changed, with many very young children behaving 'all grown up' far younger than seems appropriate. This is a *tragedy* because kids barely have a chance to enjoy their childhood before it is snatched away from them.

Also, a child of such a young age cannot understand *why* she has breasts, far less understand or be able to cope with the signals this sends out to the opposite sex. We have an inexcusably high level of teenage pregnancies and abortions in this country, and, while much of it is because girls are not taught about sex *properly* until they're well into their teens (*why* is it still considered more difficult to talk about penises and vaginas than how awful it is to be pregnant at thirteen??), another major factor is the images of supposedly sexy women our young girls see, and who become their role models.

Role models

66 *Despite everything that's so obviously wrong and unrealistic about Enid Blyton's work, I'd still rather my daughters had a feisty girl like George of the Famous Five as a role model than Tracey Beaker and her mates.* 99

Claire, mother of three daughters

When I was about fourteen, the people I admired the most and held up as my role models were – and this is embarrassing, OK, but here goes – Emma Thompson (whose performance in *Look Back in Anger* blew me away so much it was the only time I ever volunteered to tell my parents what I'd done at school), Helena Bonham Carter (remember how beautiful she was in *A Room with a View*?) and Woody Allen, whose films I watched until tears ran down my cheeks and the VHS tapes snapped. Yikes. Not exactly Guns'n'Roses or Emilio Estevez. But these people were intelligent, talented, independent and passionate about what they did – and, to me, cool for all of those reasons.

When asked, a great number of young girls today see the female characters in films like *High School Musical*, and 'stars' like Hannah Montana and Britney as powerful role models. As women they would like to emulate. God help us all. They think sex is about using their bodies to give pleasure to others, and that pouting and wiggling is what women are *supposed* to do. I mean is this how far we've come (no pun intended), that our daughters think sex is their only tool, that their bodies are the only currency they have to keep a man? Whatever happened to independent thought, to intelligence and to kindness? And where did the responsibility, the preciousness and the pleasure (for us as well, not just the men!) of sex go?

Of course there are other role models for our girls and boys to look up to. My daughters worship Emma Watson, Georgie Henley and Anne Hathaway, and I am pretty relieved about this. For a start they all look like *women*, not stick insects (for now, anyway . . .) and secondly they seem to be reasonably in control of their lives so far, not controlled by others and using their bodies to steer their course. Harry Potter has been brilliant for little boys too, breaking up the non-stop onslaught of the likes of the Incredible Hulk, Spiderman and Darth Vader for them to idolise. Harry Potter has brains, and integrity – and groovy glasses.

We need to educate our children much better about sex, to stop shoving pictures of scantily dressed women and stick-thin models in front of them, and to stop dressing them the same way. The longer girls can stay as little girls the better – you only have one shot at childhood, so you might as well enjoy it as long as you can.

YOU ARE THEIR MOST IMPORTANT ROLE MODEL!

It's easy to blame our culture, the magazines in shops and the programmes on television, and these almost certainly all influence our children hugely. But the first place we need to start giving our children positive role models is *at home*.

Never forget that the way *you* dress, how *you* speak about your body, the way *you* feel about yourself and the importance you place on your looks and the looks of others will have the most dramatic impact on your children. If you leave fashion magazines lying around, and your kids observe that you try to copy the images they portray, that will send them a message that we should look a certain way. If they see you looking at your body in a dissatisfied way, they'll pick up on that very quickly.

Be happy with yourself in front of your kids – and also when they're not there! – and, by your words and actions, teach them that kindness, generosity, respect and thoughtfulness are more important than how we look.

66 There seems to be a general feminist backlash in girls' culture with more obsession than ever with looks and boys. Depressingly my sister and I asked our seven-year-old girls whether they'd rather be Sharpay, the spoiled little rich girl from High School Musical *or a nurse who saves hundreds of lives – no prizes for guessing that they opted for the teen princess with her endless wardrobe of outfits. Aargh! 99*

Lucy, mother of two girls aged seven and ten

Mummy, I want to look just like everyone else

Granny suddenly looks exhausted. Old people are just like the very young in that way: they charge ahead at full speed for a while before turning pale and needing a power-nap. All this talk of clothing and the evils of the modern world seem to have knocked it out of her. But before she has a snooze she has one more point to make:

'The other thing with fashion, Elizabeth, is that there's no room for *individuality*. They all just want to look the same. Where are the individuals, who have their own way of thinking and their own opinions? They're like sheep! We had a school uniform out of necessity – there was no choice. But out of school you could adjust clothing that no longer fitted – trousers became shorts, dresses were made into skirts or shirts. We used our imagination, and our sewing kits, and gave garments new life.'

This point is, I think, one of the most depressing things about the fashion industry: by its very nature, it deals with things that are IN fashion. Now. Not tomorrow, not next year, but *now*. And so, if you are to remain 'fashionable' you have to all look practically the same. Hands up who bought a smock top in 2007? A batwing jumper in 1985? A gypsy skirt in 2006? Skinny jeans in 2005? High-waisted ones in 2008?

Granny's Pearl of Wisdom

Encouraging kids to think for themselves, not to just follow the crowd but to have their own ideas, is very important and one of the ways they can do this is by letting them wear clothes that are different to everyone else, and which suit them. Not what's fashionable.

Ah – individuality! I think we all struggle with this one from time to time: we know we ought to be creating a unique image, and be 'ourselves', but when push comes to shove – when the shops and magazines are bursting with one style – the majority of us tends to knuckle down and buy what's 'in' this month. Yes, even if we do look shit in it (leggings, anyone?).

During childhood this need to follow the crowd is stronger than ever, and 'fitting in' is what really matters. Yes, there are the odd few who really strike out in the style stakes, but I think playing it safe and following the crowd is a fairly natural thing for a child to want to do, and it's no big problem to let them do this. Encouraging *some* individuality, however, is really worth attempting, even if it's having different shoes or a new hairstyle or sewing some buttons onto their hat. Just something to show they can be themselves – they might even become the new trend-setter in Year One. Kate Moss, watch out . . .

CONVERSATION WITH MY DAUGHTER

I had a long chat with my ten year old recently, who I felt had become overly concerned about what she wore to school (they have no uniform, so there is a daily struggle with what to wear – this is *sooooo* annoying!) and what other kids would think about it. It reached the point of weekly tears and real anguish about her perfectly lovely clothing, and I decided to tell her something I wish I had been told when I was her age, and that has made my life so much better since I really accepted it and lived by it.

'Listen, my love,' I said. 'What you have to try and under-stand – and really believe, because it's true – is that nobody actually cares what you wear at all. It's all *here*' – I put my hands on her head – 'that matters. What you say, how you behave, how you look at people and how you treat others. I bet you can't tell me what any of your friends at school were wearing today, can you? Exactly. And they can't remember what you were wearing either. But they *did* notice if you played with

There are screams from the garden followed soon after by the sniffy, bloody entrance of my eight-year-old daughter, complete with twigs in her blonde mane and a gash on her knobbly knee. She seems to have had a fight with a sharp object – and lost. Her T-shirt has been custom-made into a bikini by tucking the bottom over the neckline a few times, and her once-clean trousers have been rolled up to make pirate shorts. Hence the gashed knee, presumably.

194

them, and if you were fun to be with. *That's* what matters. So you wear whatever you like, and the secret is, if you wear it with complete confidence, and *feel* good in it, not only will you look incredible and be very happy but people will follow your lead, not the other way around. Just say to yourself every morning: 'I look good and I feel good just the way I am now – I don't care what anyone else thinks!' and then step out feeling good in yourself.'

Then a harp started strumming sweet harp-ish music and a flock of sparrows flew overhead sprinkling rose petals on our heads in a bright ray of golden sunshine . . .

OK, it was all a little vomit-making. But I could honestly see that she got relief and strength from what I told her, and she has been happier to wear whatever she likes from that day on. Of course there are times when a little parental input is necessary (my son would go to bed wearing nothing but pants if he had the chance and my youngest daughter would never wear anything even remotely appropriate for the weather). But for the rest of the time a little individuality is to be encouraged.

A final thought from Granny, then, while I comfort the injured swashbuckler.

'The truth is, whatever we might have thought of clothing and fashion, all of the money we had went on the most important thing.'

OK, and that would b . . . the handbags? The expensive but oh-so-worth-it hair products? Friday night curries? Somehow methinks not.

I am locked in by the killer stare yet again. Here it comes . . .

'*E-du-cation*. All the money went on education: from the schooling, to the museum trips at the weekend, to the music lessons and instruments to the school books. Education was everything, and I still believe that's the key. That's what we need to focus on again. That will make children happier and healthier, and have more chances, and better lives. Not having pretty clothes!'

I try to find a way of saying 'Yes, but pretty clothes are so happy-making and I'm not going to make my children forgo the pleasures of a fabulous dress forever just so they can learn their Latin verbs!' without sounding hopelessly inane, and decide instead that this is the perfect moment to go away and think about what she has said, find a plaster, administer some TLC, have a final check to see if I've left anything – suitable or not – in any of my children's wardrobes and come back that evening for our last chat of the week, which will tackle that Most Important Thing. Education.

Looks like it's going to be another big one.

∾ *GRANNY'S TIPS* ∾

Don't buy your kids fashion magazines or let them watch pop videos. There is an OFF button on the telly. Use it! Or make sure you don't get unsuitable channels in your television package.

Don't buy them clothes that they don't need.

Don't take them shopping if you can help it. Sometimes there's no alternative, but try to keep it to a minimum.

Sexy clothes have no place in a child's wardrobe.

Encourage individuality, not fashion slavery.

— LIZ'S TIPS —

Less is more when it comes to fashion. Really stylish women don't have wardrobes overflowing with clothing they never wear: they have key pieces that last years and that *suit* the wearer. Get this message across early by buying your children fewer clothes, and you're laughing.

Banning all magazines and television watching is not very realistic, or helpful: they know they're there and sometimes you have to go with the modern flow, like it or not. But try, *try* to keep them to an absolute minimum and avoid buying any magazines you really feel are inappropriate. Once your kids have seen it, they can't *un*-see it. Try something new and NOT pink, like National Geographic Kids. It's full of cool facts and info, and despite being determined to hate it, my children all think it's great. If all else fails, there's always the *Beano* . . .

Practice what you preach: if your children see you fussing over your clothes, getting in a grump when nothing goes with anything and buying more clothing than you could ever wear, your kids are going to grow up thinking that's the way to live. Cut down, be happy and show them how it's done.

Think of the environment. Buying clothes we don't need and throwing them away is not at all PC any more. If it ever was . . . Recycle old clothes, buy second hand, swap with friends and, above all, keep things to a minimum.

Don't feel guilty for the odd time-saving cop-out. Yes, we should probably all be darning our kids' socks and knitting them jumpers, but we're not saints and the occasional trip to Primark for some new underwear and cheap pyjamas isn't the worst thing anyone has ever done. Keep these trips infrequent and you're helping already.

Chapter Eight

SCHOOL TIME

Education: n. the act or process of imparting or acquiring general knowledge, developing the powers of reasoning and judgment, and generally of preparing oneself or others intellectually for mature life.

It's my last visit to see Granny on this trip. Our bags are packed, the car looks like a strong contender in the 'can you fit the entire belongings of a medium-sized tribal village into a Volkswagen?' competition, my kids are already so excited at the prospect of watching a DVD on the motorway that they're in danger of spontaneously combusting and *I'm* already feeling slightly sick at the thought of all those bumps and bends to come. Another pleasant trip ahead, then.

But before we leave I want to broach that big subject Granny mentioned at the end of our last conversation. No, not whether it was due to turn cold again before midweek, although that had also been a subject of considerable and riveting debate. The *other* big subject: education.

Whatever her circulatory system might be playing at, Granny's mind is still unquestionably functioning at full tilt. Her Sudoku powers put me to shame, she has a thirst for knowledge and mental challenge to make most of us blush, and woe betide anyone who drops a foolish clanger into a conversation. She'll scoop it up and throw it right back at you before you've had a chance to wish you could just turn back time about thirty seconds.

And there's a very good reason for this: she believes that education is the key to getting on in life, and there's no reason why she should, or even could, start to wind down now. It's in her blood, from the way she was raised, to the path she chose in becoming a teacher, to the emphasis she put on education with her children. In her words:

Granny's Pearl of Wisdom

With a good education anyone, no matter what
their background or financial situation or parenting,
can make a good life for themselves. And that's the
core of everything.

Somewhat appropriately, I enter Granny's living room to find her full attention being given to a natural history documentary about baboons. David Attenborough is crouching in leafy undergrowth, sweat pouring down his weathered brow and looking rather as though he is either about to have a heart attack or a major scientific breakthrough. Before him, a male baboon is trying to get it on with his lady friend, and, despite not knowing much about non-human primate shagging, I can guess that it's going pretty well. Granny is hooked, and doesn't take her eyes off the screen as I make my way into the room.

'Shhhhh! Listen.' She beckons with her arm, her wide, bright eyes still glued to the screen. She is enraptured, and concentrating hard on today's zoology lesson. So is the baboon.

I now have the dubious pleasure of sitting through several minutes of baboon luurve, in the presence of my grandmother, narrated in intricate, move by move detail by our distinguished host. And I can assure you that there's very little this man doesn't seem to know about baboon sex. Very little indeed.

When it's all over and Mr Baboon has rolled over, farted and gone to sleep, the telly is turned off and we have peace at last.

'Well, isn't he just *fantastic*?!'

'Who's that – David Attenborough, or our furry friend there?'

'Oh, Elizabeth! Yesterday I learned all about hippos in the Serengeti, and I think tomorrow he'll be looking at the effect of global warming on the Polar ice caps. Mind you, he's only eighty-three. We eighty-four year olds are *much* too old to be carrying on like that . . .'

With today's wildlife class as our cue, we begin our chat about education. The relentless and often savage criticism of our education system comes from almost every level, from politicians to head teachers and from parents to the poor little buggers who are supposedly taught through it themselves. If it's not out dated and run-down classrooms and equipment it's the supposed falling standard of teaching, the poor quality of school meals, the bad manners of the pupils and the woeful size of the gym mistress's tits. No, not that one. Just checking you're paying attention.

And – shock horror – none of these is likely to get any better if less money than most of us spend on shoes every year is pumped into the schooling and university system. Politics aside, there is something else that has changed where education is concerned, according to Granny, and this is one we can influence – a lot.

She picks up a log and throws in on the fire, which spits, just as she has been known to do about irritating issues. Like this one . . .

'Nobody *values* an education any more. That's the problem. Education, Elizabeth, is the all important thing, and people used to value it above all else. When our children were growing up we were prepared to have absolutely nothing – nothing! – in order to school our kids.'

Granny's Pearl of Wisdom

Education is the one way you can rise through life. To take yourself to the next rung of the ladder, the next level, and to better yourself.

What, not by winning *Pop Idol*? Or marrying a Russian billionaire? Or sitting back and waiting for it all to happen . . . somehow?

No. Sadly not. It means putting in some effort both in the classroom *and* outside it. 'Bettering yourself', I think, does *not* mean having the best job or the biggest house or the most power or money. It means being able to have the life *you* want, and putting something back for others. And whatever it is your children choose to do, having a solid education can allow this to happen, because **education teaches children how to make good choices** – the right choices for them, to make their lives better.

EDUCATION – WHAT'S THE POINT?

Unleashing the potential within. The word Education comes from the Latin (as of course you know . . .) *E ducere* meaning to 'lead out'. It's not about cramming as much information *into* their brains as possible, but about cramming a little in and then nurturing, or leading *out*, the potential that lies within each child.

Learning from others. If you sat in a room all your life in complete isolation, learning everything there is to learn about everything, you would have a pretty poor education in my opinion. Because it's by interacting with others, learning how we all behave and live together that you can be truly educated.

Struggling to succeed. As most teachers will tell you, there is little more rewarding than watching a child who has struggled with a problem suddenly crack it and succeed. This sense of achievement, of making progress through hard work and sheer effort, is an invaluable part of a child's education, which will help them throughout their life: when the remote control breaks, the kitchen units they're installing don't quite fit, or the car won't start. As Robert the Bruce once allegedly said and I try (with limited success) to remember every day when I fail, yet again, at something: if at first you don't succeed, try, try, try again.

Thinking. This may seem very obvious, but part of what children have to learn is *how* to think. They need to learn how to order their thoughts, reason, make sense of otherwise meaningless information and apply it in the context of their world. Otherwise how will they ever solve a problem like: I have £10 in my wallet, the shoes I want to buy cost £50 and I already have a £400 overdraft – whatever should I do?? (Answer: walk away, crazy lady! Walk away!)

Getting the Master Key. My dad used to say to me that it doesn't matter which doors you walk through in life, but the more you are able to open, the better your chances of finding the ones that lead to success and happiness. Having a good education is like being given a master key to a vast number of doors. The only trouble then, is which one to open. I goofed the first twenty times or so and still do occasionally. But I plough on . . .

First time lucky. If you still need convincing of the astonishing importance of encouraging your kids to get a good education, just look at the number of adults returning to education in their spare time in order to progress in their chosen careers – often at huge expense. And what do they all say? 'I wish I'd tried harder at school.'

Look at the stats. On average, graduates tend to earn substantially more than people with A levels who did not go to university. Projected over a working lifetime, the difference is something like £100,000 before tax at today's valuation.

A study from London University's Institute of Education showed that people with more education have better physical and mental health. Those with low levels of literacy and numeracy suffer more from depression, and are more likely to commit suicide than those with more education, while older people with more years of formal education experience lower rates of cognitive decline.

A is for Attitude

OK, so how do we come into this?

It's simple: it's all in our attitude towards education. Despite all that we've just said about the importance of getting a good education (but we can't really be bothered to think about too much because *QI* is on, which is more fun), there does seem to be an attitude problem as regards schooling and education in general these days. It's all: teachers are useless, schools are crap, and increasingly I've noticed a really irritating habit people have – especially women, and in particular mothers – of pretending they were never any good at school, as though it's a badge of honour or something. 'Oh, I was never very good at maths. Silly billy me. More cake anyone?' A mum at school once said to me, 'Oh, I'm far too stupid to write a *book*' right in front of her kids, and I just thought, 'Well, to say a thing like that I guess you must be.'

I mean, why not say something ever so slightly more inspiring like 'I loved maths at school,' or 'Oooh, chemistry was fun!', or even 'I might not be able to, but I'd like to have a go at writing a book'?

We can try to ignore the problem all we like, praying instead for the day that our kids win the lottery, get 'discovered' by a modelling scout at Oxford Circus or land the multi-million-pound-earning lead role in the next Hollywood Blockbuster at an open audition on a wet afternoon in Falmouth. But the fact is that if we were to value their school and home education more, *encourage* them to learn and make sure they actually *get* an education they'd have a much higher chance of succeeding in life – however you measure that success.

Unsurprisingly, Granny has a simple solution we can all try at home, starting right *now*:

Granny's Pearl of Wisdom

Show your kids the importance of an education by
the way you speak of it and further it at home.

The knobbly finger comes out again, to accentuate her point.

'Speak of school as important, of lessons as important, of *homework* and practice as important – and fun! I got it from my parents: Dad wanted us to get the best education we could, because he knew it was our ticket to a better life, and he made this clear to us from the start, by putting our schooling above all else and encouraging us every day at home.'

HONESTY BOX

I've caught myself on a number of occasions having an out-loud moan about a teacher or a school policy in front of my kids. It's usually when I feel my child has been prevented from doing something perfectly safe because of some moronic new Health and Safety school rule. It's at times like these that a 'Yes, well Miss So-and-so is an idiot' can creep out before I've had a chance to bite my tongue. Again. If you find yourself doing the same then try and follow this with something suitably arse-licky to mend any damage to the school's cred like, 'Well, I'm sure she was just doing what she thought was best. I think you'll have to just do as she says – she is a teacher after all.' Then you can retire to the bathroom, scream into a towel and call her a fussy cow.

A photograph of one of my daughters, then aged about four, pops up on Granny's funky electronic photograph album – her hair is wild, she has chocolate on her face and yet more down her front. She looks a complete mess, but very happy! This image triggers another thought for Granny.

'And you know, we say a lot just by the way we make out children dress for school – whether they have a uniform or not. Just brushing their hair, making sure their clothes are clean – this is the starting point for a good day at school and the rest can follow on much more easily from here with such a strong message from home.'

It's a small point, but a good one, I think: I'm always banging on at my girls to *please* sort their haystacks out before school, and to tie it back! Ooh, I hate when girls have their hair dangling all over the place, especially as half of them have nits, which spread like mad – is that *too* old-fashioned of me? Sending them to school without ketchup on their jumper, tattoos on their cheeks and mud on their shoes are all simple ways you can help to give children the message that their school education is important and they should learn, enjoy and behave well while they're there. Also, the way we react to school news ('Not *another* bloody parents' evening. You go this time.)' to teachers' comments ('Maybe he should try wearing deodorant once in a while. That'd make you sit still and listen to what he's saying more') and by the way we talk about schooling in general, we give off very clear vibes about the importance of school.

Even if you don't believe all of it, it's the *attitude* you display that counts!

B is for Brains

My kids have recently got wise to the tools on offer out there to 'do the math' for them, like calculators, spell checkers, Google and the like. If they can just whack some numbers into a calculator then why bother to learn anything any more? If you don't know about something, look it up on the web. Google, cut, paste . . . school project done. Like, duh, Mum.

Granny is slightly appalled at this suggestion, and not just because of any concerns about plagiarism.

'But if you don't learn the basics for yourself, where are you when your calculator breaks, or your Gaggle – '

'*Google.*'

'Well whatever it is – when it crashes, or if your spell-checking program is written by *Americans*? You can't rely on these things to get the right answer for you, or you'll be spelling "colour" without a 'u' before you know it.'

That bad?! Cripes. Call the spelling cops! Sorry, spelling *police* . . .

Granny's Pearl of Wisdom

And what about the most important thing, and that's using the brain? If children don't exercise their grey matter they just slowly fall mentally asleep.

Without warning she starts rummaging around under her chair for a while, before presenting me with the old box of Quality Streets, shoving it under my nose and continuing her attack on our children's education – while I try to find the big, round toffee one.

'They need to keep their brains ticking over with basic maths like adding up the shopping and working out the change, and writing letters *by hand*' (I get a stony stare at this point, and guiltily recall sending my last two letters to Granny as printed word documents . . . tut tut.), 'not watching telly and action-packed computer games with no imagination. If your brain isn't kept on its toes at all, you just shut down.'

So our kids are effectively shutting down and going into 'hibernation mode' because they're not using their brains enough. Is there any way we can we re-boot them, or is a complete hard-drive failure imminent?

Granny takes a strawberry sweet and chucks the box back onto the floor. Jaffa, the bigger of her two ginger moggies, now hiding under her chair as well, eyes it suspiciously.

'What you have to do is keep stimulating their brains – not with aggressive, fast-paced games, but with knowledge, imagination and memory games. Our teachers were very keen on using the memory, and making us learn and recite poetry. It wasn't so much for the poetry itself, but for using our brains to memorise things, every day, and working the mind. We learned our Chanelle Spelling every week by re-writing the words over and over, [remember that?!], and we did a lot of mental arithmetic, which was also fantastically useful. Every day we'd have to look at the clock face and teacher would call out "six and seven!", "Two and nine!", "twelve and eleven!" and so on – quick, quick, quick! That got your brain going, I can tell you.'

The buzz you get from brain stimulation is the same for adults as it is for kids, and it's part of the reason why Sudoku and other brain-tickling games have become so popular: it *feels* good to use your brain, and for children it's absolutely vital. Assuming they get enough of this at school is a bad plan – my kids seem to spend a large proportion of their time at school waiting for unruly classmates to shut up, eating their lunch and getting changed – and then changed again – for PE. So keeping their brains working at home, in however off-hand a manner, can only be good for them and they'll learn everything so much more easily as they're not half asleep all the time.

The key is to do all of this brain stimulating without turning into a total geek parent. Nobody said you have to train them for *Mastermin*d – little and often is the key, and try to keep it real!

C is for Computers and stuff . . .

Contrary to what many of us might think, there are plenty of people in the blue-rinse generation who don't regard all modern technology as the Devil's work. Even Granny, who doesn't have a computer despite repeated efforts on our part to get her onto email, can see that the potential for learning through the internet, educational CD ROMs, interactive games and computer games is just staggering.

I am interested in the educational value of new toys, new gadgets and new technologies. Granny, it seems, has always been on the ball here.

'When a new invention comes along, you have to take the good and leave the bad it brings with it. Television isn't evil. Radio doesn't rot the brain.'

'Except for that nasty *popular* music of course, Granny,' I tease, gently.

Rumour has it that she banned all pop music from the house when her kids were teenagers, a decision, if true, that I can only see as fairly unkind and unhelpful. But there it is – damage all done now.

'Oh, I have no time at all for pop music. What a noise.'

Told you.

'But there's plenty of good radio for children to listen to. And computer games can be stimulating and interesting – and educational too. Even I know that! So use them. Use what's out there, but don't get swamped by it, and don't forget more traditional methods of learning.'

So modern technology is good – hurrah! Off we go for a three-hour surf on YouTube. Er, no. Turns out there are some very nasty side effects from sitting in front of a screen for too long, whether you're on a jolly intellectual and educational mission or not.

When children see computers as their *only* educational tool, and forget what books, microscopes, test tubes, tennis rackets and maps look like, when they can only play tennis on a flat screen and cannot use a paperback thesaurus, you know something very strange has happened.

VENI, VIDI, WII

Where technology can help their education – and hinder it.

———— ⊗∞⊗ ————

Stimulation not hibernation. Much as we may hate to see kids getting all hyper on a computer game, there's no doubt that it does at least get *some* part of their brains going. Remember the buzz from PacMan? Watch out – ghost ahead!! Go left, go left!! No wait, here comes another one – go right!! *RIGHT!* It was like taking Junior Speed. Well, so it is with whatever games they have these days. It's not great in huge doses, but a *bit* of adrenaline never hurt anyone.

Coordination. Learning how to use a mouse, type and other basic computer skills are not just useful but absolutely essential for kids these days. So letting them have a go at writing something on the computer, drawing a picture on it, printing something out or making a PowerPoint presentation is helpful, not sloppy parenting. Computer games can also be very effective at honing their eye - finger coordination and getting that reaction time up to speed.

Learning. A good CD ROM can teach and engage a child as much as anything they could get at school. If we'd had them when I was a child I'd have liked Economics a whole lot more, I'm sure. Talk to other parents about ones they recommend, and have a shop around yourself. Everything from foreign

continued overleaf . . .

languages to science to art is there for the taking – just so long as they don't spend more than half an hour or so on it per day, or an hour for older children, they're getting the benefits without the negatives outlined below . . .

Death of the individual. The trouble with computer games and many television programmes is that they don't require you to think as an individual at all. This is great if, like me, you just want to veg out of an evening and not think very much. But if a child spends a lot of his free time just watching a screen passively or doing whatever it is he has to do to get the treasure at the end of level 5, he's not thinking for himself. There is some research to suggest that this is quite damaging for child development and that such activities should be kept to a minimum as a result.

Life in 2-D. Similarly, if a child spends hours every day experiencing life in the flat, flickering world, she might find life in 3-D just a little complicated, or scary, or troubling. A child needs to connect with *real* people who don't do what they want, who have other ideas, who smell, who laugh and who cannot be got rid of by pressing the OFF button. If you think your child has more online friends than real ones, it's time to switch off the computer and do something about it.

Violent games. There is, in my opinion, only one place for games where you are a soldier trying to blast the shit out of everyone in your path: in the bin. They are aggressive, nasty and damaging and arguably cause a lot of harm in our society as a result. Who wouldn't have a peculiarly relaxed attitude towards violence if they spent four hours a day shooting very life-like people on a screen? If your kids must play games then please, please choose ones that you think won't turn them into psychopaths. Thank you.

ZIP, ZIP, ZIP. If children are raised on a diet of Google searches, blogs, websites and instant links, they risk losing a very useful – and a very *human* – way of thinking. A slow, measured, considered and thoughtful way of thinking, and of information gathering, that can free their minds, let ideas develop and lead to deeper thoughts and learning. Click, click, click is all very well, and the benefits of the internet cannot be overstated, but if this is ALL they get, to the point that they can no longer concentrate on one thing long enough to read a page of a book – let alone the entire thing . . . what a chore! – without getting restless for the next link, the next quick-fix opinion or fact, then they have lost something very valuable indeed, and will be the poorer for it.

66 *Beyond our reasoning ability . . . is our ability to appreciate, 'understand', what is happening around us. The computer, even more so than the TV, may be initiating a fundamental change in the development of a robust conceptual framework based on a wealth of different narratives...*

'*. . . If you are always working with directory-trees – where menus are offered with fixed numbers of options where . . . you have to plod up and down through various branch lines of thinking – might that pattern not impose itself on the way you think in general? Surely it would be highly restrictive.* 99

Baroness Susan Greenfield, neuroscientist and author of
iD: The Quest for Identity in the 21st Century **(Sceptre, 2008)**

continued overleaf . . .

In other words, too much computer time could have a real and detrimental effect on how kids understand and therefore, I assume, interact with and respond to the world around them. If the main way kids learn and work doesn't require or even allow them to think laterally, to move away from the limited options placed before them and to use their *own* imagination, to think of their *own* ideas and to jump from one thought to another freely, and to use their memory and powers of deduction, this could restrict the wonderful freedom to think and create that is so innate, and vital, to being a child.

Writer Andrew Sullivan described the effect that large amounts of time spent on the computer researching his blogs and articles has had on the way he thinks, in the *Sunday Times* recently: '*[before the internet] I needed a good memory . . . I needed time. I needed to think a little before I began my research. Now all I do is right-click and type a few words . . . When it comes to sitting down and actually reading a multiple-page print out or even, God help us, a book . . . , my mind seizes for a moment. After a paragraph I'm ready for a new link.*'

Just think what it's like being the brain of a child who's on the computer for hours a day . . . !

I've experienced this "pond-skater" mind syndrome too, and when you also think about the speed at which most television programmes change camera angle, you can well imagine the problem for children is much worse!

D is for Do It Yourself

Granny's Pearl of Wisdom

Education starts at home. That's the most important place you learn things – from your parents. People rely on schools to teach their kids everything, but home is where it starts.

As these words are coming out of Granny's mouth, I try hopelessly to remember the last time I checked my child's homework or made sure they had written in their school reading diaries using capital letters, full stops and all that jazz . . . and find I can't. Searching for a lame excuse for my lame parenting, I put it to Granny that we don't all have much *time* to educate our kids at home, and anyway, who wouldn't rather be relaxing in front of a good film than preparing tomorrow's 6 a.m. science lesson? Apparently this isn't quite what she meant.

'You don't have to have *lessons* at home to educate your kids! A parent should simply correct a child who uses bad grammar or who spells incorrectly – just in your everyday conversations and by correcting little notes they write with magnetic letters on the fridge or on scraps of paper. That way they just pick it up as they go along. Things like "I could have", instead of "I could OF". Or "If I were", not "If I WAS." Oh, and my pet hate "Between you and I." It's "between you and ME"!! Just basic, basic English like that. You can't expect teachers to do it all. That's what happens today: parents don't teach their kids the basics at home, and they arrive at school unable to hold a book the right way up.'

This is a bugbear of mine too. *Fewer* people, not less people, the Government *is*, not the Government are, apostrophe's where they should be (yes, I did notice that one . . .) and so on. I don't run some kind of Baby Brain Academy in my house, with algebra before baby rice, and literacy after a nappy change, and neither did I pack them all off to some pre-pre-pre school A-level cramming classes before they could hold a pencil, but somehow all three of my kids could recognise all of their letters and were writing basic words before they started Reception class, and they speak pretty damned good English now, not because their teachers do but because *we* do at home, and they've picked it up from us.

AND FOR TODAY'S LESSON . . .

Teaching kids at home does not have to be formal, or planned or agonising, but it is absolutely essential. It can happen by default, if you try a few basic things:

Literacy. Read to your kids almost from the day they are born, and continue this as long as you can – or until they don't want you in their room any more! We did and just through listening and looking at the books they got a sense of the letters on the page, and of the words these spelled, and they eventually started to ask questions themselves: Where does it say 'house'? What letter is that? How do you write 'fart'? And so on. They *wanted* to know, so we showed them and they just soaked up the information and learned stuff bit by bit, more through play with scraps of paper and picture books than anything else. All it takes from you, is time.

Numeracy. As for the third 'R', arithmetic, children can learn all their numbers just by having them pointed out in the supermarket, at bus stops, in the kitchen, on food packets and so on. You can practise this all the time around the house as they get older too; if you each have fifteen minutes on the computer, how long will it be on for in total? (The answer is 'too long', by the way.)

General Knowledge. *You* are their first port of call for this. Not their teachers. If they want to know about volcanoes, pirates, space travel or how plants grow then get out of the house, go to the local library and let them choose some of the fantastic factual books available. The internet is also an invaluable tool for this kind of home learning (because, let's face it, most of us don't know the answer to ninety per cent of the questions our kids ask us) so what's stopping you? Learn something together!

Catching them young. You know how hard it is to try and learn a foreign language when you're thirty-five, and yet kids pick them up like tummy bugs? Well, that's because their brains are making new neural (brain) connections far, far faster than our old fuzzy, alcohol-ruined brains are, so this is the point where we need to invest some time and energy into making those connections, and getting them in the right places. If you leave it until they're eighteen it's a little late. Teach them young, and they'll learn at breakneck speed, and enjoy it too.

And repeat after me . . . One of the best ways of strengthening these neural connections is by repetition, so the more times you can say 'Mummy doesn't like it when you put the cheese in the dishwasher' the faster they'll learn it and the longer it'll stick. The same goes for 'two times two is four' and all the rest.

They will, of course, learn most of what they need to know to get through the final exams at school at some point anyway – assuming they pay attention even half of the time. But passing exams is not what education is all about by any means! It's kinda handy and everything as a means of showing you know *something*, and can sit still for three hours, but there's so much more to know than what's required on a test paper, and there's just no reason why we shouldn't pass on lots of what we know to our kids while they're hanging around the house, looking bored and flicking bogeys onto the window ledge, is there?

Apart from anything else, the earlier a child can read and write the less likely they are to *be* that bored, because they can always go and pick up a book and escape into the imaginative world its words describe or write their own story about how crap it is to be the only kid in class who doesn't stay up until after 10 p.m. It's just a no-brainer to teach kids stuff at home, throughout their childhood, and yet less and less of this seems to be happening, as more and more of us work, and are busy, and tired, and stressed and just gagging to sit down after the kids are in bed.

But it's not *all* down to us – phew! Between sucks on her sweet, Granny has a word or two to say about teachers too . . .

'Of course, none of this is to say teachers don't also have a vital role in a child's education. They absolutely do! A *good* teacher can spot a bright child and help him along tremendously. She can spot talent, and nurture it – and transform a child's life forever – inspire him and set him on a path to achieving something he never thought he could. But . . .

Granny's Pearl of Wisdom

. . . if kids can't even grasp the basics before they enter the classroom, and aren't encouraged at home, you're fighting a losing battle, you really are. It's like trying to build a house without the foundations.

Education is clearly at the forefront of our children's future in Granny's mind, and I have to say that I agree with her on this one one hundred per cent. We may not agree entirely on what exactly *constitutes* an education – for me it is as much about experiencing many things for yourself *outside* the classroom, about travelling and thus learning about other people and cultures, about art, and music and film and culture of all kinds – but we do certainly agree that parents have as great a role, if not an even greater one, to play in their children's education than teachers do.

Somehow I suspect that this clever lady is in no danger of shutting down her mental faculties any time soon. Her body may be giving her grief, but a positive mental attitude can overcome much of that, and the progress seems to be looking good for now. Perhaps I have Dr Attenborough and his bonking baboons to thank, in part, for that.

Some quotes I love, about education:

❝Nine tenths of education is encouragement.❞

66 *The whole art of teaching is only the art of awakening the natural curiosity of young minds for the purpose of satisfying it afterwards.* 99

Anatole France

66 *Children require guidance and sympathy far more than instruction.* 99

Annie Sullivan

66 *Prejudices, it is well known, are most difficult to eradicate from the heart whose soil has never been loosened or fertilized by education; they grow there, firm as weeds among rocks.* 99

Charlotte Brontë

66 *The aim of education is the knowledge not of facts, but of values.* 99

Dean William R. Inge

66 *We must not believe the many, who say that only free people ought to be educated, but we should rather believe the philosophers who say that only the educated are free.* 99

Epictetus

66 *Education is the most powerful weapon which you can use to change the world.* 99

Nelson Mandela

SILENCE!

There is, of course, another major factor in learning anything at school. No, it's not having the cleanest school bag, the sharpest pencil or the Clever Dick badge proudly sewn onto your blazer. The thing that really helps children to learn at school is their surroundings: having the peace, quiet and attitude required to concentrate and learn. This comes primarily from having pupils in their class who want to learn, and who let others learn. Pupils who are well-behaved. Who are well-*disciplined*.

Talk to any teacher working in a 'normal' school today, and they'll tell you that a large proportion of their teaching time, and therefore the kids' learning time, is wasted by children being disruptive. Whether they're shouting at the teacher, throwing bits of paper across the classroom or knifing each other in the playground (OK, this is very rare, but it does happen) kids are not doing what they're supposed to be doing quite a lot of the time. This isn't new, of course, and pupils have always misbehaved in class. But many teachers now feel unable to do much about it, for reasons we'll examine later, and although by far the majority of children are very well behaved at school it's clear that a significant and troublesome minority are causing havoc in schools up and down the country. And discipline is dwindling fast.

Now from what I've heard, and you probably have too, discipline at school was often fairly tough in the old days: it was commonplace for pupils to say 'please, Sir', do their work when told to and not to draw graffiti on their chairs while they were at it. Even if they were cheeky behind a teacher's back, it was unthinkable in most classrooms to be rude to a teacher's face. Sadly, this doesn't always seem to be the case any more, and many teachers today complain that they are having a tough time simply keeping their pupils under control, let alone teaching them anything.

Does Granny have any tips from the past that we could use today to get some learning and respect back into the classroom?

'OK,' I say, stoking the fire a little before returning to my notebook, 'tell me about school discipline. I assume there was a lot more of it when your kids were at school than there is now, just from what I've read and heard. It all seems like a complete nightmare in some classrooms now, with kids being unbelievably rude to their teachers – and even violent.'

The blanket twitches as Granny's apparent annoyance at the state of affairs gets the better of her.

'I don't understand it one bit, Elizabeth, I really don't. What is going on in schools these days – teachers being talked back at, children behaving as though they own the place? There's no discipline at all. It's like going to the madhouse not school.'

Is it?

It certainly does seem from what we read in the press or hear as we walk past school playgrounds that behaviour in many schools is not quite what it used to be. Where once it was a tentative 'Please, Sir, can I have some more' these days it's more likely to be 'Oi, fuck-face! Watcha lookin' at, eh? Gi'us another load of that fuckin' rice will ya before I kick your fuckin' fat ugly face in. Yeah, wha'ever – I'm fuckin' starvin' man. Wicked.'

Charming, as I'm sure you'll agree.

But let's see if Granny and so many others I hear muttering in playgrounds, coffee shops and newspaper columns are right: have things *really* got so much worse, or are we getting all hot under the collar (or blanket) about nothing?

Classroom chaos

❋ The Association of Teachers and Lecturers surveyed 800 members across the UK in 2008 and found two-thirds believed standards of behaviour were getting worse.

❋ Three out of ten teachers said they had experienced 'physical aggression', while three-quarters said they had been threatened or insulted by a pupil.

❋ One in ten teachers and college lecturers said a violent student had caused them 'physical harm'.

❋ 'Sixty-five per cent have considered leaving the profession as a consequence' according to the ATL's general secretary.

❋ All recorded violence in England and Wales has risen twenty-five-fold since 1951. While this by no means counts only violence by young people, this rise is reflected to some degree within schools as well.

❋ In 2004 a National Association of Schoolmasters Union of Women Teachers survey suggested that a teacher in a British classroom suffers verbal or physical abuse every seven minutes.

❋ A five-year study by Cambridge University published in 2008 and commissioned by the NUT, found that teachers are under pressure from poorly behaved children, with primary teachers forced to deal with poor standards of behaviour more normally associated with secondary pupils. Teachers claimed pupils were reluctant to follow instructions and that 'a minority could be extremely confrontational, use foul language and could even be physically aggressive', according to the report.

Ring the school bell – this sounds awful! Is there any good news at all?

Well, maybe there is, from someone who really has been on the front line, so to speak:

> 66 We are not in the middle of behaviour melt down as some tabloid newspapers would have us believe. Even Ofsted agrees that the vast majority of children and students attend schools and colleges and behave in a totally acceptable manner. For many children our schools are a haven from the rough and tumble of their lives beyond the school gates. In school they do know the difference between right and wrong. They know the school rules and the consequences of not following them. 99

Hilary Bills, NUT national president, 2005

Aha, the 'consequences'. This is a kinder way of saying what I sense Granny is itching to say herself, so I ask her – a former teacher herself, remember, and who saw four children through school – what she thinks could have caused children to behave so badly in some cases, and get exactly the answer I expected.

She leans forward, and fixes me with her sparkling eyes. 'Well, you know what the main problem is, don't you?'

I look thoughtful. Harder school chairs? Meaner teachers? The Dunce's corner? Woolly tights? Granny puts me out of my misery.

'It's *punishment*, Elizabeth. Children used to be punished if they stepped out of line. Nobody can punish a child any more at school, so there's no way of stopping them doing whatever they like. They *need* to be told off and punished, if they misbehave. Simple as that.'

Now, I'm not someone who jumps to punishment as the first and best way to get some order. Nor do I think that school should be in the business of punishing kids; they're there to impart knowledge and enthusiasm for learning, and for helping pupils who are disruptive to behave better, not for doling out detentions. But unruly kids spoil the learning experience for *all* pupils, and there has to be some way of putting an end to their destruction.

Perhaps Granny has a point, albeit a dated one, that could quite easily be adapted and reintroduced today. And probably I'm feeling uncomfortable with the rather old-fashioned word 'punishment'; today we would use 'discipline' instead but mean the same thing effectively.

Whatever we're calling it, the Right Royal Bollocking technique certainly worked for me, and the threat of having to listen to Monsieur Frankenstein (not his actual name, you gather) screaming at me in 100-mile-an-hour French while spitting through his yellowing teeth and waving his BO in my direction was enough to make me behave pretty bloody well I'd say.

What has happened since I was at school is that the Right Royal Bollocking we knew, and that worked, has seen something of a decline, due to what is known, unofficially, as Right Royal Political Correctness Load of Old Bollocks.

This new theory states that a teacher can't say anything to a child that might offend it, upset it or cause expensive visits to psychotherapists in future years. Shouting 'STOP THAT *AT ONCE!*' at a child is now tantamount to child abuse, and as for sending a child to the head teacher – this would very possibly cause years of mental torture, recurrent depression and comfort eating on fast food. Much better to let the little bastard carry on throwing pieces of paper he has recently removed from his bottom down Suzy Sanderson's neck in Maths. Obviously this is a mild exaggeration, and there are still visits to the Head and detentions and all that, but you get the point. And so does Granny.

'If you let a child get away with any behaviour they like at school you are teaching in a zoo within days. You *have* to keep them under control from day one, or you've had it. That's what's happened now – children are treated as equals with their teachers, and given rights and I don't know what else. And so they just walk all over the staff and it's a complete disaster.'

This reminds me of something I heard John Humphrys saying on the *Today* programme recently. (That puts me in my boring place. Oops.) The subject was, yet again, unruly school children, and his guest insisted on referring to them repeatedly as 'students'. Humphrys tripped up several times trying to use this word, and eventually said something along the lines of 'I'm terribly sorry, but I'm having trouble calling these people "students". They are 'pupils' aren't they?'

I could have kissed the radio: yes, they are! *Pupils*. Young people who are here to learn. Not students at university, or colleagues or learning partners . . . pupils. So, while absolutely not wishing to see children treated unfairly, why can't they be treated as *children*, rather than as peers with their teachers, or adults?

Does this aspect of childhood have to be erased along with so many of the others as well?

" I can't believe the things some of the children feel they can say to me. It's like I'm one of their mates or something. Just last week I was on my lunch break, doing some work at the computer, and one of my pupils marches up to me and says, in a really cheeky voice 'That top makes you look fat, Miss,' and saunters off. I just thought: I would never, ever have said that to my teacher – so why do they feel they can say it to us? "

Claire, 35, Year Five teacher in a secondary comprehensive

Getting tough on unruly kids

* In 2006 teachers were given the clear **legal right to discipline** unruly pupils and restrain children using 'reasonable force', but many teachers feel they cannot exercise this right for fear of being attacked themselves, or of complaints from parents.

* In 2005 the then Education Secretary Ruth Kelly said schools should adopt a **ZERO TOLERANCE** approach to low-level disruption such as incessant chattering and answering back, for example by removing such pupils from the classroom.

* Also in 2005, Discipline Zsar Alan Steer said schools must be given the right to apply to magistrates for **legal orders against parents** unwilling to work with them, and extend the new powers given to heads to search pupils for weapons without their consent to include drugs and stolen property.

* June 2008: Schools Secretary Ed Balls promised to tackle parents who refuse to accept that teachers have a right to discipline their children.

This all sounds very grand and encouraging and any changes that make teachers' lives better and pupils' chances of learning higher are to be welcomed. It's a little too early to say whether these measures have had any positive effect already, but some good news came from a long-term study by educational psychologists published in 2008. They found that primary school pupils are actually better behaved within the classroom than in the 1970s. Hurray! They put this improvement down to teachers being better at 'verbal encouragement' than they used to be, and working harder to make sure pupils are 'on task' (that's 'playing some bloody attention' to you and me!) more.

Sadly though, in contrast to this apparent improvement, many teachers anecdotally report that when there is misbehaviour it can be more extreme. And at this year's annual conference of the NASUWT teachers' union, delegates heard that bad behaviour from pupils is the biggest cause of stress for teachers.

So maybe things aren't quite so rosy after all, and pupils are indeed causing a lot of disruption and stress. The fact is that the upshot of Namby Pamby Teaching is that our oh so very perceptive children realise within three nanoseconds of stepping foot inside the school gates that teachers can't touch them – metaphorically or physically (the latter being a good thing, I'd say) – and so they do whatever they bloody well like. And a lot of this is caused by our obsession with 'rights.'

Hilary Bills, former NUT president again

❝ *The balance between the rights of pupils and the rights of teachers are too often tipped in favour of the pupil. The no win, no fee culture has encouraged pupils and parents to question teachers' actions in a way hitherto unknown. The almost certain suspension of a teacher accused of any wrong doing sends out the wrong message to those who want to cause mischief and it undermines teachers' authority.* ❞

Here's how eighteen-year-old jellyellie sees it, and it's hard to disagree:

❝ *If you receive a punishment – detention, or litter picking, for example – and you know that the teacher will just forget about it if you don't turn up, then obviously you're not going to turn up and you'll continue disobeying rules. However, if you know that you will be dragged into the head teacher's office – whom you respect because he's helped you get onto the local football team and lets you go to a local college to do a mechanics course one day a week – you will go to that detention because you don't want to end up in front of the headmaster whom you respect. Get respect in the bag and discipline will follow naturally.* ❞

There's that Respect thing cropping up again. A teacher with no respect from her pupils has no chance – and punishment is futile. The two are inextricably linked, as we've seen at home. It's the same at school.

So far, so in agreement with la Grandmére, but I feel a strong divergence coming on. Though I completely agree with what Granny is saying about disciplining children, I get the feeling that she and I are again not talking about the same *kind* of discipline here. I'm talking about lines, detentions, being told to jolly well 'sit down, Fraser!' I suspect she has something a little more forceful in mind.

I make enquiries . . .

'Children are still disciplined, Granny. They get sent to the head teacher and given extra homework and all that just as they used to. It's not a free-for-all you know.'

There is an incredulous pause, before: '*Lines?* What's that going to do? They don't care about that one jot.'

Oh here we go. I feel the c-word coming on . . .

'So, you think they should have, what, the cane?'

'The *cane*? No! We didn't have the cane in *Scotland*.'

Well pardon me. Just the cruel, merciless English then. And what, pray, did the kind and civilised Scots have to discipline their tearaway louts with?

'Well, we had detentions, of course. My kids hated that. And then we had the strap.'

The strap. Oh well, that's all right then. Just the strap.

'According to your father – who I believe became quite familiar with the thing – it was about thirty centimetres long and had two tongues at the end, to make it really whip around your hand.'

There is almost nothing sensible you can say to this kind of comment, especially when your eyebrows are stuck to your hairline and your mouth is involuntarily pulling itself into a part grimace/part vomit/part scream position. (Try it.) This sort of talk, sensible though it clearly seems to Granny and probably to many other people of a certain age, is just hopelessly out of date. Corporal punishment being reintroduced into schools as a standard form of discipline? Over my caned bottom. And I can't think of one person I know and like who would disagree – we can surely instil a sense of respect and good behaviour in our children without wielding pieces of leather, cane or plastic at them?

This kind of discipline, as well as being a form of child abuse (and let's not pretend it isn't. The child is powerless, and the person hitting him with a cane is doing so in a very measured, planned way with no possibility of reprieve for his terrified victim) it is also a particularly nasty form of bullying to boot. So there's one more good reason never to bring it back: what a great example to set the pupils!

I have read many accounts from people who were caned at school, and what surprised me was that, even though most of them said they hated it, it hurt and, most importantly it terrified them, by far the majority thought it had kept them 'on the straight and narrow', 'out of trouble', 'being a model pupil' and so on. Even some who spoke of caning as something that had really upset them at the time, now look back on it as a good thing, and feel too much 'PC nonsense' has let behaviour slip.

Perhaps time heals most things, and perhaps caning really is an effective deterrant from bad behaviour but still, I would like to think we can discipline our children without beating them up!

BULLYING

——∽∽——

Bullying between children makes the headlines more frequently now than I ever imagined it could. What surprises me is not that it's new: bullying has been around as long as people have, and we all remember kids calling the fat boy, er, Fatty; making up nasty rhymes; pinging bra straps during maths; giggling in groups whenever the class geek shuffled awkwardly by. Actually, I *was* the class geek. Damn. It's that it's so prevalent, and so, so *nasty* now. Some of the worst bullying happens between girls, and is not so much violent as downright horrible. This distinction is important. Bullying used to be thought of as physical: hitting the weak kid, or beating him up after school. But it's the quiet, stealth bullying that has crept into every classroom in the land, which needs stamping out – fast.

The word 'teasing' has been gradually replaced with 'bullying', and I think this is a good thing: it's easy to laugh off childish

So how on earth has this happened? Was bullying such a problem when Granny was a child, and if not, how come it is now?

'No. Absolutely not. In my day, if you teased someone you got your come-uppance immediately and you didn't do it again. That was that. You were sent straight to the Head, and then you got into even bigger trouble at home, and you learned not to be such a nasty bully.'

pranks like throwing packed lunches in the bin every day (or, in my case, my scarf. Hey, get off my scarf, dudes!) or calling someone names, as nothing but childish silliness that doesn't cause any harm (and some of it doesn't); but when this teasing becomes persistent and if the person being teased clearly cannot laugh along with the joke and is becoming upset, then it has become bullying and needs to be taken more seriously.

Bullying has reached epic proportions:

* According to the BBC's *Panorama* programme, one home learning charity believes that up to 90,000 British school children may have been withdrawn from school by their parents as a direct result of bullying that was not stopped.

* Another study suggested that around sixteen British children take their own lives each year as a direct result of bullying in our schools, but that the true figure might be much higher.

'Isn't that sort of using force against force, rather than reason?' I say, somewhat playing Devil's Advocate because I know exactly what she's going to say to *that*!

'Reason doesn't come into it, and telling a child off is *not* bullying. You need to get that straight, and so do the teachers. Some things are just plain WRONG, like persistent teasing, and children need to know that in no uncertain terms. That's the point about disciplining children.

Granny's Pearl of Wisdom

If you don't discipline children they can't discipline themselves. They walk around with no idea of what's right and what's wrong. Punishment is not a dirty word – bullying is.

Trouble is, many children are not getting this idea of what's right and what's wrong from home, as their home life is so shattered and inconsistent. This makes teachers' lives almost impossible because they're trying to teach pupils whose parents don't enforce any discipline.

> *The number of dysfunctional families is increasing [and] all we are doing is picking up the debris of what is happening in the wider world.*

Mike Lewis, head of Bristol Gateway special school for children with emotional and behavioural disorders

So part of the reason that bullying has got so out of hand could be that there are more and more kids pacing the corridors who haven't ever been taught, at home or at school, that they can't treat others with so little respect; how to behave kindly towards others and that being a wanker is NOT OK.

But not everyone agrees with this theory of punishing bullies, and this is where it gets confusing. One strategy, which is growing in influence, recommends that bullies should never be punished, even when it's quite clear that they are guilty as hell. This so-called 'No Blame' approach brings the bullies and other kids in their class together to discuss the allegations, while the victim stays out of the room. In theory, if you can get most people in the class to agree that the bullying is wholly unacceptable – or, 'fuckin' out of order, mate', if you prefer – the bullies will feel isolated enough to change their behaviour.

There has been some success with this approach, and also with a 'house' system, which has, according to some pupils who have experienced it, helped to foster a spirit of mutual support and responsibility. The idea is to foster a more 'village feel' and create a sense of belonging for these 'lost' children.

But other anti-bullying experts strongly oppose it, preferring the punishment method advocated by Granny.

Oh, it's a tough one!

Cyber bullying

Things have got even trickier in recent years with the arrival of Cyber bullying. This is much harder to stamp out, because you can't tell it's going on and it can be much more traumatic for the victim, as it is so relentless, direct and impossible to ignore. If you receive 200 text messages a day saying you are a twat and everyone hates you, it's going to pretty tough not to feel the pressure. Cyber bullying is less in-yer-face, but can be just as intimidating; you are unlikely to get picked on by 200 kids at once in the playground, but can easily receive that many nasty emails and texts in one evening.

66 *There is no one group that is to blame, or that is responsible, for tackling bullying. Everybody, from parents and teachers to shopkeepers and bus drivers needs to take responsibility for combating and reducing the problem. We can set good examples at home and in the community, and intervene when someone is behaving inappropriately. We mustn't ignore bullying or accept it; only by standing up to it, collectively, will we help to influence others' behaviour.*

*'Cyber bullies can attack their target at any time, via email, text message or social networking sites, which means that they can penetrate more personal, and once perceived safe, areas, such as the home. It is sometimes easier to type something horrible than say it to someone's face, and cyber bullies often hide behind the apparent anonymity that cyberspace gives them. However, this anonymity is a myth and the bullies are leaving undeniable evidence of bullying, which can be traced back to the perpetrators. We also must not forget that this is the same behaviour that we have seen offline for many years, and so the way to tackle it is also the same: taking collective responsibility for reporting it and intervening. Again, young people hold the key. Working with both the bullies and the bullied, training young people in how they can change their behaviour and mentor others, online and offline, is critical if we are to reduce and prevent bullying effectively in the long term.*99

Emma-Jane Cross, chief executive of Beatbullying

Even though some of this behaviour is against the law, for example sending malicious emails or texts and harassment or defamation online, it still goes on in shocking numbers, and many children don't seem able to come forward and tell anyone, such is their fear of the perpetrators. This is possibly the most shocking part for me: kids – indeed humans in general – have always bullied each other, but how come so few children feel able to *talk* to someone about it, and to get help? Why do they so fear being judged, being criticised, or being laughed at? Where are the people they should feel safe to confide in, and to get help from?

Oh, that'll be us then. Time to make this possible.

So what can be done?

We urgently need to raise awareness and change our attitude towards bullying and, happily, this is already happening in several spheres.

Campaigns like those organised by BEATBULLYING are doing a fantastic job of this. The high profile blue wristband campaign, endorsed by celebrities like Rio Ferdinand, also sends out the growing message that bullying is no longer acceptable. With more and more celebrities coming on board to speak out against bullying, and moves such as the 2003 **Anti Bullying Charter** introduced by the Department of Education and Skills, slowly things are changing on the public perception front.

Schools also need to clamp down much harder on bullying. A leading anti-bullying charity, Kidscape, says that in three-quarters of the cases it deals with, schools blame the victim instead of tackling the bullies. And many children who are bullied at school report not being taken seriously, or being told off for wasting teachers' time.

Research from Childline found that eighty-seven per cent of young people are too embarrassed to talk about problems, while two-thirds fear getting into trouble.

I asked my children if they have come across this and was met by an immediate and unanimous 'Yes!'

66 *If I say to my teacher that someone is picking on me, which I think is bullying because, well, it happens every day and it upsets me, she just says 'Oh come on now, Phoebe, run along and play and stop being silly.' So I can't do anything about it.* 99

Phoebe, aged eight

66 *They [the teachers] just don't want to do anything about it, and they make us feel stupid for telling. So the people bullying just carry on and it's as if they've won.* 99

Emily, aged ten

There are a large number of **helplines** children can call, and it's not a bad plan to make your kids aware of some of them, as they get older. Kidscape, Childline, Anti Bullying Network and Anti-Bullying Campaign are just some.

The media. Who can forget the furore over the racist bullying of Shilpa Shetty on *Big Brother*, and also Germaine Greer's decision to walk out of the *Celebrity Big Brother* House when she felt she was being encouraged by the programme makers to partake in bullying of one housemate. Such vile endorsement, indeed encouragement, of bullying by the programme makers has to be stopped. 40,000 people phoned in to complain about the 'Shetty incident' – a good sign that people are prepared to speak out, but why wasn't the number closer to two million, and why do people continue to watch? We can act with our remote control, and switch this kind of malicious crap OFF.

The role of parents in stamping out bullying is colossal. Not only can we raise our children to have respect for others and to behave well, we can also help our own children who may have become the target of bullying.

* **Don't refer to them as victims.** They feel weak, and often guilty and ashamed enough as it is; they need to feel strong, so that they can overcome this problem.

* **Teach your children how not to be bullied, as well as how not to bully.** I recently had a long chat with my daughter who felt she couldn't wear something to school in case she got teased. I explained that the people doing the teasing are the weak ones, and they actually feel jealous of anyone who has their own style or opinion. She has to believe that the way she is, is OK, and go out there, head held high, and be herself. If they want to laugh at her they can, if they're that silly. The trick is not to react, or to make a joke at her own expense. That takes the wind right out of their sails. She did, and she was fine.

* **Be non-judgemental** and keep the channels of communication wide open at all times, so that your children feel safe to talk to you.

* **Keep your eyes open** for tell-tale signs of bullying, such as becoming withdrawn, self-harming, cutting back on social things, eating problems, being unusually aggressive or abusive, 'losing' possessions, constant anxiety, defensiveness, injury or damaged clothing.

Even though we disagree on the type of punishment children receive at school, Granny and I can at least agree on the principle of what it is trying to achieve.

She seems annoyed and saddened at the hopelessness of the situation, and I suspect many parents in the land share this sense of frustration and despair.

'What you seem to have forgotten,' she says slowly, 'both at home and at school, is that there have to be *consequences* for our actions.'

Granny's Pearl of Wisdom

Teaching children to understand that there are consequences to the way they behave, is central to their upbringing. If a school fails to do this, it has failed your child.

'And presumably the consequences are that they get into trouble sometimes?'

'Yes! Of course. There's nothing wrong with it. You all think that children are made of bone china – they are not. They are tough; or, they used to be. Today they have no backbone at all. It's all cotton wool and lovey dovey. Kids know perfectly well when they are breaking the rules if you have the punishments in place.'

This sounds a bit like 'you have to be cruel to be kind' to me, a point I make to Granny, thinking she'll smile and agree with me wholeheartedly. I'm wrong.

'No – you are not being cruel. You have to get that thought out of your head, you really do. You are being a parent, and you are *parenting*. The teachers are being teachers, and teaching. The child is being a child, and learning – from you, and their teachers, and everything they see.

Granny's Pearl of Wisdom

Discipline is very easy to let slide and very, very hard to get back. Schools need discipline, or the children will take over very quickly.

Discipline is indeed near as dammit impossible to put back once it's gone. Just like muscle tone or sex, once you've waved goodbye to it, it takes a Herculean effort, to get it back again. (Though, if I might be so bold as to point it out, the getting the latter back rather helps with the former so if you can sort that one out that's two problems solved in one go. Genius.) The only difference these days is *how* we keep this discipline in check.

But here lies another modern problem, we've touched on before:

Oh, litigation's what you (don't) need

Once upon a time if a young child cried at school her teacher would lift her onto his lap, put his arms around her and comfort her.

Once upon a time if a child fell over in the playground and cut himself he would go to the nurse who would clean it with Dettol – ow! – put antiseptic cream on it and a plaster, and send him on his merry, sore way.

Once upon a time if a child was suspected of having nits he was sent to the nit nurse who would have a jolly good rummage around to check and if this was found to be the case he'd be sent home until they were eradicated.

And once upon a time if a child misbehaved she was jolly well told off for it.

These days, giving a child a cuddle is bordering on paedophilia; cuts cannot be treated in case of a fatal reaction to the antiseptic cream/plaster/air/nurse's sense of humour; nits are left to breed at will because you can't possibly check a child's head for them – oh! The humiliation! – and telling a child off is a form of intolerable cruelty. In all these cases – and I'm sure you can think of several more from your own experience – schools are so paralysed by the fear of litigation that they have had to remove all contact between staff and child, lest anything untoward, dangerous or suggestive be suspected.

This is the same problem we saw earlier with children's rights coming above teachers' where discipline – or the lack of it – is concerned, and it's not just pathetic; it's TRAGIC. Children are given no experience at all about how normal human behaviour operates, no clue as to how to behave in perfectly everyday situations nor any idea of what their teachers are there *for*.

This would all be quite funny, too, if it weren't so true and so very, very sad. These are our KIDS we're talking about! Not puppets, or guinea pigs. They are people, with brains and feelings, who need to learn to cope with life's little wobbles. Why can't they be treated like human beings who are praised for being good, comforted when they are upset, cared for when they are hurt and bloody well scolded when they poison the school rabbit?

The fear of litigation has crept into the home environment as well: a judge recently ruled that a couple was responsible for a dreadful accident that occurred on the bouncy castle they'd hired for their child's party, and it struck fear into the minds of ordinary bouncy-castle-hiring parents everywhere, making us ask ourselves some truly ridiculous questions: is it OK to have a party at my house any more? Is it safe to invite children round for tea – what if they choke on a Hula Hoop? Should I get rid of the trampoline? Can I ever own peanuts again?

And so we find ourselves back at school again; with such fear of being sued for Random Bad Things happening, schools are clamping down even harder on the amount of fun kids are allowed to have on site. No more playing on the equipment outside school hours, no using the monkey bars without an adult supervising, no more than three children in the sand pit at any one time ... *Oh ENOUGH!! They're going insane with frustration – let them PLAY!!*

This depressing discussion about litigation is all very well, but what can we parents *do* about it? **What answer do you come up with if you ask yourself the simple question: Is this how you want your kids to be educated?**

Thought so. The bad news is that we have a fight on our hands if we want to change things, because the amount of red tape and rule-writing is enough to put out the hottest fires.

The good news is that there are enough parents in the land who want change, and that means we can make it happen. It's a two-pronged attack.

Solution 1: throwing out the rule book

Obviously not completely, but all of these moronic rules like 'a child cannot have plaster put on her bleeding knee in case she's allergic to it' really have to go. There are PTA committees, and head teachers and governing bodies. Write to them. Get as many people as you can to sign a petition, write a letter, organise a meeting and see if you can get some common sense back into your school. Hopefully while they're at it they can agree that children are actually allowed to be punished for misbehaving and we'll be getting somewhere.

To make this punishment (be it lines, detention, seeing the Head or whatever) actually have an impact we have to turn to Solution 2 below . . .

As well as punishment though, I would like to see more rewards for *good* behaviour: a child who responds not one bit to punishment often reacts much better if offered a reward for being good instead, and this can break a bad cycle of disruption with less confrontation and upset. Some kids actually *like* being punished, and seek a cross word like most of us seek a bar of chocolate; we know we shouldn't, but we can't help ourselves. (Damn that chocolate.) But very few kids are stubborn or stupid enough to persistently turn down the offer of an extra ten minutes' break time, or a turn on the computer.

I know this is easy to say, and talking to most teachers makes you despair, as they speak of teaching as little more than crowd control in many instances; if they can make it to the end of the class alive they've had a good lesson. But ignoring bad behaviour or coming down hard on kids who repeatedly behave appallingly – to absolutely no effect whatsoever – is clearly not very sensible.

Giving them something they've never had before – something to work towards and get as a reward for putting in the *effort*, could be the answer. It works wonders in my childrens' school.

Solution 2: on the home front

This is where Granny comes in again. She leans towards the fire to give it another poke, and it gives a satisfying crackle and fizz before a long, orange flame curls its way around an old log.

'But you know something – it's too easy to pin all the blame on teachers and the education system, lamentable though it is now. Parents also have a huge responsibility to give a message about school and this will make them behave better automatically.'

Granny's Pearl of Wisdom

If you don't teach your kids that school is important, teachers are important and that respect and effort is required, they won't pay any attention to what their teachers say.

Well said. This point is one that is so often overlooked as we try to pin the blame onto teachers for all the ills of their less perfectly-behaved pupils.

Hilary Bills, one more time

Schools are a reflection of society and have to deal with the issues that children bring into school. As Professor Tim Brighouse said: 'Children spend 15% of their time in lessons in school. It is paramount to recognise the other 85% of children's time is spent with parents and the community.'

There's an old story that if a child was clipped around the ear at school, he'd get another one when he got home for getting a clip around the ear in the first place! These days Mum and Dad would be round that school in a flash to complain that their child had been physically assaulted. There are even parents who storm into classrooms to complain when their unruly children are given a detention, demanding that their little cherubs be let off.

All that this kind of reaction does is to completely undermine the authority of the school and the teacher. It says to the child: 'Your teacher has no right to discipline you. You are right, and he is wrong.'

Well now, that's a terrific message to give a child, isn't it? How is a teacher ever supposed to get any discipline at school if the pupils are told by their parents that the children have more power than teachers?

> *My eldest son works with a Polish colleague who resigned from her job teaching in a secondary school because she was fed up with the pupils swearing at her and spitting. It was something she simply hadn't encountered in Poland. In the US, teenagers always call people 'sir' or 'ma'am' – it might seem old fashioned but I think it just makes the world seem like a more pleasant place.*

Joe, father of three

Now, I didn't exactly go to the best school in the country and there were the usual suspects smoking behind the chapel and trying to sleep with the Italian girls in Year Ten. But I think that the 800 or so pupils were pretty well disciplined in general, because we sort of had a sense that, when we weren't doing perfectly expected school-child things like writing 'Mr Jones has a big cock' on the walls or sticking chewing gum under our desks, we were quite happy to do what we were told. We *expected* to do as we were told. (Mostly!)

The reason for this is that there was an unspoken understanding that, even if you did take the piss out of some of the less liked teachers, and even if you did see who could get an erection out of the science teacher by sticking their tits out at him (oh come on – you never tried that?!), the teachers, many of whom we secretly did actually *like*, did deserve some respect. They were teachers; we were kids. End of story.

And where did this respect come from? It came from HOME.

From our parents, who had drummed it into us from year dot that you don't behave badly to others, that school was a place of learning, and that teachers were important people in society.

So let's ask those who are 'at home', the parents: what do they think about the state of pupils' behaviour in schools today and do they have any suggestions for what could improve things?

   There was more discipline when I was at school and we were constantly threatened with a beating – although they were not administered as much as they were threatened. I think it's better the way things are at school now because pupils are not afraid, but my impression is that there are some kids who waste a lot of everyone's time because they have no discipline at all, and the teachers can't cope. Codes of conducts drawn up by pupils themselves might be a good idea.

Pete, 41, father of two girls

66 *We had more discipline at school than my boys do, but of a different sort. 'Discipline' seems to be lost in a PC legal world, but I don't see kids rioting in the streets like my generation did – so I reckon something is working. Kids are more cynical, but happy – and many of them do still treat teachers with respect. I think the bad kids need help, not a good hiding.*99

Mike, father of two boys

Putting some respect back into the school corridors is a really tough call but there are suggestions coming in from all sides that could be implemented, as we've seen above. Perhaps if pupils were not allowed to leave the school grounds during the school day, if there were consequences for *parents* if children are late to school and that sort of thing, then maybe that would also help to underline, for those numbskulls who *still* don't get the point and go around smashing up the science labs every Friday afternoon, that it's a school not a rave and the pupils are NOT in charge – the members of staff are. And the point about *helping* those who are causing trouble is critical – punishment works for some occasions, but sorting out the root of the problem is far more useful and effective in the long term. But it takes time.

We have to work *with* schools to sort this huge problem out, not sit back and say 'Well, why can't they teach kids anything any more? How crap are they?' **It's not solely our fault, nor solely the teachers' fault. We're in this together, and we can only sort it out together.**

I'm glad I talked with Granny about this, because, after a few major disagreements with the Head of my kids' school about a variety of things, we had started to be less than polite about the way the place was run, even when our children were within earshot. I had come to not really care about this, as my feelings of annoyance were so strong. But hearing what Granny said about the importance of showing our kids that school is important and teachers should be respected really put a stop to any snide remarks about school policy, or certain teachers. We have a duty as parents to behave better, and we got back to doing this just in time, thanks to Granny's reminder.

Granny's Pearl of Wisdom

You know, teaching is a two-way street. It takes work on both sides and kids need to understand that very clearly. They aren't owed an education: they have to get it through hard work, and if they treat their teachers with disrespect then that needs stamping out.

With this final thought ringing in my ears I know the time has come to say goodbye. It's the end of another conversation; the end of a holiday; the end of another chance to spend time with this amazing lady. But we'll be back for more as soon as we can: there's still so much she can teach me, I'd be a fool not to keep asking.

Here's a reminder of some simple ways we could all try to get discipline in school back on track. If we can't, it's 500 lines and a trip to the Head for the lot of us.

Teach your children that school is important and that teachers are to be respected and listened to.

Talk to your school's Head if you feel that Namby Pamby Teaching is getting out of hand, and see if a big group of you can make some changes here. I've yet to meet a single parent who doesn't want it all to stop – but we aren't doing anything about it!

Back up your child's teacher (if you feel the punishments she gives out are justified!) in front of your child. Contradicting them undermines their authority, and once it's undermined, it's GONE. Yes, you might feel they are a little out of order sometimes, or heavy-handed or even unfair. But keep it for private talks with that teacher, not for general discussion with your kids.

Make some effort with how you and your kids dress for school. This includes tying their hair back, making sure clothes are clean etc. I'm not saying *ironed*, necessarily (I haven't ironed anything since about 1995, favouring the 'buy garments what don't need ironing' approach instead) but at least clean and smart for school. Turning up in muddy tracky bums and hair all over the place sends a pretty clear message that you ain't bovvered at all. And so neither will your kids be.

Talk respectfully about teachers in front of your kids. Even if you do think Mr Holmes is a git, try not to say it in front of the kids, or they'll ignore everything he says.

Chapter Nine

'TIS WISE TO BE THRIFTY

The curse of consumerism, and how to escape it

Two weeks have gone by without my phoning Granny once, and I'm beginning to feel miserably guilty about it. The pace of my life has crept back up to hyper speed and if I'm not working like a crazy bee I'm tidying or washing or cooking or helping with homework or reading stories . . . You know exactly how it is!

Today I am tidying my kids' bedrooms, and in between picking up hair bands, Power Ranger arms, swords and gel pens I take a moment to look around me at the colourful, strewn-about array of *things* they have. Now, let's get one thing straight: compared with many kids I know in what is, rather amusingly I think, called the Developed World, my children have remarkably few toys. They have enough to keep them occupied in their free moments, but their bedrooms are not reminiscent of a gargantuan toy emporium and you can actually move about in there without knocking over half a ton of unwanted plastic.

But despite my concerted efforts they still have what I think I can safely call 'a lot'. And they're not alone. How many of you can honestly say *your* kids don't also have too many, often barely used, toys? And we've all collected our kids from a friend's house, poked our head nosily into what is increasingly not a bedroom but a separate playroom to house all the merchandise, and been hit by an avalanche of toys: shelves upon shelves upon *shelves* of boxes and crates, bags and baskets crammed and overflowing with every game and toy a child could ever dream of. From simple games and jigsaw puzzles, to dinosaur models, mini tents, dressing-up clothes, the latest electronic gadgets, Disney figurines, pirate ships, dolls' houses and so on, I know kids who have more toys than they could possibly ever play with, even if they chose a different one every day for two years. The average child in America gets seventy new toys per year, and I don't imagine it's very much less than this figure for many kids over here.

Fun though this may sound, it raises an important question: what is such over-indulgence – if indeed it is over-indulgence – doing to our children? Is it lovely that they have so much to play with, or could these astonishing playrooms be the very tip of the vast consumer iceberg; the training ground for a life of buying, buying and buying some more – without learning how to imagine, make and play – and consequently learning very young that buying actually brings nothing but disappointment and an unquenchable desire for even more? And if so, what can we do to stop our children being sucked into the consumer orgy of a life of 'wanting more' before they know any better?

I exchange my duster for the phone immediately and call Granny. She answers after more rings than usual and sounds a little groggy to start with – probably the first of the many winter colds to come. I learn that there is a fresh covering of snow on the hills and the thermometer has rocketed up to a whopping five degrees. Quick, get the bikini out, Granny. I mumble a pathetic apology for not phoning sooner, and we begin talking about the joys of consumerism.

From what she's seen of her eleven grandchildren and three great grandchildren, does she think children today get more toys and presents than they did when hers were little? There is a pause of approximately three nanoseconds before the animated reply comes down the line.

'Oh, about two hundred times more! I was horrified when your cousin Ian went to play at a friend's house many years ago – the things that child had! Train sets and boats, little toy figurines of Star Wars or something, and racing cars and I don't even know what else. He could hardly move for toys. And it's only worse now – the things children have – how can they play with it all?'

Granny's Pearl of Wisdom

We had so little, you know, but it didn't worry us. We were happy and we played more than any kids I see playing today, despite all that they have. It's the playing, not what you play with that matters.

This point is an interesting one: when did you last take the time to watch what your children actually *do* with their toys? You know – those really expensive ones you bought under duress, or through guilt, or because you thought it'd keep them quiet for a few weeks . . . Well, if it's been two weeks or more then make a date with the playroom because you might be quite surprised by what you see. Often, children spend more time just playing imaginary games with odd bits and bobs they find lying around (string, bits of broken cars, an old cuddly toy who seems to need some love and so on) than playing with the toys they have scattered everywhere rather than as they were designed to be played with. Many of these 'toys' have so little play potential it's mind-blowing, and you end up spending a fortune on plastic or electronic tat that becomes boring within minutes. It's ridiculous!

Watching how they play is as important as buying them the things to play with, so watch and learn . . . and buy (or don't) accordingly.

So what kind of toys did Granny have?

GRANNY'S TOY BOX

'I had a nurse's uniform, and we'd play hospitals for hours in that. We also played shops a lot – we'd set up a wee shoppy outside with tins of this and that, and bread and packets. And I had a tea set, with little tea cups. Oh, and I loved my nightie bag: it was in the shape of a . . . oh, what do you call those Chinese dogs... Oh, that's it, a Pekinese! I had a Pekinese nightie bag, though it was never used as such – I took it *everywhere* with me. And I had a soft toy Kiwi, and a teddy bear. My father-in-law called it "the diseased rabbit" but I loved it – it was my companion for years.'

Moving on to more recent times, I'm expecting to hear that things had changed somewhat by the time she was a parent herself.

'And Dad? What did your kids have when they were little?'

'Oh, not that much at all – but enough. Your father had one tin engine, and I probably have that somewhere upstairs. There was a cart with wheels – he probably tried to sit in it and broke it, knowing your father! – and of course there were Dinky cars. They were very special, and we collected quite a few over the years. Alison had a dolls' tea set, I remember that. There were not many wooden toys, now I think about it. It was mainly tin or plastic, latterly.'

I pause, waiting for the rest of the list. The pause continues and I begin to wonder if we've been cut off. But no. That is quite simply the end of the list of toys. There is no more: no collections of hundreds of dinosaurs, no silly little toys you get in magazines that you never play with but that Mummy stands on in the dark of the night and swears at, no Thomas the Tank Engine collection or Spiderman DVDs. That's *it*.

'But, Granny, were they *really* satisfied with a few toy cars and a cart? I mean, didn't they want more, or get bored with their toys? Mine do quite often, and then I feel I ought to get them something new to keep them amused or to keep up with what their friends have or just to make them stop pestering me if I'm honest. Didn't yours want more too?'

My ear is blasted by a loud, nasty cough, before Granny exclaims, 'No! What would they want more for, if they already had plenty to play with?'

'Ummm, because everyone else has lots more? It's basic child psychology: they see – they want.'

'Well, there's the problem. You have to buck that trend if you're to teach them anything useful at all – and have any money left! Teach them to enjoy their toys – that's much better than buying more and more junk.

Granny's Pearl of Wisdom

Give them less and they'll play with it more, and use their imagination to make up new games with it.
That's playing!

THOUGHT BOX

IMAGINE, IMAGINE

Amongst the rigid, action-packed structure of our children's lives there is also a vital place for regular playtime *without any structure at all*, which lets them explore one of the most special things kids possess naturally: their *imagination*. Boredom, a word often spoken with derision, like it's a disease or something, is not a dirty word, and it can sometimes be the trigger for some of the most creative and amazing play children ever have.

We did a rather cruel but ultimately very successful experiment on our daughters when they were about six and four years old. We went on holiday for a week and, instead of the suitcase full of toys and games we usually lugged to the airport with us like all the other parents terrified of holiday boredom setting in, we took nothing with us but paper, pens, scissors and glue.

And what happened? Well, there was a day or so of 'Mum, I've got nothing to doooooo!', which put me into a foul mood, but this was very soon followed by blissful, and very unusual, silence. Had they run off to Paris to find luurve? Were they raiding the local *Magazin des Jouets*? Nope – they were just *playing*. They made paper plates and paper people with paper hats. They collected stones on the beach to make furniture and cars and played so happily with their make-believe world that they never complained of boredom again – and it cost us nothing. In that week their imagination was used more than it had been in the whole of their lives, and Mummy and Daddy got a holiday . . . result!

It's also important to remember that there is no 'correct' way to play! Some kids do exactly what it says you should do on the box; others prefer to use their imagination and invent games using toys that were actually meant for a totally different purpose. That's fine. Just see what works for your child and don't feel you have to encourage them to play with a toy in a certain way. So long as they're playing, that's the important thing.

If children always play with toys that have one action, or one purpose, they have very little scope for the imaginative play that's such a vital part of childhood. Let them imagine; let them PLAY.

—— LIZ'S FAVOURITE IMAGINATIVE TOYS ——

Doodle Pads, Rosie Flo colouring books. I had something called the Anti Colouring book back in 1978, which is along the same lines. They start you off with a picture but leave much of it blank for you to fill in as you want. Much more imaginative and interactive than just colouring in and you'll be stunned at what your kids come up with.

Dolls' house, Sylvanians and other toys you can 'make up' home-like games with.

Art and craft toys: clay, card, stickers, pencils . . . every child can make *something*!

Dressing up. It's old-fashioned. It still works. I also think it's best not to buy fancy and expensive costumes off the peg: let them create their own using your old hats, Dad's shirts and so on. It's all part of the imaginative game of dressing up.

Shops. For younger kids, emptying out the tins and packets in the cupboards onto a table or bench to make a shop is still a winner.

Dens. Whether it's in the garden or made out of sofa cushions or some chairs and a sheet, building a house, den or cave is pure childhood imaginative heaven.

∽ *GRANNY'S TIPS FOR GOOD TOYS* ∽

'Well, I suppose anything that they can *do* something with is a good toy. **Something to keep them occupied and thinking and imagining.** Lego, or other construction toys are good. What I think is so bad for children are toys they just play with for five minutes and then leave lying around. They often look so tempting, but really there's nothing to *do* with them. **You have to have a good look and imagine what they can get out of it – if the answer is "not much", then put it down.'**

She pauses to get another frog out of her throat, before offering one more tip about toys, which I think is very helpful:

'One thing I don't understand is why children have so much, and yet so few toys are left out to play with. People are so concerned about keeping their houses looking neat and tidy there's no opportunity for children to actually play because the toys are put away. If you **have fewer toys but actually leave them accessible** for the children to play with that's much better than having 200 and sticking them all in boxes.'

I think this is a fantastic point, and applies particularly to things like dolls' houses, car racing tracks, pirate ships and so on. If they are all hastily tidied away after each play – and I used to do this a lot when my kids were younger – it means the toys are not there, at the ready to be played with. If you have a gazillion toys you have to pack most if it away, or you'd be swamped; but if you have very few, you can have more of them out and ready to play with all of the time. And then, surprise, surprise, the kids do play with them!

I've been trying this simple tip recently and to my complete delight my daughter has started playing with the Sylvanians she's had for two years, but has barely played with because they have always been tidied away in a box! Now that they're actually on her bedroom floor she's in there every day after school playing. I felt like a bit of a clot, actually, for not doing this sooner.

'The price of everything – and the value of nothing'

I'm not sure how many toys Oscar Wilde had as a child, but the well-known line above shows he certainly learned a beautiful thing or two about language. Something tells me it wasn't from a 'Speak and Spell' machine . . .

Whatever he did have, I think it's a safe bet to say it wasn't very much, and this, according to the lady at the other end of the phone line, is a very good plan.

'What's silly is that you all buy so much for your children, and then expect them to be so grateful and to play with all their toys. How can they? There's so much to choose from, so half of it is unused, and then you throw it away! People always used to keep toys and pass them on – they had less but they valued it more and looked after it because it *meant* something to them.

Granny's Pearl of Wisdom

The more you have, the more you want and the less satisfied you are.

I spend a few moments thinking back to the toys I had and realise with happy surprise – and a smidgeon of shame – that every single one is currently in my mum and dad's house, in almost perfect condition, and is played with by my children every time we visit them. I'd never really thought about how little I had – I was quite happy with my lot! – but as soon as I start remembering I realise what fond, fond memories I have of each and every toy, because I'd played with them all so much over the years.

MY TOY BOX

Every item on this list I still have, and my kids still play with:

A teddy bear called Bearly. He only speaks German, which is how I learned German too. Clever trick, Mum.

Some traditional Czech marionettes – and their less traditional recent addition: Harry Potter.

A very basic dolls' house, which my mum made, and in it lots of furniture she also constructed herself, to which I added several kitchen units and beds made from matchboxes and old off-cuts of material. (Thank you, _Blue Peter_.)

A glockenspiel.

Colouring books – who keeps half-complete colouring books any more? But there are still some pages to fill so there they still are, in great condition and waiting to be added to every so often when the mood strikes.

A doll's pram and three dolls to go in it. (Those that escaped the eyeball removing precision of my brother's swords . . .)

Two Cindy dolls and clothing (that, you guessed it, my mum made), who each got married many, many times to my brother's Action Man – such a tart, he was.

A healthy collection of games and puzzles.

A microscope.

Lots and LOTS of books.

During this reflective pause I hear the unmistakable sound of tea being sipped, before Granny continues her sound advice for those of us who overindulge and overspend.

'And you know another thing? Toys and presents were for birthdays, not any day. We didn't just buy toys and presents all the time, as seems to happen now. We didn't have the money for one thing, and also, what good is it to give children things all the time, Elizabeth? They cannae appreciate any of it, and it doesn't make you any happier, having lots of things.'

This annoyingly simple last remark reminds me of something an Indonesian man once said to me so simply and so clearly that I made a note of it in my diary at the time.

I was seventeen, and staying on a tiny island off Lombok. It was a little piece of heaven on this earth, and the local inhabitants clearly thought so too. I was really struck by how happy the local children were, playing together on the beach, splashing playfully in the water, kicking a ball on the dusty road. No arguing, no nasty bickering, and none of the constant competing over who has what that we are forced to listen to in supermarkets and on street corners everywhere in this country. It was simple: they had nothing, and were content with that because they didn't know what they didn't have. When I pointed this out to the man in question, he said with a gentle smile: *'In the West you have many problems and possessions: TVs, cars, houses. Here we are simple but laid back and happy. That's why we all smile and are friendly.'*

I doubt there are many people reading this book who don't feel at certain times that we have too much, and it's making us unhappy. Yes, that's you with the forty pairs of shoes, you with the clutter of kitchen gadgets that just make you cross because they're so messy, and me with a stack of unread magazines on the kitchen table that I *had* to buy because it made me feel special at the time.

We've all lost the feeling of *valuing* something. Of waiting for it, looking after it, loving it and keeping it for years. It's part of a bigger condition, almost a sickness that many inhabitants of richer nations are experiencing in increasing numbers. It's called consumerism, and it's probably got a hold of you already.

Read on for a pain-free cure . . .

THE CURSE OF CONSUMERISM

The nub of this problem was neatly summed up in 1964 by Lennon and McCartney: money can't buy you love. Turns out, dammit, that it also can't buy you happiness, or contentment, or health. It can just buy you *stuff*.

But just a sec – isn't that OK . . . having lots off stuff? I mean, it's better than *not* having any stuff, isn't it?

Well, beyond a roof over your head and food on the table, that's questionable, I think. Our obsession and apparent *need* to acquire STUFF grew substantially in the 1970s, as new-found wealth and the associated social requirement to 'own' took over most people's rational thinking. Washing machines, cars, Scalextrics, dodgy shirts with unfeasibly long collars . . . and the more everyone *else* had – you guessed it – the more they felt *they* ought to have. So the more hours they worked; the more money they had; the more they bought; the more everyone had; more they all wanted. And so the cycle went on. And still does.

Families, unsurprisingly, break down under such self-inflicted pressure, as working hours extend well beyond what

continued overleaf . . .

any family can sustain and people spend no time just having fun with all their STUFF, leaving millions of kids – and their parents – somewhat unhappy.

Wrong. All of this manic consumerism can have distressing affects on mental health, as illustrated here by Oliver James, in his excellent book, *Affluenza*:

> 66 *The Affluenza virus is a set of values which increase our vulnerability to psychological distress . . . Infection with the virus increases your susceptibility to the commonest mental illnesses: depression, anxiety, substance abuse and personality disorder . . . with younger generations more afflicted than older ones.* 99

Here are some stats to make you think before you next shop:

One in ten young people suffers from significant mental health problems according to the children's charity NCH.

The same charity said it found the prevalence of emotional problems and conduct disorders had doubled since the 1990s, citing studies of 8,000 children.

A report in 2008 by the Good Childhood Enquiry concluded that **failure to protect children from commercial pressures** is partly to blame for deteriorating mental health among young people.

Hundreds of submissions from children in the report showed that they **felt overwhelming pressure to keep up** with trends in clothes, music and computer games.

Adults are affected too: mixed anxiety and depression is the most common mental disorder in Britain, with almost nine per cent of people meeting the criteria for diagnosis, and there is growing evidence that disillusionment and pressure from our consumer-oriented society shoulders much of the blame for these conditions.

Shit, this all sounds nasty. Is there a cure?

Well, yes, I think there is one actually: it's free, anyone can have some and you can start it straight away. It's called *restraint*.

Turns out some people have already got here, hence the swell in the number of so-called New Aspirationals. This is a very annoying term for the quite sensible and growing number of people with expendable incomes who are at long last turning their backs on buying new, funky, expensive, covetable 'stuff' to, sup-posedly, make themselves feel good, and who now want some-thing simple, real and lasting instead, which actually *does* make them feel good. So instead of the latest computer gadget, they'll buy a water pump for a village in Africa. Instead of a new sofa, they'll plump for an allotment and watch their crops grow.

Yes, we may well snigger and scoff and say how horribly worthy and 'Good' it all sounds, but excuse me . . . since when was doing good actually bad?? That's just insane and bred of jealousy and feelings of deep insecurity and inadequacy. If you want to do a good thing, you just go right ahead and be happy about it!

See tips overleaf for how to beat the consumer disease . . .

After another coughing session, Granny continues to speak between audible sucks on what is presumably a cough sweet.

'If you buy your kids all the toys they could ever want, you are teaching them at the youngest, most influential age, that acquiring things equates to happiness.'

'The problem being,' I reply, rather wishing I could have a sweetie too, 'that when they discover this is just not true, because the Nintendo they got last week just isn't cool any more and they have to have the next 'must have' item, they get their first taste of deep dissatisfaction before they're old enough to even know what the word means?'

'I couldn't have put it better myself. And is that *really* what you want for your children?'

No, it's not. By a very twisted blow of fate, something might already have arrived that could help. It's a bitter medicine, but the most effective ones often are . . .

Yes, it's credit crunch time

As we've just learned, money is what enables us to buy too much for our kids. So what is going to happen now that global economics look set to have us all tightening our purse strings for the next few years? Well, the Credit Crunch and the recent onset of global recession have already had a noticeable effect, with many retailers noticing a dramatic downturn in sales of consumer goods. Could this have a positive effect on our kids, cut down on the toy explosion in many front rooms and force us to waste not, want not?

'Granny,' I ask, adding a mini Vespa to the overflowing box of toy trucks, car transporters, helicopters, skidoos, motorbikes, and

266

quad bikes that lurk all around me in my son's room, 'was this lack of toys all because of money? I mean, did you buy very little because you *couldn't*, or because you didn't think it was right?'

'Oh, I suppose it was a bit of both, but the money factor was very real.'

Granny's Pearl of Wisdom

We never bought anything when we couldn't afford it, Elizabeth, and I still don't to this day. It's a terrible way to live.

'What – *never*? Not even at Christmas?' (When the rest of us are driven into debt quicker than you can say 'another Bionicle for the collection please, Sir.')

'No, not even at Christmas; we went as far as we could go, but we certainly didn't splash out. There were always the school fees to pay in January, and then there were rates in February to worry about. I remember your grandfather used to go hurrying down on the 28th February and shove the cheque through the letter-box! If we could just tide things over until March, then a £50 cheque would come in from the University – we got a small allowance for each child back then – and we were OK for a while. That's how we lived – and how many, many people lived. And we were very lucky, because we had one holiday a year, for three weeks in the summer – that was luxury.'

'What, no credit cards?' I'm joking, and she knows it, but the subject is not one she finds humorous.

'Absolutely not. What nonsense – spending money you don't have. It all comes from advertising, I think. Advertising is so evil: they tempt you, and make you think you want to have it, and need to have it, and some poor fool's going to fall for it. And advertising to children should be stamped out immediately – that's what makes kids want everything they see. There was no 'must-have' anything when I was a child. None at all.'

'I'm guessing you didn't have what we call Pester Power, then?'

There's a rather loud Tsk! noise in my right ear.

'Oh no, no we absolutely did not. Of course the kids wanted toys sometimes, if friends had them or if they saw them in the toyshop. But we never had things laid out in shops that kids wanted – at eye level. There were no sweeties by the checkout, and magazines down at floor level like you see everywhere now and adverts everywhere from cereal boxes to the sides of buses. It's so unfair, unnecessary and unhelpful to you all.'

Pester Power

Pester Power crept its way into the Book of Common Parenting Parlance (which I haven't written yet, but I'm working on it . . .) somewhere between my own childhood and my children's. It's hard to say *exactly* when it arrived, but it's fairly clear that it was a gradual evolution in parallel with the rise in what is now almost relentless advertising targeted at young children, coupled with the relentless inability of their parents to say '*Mais non, ma chérie! Tu as déjà assez!*'

Where previous generations (that's us) were happy with a second-hand dolls' house or a hand-me-down BMX, now it's all

'I want this! I want that!', where 'this' and 'that' are inevitably brand new, very expensive, often fairly useless and, *most* often of all, what somebody else has.

If you are crumbling under the pressure of Pester Power, whether emotionally or financially, try, try, try to remember the following and put some of it into practice:

Advertising is designed to sell the maximum number of products whether or not they're suitable, worth the money, or of benefit to your child. You don't have to be the mug that falls for it.

This year's must-have toy is next year's reject. If you can sit it out for a month he won't want it any more.

Expensive doesn't mean better. We remember toys because of the fun we had playing with them rather than how much they cost. Cheap can be just as much fun.

Give your kids extra time and attention – this can really cut down demands for things.

Acknowledge the strength of their desires. 'Yes, that does look brilliant,' while preparing them for possible disappointment, 'but you do know you probably won't be able to have everything you want.'

Explain to older children how advertisements try to influence what we want and buy and try to make them understand that saying 'no' is empowering, not a sign of poverty or meanness!

Talk to older children about the cost of items and whether you can afford them, without worrying them. They can understand that money doesn't grow on trees, or just pop out of the wall.

'Come on now, Granny, you *must* have had some issues with my dad begging you to buy something, or pulling your sleeve and saying 'please, please, Mummy,' didn't you?'

I am thinking of my own kids' badgering to get something they want (it almost never works – I'm a real meany) and other children I see on a weekly basis in town, and I just cannot believe this didn't go on to some degree in the past.

Apparently it did: 'Well, of course they tried it on sometimes, but it never lasted long.'

Granny's Pearl of Wisdom

We had a simple rule, and that was 'I want doesn't get'. There. Simple and effective, and they didn't ask again.

'They didn't?!'

'No. They had to wait for their things. I remember your Aunt Alison wanted a red dressing gown – she really did. She wanted it so much you could almost see the dressing gown in her eyes. And she waited, and she got it, and was so, so happy with that until the day she grew out of it. The kids were all happy with what they got, because they waited for them.'

It's just possible that the credit crunch could see the resurgence of 'I want doesn't get'. We never shy away from saying to our kids 'We can't afford it, so you can't have it. Maybe some other time.' And, surprisingly, they seem to accept it perfectly happily. It's as if 'no' means 'maybe, keep trying' to them, but if we say 'We haven't the money,' that really is the end of the line and they accept it.

It's a shame it has to come about this way, but whatever works . . .

Playing 'green'

Another positive thing to come out of not having so much spare cash lying around is that people tend to go back to what people always did years ago – they stop being so wasteful. Really, in terms of Being Green our grandparents were streets ahead of us, and are probably all laughing into their sherry at how clever we think we are to have thought of Reuse; Recycle; Reduce first. The shame of it.

But any moves to waste and use less can only be a good thing, in environmental and emotional terms, so here are some ways your kids can get plenty of play opportunity, without trashing the planet or your wallet:

∾ GRANNY'S TIPS ∾

Share or swap toys with friends.

Don't buy it if you don't need it.

Join a toy library. Your kids can play with hundreds of toys and then give them back.

Look after the toys and pack away the good ones for your grandchildren . . .

Take unwanted toys to the church sale.

Recycle what you don't want any more – take it to a charity shop, sell it or turn it into something else. Just don't throw it away!

Make something. *Blue Peter* was my inspiration, but there are other programmes and magazines that have some fantastic ideas for making toys. The effort makes them all the more loved.

Find websites that reuse items (gumtree, freecycle etc).

Birthday parties – noooooooo!

The crème de la crème of over-indulgence where kids are concerned is the children's birthday party. Once a place for jelly and ice cream, now the showground for the grossest overkill.

When Granny was a child, parties were, weirdly enough, to celebrate a child's birthday. Nowadays they are to make other parents feel crap.

'Oh, we'd clear out a room in our house,' she reminisces down the crackly line, 'and hire trestle tables for all the sandwiches, jelly, sausage rolls and the like. We'd invite twenty or so friends, and play games. But only when we were little – by twelve or so we didn't want parties any more, and we'd just have a few friends over for a play.'

Even in the 1970s (my day, in case you're wondering) things weren't so different: a small group of kids in hand-made, smocking-heavy party frocks or Cowboy outfits played pass the parcel (the traditional kind where not everybody wins a Nintendo DS in every layer. Cripes . . .), musical bumps and pin the tail on the donkey in a beige sitting room to the tune of Simon and Garfunkle. Tea was sausages on sticks, triangle sandwiches and jelly; throw in a few presents, hand-made birthday cards, and a balloon or two and you've got yourself a party to be jolly pleased with.

And I was. Very pleased. (Except the one where Talia ate all the raisins and I cried.) But today my kids would accuse me of Complete Failure, Humiliation and Patheticness for laying on anything so simple, unadventurous and . . . cheap.

Or, just one minute . . . would they really?

Have we parents been duped, cajoled, pressurised and terrorised into putting on lavish birthday parties, when really, going back to something simpler would be just fine with everyone, and not, as we so fear, social suicide?

Let's take a look at the lavish status quo:

A party these days for a child above the age of two is likely to involve no fewer than three of the following: an entertainer (at about £150 a pop), a disco, a bowling alley, an ice rink, a make-over lesson, a private performance by the cast of *High School Musical*, a sleepover for thirty.

* The average amount of money spent on a child's birthday party in 2007 was £154 according to one survey.

* Presents cannot come in at less than the price of a weekend in Rome.

* *Everyone* is invited. Even the kids your child hates.

* Present opening can go on long into the night, by which time your child hasn't a clue who gave what, and has barely the strength to carry on paper-ripping any more.

* Everything is bought, coordinated and impressive: from the invitations to the table-ware, to the party bags to the thank you cards.

Reversing this trend

I have talked to more parents than I can count who agree with me that kids' birthday parties have gone way, way over the top. But still nobody seems to be *doing* anything about it! Well, now you can.

A few years back I decided to bring a bit of normality back to our children's birthday parties. First stop: we did away with shop-bought party bags. Nobody minded. Next, we stopped buying invitations, and went back to making them ourselves; the kids' friends all liked them. We have come right back to the simplest of parties for our kids, with a few friends, some games and activities or a trip i.e. ice skating or swimming for the older ones. Party bags (which we make ourselves, either during the party as an activity or by decorating brown paper ones from the local green-grocer) contain a slice of cake and a lollipop. Recently we've started to add a bag of seeds, thanks to a suggestion by a Green friend of mine. No electronic toys, no mountains of waste packaging and no sad faces. Presents are optional and shouldn't cost more than a fiver or thereabouts.

And guess what? The kids honestly don't mind at all. Even without hiring the Albert Hall, they seem quite able to have a good time if they are able to run about and play, particularly if there's a decent chocolate cake with candles at the end of it.

Granny says in her day it was even more spartan, with presents being turned down as well.

'We used to write on the invitations "No presents please". The children are getting enough as it is from their own parents, and it's not fair to ask people to buy a present for every party they go to – for some this is a real financial strain. It also teaches kids to expect something, rather than being happy that their friends have come to play.'

I'm not sure we're ever going to resurrect the 'no presents' idea, but wouldn't it be great? I'd save about £200 a year on tat for kids I don't even know! But there is a middle ground and you don't need to feel you can't inhabit it. Sure, the occasional two-hour sweat fest at Spy Masters is great occasionally, or swimming or a trip to an indoor play area. But just by cutting back, keeping it real and NOT trying to keep up with the obscenely wasteful Joneses you too can join the **SAVE OUR BIRTHDAY PARTIES** movement, and bring back some simplicity to the whole obscene affair.

If you don't, then please don't be surprised or expect any sympathy when your fifteen year old wants to hire a stretch limo and be kitted out with a new ball gown, a £100 hair do and a full make-up session to celebrate her GCSEs, where the rest of us had a tacky disco in the village hall. *You* set the standards from day one, so keep them real.

Sausage on a stick anyone?

Pocket money

Of course, one way kids can get around Mum and Dad not buying them things they want, is if they have some dosh of their own saved up somewhere. Then they can buy whatever they like, neatly dodging the 'no, you can't have it' barrier. I had pocket money, and my kids do too, only we forget to give it to them half the time. Oops.

Granny, however, thinks otherwise, and has something to say about pocket money. 'I had no pocket money as a child at all. Money was not part of a child's world. I got swimming money and money for the bus, and for sweeties at the end of the week or at weekends. I would never have asked for money – that would have been shameful. I knew I'd get money if I really needed something, and there were sweets and treats here and there, but no money of my own. Oh no.'

'And your own children? Did they get any spending money?'

I'm trying to imagine my dad, who seems to have been born with a depressingly astute business head screwed onto his shoulders, which unfortunately I haven't inherited at all, getting by with no pocket money. It wouldn't have taken him long to dream up a scheme to make money elsewhere: that's just his way. So pocket money was probably a good idea for him to keep him out of trouble, and his parents had obviously realised this.

'I think we did give them a little something, to teach them about saving up for something they really wanted. But you know,' I can hear her smiling wistfully at a memory long forgotten, but now recalled, 'I remember your Uncle Neil saying to me one day, with a sad, sad look in his eye: "But, Mummy, by the time I save up all my money, it's gone up in price and it's too expensive!" He was quite right too!'

Her laugh is warm and full even down the phone line, and I can picture her sitting in her chair, telly on in the background, stroking one of her cats and fondly remembering her now forty-eight-year-old, six-foot-four, rugby-playing son being so small and sweet once upon a time. I try not to think of my own little boy being so grown up (I daren't say 'old'... I'll get in trouble!) one day.

But I'm not so sure I agree with her on the pocket-money front. I think there are some very valuable things to be learned from being given your own few pennies every week as a child, and here they are:

—— LIZ'S POCKET-MONEY TIPS ——

Saving: Giving kids a little bit of pocket money teaches them that you have to save up for things you want. Good things come to those who wait, and all that . . .

Choosing: It also means they have to practise making *decisions*, which is an essential but oft overlooked life skill. Do they want the toy car *or* the £1 in their piggy bank for something another time? It's sometimes quite painful watching as they struggle to decide, but eventually they will and getting used to how it feels to spend and then not have the cash any more is quite useful for later on when it turns into 'now, do I buy the DVD or still have the £17.99 in my bank?' And worse . . .

Ownership: It also means that the thing they buy is all theirs – they chose it, they bought it, so they don't need to be grateful to anyone – they can just enjoy it!

Keep it small: Pocket money doesn't need to arrive on a lorry bearing gold bars. We give 50p for five years old, 60p for six years old and so on. Then we do a bit of a jump to about £1 from then on for a while, because let's face it – you can buy bugger all with 50p these days!

Do you really want it? When our children beg us for something, we can simply say 'You have the money – so if you want it, you buy it.' Nine times out of ten the response is: 'But I don't want to spend *my* money on it,' to which we simply say 'If you don't want it enough to spend your *own* money on it, don't expect me to spend my hard-earned cash on it either because you clearly don't want it all that much!' Ha.

It's good that Granny and I can disagree about some things – I don't want to be an old lady just yet! But I think her point that money is not a part of a child's life is a sensible one, and I'm going to try not to talk about how much things cost, or to talk about money much in front of them any more. They can have pocket money, and if I can't afford to buy them something I'll say so, but other than that I think kids and money are probably best kept apart as long as they can. There's plenty of time to fret about savings (or the lack of them) when we're grown up. Help . . .

The sound from my kitchen of small hands trying to open a biscuit tin reminds me that dinner time is fast approaching, so I begin to wrap up. If my kids get hungry all semblance of good manners vanishes in a flash, and we have a house full of murderous lunatics before I've had a chance to open the fridge. 'Granny, I'll have to go now. The troops are getting restless and hungry.'

'Oh well, we can't have *that*! You've got some lovely children there, Elizabeth. You make sure they eat properly, as they're all growing so much.'

I hear a cup of something being stirred.

'Will do! Speak soon, Granny, and you look after that cough, will you?'

'Auch – away with you. I'm fine!'

And with that we leave it for another day, and I go back to the madness of my family life, thinking about all I've heard today. Now then, is there any toy I can find for them to play with while I make their dinner, I wonder . . .

∞ GRANNY'S TIPS ∞

I want doesn't get. You don't have to say this in an angry way, just be firm and consistent.

Let them use their imagination, rather than always playing with a toy that has one action.

Less is more – they don't need every toy in the shop!

Leave some toys out for kids to play with any time.

Don't buy toys if you can't afford them. The kids don't mind.

—— LIZ'S TIPS ——

Keep the numbers down. We moved house recently and almost all of my children's toys were packed in boxes for well over six months. They literally had a couple of games, some paper, their Sylvanians, a few swords and shields and books. And you know what? They didn't miss the other toys AT ALL. In fact, I honestly began to wonder if we actually *needed* any of the rest.

Rotate toys. When I did finally get around to unpacking a few items, they played with them as though they were new, and were so excited to see things they had previously completely ignored. If you can do this, and put away some toys for six months or so, you can have the 'new toy' sensation without having to buy anything new at all, and even better – these toys bring back some memories.

Surprise them with a completely unexpected treat every so often. It will have a much bigger impact than the times when they do expect it.

Chapter Ten

...AND DON'T COME BACK TILL TEATIME

A train ride

Two months later I get a call from my mum to say (among a great number of other things, all relayed without pause for breath) that Granny has got to go back to the hospital in Dunblane where she had her operation for the follow-up appointment, which will reveal if things are ticking along nicely in the foot/leg department. If yes, she'll be free to go home. If no, she stands a very good chance of losing her bad toe, or possibly her foot, and possibly *even* her leg from the knee down. Unless it belongs to a chair, a leg should definitely have a foot at the end of it in my book, and any amputating at all would be very, very bad news, as it would see the end of Granny's physical, thus emotional, independence. And we all know what that can do to independent-minded people . . .

At a frightening, uncertain time like this, Granny needs moral support, and so I decide to take the delightful GNER train from

London up to the cold, windy, granite-hard town of Dunblane. It's been seven years since I've been without my children for more than one day, so to say I'm a little bit excited at the prospect is an understatement of FF-cup proportions.

The journey itself proves to be almost as pleasant as having a limb removed:

First, an hour in the Filthiest, Most Overcrowded Carriage Known To Man; then twenty minutes freezing to death on Platform 2 waiting for the 09.00 to Edinburgh with a crowd of pasty people who appear to be suffering from either secondary pneumonia or Asian flu; finally, discovering that my reserved seat is next to that of a man emitting more alcohol from the pores of his face than an England football supporter could drink in a week, and who slurs garbled stories at me for 200 miles, before falling asleep somewhere near Newcastle and dribbling on my shoulder.

But my greatest interest is not in the pissed drooler – it's with my travelling companions opposite. There, sitting at a table, is a family of two young kids and a visibly exhausted dad. Now, you think I'm going to say how horribly behaved they were. How rude and loud and typically obnoxious. But I'm not. Forget scenes of screaming, hitting, swearing and 'If you do that again I'll smack you.' This Wonderdad has pens, paper, magazines, comics, and more patience, humour and generosity than most parents could squeeze into a lifetime. His kids are happy and friendly, and chat with a kind old lady who has joined them at Ely.

I decide that this family is just about the best example of how a family should travel together I've ever seen – and that I miss mine so badly already I wouldn't mind jumping off at the next station and going straight back home again.

We curse our children, our family life, our husbands, our jobs and our whole set-up so often, that it's easy to convince ourselves life really is that shit.

It's not until you leave it behind for a while, and think about how lucky you are, that you can say 'I *like* having kids, and I *like* being a parent. And I'm bloody well going to do the best job I can of it.'

I vow to try and remember this when Charlie then whacks me on the back of the head with a plastic Samurai sword . . .

When I finally stumble out of the train carriage seven hours after setting off, Granny is waiting at the station in her car. And whaddya know? She looks fantastic! Smiling, with a little colour in her hollow cheeks – which on a freezing December day in Dunblane is saying something – and a clean, ironed shirt beneath her cosy jumper, I see plenty of signs that this lady has turned a corner and is feeling much, *much* better than even a few weeks before. I get a big hug and a kiss, and then a car ride that would make anything on the high mountainous passes of the Himalayas seem relaxing, to my aunt's house just a mile or so away.

If we make it that far alive, this is going to be a lovely break.

Kids in the community

I sleep like a baby (which is understandable, since it's the first time in years that I haven't shared a bed for any length of time with a bony, wriggly toddler) and by the time I get downstairs the next morning, breakfast is underway and Granny is standing in the kitchen talking with much animation and gusto to her daughter, my Aunt Alison, while munching on toast. Considering she still has an unbearably painful foot and is due to go to the hospital in two days to receive what could be devastating news,

I am put to shame by the fact that, after a ten-hour sleep, I feel and look like a wet dishcloth.

I am immediately offered more food than I could eat in a week, and plump for toast and a cup of instant. On the cluttered stove, a huge pot of mouth-watering chicken with lemon, ginger and cashew nuts is already bubbling away: yet more remorse for my lie-in.

My come-uppance comes, however, when it's discovered that the milk has run out and it falls to the last person out of bed to go to the shop and get some more.

As I saunter back ten minutes later, dairy produce in hand, I wonder how many children I know who just pop down the road to run such a simple errand? Obviously, I'm not technically a child any more – though I do behave like one with worrying frequency – but when I *was* a child, I did go to the shops by myself, and walk to the school bus stop, and cycle by myself into town to my violin lessons, and latterly to the pub. (The cycle home was always a little wobbly . . .)

But it's something you see very little of these days: children walking about by themselves doing odd jobs or running errands. They are always chaperoned, watched, protected by a parent, a nanny, a teacher, a herd of friends. But *why*? What are we all so afraid of, why are so few children allowed any freedom in the community any more, and how are they ever going to cope with the simplest tasks, such as finding their way around a strange town, if they never get any practice?

And most importantly: what can we do to allow them some freedom once again to enjoy their childhood and to learn about the world around them – safely, but in relative freedom?

Questions, questions. Time for some answers.

THE BIG RISK DILEMMA
OF PARENTS TODAY

How much risk we should allow our children to take, and how much they should be allowed to go out by themselves in the community is a subject that I know worries a lot of parents these days, and many of us feel torn:

On the one hand we want them to experience some sense of freedom and to learn how to 'get on' in the world without Mummy wiping their nose every five minutes.

On the other, we are worried about 'bad things' happening to them, feel that there is more of a chance of this than when we were young, and feel we should protect them.

66 *I just don't feel that I can let Jake walk to school by himself – he would have to cross two roads and it's quite a built-up area. I don't know who lives in the houses he walks past, so I'd rather be with him. It feels silly, but if anything happened I'd never forgive myself.* 99

Claire, mother of Jake, eight and Archie, five

66 *I had much more freedom than I give my own children. I don't know why, but I feel there are more risks out there now. If it's not traffic it's weirdoes, but it makes me sad because deep down I know I should be letting them learn about the world more, by themselves.* 99

**Helen, mother of Sophia, ten, Robert, eight
and William, four**

My hope is that by talking to Granny, who was raised with far more freedom than our smothered 'cotton wool' children are allowed now, I might find some sensible, workable answers to this dilemma. It's a big hope . . .

As we take our toast through to the next room where the comfy chairs are and Granny sinks into hers with a relieved 'Aaaaah!' I bring up the question of risk.

'Granny, you know we '*modern*' parents like to fuss over our kids quite a lot, and worry all the time that they're OK, and not let them out on their own even, say to fetch some milk . . .'

'Well, only because so many '*modern*' parents are hardly ever there at home looking after them. But anyway. Yes?'

Ouch. It's not the best start, but she is partly right and I make a note to come back to that in a while . . .

'Right, well anyway. Is it a new phenomenon – all this worrying and protecting our kids and not letting them take any risks? You know – all these 'cotton wool kids' they talk about?'

A piece of hot, buttered toast comes to rest in mid air, held by a gently trembling hand.

'Is it a *new* phenomenon? Yes, of course it is. We didn't fuss and molly-coddle our kids like people do now. And I wasn't wrapped up in cotton wool – my mum was too busy and too sensible! Oh, but it's just everywhere nowadays: kids can't even walk to school on their own for fear of being mugged or kidnapped or I don't know what else – and the irony is, it's so bad for them!'

Granny's Pearl of Wisdom

If we watch our children all the time it just makes them more vulnerable later. They have to learn to stand on their own two feet, or how will they cope in the real world one day?

She takes a big shlug of tea and settles into reminiscing mode, shaking her head a little.

'I remember all of my kids getting into the most dreadful scrapes, falling out of trees, cutting themselves on brambles and playing on their own in the street. Your father, particularly . . . If two kids played on a swing and one got hit on the head, oh, it'd bleed like a stuck pug for a while. But it was part of growing up and *learning* – and they grew up just fine.'

'So you think they should be allowed more freedom to climb trees and take risks?'

She leans forward and I get the full Granny Eyes treatment.

'If you want to climb a tree you go and climb a blimmin' tree! That's what I think. Just go, and fall and hurt yourself and then you'll know for next time to be more careful – or just not to climb that one. If you are a reasonably caring parent you make sure there are no obvious dangers to your children, and you always know where they are anyway, without hovering over them all the time.'

Ah, an unintentional but perfectly timed reference to what is known as Helicopter Parents. This exasperating breed is so-called due to their habit of 'hovering' around their children, making sure they know what they're up to at every second of the day. When the kids are little it's never letting them out of their

Helicopter Parents' sight. As they get older it's texting, calling and emailing them twenty times a day. 'R U OK?' Where are you? What are you doing? Why aren't you calling me to tell me?? That kind of stifling thing. Being of a generous nature, I'm prepared to believe that all this helicoptering has entirely good intentions, but this is surely a dreadful way to go about raising children?

Where is their privacy? Where is their sense of being alone and working things out for themselves? Being there 24/7 for our kids not only makes them desperately dependent on us, it also gives them a tendency to treat us as their servants. How many houses have you been in where the telly is tuned to a children's channel, there are toys everywhere and mum and dad haven't had a night out for six months because they're so busy running rings around their kids, taking them to extra classes, sleepovers and birthday parties or are just too afraid to leave them with a babysitter? All of this attention is almost certainly very well meant, but it doesn't make kids any happier, show them we love them any more or help them to grow up. Sometimes a little 'benign neglect' can be a good thing – why can't we just butt out and let them BE?!

My mum is a control freak!

One of the reasons many parents have become so unable to let their kids go, is because we are a generation of control freaks. Every moment of every day of our lives is planned and executed to minute-precision, and if anything should throw this the tiniest bit off course, we have a full scale panic attack.

From ordering a coffee (double tall, skinny, soya, dry, extra hot cappuccino with hazelnut sauce and low-calorie chocolate on the top) to buying jeans (bootleg, high waisted, flared, skinny, boyfriend, straight-legged . . .) to planning the evening's enter-tainment (woe betide the programme controller who makes a last-minute change to the schedule), control freaks are so highly organised it leaves them paralysed if anything should not go according to the detailed plan. This, in turn, makes them less and less able to deal with little surprises, and so the cycle continues. I'm a bit of a control freak myself, and have been known to throw a small fit when they run out of my favourite porridge in Sainsbury's. *No porridge*?! But, but . . . now my day is ruined!

BUT KIDS CANNOT OPERATE LIKE THIS. They can't be planned: by their very nature they are unpredictable, changeable and impossible to control – that's the beauty of kids, so why try to quash this wonderful unpredictable freedom?

Because we're not used to it, that's why. What's so sad, is that trying to control what our kids do all the time – by adopting what is sometimes referred to as 'Scheduled Parenting', where every-thing they do is planned, timetabled, scheduled and organised as part of a grand 'plan' for the day/week/month/year. Ugh! – is killing the very essence of their childhood, and if we could just chill out, let go and see what they come up with next (within safe boundaries) they would be a lot happier and healthier. And so would we. Not only that but when they finally leave home – running! – they'll stand a chance of coping with whatever a day at college or work might throw at them. Assuming Mummy doesn't have their tutors, lecturers and employers on her speed-dial, as seems increasingly to be the case . . .

Of course, there is room for a *little* organising of kids' lives: if you just say to a child of five 'You do whatever you like all day today – we have no plans' they'll probably spend ten minutes having a whale of a time doing something you disapprove of, before slipping into 'I'm bored and I've got nothing to *doooooo*!' behaviour quite fast. Some guidance is very helpful here: suggest a trip to the park, get a toy out that they haven't played with for ages, go and make something together in the garden. It's the level of obsessive organising that has got out of control.

HOW TO STOP IT

Confront it. The only way to break this nasty habit of wrapping your children up in cotton wool all the time is to take a leap, confront it head on, and TAKE A SMALL, CALCULATED RISK. Let your school-aged child pop down the road to post a letter. Let her make her own toast, if she's old enough to do it safely. Say 'yes' when he asks to walk to school with a (responsible!) friend if it's within a safe mile or so. Then, when the Worst Thing in the World Ever *doesn't* happen, you'll realise how silly you were to worry, gain huge confidence that things can turn out OK and feel able to move on to the next level. And your children will be delighted!

Let go of your security blanket. One of the things that control freaks rely on are small habits that they use for emotional support: always having a mobile phone on them; writing lists; looking at the clock a lot; having routines and strict schedules. If you can try to rid yourself of some of these, for example reading stories *before* bathtime instead of your usual 'after bathtime' once in a while, or stopping off in the park on the way home on a whim, even though that wasn't the 'plan', then you can slowly start to enjoy yourself a lot more and so will your kids. Routine is important but rigid over-controlling isn't.

There is, of course, the antidote to Helicopter Parents, called Absent Parents. Granny has a thing or two to say about them as well:

'When my children were growing up, even though we didn't watch over them twenty-four hours a day we were still *responsible* for them, and *present*. I was at home: I was there when they got home, and I was there when they left for school. I didn't "mother" them in the smothering sense: I was mothering them simply by being *there*. That's what so many kids miss: having a parent at home when they need them. Not when their parents choose to be there.'

Granny's Pearl of Wisdom

If parents spend very little time with their kids, it's no wonder they don't let them take any risks: they hardly know their children, far less know what they are capable of. Spend time with your kids – have fun together and learn something new from them each day.

It would take a very severe workaholic indeed not to see the value of what Granny has just said. Children do need their parents to be around; not in their face telling them what to do, but just being there. Even if you're busy doing other jobs in the background, at least you're *there* providing a sense of security and constancy, which are both essential for happy childhoods.

But this isn't the 1940s any more; many families need two incomes and it's far too easy to come down hard on all of us parents. The realities of the modern world are that many of us live in families where *both* parents have to work in order to pay the extortionate bills that fly through the letterbox every month. And, let's be honest here, many of us Working Mum types actually love our jobs because it allows us to be not just Mummies, but also thinking, intelligent beings who are able to talk about more than just the finer points of nappy disposal and playdates. Crazy, I know – but we can! And don't worry: it doesn't matter if it's *you* at home every day after school or a nanny instead – so long as your child has someone *with* them who they feel safe with, and who keeps an eye on them.

Where the problem can lie is if you have reached the point where you're spending so little time actively looking after your kids that you don't even know how able they are to look after themselves, and so racked with guilt at being away so much that you daren't let them out of your sight lest a passing bee puts an end to the only hour in the day you actually have together, you've really missed a trick and it's time to make some changes.

Granny's Pearl of Wisdom

Remember that observing kids is as important as teaching and telling them. Watch them, and let them take gradually bigger steps to be able to stand away from you and survive by themselves.

Community parenting

One of the biggest changes in our society in the last fifty years that has made letting kids take small risks outside the home very difficult has been the breakdown of the community. Unless you live in a Mister Men book and own one of the lovely detached properties on Friendly Street, in Happy Town, the chances are that your front door remains pretty damned shut, chained and bolted most of the time. In fact, it's also depressingly likely that you don't know the people living next door to you very well, if at all.

This is a far cry from how things used to be, in many towns and cities, and Granny remembers it well.

'We didn't have to worry about our children playing out on the streets, not just because there was less traffic but because other people in the neighbourhood used to look out for your children too. There was a real sense of community and we all made sure *all* the children were safe.'

Granny's Pearl of Wisdom

If you shut yourself off from the community and don't know your neighbours, you make it almost impossible for your children to feel safe as part of a community – to feel looked after, and a part of something bigger than themselves.

This reminds me of a beautiful and wise phrase that I absolutely love:

It takes a whole village to raise a single child.

Children should be 'raised' not only by their parents but also by those people who live near them; people in their community. We *all* have a responsibility to look out for *all* the children we know, and to make sure they are safe and happy – to step in if they're causing trouble, to help if they are hurt or in trouble. To look after them all, basically.

Sadly, this doesn't seem to apply to suburbs, cities and busy roads, but it doesn't need to be as bad as it has become. We *can* trust each other more and create a sense of community wherever we live – it just takes some effort on everyone's part.

Granny's Pearl of Wisdom

You must make the effort to get to know the people around you. It can take as little as a nod and a 'hello' to start, but otherwise you lose all sense of community very fast.

But can such community parenting really work in practice for most of us any more? It's all very well in theory but half the people I know don't even *know* their neighbours, let alone feel they would keep a lookout for their kids. There has been a tremendous loss of community in the last few decades, brought about by a number of factors such as, from people moving frequently, working further away from home, living in bigger houses or on busier streets where front doors are closed and neighbours hardly know one another.

The 'village' spirit lives on, however in, erm, villages, such as the one Granny inhabits.

COMMUNITY PARENTING OR
NOSY NORAHS?

~~~

We are all pretty paranoid about Nosy Norahs in this country. Between net curtains twitching, peeping Toms peeping or interfering old busybodies muttering under their breath, we're a nation of nosy neighbours who gossip-monger and bitch behind closed doors but rarely actually come out and say anything directly.

Well, where raising children is concerned, I'm not sure that the British habit of turning a blind eye is always the best option.

How many times has a news story come out about a child who has been dreadfully treated at the hands of cruel, neglectful parents, only for it to turn out that people had had their suspicions for months but nobody thought to say anything? How many times have *you* noticed something about a child's behaviour that just makes you think that doesn't seem quite *right*? How many times have you walked on by when a child has been cruelly treated by a parent on the street?

I had such a dilemma recently, involving a child at my children's school, and I didn't know what to do: ignore the concerning signs I observed as, basically, they're absolutely none of my business. Or tactfully say something to the headmistress who could then make enquiries, because it's my responsibility as a citizen to do so?

Having wrestled with my conscience for a few days, and after asking a number of other parents about it, who all agreed

continued overleaf . . .

that I *should* speak up, I decided I had to. Whether it did any good or not I don't know, but I do know that it felt like the right thing to do and I hope everything is OK for that child now.

Even on a much lower level we can and should look out for all the children who live in our communities far more than we do. If this were to happen, it would become OK to leave them in the park for ten minutes, knowing that a responsible adult would help if someone got stuck up a climbing frame, instead of turning away and pretending they can't see it, lest helping out could somehow land them in trouble.

It's the fear of litigation, and of violence, that has made us all terrified to intervene – a change that is costing our children dearly, and one we must try to resist as much as we can.

'In a village, looking out for all kids still holds good, you know? A child here knows he'll be seen and reported if he's up to no good. They still manage to get into trouble, but there is a sense that they have to try and be well behaved, or they'll get told off by the whole village, not just their parents, and that's a much greater deterrent. *And*, not only are they respectful towards the adults, they also behave properly because they never know who's going to spot them causing trouble!'

I put it to Granny that not everybody is lucky enough to live in a beautiful village where everyone looks out kindly for everyone else. What can the rest of us do – those who live in towns and cities?

'It's a terrible shame if you have to live in a place where you don't feel a part of a supportive community. But you know you mustn't give up: you can still *try* more than you do to communicate with your neighbours and get to know them. Just knock on the door; invite them in for a cup of tea; smile at people who live near you. It doesn't take much, but it can change everything. For your children's sake.'

∾ *GRANNY'S TIPS* ∾

When you're gardening outside, say hello to passers-by.

Talk to people in the street who have lived there for years. They'll know everybody, and put you in touch with others you could know better.

Go and knock on the neighbour's door and make sure they know who your children are, and your children know them and theirs.

Make the effort. It's your community – you have to make it work!

We moved house recently and have done that classic thing of saying hi to a few new neighbours – especially those who might be able to offer sugar in times of need – but then not making any effort to really get to know them better. Now, after talking with Granny, I'm using some of her tips to change this. We've had the neighbours round for a few dinners, we've had some chats with the elderly lady opposite and in general I'm trying to be much more vocal in front of my kids about living in a *community*, rather than a house. So far, so very much improved, and they walk off to school by themselves, feeling safe, not worried.

Fear of other people

There is, of course, another reason that so many of us worry about letting our children out alone. Fuelled by the screaming, relentless tabloid headlines, scare stories and fear, it is the very thorny issue of STRANGER DANGER; the danger (perceived or otherwise) of abduction, attacks and, increasingly in parents' worried minds, of paedophiles.

But is this really new? Didn't people worry about other people harming their kids when Granny was young? I put it to her, and her answer is categorical and without hesitation:

'Absolutely not. That kind of thing [child abduction] was unthinkable in my day. We had never even *heard* of paedophiles when I was a child. Never ever.'

Hold the front page – you *what*? You'd never *heard* of them? Much as I'd love to believe it, this seems about as likely as saying that no women thought their bottoms were fat. There *must* have been paedophiles when she was young. They didn't just pop up overnight with the invention of the miniskirt or porn on TV. Sad to say it, but adults have been abusing children since time began, surely.

'But Granny, paedophiles haven't only existed in the last twenty years. They must have been around in your day, don't you think?'

She's not going to budge on this one. And neither is the piece of toast now wedged between my back teeth.

'Well, that may be true,' she says, unconvinced, 'and there may well have been some bad things that happened, but we didn't know about them. I honestly can say that, as a child, I never heard about a child being taken, or attacked. There was no such terror and worry for us as children, or when we were parents.'

Granny's Pearl of Wisdom

Ignorance is sometimes bliss, and the less you torment yourself by reading every last detail of dreadful incidents the more you can get on with living your life and not being paralysed with fear.

Now that's *certainly* a good point we should all bear in mind more often. If I didn't know about every incident of child abuse or sexual assault I would be a lot calmer about letting my girls walk to school by themselves. The 'not knowing' wouldn't mean the chances of anything bad happening would be any greater or smaller, nor that I would be less responsible; I'd still make sure they knew about safety, not taking sweets from strangers and all that stuff we were told, which still applies today. But I wouldn't be constantly on paedo-alert, in abduction fever, *frightened* of bad things happening, and thus – and here's the nub of it – passing this unsettling and unnecessary fear on to my children. The media want to report every unsettling incident – but we don't have to read it all.

Nor do we have to search the internet for the gory details of awful crimes, or leave the twenty-four hour news channels on as permanent background terror monitors.

Of course you'll hear about some bad incidents but try to keep them in perspective and don't store every bloody detail about them all with your children.

THEN AND NOW: COULD YOU?
WOULD YOU?

———————⧟———————

Most over-thirties you know have memories of something unsupervised and potentially 'risky' they did as kids. You know, the kind of dumb-arse, 'almost get killed but escape by the skin of your buck teeth' stuff you did on a regular basis. Stories of dangerous escapades on rooftops, making secret potions in back bedrooms out of shampoo and food colouring, getting lost in the woods for five hours and eventually having to hitch a lift back with a sword-bearing tiger trainer. Once perfectly ordinary childhood capers, in other words. (Well, almost.) These stories are usually recounted with a sad 'you can't do that nowadays' expression, before the teller heads down the pub to drown the nostalgia in strong lager.

Here's one of mine: I used to cycle two miles away from my house in Oxford when I was about eleven years old, down a narrow, very isolated country lane with fields all around and a stream running down one side. I would bring a fishing net, a glass jar and a book about marine life – yes, I really was *that* cool – and spend hours lying on my stomach on an old iron bridge that crossed the brook, fishing out all manner of revolting water creatures and examining them with a magnifying glass. I was completely alone; I had no mobile phone or way of contacting my parents; and I was deliriously happy with my pond-skaters and snails. My parents knew where I was, and what time I was due home, and it was a dream-like place of escape, adventure and learning for me.

So the big question for me as a parent in the twenty-first century is this: would I let my daughter do this now?

It's a really tricky one for me to answer because, like most parents I know, I want to say 'yes', but if I'm honest I'm not sure if I'd feel comfortable about it. I mean, there are enough 'what if's to scare the beejeebies out of the lot of us: what if some crazy lunatic comes along and tries to take her away? What if a paedophile comes and rapes her? What if she falls in the stream, knocks her head and drowns? What if a car comes off the road and runs her over? What if a whiff of a superbug flies across the field and up her nose and she dies of an incurable viral disease? What if . . .

These are the kinds of ridiculous and highly improbable (or even impossible) scenarios that fly immediately through the minds of many otherwise perfectly sane parents when faced with a question like this, and we are left torn about what to do.

Well, what would YOU do?

I put this modern struggle between what we did then and what we feel we can do now to Granny, and am surprised to hear that she sympathises with our situation more than she'd previously let on.

'Look, we weren't foolish about letting our children go out alone. We did worry about them, and we didn't let them do things we thought were dangerous or silly. And of course, things changed as time went along: I didn't let Neil [the youngest of her four children] have as much freedom as I did your father [the eldest]. There were more cars, for a start, but there was also a new violence creeping in that made us more wary.'

Ha! And there was me thinking they just opened the back door, waved goodbye and hoped to see their kids again some time without so much as a flutter of parental concern. More fool me. I feel like an excited archaeologist who has unearthed evidence of the very earliest example of Cotton Wool Man. (Or Parent.)

The last taste of Marmite dissolves in my mouth along with any notion that all Olde Worlde Parents were fundamentally neglectful.

'So you *did* worry, just as we do. I guess the difference is that you let them do it, and we don't. Maybe we're just silly!'

Granny puts a cold, old hand on mine and smiles.

Granny's Pearl of Wisdom

You're not silly. Times have changed and you mustn't feel too bad about being more cautious. Protective is sensible: overprotective is not.

A new kind of risk: the internet
Be informed, not afraid

Every time brings with it new inventions, and, just as vertiginous heels can lead to broken ankles and alcohol results in liver failure (eventually), so a good number of these developments have their own new dangers. In our time, one of many new bringers of Good and Evil is the internet.

Any parent who has a computer in their house that is connected to the web needs to know about the potential risks to their children when they're playing around on it.

DON'T BE AFRAID, BE INFORMED

Secrecy: A child doesn't always know with whom he or she is interacting. Children may *think* they know, but unless it's a school friend or a relative, they really can't be sure.

Sex: In 2001, in a US report on online victimisation, one in five children said they had been sexually solicited on the internet.

Abuse: In 2002 the number of reports to the Internet Watch Foundation of child abuse on the internet increased by sixty-four per cent.

Antisocial issues: The number of violent, racist and hate websites as well as gambling sites is increasing steadily and there is a strong belief among many educators and psychologists that looking at violence on a screen, and behaving violently, are linked.

Data protection is another important issue for the safety of children using the internet. Children should not be asked to give out personal information like their names, telephone numbers, addresses or names of their schools in order to be able to participate in games or enter other areas. It is possible that someone dangerous could use the information to try and find them in the real world.

Now you see it . . . One of the key risks of using the internet, email or chat services is that children may be exposed to inappropriate material. This could be pornographic, hateful or violent in nature, it might encourage activities that are dangerous or illegal or it might be just age-inappropriate or biased.

continued overleaf . . .

This may all sound quite scary, but the internet is, despite its dangers, still a wonderful tool for children to use – if you use it wisely. There is a simple solution to the problem of kids getting into trouble online, and it's the same solution as there has ever been to counteract any potential harm: **calculate the risks, and take steps to minimise them**.

* Have the computer in a family room, and never, ever in a child's bedroom.

* Know what your child is doing on the computer at all times. You don't have to loom over them to do this. There are systems that log all chat-sites visited so you can check where they've surfed. Clever.

* Talk about what they do there, friends they have chatted with online etc.

* Use a child-friendly search engine, like www.askforkids.com, www.yahooligans.com, www.kidsclick.org or www.factmonster.com.

* Assuming that your child will, at some point, get onto an adult search engine like Google, then you must **get parental control installed**. For example, Google allows Safe Search Filtering that can be accessed by selecting 'Preferences' from its homepage. MSN's Safe Search Filtering is accessed via the Settings page and Yahoo's through the Search Preferences page. Alta Vista's filter can be found on the Family Filter Setup page and Lycos' on the Advanced Search Filters page. **The best filter, however, remains a parent's own good judgement**.

* Limit the time to twenty minutes a day for younger children, and an hour or so for older kids.

* Keep the dialogue open. If you demonise the internet as a whole, your kids will want to go on it more and more, just to piss you off.

Granny stretches slowly down to put her empty coffee cup on the floor and then lies right back into the deep sofa, her bad leg stretched out in front of her, and sighs.

'When your father was wee it wasn't such a problem: he'd take the bus on a Saturday to his music lessons aged eight or so, all on his own. It's a long way, and then he'd have to cross a main road. And he used to come home on his own from school on the bus, and spend hours collecting conkers on the way home. I wasn't worried then, and there was little fear of other people and of violence.

'But by the time he and Alison left school things had really changed: I remember her being warned by her university teachers not to go home alone, but to come out of classes as a group and go home together. And that was in 1963. Then the worry really set in, parents started to give their children less freedom, and I can only imagine it's much worse today.'

It is. 'Worry' has reached epic proportions and it must be about time we tried to calm our fears – rational or not – a notch or two before we raise a generation of kids who can't cross a road without a ten-man entourage.

Where to start? With some statistics, of course.

Abductions and sexual assaults – the facts, and how we miscalculate the risks

It's surprisingly difficult to say whether incidents of child-abduction, abuse and so on have actually gone up at all in the last fifty years.

The first problem is one of recording: the way incidents are recorded has changed over time with some including any child abduction, others omitting those where the child is killed, as that counts as murder and so on.

Then there is also the issue that by far the majority of children who are abducted are actually taken by a member of their family, and this is often not for sinister reasons. It could be to help a child who is in a dangerous home situation.

What *is* clear is that the number of internet sites featuring child pornography has increased infinitely (there were none at all until about ten years ago) but again this doesn't mean there are more paedophiles; it just means there are more paedophiles on the internet. Hmmmmm. All very fuzzy so far.

We humans are good at many things, but we are inherently *dreadful* at weighing up risks and calculating probabilities. (How do you think Casinos survive . . .?)

Here are two classic examples:

A child is far more likely to be killed by a car than murdered by a stranger passing in the street, and yet increasing numbers of parents choose to drive their kids to school to keep them 'safe'. Just think about it for a moment. It's totally flawed logic, yet it seems to make sense in some way to many.

A child hit by a car at twenty miles an hour is going to come off a lot less well than one who is flashed at in the local park (who may well suffer emotionally, but at least won't be taken to hospital in an ambulance and possibly never be able to walk again . . .) so we should be far more concerned about traffic than sexual perverts and child-rapists, of which there are actually very few. But we fear bad things happening to our children at the hands of others so much that we cannot get this fear out of our minds because of the stories we've heard in the news or watched in films. Somehow a car accident seems like just that – an accident that is unpredictable and unavoidable, yet keeping away from paedophiles and other horrors seems more in our control because we *can* keep our kids away from strangers if we try hard enough. And so we over-react and rarely let them out alone in case the highly unlikely happens

So, as you can see, it is very hard to get any clear sense of whether such incidents really have increased or not. What *is* clear is that our concern about them has increased dramatically, and that's stopping children from being allowed to play freely.

66 *Research commissioned by Play England for Playday 2007 showed that 71 per cent of adults played in their local streets every day as children, compared to 21 per cent of children today. The perception is that the world has become a more dangerous place for children. Some perceptions are well founded, such as the threat from traffic. Others, such as the widespread fear of stranger danger, are less justified. These factors, along with a decline in public playable space and reduction of acceptance of children and young people in public spaces, are all hindering children's opportunities to play. Playing is an essential part of growing up. Children both need*

*and want to push their boundaries in order to explore their limits
and develop their abilities. Adventurous play that both challenges
and excites children helps instil critical life skills. 80 per cent of
adults agree that children should be free to experience adventurous
play even if it puts them at risk of minor injury [and] we are calling for better, more imaginative and more widespread measures to
allow children to experience risk in play.* "

Adrian Voce, Director of Play England

If such a large number of parents say they want their kids to
be able to play more freely and take more risks, how come this is
exactly what so many parents don't let their kids do?

Here are some suggestions both from me and from many
other parents I've talked to about this issue:

We hear more news stories about attacks on children, muggings,
gangs and so on, so our *perception* of the risks is exaggerated and
our concern is constantly reinforced.

Internet news websites allow us to re-read the horror stories as
many times as we like and also find out lots of frightening and
detailed information about paedophiles and potential wrong-
doers in our area, while we sit in our own homes. This feels inva-
sive and directly relevant to *us*.

There is a serious drinking problem in young people today and
this has led to more violent behaviour being visible on the streets.
Even though this doesn't directly affect younger children, it leads
to a feeling among parents that society is more dangerous and
our kids are more at risk in it.

There is more traffic and cars go faster than they used to.

We feel guilty that we work so much that the fear of something happening to our kids is wildly exacerbated and is partly a fear of even more guilt for not looking after them enough.

We fear the criticism of other parents, and of the public at large if something bad, however minor, happens to our kids while we weren't with them.

Many things in our lives are so transient and have little real value, so the importance of our children and their welfare is heightened, as they are the only things that really matter, for which we have full responsibility and for whom we should provide stability and constancy. Losing them is the worst thing any parent can imagine, and so we fear it constantly.

While some of these factors are very real (increased traffic, binge drinking) many others are either imagined (hearing more stories on the news about muggings does not mean there *are* more muggings) or brought about by our increased levels of stress in a busy, fast, insecure world.

What is not in question, however, is how our perception of violence in cities, and our consequent actions in certain situations or tendency to avoid certain situations, has changed. Here's an example of something that happened to me recently, which you might identify with:

I was at a bus stop one morning where three women (and I use the term 'women' in its loosest possible sense. They were barely human, in fact) were abusing a two-year-old boy in full view of everyone passing by. They pulled him along the pavement by his tiny, soft arms, shouting at him to 'Stand still!!', 'Shu' up' and 'Come 'ere!' and the eyes in his grubby, pale, frightened face, said it all: this was the norm for him, and he was living in terror daily. It was shocking, truly sickening and frightening and all I could think was 'How can we all stand here doing NOTHING about this?'

I wanted so badly to march confidently up to them and tell them to leave the poor kid alone. But here's the thing: I was there with my two young children, and, truthfully, I was frightened of what could happen to *them* if these monstrous people turned on them instead of their own. What if they had a knife, or physically attacked my kids? It was one against three, and they were each several stone heavier than me. So I did what every other frightened person present did: I was a coward and I walked on by. And then I cried. Pathetic? Maybe. Sensible? Probably. But I felt deeply ashamed of myself, and deeply upset that I could live in a society where I *dare* not confront unacceptable behaviour; where fear has got the better of morality.

What's a parent to do?

Crikey, this is all getting a little depressing! Let's try to focus on the positive: what, given all of this fear and concern, can and should we parents do? Let our children go out and see what happens? Keep them within our sight at all times and never give them any space to take risks? Hope? Pray? Ask Jeeves?

The answer, I think, is a mixture of all of these, in rather less extreme form. And not including the last one, though I'm sure Jeeves would have a beautiful, sensible and cunning answer for us all, if only we could ask him.

Let's ask Granny instead: what would *she* do?

'Well, you know,' she says, shaking her head slowly, 'I do feel sorry for you parents now, with so much terrible violence everywhere. I would be much more cautious now than I was back then. But,' she adds, sitting forward for effect, 'we took precautions in our own way: your dad didn't cross the main road on his own until he was eight or so. We weren't careless. But they had their freedom, and their space to play without adults always peeking in, and if you take all of that away from a child you leave them with very little of a childhood.'

'So making sure kids have the chance to experience the world by themselves is important enough to take a risk sometimes?'

'Oh, good Lord yes.'

Granny's Pearl of Wisdom

You have to let your kids go and get your nose out of their affairs some of the time. Let them be without adults and just be children. Playing made-up games and being free from the constraints and pressures that we adults put on them. That's a childhood.

'A childhood is not about being mothered and supervised and told what to do all the time. You have to let go. You have to take some risks, of course, just not silly ones.'

She looks up at last with a laugh.

'You know what you parents have to do?'

'Chill out?' I suggest vaguely.

'Yes! Exactly that. You just have to use your common sense – you all have a brain, so use it!'

That sounds about as sensible a thing as I've ever heard, and it's something I've been writing about for years – though it's very comforting to hear from a member of the older generation who agrees. **Parenting is not just about rules and methods and lists of facts and figures and statistics, helpful though these can be. It's about common sense, sensing what is right for each child in each situation and letting a child grow and develop. Sometimes this means protecting them from things and sometimes it means letting them have a go.**

Preventing kids from doing things for themselves is exacerbated by issues over fear in schools. Due to budget cuts and fears of the risks of litigation, fewer schools are allowing kids to go on school trips, so they learn even less about how to behave away from home and how to be responsible and keep safe.

And so we have a whole generation of frustrated, naïve, sheltered and angry children growing up in our cities and towns who grow into frustrated, rebellious and often drunk teenagers, wandering around the streets looking for trouble because it's a lot more exciting than being cooped up at home all the time. And so the rest of us let our kids out even less! It's crazy.

We must try to overcome our fears and to be rational. We must *try* to remember just how unlikely it is that bad things will happen to our kids on the way to school or to the shops, or when they're playing with friends in the park, if they have been raised to understand the dangers and to take care. And we must try to give our children more space to be by themselves in order to learn what's safe, in such relatively safe environments. If we never let our children take risks and push the boundaries we are doing them no favours at all, and it will only come back to cause problems later in their lives.

∾ GRANNY'S TIPS ∾

Use your common sense and don't be a panic-monger. You *know* what is sensible and what isn't. Stick to that.

Guard against real dangers where you can – for example crossing busy main roads by themselves – and try to realise when the dangers are imagined or exaggerated. Protecting your kids against everything they could ever encounter is impossible and unhelpful.

Try to remember what you were allowed to do as a child, and imagine how your parents felt about it; they were probably worried too, but had the good sense to let you try it.

—— LIZ'S TIPS ——

If you really can't stand the worry, then **get a mobile phone** that your children can use if anything goes wrong. You have to be a little cautious here though, as mobiles can attract unwanted attention and cause more trouble than they prevent if they're on show, so make sure your child keeps hers out of sight when she's not using it. They exist, so use them to your advantage. Just don't phone your child every five minutes to check up, or it's to everyone's disadvantage . . .

Enrol your child into a group that does adventurous activities under some supervision: the Brownies, Scouts or something similar. This could be a perfect balance of freedom, playing, learning and adventuring that your child craves while you have the peace of mind that they are in a safe environment.

Don't freak your kids out about 'stranger danger'. Not all people your kids meet in the street are bad: in fact by far the majority of them will be very good, helpful people. Teaching children to fear people they don't know is to make them very frightened indeed, and socially awkward. Teaching the basics like not getting into stranger's cars or accepting sweeties is essential: scaring the shit out of them is not!

Test yourself. Let your kids have some freedom that stretches you a bit: let them walk to the letter box, or go exploring in the woods without you running about after them. You'll both gain confidence, and your fear will drop dramatically.

I've been quite good about letting my kids take small risks that I'm not totally relaxed about, such as walking to school alone, or going to the shop down the road for some milk. But since talking with Granny I've made even more of an effort to keep this 'letting go' part of my weekly life with my kids and to remember that it's really good and important for them. I also feel comforted by the fact that we're not the first generation to worry, and if I really don't feel OK about something, then I can say 'no' and not feel I'm too pathetic. As she said, we still have to guard against the *real* dangers – we just have to be more relaxed about the ones that are mainly in our busy heads.

Chapter Eleven

OH I DO LIKE TO BE
BESIDE THE SEASIDE...

Family holidays

The following cold morning I am invited on a day trip to the seaside. The *seaside*? Me? Today?! Much whooping with uncontainable childish delight follows, which seems to me to be only polite and to Granny, apparently, to be annoyingly noisy. But I can't help myself: it has been so long since I've been to the seaside that I can barely remember what salty air tastes like. The seaside?! Hell yeah – let's go.

Of course, what my excited mind has forgotten to register is that we are not in the Caribbean. Nor the Med. Nor even on the Cornish coast. We are in the East of Scotland, and as the tempting photographs you may have seen of unmarked sand and crystal clear waters off Scotland's coasts cunningly cannot indicate, the water temperature never rises above 'cold enough to freeze your nipples off'. Given that there is frost on the grass, my own nipples are probably in for a bit of a shock.

By late morning we are off to North Berwick: Granny is in the driving seat – words that should put the fear of death into any passenger – with me in the front beside her to secure the best view of my vomit hitting the dashboard, and Alison in the back to provide an unbroken stream of in-drive entertainment.

And then it dawns on me quite why I am feeling so excited about this trip: it's not the going to the seaside itself, novel thought that that will be. It's that I'm going on a mini family holiday. A very old-fashioned, simple day at the seaside, with an ageing granny and a not ageing at all aunt (that'll make her happy). It's not quite a week in Tuscany, but maybe that's why I'm so excited: this is simple, cheap, almost hassle free, and fantastically refreshing – which is a lot more than I can say for the last twenty-odd family holidays I've taken, struggling through passport control, waiting for delayed flights, packing half of my children's belongings just in case they need them. (They never do.)

Family holidays, as anyone who's ever dared to take one recently will empathise, are increasingly talked about as though they are a form of torture: expensive, exhausting, disappointing and not worth the hassle one bit. And most of us tend to put on weight on holiday too, which is the final straw. Hassled *and* overweight? What's not to like?

As we sway at alarming speed along the A9 I take my mind off the tumble dryer lurking in my stomach by talking to Granny about holidays when she was a child. Were they always so fraught with anxiety, so hard to organise, so expensive and so complicated? First up: did they even *go* on holiday?

'Oh, well, we were very lucky because we could actually go *away*, every year, on a holiday. Not every family could, don't forget.

There was not so much money around as now, and people would never *borrow* to go on holiday.'

'Borrow' sounds on a par with rape, murder and pillage, incidentally, and I guiltily remember borrowing money to go on our honeymoon. As neither of us was intending to go on another honeymoon any time soon, and we were completely skint at the time, I think borrowing a little to spend two weeks on our first and last opportunity (till the kids leave home anyway) for us to shag day and night on deserted golden sand was the right decision. I decide not to bring this into the conversation, however. The driving is erratic enough as it is.

Swerve left a little . . . and back right again . . . and we're back on course. Mum, how many miles to go?

So, on these annual holidays, where did Granny's family go? Morocco? Corfu? Grenada? Pluto is as likely.

'Well we didn't have a car of course – only the doctor had a car – so we'd take the bus from Aberdeen to Tarland, where your family's originally from.'

Aha. Not quite the 'going away' on holiday many kids are used to now. A bus to Tarland?! Move over Phileas Fogg. Flying off all around the world for the annual family holiday is what our junior travellers today have come to enjoy – indeed to *expect*, if we're honest. Italy, Spain, America, Greece, the Caribbean... you name it we've trekked out there with our family sized suitcases, sibling squabbles and pasty skin to return two weeks later with a snow dome or two, ha'penny flip flops, a nasty stomach bug and sun burn. For many kids, going to Sardinia for a week is no more impressive than a trip to the London Eye. They've been there before, they'll go again, and they're as familiar with mosquito nets and eat-all-you-can buffets as we used to be with a stick of rock and bashing in tent pegs in Wales.

I open the window a fraction and sniff the cold, damp air, wishing I'd brought a plastic bag with me. We always travel with several spares in the car for puke emergencies (N.B. not the supermarket varieties with holes in!) and we've also instigated a rule whereby children must, must, *MUST* tell us when they *start* to feel sick, and not leave it until three nanoseconds before their last meal hits the back of Mummy's seat. I advise you to do the same.

I've been the car-sick type since I was very young, and still can't look down for more than a minute at most, even on poker-straight roads, before my stomach starts turning somersaults.

Talking is the only way to take my mind off my growing queasiness.

'Did so few people go on holiday because it was too expensive?'

Gear crunch… Hard right turn…

'Oh yes – that's why we had such very simple holidays. There was no flying here and there like you all do now. It cost four shillings return from Aberdeen and we stayed in the same village in the same, simple house every year, with sheep all around and just perfect peace and quiet. But it was a blessing in disguise, because it meant we had a proper *holiday* – quiet, rest and fresh air for us all, and the kids were free to run around and explore by themselves because they knew the place so well.'

Four shillings. Blimey. Even though that did count for something back then, it isn't even in the same league as the thousands of pounds we throw at package holidays, hotels, flights, trains, food and entertainment every year on so-called 'holidays' from our already costly and busy lives.

But, dear traveller, things they are a-changing. There has started to be a shift back to just what I am doing today: to old-style, UK-based, no frills holidaying. Just as Granny used to do seventy years ago.

Could it be that we have reached the end of the stressful family holiday from hell, and just want to get back to windbreakers and flasks of Campbell's tomato soup? Could it be that jetting off to Val d'l sère for Easter, Majorca for May half term, Sardinia for the summer hols and the Canaries for a last blast of sun in October could be replaced by simple séjours in Wales or Cornwall, and camping in Brittany? Well, from the following evidence, I think it just could be.

THE CHANGING FACE OF
FAMILY HOLIDAYS

—⟨⟨⟨⟨⟩⟩⟩⟩—

After decades of holidaying in exotic locations and tropical climes, it seems that more and more Brits are choosing to holiday at home:

✳ In 2007 UK residents took 53.7 million holidays of one night or more in this country, spending 11.5 billion pounds.

✳ According to Direct Line and the Future Foundation, the number of domestic holidays taken in the UK is set to rise by 21 million by 2027, boosting the domestic tourism market by an estimated 15 billion pounds.

✳ Ancestral tourism – when people visit an area to trace their family history – is also on the rise in the UK.

✳ Try websites like: www.babygoes2.com; www.greatlittleescapes.co.uk and www.travelforkids.com, and don't forget websites like www.mumsnet.com where you can pick up invaluable tips from people who've been there and aren't trying to sell you anything!

❝ We have one annual Easter holiday in a cottage by the sea in Dorset: we listen to tape books, play games and sing songs on the journey down; then we breathe the fresh air, see old friends, build sandcastles, collect pebbles and shells, paint them, build boats out of driftwood, have picnics, walks on cliffs and around the woods, play cards and so on when we get there. This trip is partly based on my favourite childhood holidays and it's the best week of the year.❞

Esther, mother of Sam, ten and Claire, six

Searching for that missing 'something'

It would be tempting, and easy, to assume that this change in the way we holiday has come about simply because of our old friends, Mr Credit Crunch and his partner, Recession. If we're all feeling the pinch, holidays are one of the first luxuries to go.

But, interestingly, saving money does not seem to be the main motivator. For a start, contrary to what my white-knuckle-ride driver assumes, many foreign holidays are actually still very affordable, while renting property in this country can be exorbitant. And shit. Proof of this is that it's no longer uncommon to go camping in darkest Wales and find yourself sharing the camp fire with a wealthy barrister, a merchant banker or the director of a multi-million-pound organisation. And if you're really lucky he's also recently divorced and on the pull and you can bag yourself a millionaire. Whoopee, let's go, baby! (OK, I didn't just say that.) We recently found ourselves at the summit of a peak in the Cairngorms with a man whose annual bonus was more than I have earned in my entire life, or am ever likely to.

So just what are these obscenely rich people *doing* there? They could quite easily spend their week off lounging on the beaches of Mauritius, the Seychelles or Mustique or exploring the remotest regions of Vietnam, Africa or the Far East in five-star conditions.

Granny has an answer that I think is as near to the mark as the left side of our car is wide of it.

'A lot of people, in their rush to have the "perfect holiday",' she tells me while keeping one set of wheels firmly on the hard shoulder, 'have lost sight of what a holiday is supposed to be *for*.'

'I ... uh ... what do you mean?' (Please can we pull over now?)

'Holidays are not for cramming in as much as you possibly can. They are for stopping, thinking, resting, having fun, and just *being*.

Granny's Pearl of Wisdom

People talk about the need to escape on holiday. But actually what you need is to find peace, with yourself and your family, in a place that brings you closer. That's where establishing childhood holiday places is so important. Escaping is about getting away from. Holidaying is about being present.

So maybe that's what our wealthy campers are doing: just *being*, rather than escaping. They could easily go to the most luxurious places on Earth, and most of them have, many, many times. But now they're bored, dissatisfied and searching for something with meaning for them, and that brings a connection to something. Often this 'something' is their childhood – their simple, carefree childhood, and they are coming back home in droves to share this with their own children.

And, if you're like me and the many fed up, travel-weary, lost parents I've talked to recently, you'll be doing just the same before the year is out.

❝ We travel to North Devon in May every year, and have done so ever since my daughter was four months old. There are ten of us in total – of which there are five kids – all cousins, their grandparents, and parents. We share a self-catering cottage and all don *our wetsuits, and boogie-board come rain or shine. And we love it! My daughter loves it! She is with her cousins and close family for seven days and nights. There are no bright lights, big city, or must-see tourist attractions to visit, just a simple retreat in Devon where work and life seem a world away.*

'It is a simple holiday but one that will provide my daughter with long lasting memories and shared experiences; a strong bond with her family that will last a lifetime. "

Alison, mother of Amalie, six

Everything but the kitchen sink (and sometimes that as well)

In the madness of trying to 'get away from it all' we often end up taking most of 'it' with us, in the form of bulging suitcases, rows with spouses, bickering with children and head lice.

Rows and lice we can work on gradually, using charm and patience (in either order), but luggage we can cut down on instantly. Just check out the scenes at the check-in desks at Stansted: I've seen kids checking in two bags *each*, leaving me unsure if I should feel jealous that someone half my age has twice my wardrobe, or depressed that they can't seem to do without it for a week ...

Did Granny take so much with *her* on her outings to deepest Aberdeenshire back in the 1940s and 50s?

I almost wish I hadn't asked, such is the lurch this enquiry brings on. (Stay on the road woman!)

'No! We had all our clothing in one trunk – and a small one at that – and a "carrier" brought them off the bus, I remember that. But we brought almost nothing.'

Granny's Pearl of Wisdom

What do you want to be bringing all your rubbish from home with you on holiday for anyway? It's a holiday – leave it all behind, and see something new. That's half the point of it, isn't it?

It is. We spent the first few holidays with our kids literally bringing along every favourite toy, book, activity and item of clothing they had ever given a passing glance to, lest one of the little darlings missed anything dreadfully and the whole holiday ended in catastrophe. The result was that I had no room for any of my stuff and lived in a grubby, stretched T-shirt all week.

We've learned though. Now we take two changes of clothes each and no more, one toy per child, pencils and pens, paper and books. And that's it. All the rest is left at home where it belongs and it's up to our kids to use their imagination to create new games, invent stories, write, play and get *away* from all their stuff at home.

Try it. You might just discover you don't need ninety per cent of the stuff clogging up your home.

But there's a whole world out there!

Now fear not, my travelling friend: this is not a 'why can't we all stop trashing the planet and just sit on Blackpool beach eating chips' type of a chapter. No, no and no! We are *lucky* to be able to travel so easily, and we should jolly well continue to do so, to see the world and learn from it, and just to have some warm, sun-shiny, adventurous FUN during our hard-earned breaks. We're not saints!

But – oh here it comes – there is the somewhat pressing issue of CO_2 emissions and Global Warming to consider, and consider it we must.

A return long-haul flight creates about three tonnes of carbon emissions per person. According to some estimates thirty trees are needed to absorb that carbon. Therefore, if we were all to cut down to one flight per year, from say, a fairly typical year for many involving four flights, that would save nine tonnes of carbon emissions *each*. That's a whole lotta emissions reduced!

You notice I didn't say cut *out* air travel. We have stressful lives and very little holiday. Life is there for living, and for learning, and I don't subscribe to the Total Ban On All Fun approach to planet saving. We all have to do our bit, whether it's buying local food, recycling as much as we can, growing our own tomatoes or having showers instead of baths. The best thing you can do for this planet is cut down on *all* of your consumption and wastage. Period. Making an annual SOS call to the sanity-saving people at the holiday company Essential Italy is my guilt-free reward – so what's yours?

Granny, however, is one of those people from another age who have managed to get through a very long life never owning a passport. It's a concept that I find deeply miserable-making: never seeing another country, another way of life, never hearing a cicada chirp, never smelling a hot, ripe tomato straight off the vine, never listening to a bunch of people hurling abuse at each other in a language you understand absolutely none of on a dusty road in a strange land. What wondrous things to miss out on! But many elderly people are like this, and think we are bonkers for wanting to travel as much as we do.

'Granny,' I ask, as we pass the welcome signpost indicating there are only three miles to go to North Berwick and the end of this nauseous trip. 'Do you not wish you'd travelled abroad? I mean, haven't you ever wanted to see Italy or Canada, or Denmark?'

'No. Why would I want to? I have everything I could want here, and I can see it all on the television, so I know what it all looks like.'

'But it's not the same – on television. It doesn't smell different, and you can't taste the foods and meet the local people. Don't you think we should travel with our kids, and teach them about the world, and other people?'

We bump along the last stretch of straight road before the beach and I congratulate myself heartily on not being sick – yet.

'I know there's so much to see out in the world,' she says, narrowly missing a passing truck. 'But I've seen a lot of people come and go and they never look any happier with their lot back home.'

Granny's Pearl of Wisdom

The more people wander the less satisfied they are.

Now, I've put this down as a pearl of wisdom, but it's not actually the wisest thing I've ever heard anyone say. The principle is right, I think – you can search and search for happiness but you will always find it right back where you began, with yourself, and being content with that.

But much as I champion the good old British holiday, I cannot disagree with Granny's attitude to foreign travel more. She seems afraid almost of what she might find out there if she looked – afraid that it might reveal some places to be better than where she lives, and that this could make her dissatisfied. My own pearl of wisdom (I'm allowed one, surely!) found through my experience of world travel would be as follows:

Liz's Pearl of Wisdom

The more we travel and see what's out there,
what kind of a planet we live on and how we are
all connected by sharing the same human needs and
the same Earth, the better educated we become
about our own country, its place in the world and
how we can live better in that world.

Yes, some places are spectacular and beautiful and all the rest, but they have their problems too and it can be a pleasure to come back home to what you know, and appreciate it all the more – and maybe improve it with something you have learned abroad.

For kids, seeing more of the world couldn't be more important now than it is, as global economics, social, political and environmental issues will come to dictate so much of their futures.

My future, and my children's future, requires understanding foreign languages and cultures so much that *never* going abroad on a holiday if you have the chance to seems not just boring but also rather silly. Their classes are full of foreign kids from Eastern Europe, Asia, China and many more faraway places, and it is vital that they understand and visit lands far away from their own in order to understand the new multicultural society they live in.

But I can't convince Granny of this, ever, nor would I ever try.

As the car swings around the last bend to reveal at last what my nose has already detected – the windy beach front, the salty sea and the vast empty space beyond – my breath is taken away by the beauty and timelessness of this place. Book deadlines, financial pressures, marital gripes and schooling concerns vanish in an instant. Hell, I don't even feel sick any more – I want to jump out, run across the golden sand, throw my shoes off and splash through the bastard freezing water.

I am a child again, and that's what going on holiday with kids is all about. Renaissance churches, Florentine frescoes, Moroccan souks and freaky Japanese fish dishes are unquestionably fascinating, but walking along a beach with your granny – that's invaluable.

Holiday clubs – love 'em or hate 'em?
Probably a bit of both

Here's a funny thing lots of otherwise sensible people do: they moan about how little time they can spend together as a family, and then go on holiday, only to pack their kids off into a holiday club.

Ummmmm, but isn't that . . . kind of *stupid*?

I know, I know, you want to get some peace and quiet, blah de blah, and you want to read a book and your kids drive you nuts . . . blah blah. I know. I have three kids. I can sympathise. But here's the thing: if you don't spend any time with your kids while you're on holiday, when the bloody hell are you ever going to spend any time with them? Ever?

No wonder they drive you insane – you hardly know each other.

Kids' clubs range from the truly fantastic to the staggeringly awful. Some offer the chance to learn anything from abseiling to archery, windsurfing to wax modelling. Others are little short of a sweaty parking space for abandoned children.

Just for a laugh, and since we are no longer in a moving vehicle, I ask Granny what she thinks of holiday kids' clubs.

She kind of looks at me sideways, with a withered, 'I can't believe what I just heard' kind of face, before asking quite slowly:

'Holiday *WHATs*?'

'Ummm, kids' clubs. They're, sort of places where you can, um, put your children . . . well, I mean not where you *put* them, as such, but where children can go, and play and learn stuff and have fun. While you have a break. You see?'

She does see. She sees it all, in this one feeble attempt to defend our feebleness.

'That is just about the saddest thing I've ever heard, Elizabeth,' she says as the three of us walk very slowly towards the pier.

I feel a sudden need to defend my kind. The frazzled Modern
Parent. The stressed Mum. The overworked Dad. The . . . the desperately lost and confused person who is basically still a small
child but who somehow seems to have small children of her own
to look after. We're doing our best here you know!

'Actually, some of these holiday clubs are really quite good. The
kids love it and they learn lots of stuff there.' I decide not to say
'And their parents might even feel revived enough to have sex with
their partner for the first time since the last year's holiday . . . '
Maybe she already knows this is part of the idea.

She pauses to catch her breath and give her leg a rest.

'I'm sure they do learn all sorts there. And probably a few
mornings a week would be good all round. But they learn at
school all term long. Why not teach them something yourself?
Why not have a *holiday* with them?'

Drat. She's right. Kids aren't stupid and they know a lame excuse
to get rid of them when they see it. My own kids occasionally drive
me up the very high wall, but I don't hate them so much as to banish
them from my sight every holiday. In fact, I love their company most
of the time, and *especially* when we're on holiday together. Drinking

yourself into a Sangria-fuelled stupor to 'get away from it all' isn't the answer; you only have your kids for about twelve years before they decide you are too embarrassing to be associated with, so make the most of them!

> 66 *Every summer I take my kids on a week's canoeing break. We just take off down the river with our tents and food. The first time they thought it was going to be soooo boring, but soon we were gliding along peacefully, passing herons and seeing fish and king-fishers. They fell silent in wonder and you could see the pressures of town life melting away. Now they love it and it's the most special week of the year for all of us.* 99

William, father of Esther, eleven and Jake, sixteen

So what of family holidays? Blackpool or Bangkok? Lake District or Lake Garda? Scotland or Nova Scotia?

The answer, I think, is ALL of these. Sometimes a foreign holiday is just the ticket. Other times staying closer to home and getting out the lashings of ginger ale is what's needed, or possible, instead. But the important thing to remember, wherever you go on holiday with your family, is what the holiday is *for*. It's not for cramming in as many sights and destinations as you possibly can, for sticking your children into a holiday camp while you finish your book on a sun lounger in peace or for keeping up with the Joneses who go to Majorca for a month every summer.

It's for spending time – unhurried, uncluttered, un-spoiled time – with your children and partner, and feeling that you will remember this forever, and cherish the memories. This can happen just as well on the beaches of Norfolk or the forests of Wales as it can in Rio or the Riviera, and if you can find a spot that you want to return to year after year you might just get more out of your holidays for decades to come than you ever imagined – and your kids will always have a magical place which, for them, spells Childhood.

Flashy holidays are all very well, but it's the cheapest, simplest, happiest ones where they can be with you, play freely and have a HOLIDAY that they will remember and cherish for far longer.

∾ *GRANNY'S TIPS* ∾

Keep holidays simple. They are for peace, not getting exhausted.

Try to find a place to revisit time and time again.

Leave all your junk at home, and discover something new while you're away.

Remember: a holiday is for being together, not for getting away from each other.

—— LIZ'S TIPS ——

For many working parents the annual holiday is the only time they get to spend together, without their kids. Don't feel awful for enrolling your children in a club for a few days. You need time together too. Just make sure you get a LOT of time all together, WITH the children.

Go with the flow. Package holidays may seem like a good idea, as everything is taken care of. But it leaves you with no scope for doing things your way, or being flexible. Try to take a trip without planning it, and see where each day takes you.

Get advice from friends. It's hard to trust websites and adverts, so talk to like-minded parents and find a place that they loved, and you might too.

Chapter Twelve

MOVING WITH THE TIMES

The ups and downs of the modern world

The last morning of my horribly short trip brings a classic 'older generation trying to get with the times' comedy moment. Alison has decided to take a photograph of me and Granny sitting side by side on the sofa. So far so unproblematic. Anyone can take a photograph. Where it all starts to get a bit Fawlty Towers is when she decides to take things one step further – and email this snap to my children to show them how their mummy is getting on while she's away. (Like they care . . . !)

I'm not the most technologically minded lady but, living as I do in the twenty-first century, I have had to at least *attempt* to move with the times and get myself techo-sorted. I now have broadband internet access at home, and Skype, and a mobile, and a laptop and email and all that fairly essential jazz. Essential, that is, if I want to keep my job. I don't have a BlackBerry (yet) or a palmtop, I have no idea what Wi-Fi means or what the difference between Bluetooth and blu-ray is, but for now I don't need to:

I've got everything I need to get by and not drop off the edge of the Modern World into the abyss below.

As I watch Alison crouch on the floor, hear her computer dialling up to the internet, see the email address failing, the connection terminating mid-transmission and the mass of cables from camera to computer to socket, I wonder if today is perhaps the day to leave all this talk of olden times behind, and look firmly to the future. I would not want you to conclude that this book is for, as Waldemar Januszczak described the 2008 Summer Exhibition at the Royal Academy, 'white, middle class, middle-brow, allergic to progress' readers. No siree! Turning back the clock is never what this book has been seeking to do. Rather it tries to take all of what we've learned from times gone by, and bring it into the world of today, and of tomorrow.

And what's one of the biggest headaches facing any parent in any period of time? Quite simply, how far to go with all this 'modernity'.

'Granny,' I venture, as we watch the spectacle going on in front of us. 'What do you think about keeping up with all the new things any current time brings along, be it technology, or clothing or toys or whatever?'

She doesn't answer, busy as she is writing a text on her very flash mobile phone. How very ironic.

'What's that?' she says eventually, tucking it into the pocket of her old cords.

'I was asking about moving along with the times – does every generation worry about New Things and just have to move along with it, or should we put the brakes on and try to keep our children away from it all, and keep them innocent and uncluttered by it all?'

'Oh, you have to move along. Of course you do. But within reason. We thought radio would be the end of live music – but it hasn't been. In fact it has opened up a whole new musical world for thousands, who all appreciate it now; there is in fact more live music now than ever. And the same, in a way, for television; just look at all the incredible things I can watch that I'd never see without it. '

'And you'd *love* the internet, Granny. You could find out anything you've ever wanted to know about anything, if you wanted to.'

'Ah! But there's the thing – I *don't* want to. I'm happy with my television and radio and that'll do me, thanks very much.'

Granny's Pearl of Wisdom

You have to know where to stop. The world is moving on at an incredible rate, faster than ever before, but children don't have to be up to speed on ALL of it. You have to decide what's sensible, and not go overboard with it. They have time to learn as they grow up.

The internet connection crashes again, accompanied by a 'Blast!' from Alison.

I love this modern edge to my very old-fashioned Granny. She has embraced mobile phone technology with an ease and interest that really shocks me, and I regularly get messages which read things like 'A77 f1ne here. SNoww on hils and 4deg7ees out3ide.luv grnny xxxxx'. I don't think the designers of writing recognition made allowances for the shake of an eighty-four year old. Still, they make me laugh.

She can also record stuff on her Sky Plus box and has no bother programming in telephone numbers into her phone memory.

For our children, keeping up with modern tchnology is not just fun – it's essential. I put this point to Granny, knowing she'll mostly agree.

'There's no possibility of falling too far behind these days though, Granny – for our children's sake, more than anything else. They have to learn to type now and use a mouse to click and drag and all that stuff at a very early age. It's a basic skill they use at school all the time, and they'll need it for just about any job, or even to set up a mortgage, or book a holiday or just about anything else now.'

'Oh, absolutely. They have to be a part of the world they're living in. But this does not mean they have to spend all their free time on the computer, nor do they have to wear all the latest clothing or eat the latest trendy food or go on holiday to the most fancy new places. You have to control it, and make the balance right, for them.'

But everyone else does!

My kids often say this to me. Everyone Else goes to bed later than them, and watches more telly than them, and eats more crap than them, and has more toys and gadgets and clothing than them. In fact, according to my children Everyone Else seems to have everything that my kids want, and can't have.

Ahhh, poor them.

This is not new – and nor is it true! Kids have tried for years to convince Mummy and Daddy that Everyone Else has something. But here's a revelation: if you talk to other parents about what their kids really have, often it's not a tenth of what your offspring would have you believe. Nor do they go to bed at midnight or eat cheesy strings for breakfast, incidentally . . .

The trick I've learned with my kids is to convince them that everyone else thinks *they* are the lucky ones, thus not having to sell my soul to the Tempting Packaging and Advertising Devil – or find myself in debt.

Granny has some more tips for me.

'Do you think that worrying if your children are keeping up with their friends is new? Well, it's not. We had plenty of that too, but you have so much more to deal with than us.'

'I know, and I just worry so much that they'll either fall behind, because I'm so bloody-minded, principled and mean about what they are allowed to have, or get totally corrupted by the amount of mindless junk out there that they seem to want so much.'

'Then you're just like any normal parent, Elizabeth! You will always worry that your children are being exposed to too many bad things, and also that they are not 'fitting in' with their friends. It's totally normal.'

Granny's Pearl of Wisdom

What you have to do is try to relax about it, let them have a go at the new things but keep an eye on it so it doesn't get out of control. It's a juggling act and requires some compromise – some things they can do, even if you'd rather they didn't, and others they can't.

Does this include computer games?

'Well, I suppose it has to, yes. But again you have to careful about which ones, and how much time they spend on them. You used to play computer games I seem to recall.'

We did indeed. I whiled away many an hour on all the old classics – Defender and Packman, Space Invaders, Frogger, Snakey and Donkey Kong. But the funny thing was nobody seemed very hung-up about them. My parents were perfectly happy for us to play, and I don't remember any talk at all about computers being Bad, or problematic in any way.

The reason is probably simply a matter of scale. The choice of games and gadgets on offer is vast, and growing so fast you can hardly keep up (and it's all so expensive!), and while there are lots of great ones for little kids, many games have also got more violent, frenetic and less child-like. It's the same with films. Yes, there are some fantastic films for kids, but there are also loads and loads that are utterly dreadful, and should never be seen by anyone, let alone kids who mop the entire thing up on first viewing. We had *Cinderella*, *Back to the Future* and *Chitty Chitty Bang Bang*. Now it's all sexy girls, love stories, terrifying stunts and high octane explosions. And that's in the first ten minutes.

The kinds of films being made 'for children' is something I feel passionate about. There are occasional gems, like *Nanny McPhee*, the Narnia films or *The Golden Compass*, and the likes of *Finding Nemo* and *Ice Age* for younger children. But amongst such greats are reel upon reel of mindless crap, filled with complicated story lines, sexual references, overdone dramatic tension, fear, violence and jokes that fly above the heads of ninety per cent of the target audience but have to be included to keep the money-holding parents happy. And we feel under such pressure, thanks to relent-less advertising on all media, to take our kids to see this nonsense, shelling out a small fortune for the pleasure and then wondering why we bothered. Actually, why *did* we bother?

Granny knows, and is sympathetic.

'We felt just the same about some things. But you mustn't worry yourself sick about saying 'no'.'

Granny's Pearl of Wisdom

Nobody wants their child to be the odd one out. But there is nothing wrong with being different, and with not having what everybody else has. Maybe your children have something else that nobody has, and that makes them special.

This is just what we have had to learn to do in recent years, as our kids have started to turn the pressure up to MAX about what they can and cannot do on the internet. I have to admit here that I am probably leaning slightly too far to the 'no, you can't watch this or that' end of the scale, and this has caused some problems for, in particular, my eldest. It's something I'm trying to be more laid back about, and we're finding a middle ground somewhere between spending six hours a night on the web, and not going on it at all.

Because have a go on the computer they must, if they are to feel 'part of' their peer group. Below is a list of websites, games and television programmes that we and some of our friends feel comfortable about our kids playing on and watching. Some are for slightly older children than I have (I wouldn't be happy with my five year old watching *Dr Who* for example, but I realise I am almost alone in this!) but have a look for yourself and see if anything seems suitable for your kids. And do talk to other parents and use websites like NetMums for more ideas. It's by listening to other parents' experiences that you can learn a lot!

SCREEN TIME

WEBSITES

www.clubpenguin.com
www.bbc.co.uk/cbbc
www.nickelodeon.com
www.bored.com

www.bbc.co.uk/schools/
   scienceclips
www.kidsites.com/
www.bbc.co.uk/cbbc/bluepeter

GAMES

Super Mario Galaxy
Wii Sports
Buzz
Lego Star Wars, and Lego
   Indiana Jones
PES (Football)

Mario and Sonic Olympics
Guitar Hero
Rock Band
Sims
Where in the world is Carmen
   Sandiego?

TV PROGRAMMES

When they've outgrown Cbeebies and aren't quite ready for Silent Witness yet (!) here are some suggestions from parents of slightly older kids:

Bamzooki (excellent, for boys
   AND girls!)
Dr Who (we're battling with
   this one, but for slightly
   older kids it's an obsession)

Strictly Come Dancing
Raven
BBC Newsround

And of course many more!

Once I've found a website that I'm happy with, my kids pretty much have a free rein and I don't watch over them like a neurotic hen. But for others we have a No Go policy, and these include YouTube and any Google surfing. Even with parental control, I'm never confident that they won't come across something innocence-shattering, and I'm not ready to take that risk just yet. The day will come, I'm sure, but they are still very young and those are the rules in our house. Tough luck.

When it comes to clothing I am relaxing a lot where my eldest is concerned, she can choose many of her outfits, and she wears pretty trendy stuff that is still, in my old eyes, suitable for a little girl to wear. Heels are OUT, as are skirts shorter than mid-thigh or trousers lower than midriff.

As you already know, we're pretty careful about the amount of toys they have and we don't have many of the must-have (see, not *must* have after all . . .) toys they would like. Instead, they have other things that some of their friends don't and that are a big hit when they come round to play. They are different, but they're also not falling so far behind that they are social outcasts. Somewhere in the middle lies the happy zone. You just have to find it for your children and not worry too much.

There is a victorious cry of 'Done it!' from the floor as the incredible moment of digital communication takes place. We may not be the most advanced people in the world, but in our small, slow way we've managed to keep up with the times. Just.

When I leave later that day Granny is uncharacteristically jumpy. Nerves about her appointment are starting to kick in, deny it though she may. I wish I could stay and come to the hospital with her, but I have a family back home as well, and a train to catch. I promise to phone her in a few days when she has news. We hug, and wave goodbye – and I make it all the way across the road before I cry.

Conclusion

Things don't always go according to plan. Granny's appointment at the hospital does, which is just the news we are all hoping for – as she puts it 'Oh, they said I'm doing just fine. No bother at all. Right as rain.'

This encouraging progress is enough to keep us all buoyed up until our next trip to visit her, which is planned for Easter. Unfortunately, this is where the plans all go a little 'not according to': the weather is so bad, with snow covering most of the country and closing the roads near Granny's village, that we are forced to postpone.

But a few weeks later a free weekend presents itself and we seize it; I mean, who wouldn't want to sit in a car for an entire day listening to a dreadful production of *Five go on an Adventure*?

But as ever it's worth it. Granny looks sensational. Not only is she now walking to the end of the road almost every day, but when we arrive she is in her shed at the bottom of the garden lifting out big, heavy bicycles for my children to ride on.

Having told her to 'stop it at once and sit down!' we spend the day lazing in the warm sunshine and admiring the two new crazy bird feeders that have arrived and been set up in the flower bed, and are causing much competitive behaviour among the local tit population. The blue ones are winning, feet down.

Then all of a sudden, I notice something.

'Granny! You're not wearing your furry boots!'

It is the first time she's taken them off (except for bed time I hope) for nine months.

'Oh yes,' she says proudly, wiggling her ancient toes. 'I can fit into my sandals now, my foot is so much better. It's wonderful.'

It *is* wonderful. She is a new person, with sparkle, and hope and enthusiasm. If I could find the surgeon who operated on her he would get a big sloppy kiss from me right this minute. Not only that, but I also spy what looks like the shoots of a beautiful purple-flowering clematis climbing their way up the fence . . . maybe it did just need a good prune after all!

As we all take part in a family Frisbee throw-around, I reflect on all the things Granny and I have talked about over the last year or so.

About childhood, family, respect, food, discipline, love, rushing, buying, wasting, holidaying and living. It's been a lot to take in, but a fantastic chance to put something back into my children's lives – before it's too late.

'It's great, having kids,' I say, as two of mine fight over whose turn it is with the Frisbee. 'Hard, and scary, but great.'

Granny takes me by the hand and says in a hushed voice, 'If I hadn't had children, I'd have nothing and nobody now. I couldn't chat with you, or play with your children and watch them grow

344

up. People who don't have children will regret it one day when they're old, like me.'

'And yet we all curse them so often.'

"Oh, we all do from time to time. But so many people speak of children as *nothing* but a nuisance, and it breaks my heart. They hear it all; they pick up on it. And they suffer; we all suffer from bad child-rearing.'

A Frisbee hurtles through the air at knee-height and decapitates two daffodils as it lands. I resist the temptation to chastise the thrower. He's just being a kid. Just playing. Let it go, Liz.

Granny's Last Pearl of Wisdom

Children are the most important things. They're in your hands, and you decide how they turn out. So look after them – and enjoy them!

Final Note

On 20th November 2008 I receive the following email:

> It's Elizabeth. Yours is is my very first email. The BT man left
> only an hour ago. Alison is here but is leaving very soon. My
> poor brain is seizing up and I need a cup of tea badly. She is
> a very hard task master. Love to you, Granny.

And with that, Granny and her new shiny, broadband computer
took a flying leap into the twenty-first century. She may be old-
fashioned, but she always moves forward and she never ceases to
amaze!

Acknowledgements

As with any activity involving large amounts of time spent swearing, crying, being in alternate foul and euphoric moods – often without warning – and drinking far too much coffee, an army of people is required to keep those involved from spontaneously combusting. So, my enormous gratitude goes to the following lovely people who have helped me to survive the last year and get this book written:

To all the friends and professionals who were so kind as to give me quotes or let me use their wise words in this book. Without these it would have been a very one-sided affair, and I've learned a lot from you. To Lynne Drew at HarperCollins for being brave enough to say 'YES!' to this project and for her invaluable guidance; to my editor Claire Bord for bearing with me through the four hundred re-writes and embarrassingly anal checks, double-checks and triple-checks I insisted on doing; and to Victoria for her tireless efforts chasing the quotes and permissions. Also to my brilliant and patient agent Euan for continuing to have faith in me, and to my astonishingly efficient and hard-working publicist Mars who is worthy of at least one medal, not least Fastest Email Responder.

I'd also like to shower great waterfalls of deepest, loving thanks to my three astonishing children who teach me something new every day and fill me with obscene amounts of happiness. You are truly beyond words. And now you're wet. Sorry.

Finally, I would like to thank my Granny. For her time, her patience, her words and her honesty, for sharing so much with me and for being such a lovely Granny and Great Granny. Keep the fire burning – we're coming to see you soon!

Permissions

The author and publisher wish to thanks all copyright holders for permission to reproduce their work, and the institutions and individuals who helped with the research and supply of materials.

Extract from article in the *Independent* by Deborah Orr. Reproduced by permission of the *Independent*

95 words from *In Defence of Food* by Michael Pollan (Allen Lane, 2008). Copyright © Michael Pollan, 2008

Reprinted by permission of HarperCollins*Publishers* Ltd. © Alex Richardson, 2006

Reprinted by permission of HarperCollins*Publishers* Ltd. © Tana Ramsay, 2007

Extract from *Enough* by John Naish, published by Hodder & Stoughton 2008. Reproduced by permission of Hodder and Stoughton Ltd.

Extract from article in *The Times* by Andrew Sullivan. Reproduced by permission of *The Times*

From *Affluenza* by Oliver James, published by Vermilion. Reprinted by permission of The Random House Group Ltd

Index